Elfriede Jelinek was born in Austria in 1946 and grew up in Vienna where she attended the renowned Music Conservatory. The leading Austrian writer of her generation, she has been awarded the Heinrich Boll Prize for her contribution to German Literature, the Georg Buchner Prize, and in 2004 she was awarded the Nobel Prize for Literature. The film by Michael Haneke of *The Piano Teacher* won the three main prizes at Cannes in 2001.

**Also by Elfriede Jelinek
and published by Serpent's Tail**

The Piano Teacher
Lust
Wonderful, Wonderful Times
Women as Lovers

Praise for Elfriede Jelinek's work

Greed

'For anyone who wants to write or read daredevil, risk-taking prose, it was tremendously encouraging that Elfriede Jelinek won the Nobel Prize for literature in 2004... Jelinek seized the novel by its bootstraps and shook it upside down... Her dynamic writing gives a sense of civilization surviving against the odds... Jelinek's work is brave, adventurous, witty, antagonistic and devastatingly right about the sorriness of human existence, and her contempt is expressed with surprising chirpiness: it's a wild ride... wonderful, defiant mischief-making' *Guardian*

'This is complex, destructive literature that is defined then torn apart... *Greed* is another intriguing and challenging novel from Europe's cleverest, most visceral social phobic' *The List*

'Jelinek's pages pullulate with weird but wonderful lines that only she could have written...[She] is famous for her seriousness, metaphysical, political, ecological. But she is really a comic writer, like Beckett: a joker in the dark... So is it worth it, and is Jelinek worth her Nobel Prize? Yes: for those weird and wonderful lines, and for those jokes in the dark' *Literary Review*

'*Greed* has considerable energy and force. Its moral urgency is beyond doubt' *Independent*

'The real thrills lie in Jelinek's droll, penetrating insight... Her challenging words boast a lingering impact; through to its denouement, *Greed* is – like the writer herself – relentless and remorseless' *Metro*

'Global ecology, ageing and disturbing late-middle-aged

female sexuality eat at the heart of Nobel prizewinner Jelinek's provocative, mesmerizing, multi-level detective story of murderous evil' *Saga Magazine*

'The power with which Jelinek creates such a claustrophobic, disturbing narrative is impressive' *Scotland on Sunday*

'A poetic mystery. Jelinek writes from somewhere else. She never wavers. She is steadfast...there is nothing accidental in these pages. Their darkness rings, the reader echoes. It is an enduring achievement' *Scotsman*

The Piano Teacher

'Jelinek's fragmented style blurs reality and imagination, creating a harsh, expressionistic picture of sexuality' *Scotland on Sunday*

'As a portrait of repressed female sexuality and a damaged psyche, *The Piano Teacher* glitters dangerously' *Observer*

'A dazzling performance that will make the blood run cold' Walter Abish

'A brilliant, deadly book' Elizabeth Young

'Michael Haneke's jarring and bleak film of the book doesn't really prepare you for the original story, which manages to dig even deeper into the depths of sexual obsession and savagery' *TNT Magazine*

'Her work tends to see power and aggression as the driving forces of relationships, in which men and parents subjugate women. But as an admirer of Bertold Brecht, she sometimes brings to her dramas a touch of vaudeville' *Guardian*

'With formidable power, intelligence and skill she draws on the full arsenal of derision. Her dense writing is obsessive almost to the point of being unbearable. It hits you in the guts, yet is clinically precise' *Le Monde*

'Some may find Ms Jelinek's ruthlessly unsentimental approach – not to mention her image of Vienna as a bleak city of porno shops, poor immigrants and loveless copulations – too much to take. Her picture of a passive woman who can gain control over her life only by becoming a victim is truly frightening. Less squeamish readers will extract a feminist message: in a society such as this, how else can a woman like Erika behave?' *New York Times Book Review*

Lust

'A thorough rubbishing of romantic love, *Lust* is intricately written with a tumbling pace, sustained and effective word-play and plenty of sharp, cynical authorial observation. More than good' *List*

'Sport, capitalism, male penetrative sexuality, bourgeois consumerism, the family – are pilloried... Extraordinarily well-written, with many brilliant turns of phrase, this remains in my mind as the most disturbing European novel I have read this year' Robert Carver, *New Statesman*

'Elfriede Jelinek's *Lust* is an unrelenting look at the bleak correspondences between marriage, capitalism, and sex. Every sentence slams home a truth so trenchant that it's difficult to read *Lust* in large doses. An almost unbelievably confrontational and blunt writer, Jelinek dares her reader to wince and turn away from these pages; it's testimony to her witchy skill that one can't' *Voice Literary Supplement*

'An extraordinary, violent book… *Lust* is the unmasking of sex –
all "innocence and privacy" – as power' *Observer*

Wonderful, Wonderful Times

'A chilling and truthful vision of women's precarious position in a
society still dominated by money and men' *Kirkus Reviews*

'A dozen years after the collapse of the Third Reich, four
adolescents commit a gratuitously violent assault and robbery
in a Viennese park. So begins Jelinek's brilliant new novel, an
unrelenting and horrifying exploration of postwar Austria'
Publishers Weekly

'The writing is so strong, it reads as if it wasn't written down
at all, but as if the author's demon spirit is entering first a boy
and then a girl, a structure, a thing, a totality, to let it speak its
horrible truth' *Scotsman*

'With all the stark immediacy of Burgess's *A Clockwork Orange*,
Jelinek weaves a spell that is both enchanting and terrifying…
With an extraordinary power, Jelinek has crafted another
awesome portrait of the modern city overwhelmed by the turmoil
of its past and petrified by the horror of its future. Discomforting
in the extreme, but truly essential reading' *Blitz*

'Jelinek's characters, and the voice she uses to tell of them are
fashioned with black irony and jarring distortion. Yet the ultimate
effect is grace, a dark image delivered in terms appropriate to
it, but in a draftsmanship that conveys a hint of delicacy and
lyricism, as if these had been ejected from the room but continued
to haunt it' *Los Angeles Times*

'*Wonderful, Wonderful Times* probes, in a series of hallucinatory
episodes, what happens when there is no past to illuminate the

present, when history has become a mere hole, which no stuffing, not even the best straw, can fill' *Bookforum*

Women as Lovers

'A chilling and truthful vision of women's precarious position in a society still dominated by money and men' *Kirkus Reviews*

GREED

Elfriede Jelinek

Translated by Martin Chalmers

A complete catalogue record for this book can
be obtained from the British Library on request

The right of Elfriede Jelinek to be identified as the author
of this work has been asserted by her in accordance with
the Copyright, Designs and Patents Act 1988

Copyright © 2000 by Rowohlt Verlag, Reinbek

Translation copyright © 2006 Martin Chalmers

First published as *Gier* in 2000 by Rowohlt Verlag, Reinbek

First published in this translation in 2006 by Serpent's Tail
First published in 2008 in this edition by Serpent's Tail,
an imprint of Profile Books Ltd
3A Exmouth House
Pine Street
London EC1R 0JH
website: www.serpentstail.com

ISBN 978 1 84668 666 5

Typeset by Martin Worthington

Printed in Great Britain by CPI Bookmarque,
Croydon, CR0 4TD

10 9 8 7 6 5 4 3 2 1

This book is printed on FSC certified paper

GREED

The translator wishes to thank Peter 'Bär' Gattinger, Esther Kinsky and Alex Schmidt for making this a better translation than it would otherwise have been. M.C.

1.

Today country policeman Kurt Janisch is once again looking at the photo on which his father, Police-Colonel Janisch, saluted the King, thirty years earlier. Look, his father is still standing there, evidently forced to draw back just an inch from his own enthusiastic motion of standing to attention, but why is there nothing to check him? - there's something soft, indecisive about his shoulders, which then seems to push him forward again. Perhaps it was no more than an involuntary bow before the monarch, more or less as an encore to the frequently rehearsed salute. There's nothing at all subordinate about the son any more, standing there in front of the cabinet in his striped track-suit harnessing his body by slowly warming it up before going running. His father had still borne his subordination, with drooping shoulders, but capable hands, down the dusty country roads and to smashed up car wrecks. Perhaps the son is more versatile and can also give orders, the way he looks makes me curious: a somewhat angular face, across which the thoughts, which in all people like to spread out, merely seem to shyly slip through. Well. But the will would be there now, what is he going to use it for? The boat has heaved to, the traffic lights are switched on and are permanently at green, the fine distinction between him and other people is growing.

The country policeman is meanwhile completely dominated by a kind of greed, which came unnoticed, but was finally noticeable even to the neighbours (astonishment at plant progeny in the front garden, no one knows where they come from, he can't have bought them!). Occasionally someone looks up the land register, to see what the country policeman tried to camouflage with the book of life. Now he has moored, he has spied out his targets. The oars have been taken in, the line, the nets cast. Perhaps originally there was room for something else, beautiful, decent in the country policeman? A good-looking and seemingly light-hearted man, the country policeman, just the sort we women like. Something to work with. It's not just to keep world peace, that men dish out a load of lies to women, to make them dependent, while women indeed have something better to offer, all their thinking and feeling and a lot of things made of brightly coloured wools. It's understandable, of course, that we, especially those of us with the older sex organs, who haven't seen much through the little escape hatches of the body, must remain strangers to ourselves nevertheless! we love-hungry ladies, unfortunately we don't know this country policeman (the flower of the country road goes down right in front of his marked car and we're not there) personally. Not to worry, I'll take care of that: So as not to jeopardise your little bit of lover's bliss which depends on deception, like every other kind, I'd better take over the telling of the story myself now. Don't interrupt! At the moment in order to prevent war between the bodies, I can't even exactly tell their functions. Not even this determination in the man, which I already sense, properly knows its goal yet, but I know it's been looking for a long time and will find it in what corrupts most easily, the human body. Whoever knows himself, will immediately want a bit of the other, but then the others immediately want it, too.

Incidentally they're both dead now, the king and his guide and guard, the father of the country policeman, who that day proudly escorted the prancing black coaches from Graz main station (the state visit came from Vienna by rail over the Semmering Pass) across the foreordained Mur Bridge and then casually flung them into the armoury, where already centuries ago rich people had handed over their metal clothes for safekeeping. How can one hate life, the son is just thinking, who was left over from his father's table, and turns his face to the mountain wind. High up there, through the attic window of his house, a small trough for animals can be seen, into which soft muzzles dig, whose owners, male and female, will later be shot, many of them, except for the mothers, which at this time of year are still protected by their motherhood. Others are alone. Even animals, wrongly, often, seek out the nearness of the other, and the country policeman also likes to be sociable in the public house and does small deals on the side (with watches and jewellery preferably in the county town! Where not so many people know one's face). Therefore many people regard him as a good mate, who can get you second hand building tools along with building materials more cheaply. Yet if he honestly travels around inside himself, he has to conclude it's so dark in there, one doesn't even know exactly where one is. No wonder, that again and again, at intervals of about a month, he has to light himself up a bit through belligerent, but not very purposeful indiscriminate drinking. His colleagues don't see this darkness in their chum, perhaps they suspect it sometimes, and they don't want to believe their wives, who sense something like that and are strongly attracted by it until they end up in a heap on heat. Whoever only learns about everything from reading, should please do so now.

Am I mistaken, or was something found here years ago, that was never cleared up? What am I forced to look at, when I open this old newspaper? A pale face glimmers there beneath the lowest fir twigs, like a little moon, the face has something to tell, but can no longer tell anyone, because a heavy hand was laid on the throat, clothes were pulled down, the features of the face convulsed; tracks which might good-naturedly have given the green light, if only they'd been asked, arched up, broke, as the roots of the body, the legs, were tugged and shaken, until enough was enough, until the crumbly earth was loosened. So, now where's the bag with the humour, which we still had with us when we gave information to the police earlier? Where is the humus for the potting? Jeans into which absolutely nothing seems to fit any more, come apart at the seams, a skirt flies up, falls down to earth again from heaven, reluctantly, because not cut out for it, becomes a sack, into which goes the woman's face. Well, and now where will we put the stamp, so that this one, originally with such varied interests, will in future only long for sleep, because she has got to know and learned to reject fundamentally, down to the last root fibres of being, the opposite of sleep, extreme activity?

It sometimes makes the country policeman nervous, that the villagers don't really know him at all, although the camouflage he originally strove for was kindness and friendliness after all, and then he goes on drinking far too long, alone if need be. The ground beneath and between his feet has already been caressed by women until it got too hot for him, women on whose grounds he has cast an eye. Such a forceful, big man, who is capable of unleashing almost any kind of event. A chosen woman, who previously had been lying a little too long in the shop window, until too many had seen her and not taken her away, meanwhile knows only the square yard in front of the telephone, and it, too, has by now been burnt right through from all the running back and forward, and then the way from the door and the nice bed, which, together with new satin bed linen has been specially bought for two in the county town. What does one need the rest for.

It's not good to hate, but only if you tell me who, can I really say, if it's good or bad. It gives some people the energy they need, like a Mars bar, which comes straight from the god of war and plunges into a human figure, until the latter has melted away. The pilot can no longer save himself even with his ejector seat. But with hating one can grow nice and old. It passes the time, which in any case runs off, as soon as it sees us. Of course, everyone thinks they must be among friends, if they happen to run across someone outwardly tranquil, who holds public office and takes it out of women, they're always really finished afterwards. So why hate, except in a war, which is being organised once again at present, which makes everything inside us, and that's a great deal, depending on the anger of the other side, shoot out and could only be dammed up once more by the utmost love of life and a home-sewn iron curtain. But we don't have anything like that in stock in our store, we've only got two very soft down duvets there, in case someone happens to drop by. Instead we have reciprocal campaigns on offer, until the field between us is trampled down. Now it's been softened up as well by the rain and our desires for our neighbour's property. It's no longer good even as a field of slaughter. But the neighbour has to give way anyway, we've threatened to get the police onto him, if he doesn't take down the wall with the ugly fence on top, because it's spoiling our view. Frankness, diligence and cheerfulness, which the country police-man likes to feign for others, is intended to give rise to the love of life of others towards him, but there is little of this commodity in stock. The flames are already shooting up in the Gameboy, in which our own life is simulated, but what a frightful face is look-ing back at us from it? No face looks back from us at the country policeman, who is fast asleep with sweet dreams of power and greatness, because, wrongly, this man doesn't interest us yet. That could soon change once he has got hold of the building plan of our circuits and our little house and the apartments we own. I hope I'll manage it so that you too experience one of his happy moments! But I doubt it, I already don't like him. It's a frequent reproach, that I stand around looking stupid and drop my char-acters before I even have them, because to be honest I pretty quickly find them dull. Perhaps at this very moment, as the servant of the state is bending over someone else's building plan, which he has stolen, perhaps now he is happier than we are? And we're supposed to be interested in that?

Yet I fear, only if he were addressed in the Name of the Republic would it be a matter of concern to our community of the living, and that can take a long time. I am filling the time in between with my unproductive song. There is a limit, but it just isn't given to some people to be happy wanderers, although the snowdrops, that's right, it's spring now and that makes us happy, are stretching out their little digger claws towards the soil, as if they wanted to pick up the soil instead of your shoe sole doing it sooner or later. Even Kurt Janisch sometimes asks himself, where this dark side comes from (for which he has a certain warrant because of his profession, and which, whenever one thinks, now the lightbulb's gone, grows even darker still. Who on earth lets down the blinds in the middle of the night? Only someone who's going to shun the light of day come the morning!). He can't work it out. His parents didn't really ignore him, they didn't encourage him either, in any respect, not even to keep going with that smart appearance of his, which was already there quite early on, someone was bound to come and hitch a ride with him, a nice girl perhaps. Someone is sure to be able to make use of it, this ghostly, pale, curly-haired and yet nevertheless robust figure, which a person can't help, but the country policeman can, because he's constantly exercising it. God has given it to him along with the commandments, so that a man forgets obedience again, because he's so busy with his appearance. Women in particular do a great deal for their appearance, so obeying an industry prepared to go to any lengths, whose products constantly contradict one another, otherwise why would there be so many? The country policeman only rarely thinks about his actions, with which we shall have to concern ourselves, prefers to stay on the surface of things, where he passes his comb through, drawing furrows in his dark-blond hair like hammers in a rock. The comb has been moistened first, on his head then it looks as if there's rain, from which one should have protected oneself. Now the country policeman has himself risen to quite a high rank, and even his grown-up son already has a good post, even if not at the station, where he would unfortunately collide with his father's position. Yes, and something else I wanted to say: His son already has a little house, too, great, even if it doesn't properly belong to him yet, it's been acquired on a life annuity. But the life, which at this point is still owner of the house, has subsequently, unfortunately and unexpectedly, with varying success, but by and large rather vigorously, gone on living, although originally it seemed no more than a ruin: an old woman, who now only rarely gets a breath of fresh air, although it really should be the duty of the country policeman's daughter-in-law to take her for walkies every day, but one can't do everything oneself. Nor can one yet kill her e.g. with lily of the valley leaves, it would be too soon, there would be talk in this tightly defined community, and the clusters of people would grow together into an almost impenetrable hedge (though loaded with good fruit!), which like a net first protects the wrongdoer from himself and then, if he has not harmed himself, hands him over to justice. The country policeman's son has a wife, who belongs to God and the Virgin and every Sunday morning and every evening bloodlessly sacrifices herself in church in front of the tabernacle. That's how she was brought up, and she has arranged with her will to go on in the same way voluntarily, even without the coercion of the nuns, who fine-ground her, so that some day she will fit through heaven's gate. Ten years ago she gave birth to a child, a son, which is the sole meaning and purpose of marriage. A daughter, a few more kids even would have been welcome, too. God said nothing about having to change the nappies of an old woman. That's why the young woman is so pig-headed, there's nothing more solid than the views of the Church, so the old dear can just lie there in her own shit until evening, or until she rusts, we're going to evening mass now, she has to stand firm until it's time to go to bed, the old dear, not the Church, it has already stood firm for much longer and doesn't need any nappies either. Because it takes and takes and never parts with what it has. Perhaps that's where we learned it, no, we could do it already. And the son, let's just say what his name is, his name is Ernst Janisch, and he in his turn has a son, Patrick, but the wife belongs half to God and the ancient woman three quarters. Every day she swallows two litres no problem, she has to be given that, otherwise she throws a fit; that results in a lot of excreta, if one's not allowed to go to the john because it's one floor down, built-in to the present home of the country policeman's children, where it's used much more often. That's not how the old woman imagined it, when she indirectly put her fate in the hands of an official. But what I'm writing here is not intended to be an investigation. The diagnosis 'initial stages of liver cirrhosis' is anyway certain, I think. If God still manages the last drops of the old dear, he will himself be so far gone, that he won't be paying attention to anything any more and overlook many sinners. Never mind. This house will then at last belong entirely to the country policeman's son, he'll never share a thing again, not even with this God, we can collect the money ourselves. God will get our sins, he'll have to make do with that.

None of all the promising properties of which there are expectations, there are considerably more than I was able to enumerate here, is at the moment completely paid off or has paid off or is even really in prospect, with the exception of the old woman's share, who, if nothing out of the ordinary occurs and the Lord works a miracle, seems to be declining into eternity and otherwise. The country policeman's daughter-in-law has anyhow made a nice down payment on this eternal bliss, in the shape of a son, who is still a child, especially pleasing to God. God scrubs his soul in confession, the priest scrutinises it for dirty thoughts, and tells the son, after he himself has had a good wank in the darkness of his soul, his favourite place, to join the queue of little children at the back, where it's easy to get at him; the queue, which the priest receives for children's mass once a week, snakes round there, hissing and scuffling and, making use of the flat of his hand, if someone chatters or passes on unpleasant truths, he sends them home again. Are these personal belongings not perhaps burdens on the development of a still young man, who would urgently need a few mortgages, in order to unburden himself a little? To him even curtains are already a revolutionary decision, he's always saying he only needs the bare minimum, and that's the ownership of house and real estate. Otherwise he's stingy, the mechanic, the engineer, and his father even more so. His wife has to embellish the front garden with cuttings which, as if something like that were not constantly happening in the world on a grand scale and as a warning to us, she secretly plucks out from the pots at the nursery. Does this son of man perhaps want to keep the little house, but get rid of wife and child? Can all his faithfulness so quickly be over and done with? He hasn't had the family so very long yet! Perhaps there'll be more children! We shall find out or again maybe not, depending on whether I can express myself intelligibly or not and don't mix up the dramatis personae all the time, at the moment it doesn't look as if that's going to happen. Why on earth did I start off with three generations, in fact there are even four? Oh well, they're not all present at the same time, after all, and anyway they're all the same. Are we all going to get into the same boat, what do you think? Who wouldn't like to have at least one little house for themselves alone? He could drive through under the bridges or drive along on the motorways up above, but the house would stay patiently at home and wait for him.

The son of the present country policeman is employed by the Post Office as a telephone maintenance man and mender of faults, he attended a technical secondary school, whose graduates call themselves engineers and are everywhere much sought after, in particular by the telephone companies, shooting up everywhere, soon there'll be just one, hot for our voices. In order to consolidate and shield his permanent job, the son goes every week without fail to his bank on the main square, as if his determination would bring in somewhat more than his securities justify, horns lowered in anticipation of contradiction, inflexible, immovable, his hands, however, pleading, raised almost hesitantly, off he goes to the bank, which gives him credit, until he will have lost every security, and finally will only be able to dumbly, imploringly hold out his hands, they stay where they are. To be rich depends on a precise knowledge of what one has and what one could still get. Why does the Church do so little for its own, who fill its buildings so assiduously with flesh? The church doesn't care, whether people come or not, it's nearly always locked up anyway, except during mass, when the holy Eucharist listlessly does its duty in its cubby hole. It should be possible, for example, that pious vergeresses like the young daughter-in-law of the country policeman, in the course of selfless activity in the service of the parish, could spy out little houses becoming vacant more quickly than others, why not, and why then don't they inherit? Why then does a nephew from Linz inherit, who has never even seen a church or his aunt's little house from inside for years? And why are we not all wealthy film stars, who go home and wipe off our desires with our make-up, in order to have bigger, more beautiful ones the next day and particularly in order to have a good night's sleep, so that you can't tell our lives by looking at us and we can all candidly display ourselves in the magazine? Luckily crimes of violence only rarely occur around here. You won't believe, just how few people there are, who have no relatives at all any more! Then there are others again, who disguise themselves as widows with perms, and who turn out to have a faraway son after all, who slunk off in good time, but who, at the crucial moment, changes the course of events, which most of the time were themselves slinking along. What a bore! There comes this son, from Linz or what do I know from Recklinghausen, Germany, or Canada, where he had been thought to have gone missing in the smelting house of a steel works or underneath a gigantic stack of wood, and the fatted calf together with the house are already waiting for him, without him having done a thing for it. The will is now challenged with a heavy sword, just wait a moment, thwack, and the air's out of it. Perhaps the Church only exists to knock reason into the old folks, who have to die soon anyway, to ensure they step into its marquee in good time and to prettily illustrate the dark abyss of hell. Heaven is always other people, when they benevolently take our property off our hands. Hell is in us. The Church itself prefers to inherit, instead of its half-witted employees getting anything.

The son of the country policeman remains sitting immobile in the customer's easy chair of the branch manager, afraid of inadvertently betraying through the language of his body, which even he doesn't quite understand, anything, even the tiniest bit about his true and presumptive properties which the bank doesn't absolutely have to know about. What do you need this scrap of paper for? What's on this bit of paper doesn't interest me in the least. Only the signature counts, and what's printed above it. Only then is the truth also legally binding. Today the bank is to be informed of the prospective salary rise, which was notified in an informal letter. Of course all this is merely a provisional state of affairs for this employee, because soon his properties will be more numerous than the grains of sand on the vegetables freshly pulled from the garden, with which you can save money shopping. The wife pulls it right out of her heart, in which no one lives any more, because her husband moved out years ago. Yes, this house is yours to hold, says God, and means the body of a human being, even several houses together wouldn't make a knight out of me, thinks the country policeman, who knows about such a tin man from a book of tales from this area. His son is already as zealously greedy as his father and he would stop at nothing, if people didn't voluntarily die beforehand, sometimes admittedly pretty late in the day. If the Dear Lord knew, to whom they raise up houses, instead of Him having to steal them, as His children do, who even have to take care of that themselves.

The rage, which is sometimes hidden behind a cheerful smile, may then suddenly, but all the more powerfully shoot out, if the old body, which goes along with every pension, shows itself unasked in the hall next to the toilet door, where it doesn't belong, it belongs once and for all up in the attic. This old woman has a pretty thick skull, but a plastic screwdriver handle, which has many smaller, interchangeable heads, its changelings so to speak, is after all not made of cotton wool. It's good and hard, even if not fatal. Saints sometimes yield and concede something, but not this head. If you please, here however we have a corresponding bruise on the temple. Why does the old dear have to keep on falling down! Come a bit closer again, you old heap of shit, then we'll show you, how wretchedly you can bleed behind the bright and cheerful geraniums on the window sill, which are on the outside, so that no one can see in. The people in the bank yesterday irritated this man impermissibly with their glances, and he has a very violent temper, aha, he's got another appointment with the branch manager, he must be short again this month! He must've taken on too much with all those mortgages and bills of exchange and foreign exchange credits! Janisch jun. feels their looks like branches prodding the wild beast of prey inside him. But if it really came out, they would be the first to run away screaming. He says to the branch manager: It'll break my wife's heart, if it's not possible for her to open a knitted goods boutique downstairs in the basement. For this purpose the cellar requires large-scale reconstruction, damp coursing and internal and external fittings, all depending on the available cash, which you and your bank will hand over to me today, otherwise I'll be even less successful with my repayments than before, and then you can forget about the total amount, because then you'll get nothing. Yes, Frau Eichholzer is still alive and we hope for a long time to come, my wife's looking after her and the Church isn't going to come to my wife and take a look because of an incontinent old woman. My wife sees the inside of the church every day anyway. Smile, smile, my wife would be like an open book for the Dear Lord, if he needed to read it, but he wrote the Book of Books, so from one eternity to the next he doesn't need another one. But he knows everything anyway. Smirk! And: No need to worry, for all that, we've already got an eye on the house after the next one, although we will already have taken on too much with the last one and its renovation. The land it's on will provide enough security for the mortgages on the first. We can acquire a whole string of houses, one always secures the next (they'll be real castles, when we're finished with them) even if not quite legitimately and if we only knew which. We already know what we'll use for the back-up copy, the money from the bank, your money, a sweet mixed community of several mortgage, discount and other loan providers, yes indeed, we will get houses and homes, and we'll rent or lease shops in them, we'll paint windows, we'll seal floors, we'll agree on built-in cupboards, we'll mislay tiles or trample on them in a rage, because they don't make up the desired pattern, one way or another. The point of these little houses inhabited by organisms will be, that each preceding model can be taken as security for the subsequent one, well, isn't that a good idea to stimulate our economy and remove superfluous living beings? With people with a weak heart it's even possible to use bulbs, e.g. of the pretty lily of the valley, we already said so, really everyone knows that, and the patient will have such a delighted look on her face, when we mix it with the wild garlic curd and spread it on her slice of bread. Snigger. Snigger. Thank you very much, now I'll go again, to hurry along the building work. You'll see how nice it'll be when it's finished, after all, it'll still belong to you for a while, dear bank, trust is good, supervision can hardly be better. You'll surely understand, once I've laid the foundation stones for the extension of this home right up to the attic! Often things that happen nearby, have an effect far away. If you don't believe me, then just place a small coin in the bulb socket and turn the light on!

Sometimes the banks keep watching far too long, before they withdraw to their uneven path. Until the branch manager loses his post and the debtor, who has to take the penultimate path, has turned into a whimpering wreck, because now he even had to sell the car, which was still whole, his only friend, who always ran decently alongside him, because there wasn't enough money for petrol any more. Now the debtor has to try to be a light in his own darkness, in order to offer the bank manager a good picture. All of this with his meagre talents, so that the extension under which every joint is already groaning, will be stretched once more on this rack. And they all watch as one desperately negotiates, as everyday troubles turn into catastrophes and get into the paper if one doesn't keep quiet. While a whole house floats away. The branch manager will have to chuck money at it again, otherwise the whole lot will be gone; usually the auditor checks up on every peanut, which good children have set down, and which mark an ever broader sloping path, at whose end stands the most beautiful of all houses, the witch's gingerbread house. Where plump little fingers probe helplessly in the air, basically long ready to roast, so why hasn't the witch laid the table yet? Because she wanted one more side-dish! Visit the fairy tale world of Police District Mürzzuschlag (Styria): Mon. to Fri. 8-12. That's what they look like, don't they, reality and its dreams? Why don't human beings just explode, except with anger? Surely they should have gone to pieces long before. So that's why the term really can't be extended to the twelfth of never, you can be sure of that Mr Janisch, even if your father is a respected member of whatever the club is, oh yes, of the Country Policemen's Club and of the Country Policemen's Sports Club and the Country Policemen's Canine Sports Club, every one of whose members ended up hanging on the tap at the inn after a dinghy training exercise, I mean, who ended the exercise correctly. When it comes to emergency operations we recently also had the real thing, when that big blaze was raging, as a result of which in the town centre of K. a whole number of roof timbers and furnishings with a total loss of more than one and half million pounds went up the creek, so that's when these men had to carry out their perilous duties, apart from the

Country Police more than 29 fire brigades from the whole region, well, is that not something? And all the farms set alight by children and little more than children, well, is that not something, too? Children are stubbornness personified, after all. So that's why, for the sake of your father, we're giving you one last extension, Mr Janisch jun., who knows if some day the roof over our own heads won't be burning, we've read that the Fire Investigations Officer of the precinct where your father is stationed, finally established that a rusty little stove door was the cause of the fire. Man walks, who counts his steps? No one, there would be no point, whomsoever God wishes to show favour, He drops down a detached house from heaven and makes sure that the new owner is standing right below it. The debts will eat us all up, if we don't turn into beasts beforehand.

And we don't even want to start on about the clearing-up operations after the mudslide last autumn, we really must draw a line under this chapter, although we're still so stuck to it. Even the police cadets spent five days helping out then, to say nothing of the tons of hair in the ground, which no one has yet been able to explain. For that we had to bring in units of the Federal Army, didn't we? After last year's fire the plots of land are once again firmly in the hands of our bank. Those are no grounds to be against the banks or the Jews, although that's a fine tradition hereabouts, there's simply no ground that belongs to anyone else, that's it. Small cause, big effect, as NATO always said about the Kosovo War. Just imagine, there are even people who want to open a DIY superstore in the darkest and most inaccessible hills of the Bucklige Welt in Lower Austria, you wouldn't believe it, while huge loads whizz past them with a whistling slipstream and straight over the southern or eastern border, where there are people living, whom one despises, whose language one doesn't speak, whose laws one doesn't know, but where everything costs exactly half, which usefully one had already saved up. For dessert one can eat and booze really well and go to the hairdresser for the same money you pay for a couple of rolls here. The people on the other side of the border, who were rotting alive for too long in a gloomy state, don't yet know how one has to do business and our light will take a couple of light years yet until it has reached them. So they do their own business, but which is also already quite effective and even fills up petrol tanks, until they burst. Our bank however already knows it all in advance, it inspects the new house which reminds it of every other one which already exists, except that it's already falling apart while people are still living, and even takes our folks' furniture off the floor. It has to watch out too, that it keeps its feet on the carpet, which the debtor also has to pawn. A pity that it allowed that final loan, that penultimate support, but there's nothing to be done. Now all that good money has been spent and for what? Not for us! We're certainly being spoiled! Nothing's going on here, for which I would even stroke a person's head, to get it.

Well and bad: Son Janisch, himself a father, with a son of his own who already cheerfully changes into his kit, when banners flying it's time to go to battle on the football field, has already removed a small, but important part of the bank's riches, dropping by with a couple of cases of wine and a couple of nice plump lies for the branch manager, which have to be washed down with even more alcohol, we'll see each other at our table in the pub. Together with our sons and heirs, no our house will never die out, we've founded a party for it and wish everyone else all the worst, while we, gossiping, play our own jokes. All of this is my final argument, which is far too impatient to settle down here and now. They're all sneering at this by now veteran party, but they all vote for it. Now are we sitting comfortably? Kurt Janisch (at present senior director of the company Housegrab and Son) is already working himself half to death and has taken on two part time jobs as factory security guard in the small town. His father found them for him in his day. Here, where the generations still properly follow one another, tradition still counts for something. And son Ernst, too, the crown prince, has brought the bank, which anyway has a tendency to ampleness, because it so much likes to clear up and then eat the default interest from other people's Christmas trees, which, deceptively were only lit up for a week, something as a chaser: The bank can swallow it or not. Ernst doesn't care. This money, too, was finally drunk up, we're not going back to the house, first we have to have the house to go to - and now the money's gone. And the house is not yet really there, that is, it would be, but it looks so far away as if it was about to disappear and take a coffee break, before the interest has properly begun to work. A screaming old dear in a hole under the roof means, that one's not exactly acclaimed by public opinion, that has to change. Word must not get round. Otherwise payday would come around after all, the car park lit up, where it's all supposed to happen and where the other wrecks are already waiting to be towed away. She mustn't go into an old people's home, she must stay here and show a return, until she's nothing more than a transparent rustling mummy, swinging bags of flour, to kill rats dancing at night on the hot plate, because the rats want to attack her and she's got nothing else to hand except this white powder, which she secretly stirs into dough, yesyes, the wine's good.

So the agricultural credit bank is sticking out its hand too, no, both hands, and our throat between them. No wonder, when this patient institution is constantly and again and again being told more and more gloomy stories, fortunately all made up, at the same time as more and more riches, which were never there, are depicted. There's someone who's in debt to us, but he doesn't make himself available for the repayment, what can we do? We like to sit in the comfortable colourful easy chairs in the appropriate branch, have fun and look cheerfully at the glacé cherries on the frothy abundance (achieved through folding in of quite ordinary air!) of our demands. And then we look out of the window and straight into the window of the café, and there they are, the real cakes. Afterwards, full of cholesterol, in our grave, we'll feel better. But we already have to spread optimism around now, while the bank still has to learn how to deal with adolescents, when they have debts the size of future annual salaries with four different telephone companies. We're sticking to more solid assets, says Kurt Janisch and says his son Ernstl. One of those bronze turrets on the detached house, that would be tiptop! that would be really smart, would really add something to the house, why don't we just cap it? Exactly: We'll put on a tower as well. We won't put on the matching Spanish boots. The long and the short of it is: The bank wants something every month. The funds are always only in prospect, and there's never a telescope there, so that they finally come closer and look bigger than they are. But that's going to change! There are quite different times coming for the hard-working, the decent and the able, who want to take power one day, too, they've waited long enough for it and have gathered in a movement which, congealed as a cold fried egg, would at last like to add us, yes indeed, just US! as a toy or a greasy side-dish to an even greasier roast. I wouldn't vote for us, we would be too lazy for everything, war would always follow us, because we possessed no sense of judgement. At some point perhaps it will also acquire manners, this party, but it's not really necessary, because the big money, which sets great store by something like that will board this train anyway, even if still hesitantly, no matter who's driving and where to, but capital always keeps one foot on the ground, so it can jump off in time and look for another engine driver. But that's where capital doesn't know our Janischs! Going along with them would have worked out all right the first time. Marx, too, would have written something a bit different, better even, if he had known about them. Admittedly Janisch & Co. didn't set up housing mortgage companies for long enough, although people like them in this party certainly did, and fell on their faces with all of them. The companies had to be wound up again, a pity really. Now Messrs Janisch are trying something else! They want to make their own mistakes, but always ones which others would make too, if they had the chance. Indeed all human qualities are tied up in this community of the like-minded, and this bundle will then fall heavily on all our heads, I can see that already. Well, soon they're going to collect people, they already have the houses. You'll see!

So the funds: But first these have to be snatched from greedy arms and passed on to other greedy arms. The son of the country policeman, however, absolutely must have them right now, so that in association with his father (it's the Association of Austrian Building Society Investors, which has reproduced in full colour in its house journal pictures of British country seats or at least of doctors' houses in the Austrian provinces, converted peasant cottages made of beautiful old wood, grown honourably grey without a lick of paint. We'll surely provide our building society investors with this nice little magazine after having taken their billions! Then the Austrians, men and women, will save even more. Interest at less than one per cent! We'll move over to shares but still can't sleep any more. If God created men in his image, why should man not be allowed to design his little house as a likeness of Buckingham Palace?) he can pursue his hobby of collecting houses and plots of land. The branch manager also has a hobby: speculation. The coming bad times have encouraged him to take it up. He is a brave and clever person. But that's a nice hobby, which you've been given there! Other people have to go to play tennis or go to die or go jogging, and indeed the rightful owners of the adjoining properties must die, owners, for whom their property had likewise once been a heartfelt concern, and which lay together like two peaceful villages before finally being gathered together in a cosy residential landscape, large enough to be entered by a country policeman and his son, but not by their families, whom they are also meanwhile fed up to the back teeth with. First they would have died, if they hadn't been able to get them, the families, women and children. And now they no longer fit, because their own demands have grown bigger, but the children too, unfortunately. Now they suddenly need much more! People grow out of their demands and are so stupid as to tend towards violence when they have new ones. We're still there too, unfortunately, a kind of elite, who put garden chairs on their balconies. Please be a patient for a moment. One thing at a time, one house at a time, one woman at a time, one setback at a time, in order finally after all to grab the opportunities by the somewhat grey short and curlies. Ouch. The skin comes away, too. I call that the art of war! People die one way or the other, no fear, but their houses remain, unless we were in Kosovo, there it would be the other way round, but no, nothing at all is left there. Nothing of anyone. Whoever can do so wants to leave. Yes, something has to be done with the people, so that they don't rest and rust. They must have enough time, so that they can get their possessions to safety beforehand, before the war starts, which dreamy people have long longed for. They foresaw it, after all! Where is the truck, the tractor, the little horse, now it's time to go over the mountains. Before the properties crumble away, if you please, we'll just take them, if no one else does it. Abandoned property cannot bear the emptiness in itself, it wants to belong to someone again. Up there a horse is lying under the tractor, because they didn't want to take the pass road in proper order one behind the other. Some possessions are too big for any means of transport. If one doesn't take the wheel oneself and steers everything down to the smallest detail, even if it's down to the bottom of the roadside ditch, then someone else will take what belongs to one. Sometimes it'll be the duties, sometimes a distant relative whom one could not have reckoned with, because one's never heard of him. These two men, Janisch father and son, altogether making the best impression, I can't say any more than that, the first as a country policeman, the other as tamer of telephone lines, to which one has to tap up to the top of tall masts, have discovered a fine method of living, so that property lies down sighing at their feet like a tired dog. Except no one is allowed to visit otherwise it jumps up and bites, as a sign, that the property belongs to us alone:

They pay court to women. Both of them actually. But mainly Janisch senior, the country policeman. That's so easily said, but he has already made so many people in this town and in this part of the country unhappy. Well, would you have guessed it? Preferably women who own houses or apartments in the nearby small town. These female proceedings have to be conducted and intimately handled, even if what the Janischs do is not described like that. They combine the pleasing with the useful. Well.

It's a good thing if one gets around in one's job and the hours are a bit flexible, so that one can go for a wee drive in between. The husbands of these wives should be deceased if possible or never have existed in the first place. There should never have been children present either. Who knows something like that (that a lady has to make an exit at a given moment, otherwise there's one too many around for her property), if not a policeman, priest, neighbour, telephone engineer or the appropriate grocer, who himself, however, has cast an eye over this emptiness, which in his mind is becoming populated with ever more bricks, until one's heart grows heavy? However, only the margins in retail trade are worth talking about, not actions. This box of tropical fruit must not be knocked over, the ease and naturalness with which the venomous red leaping spider, but no, it's called a crested spider, will hop out, could produce expressions, which would become sights worth seeing. The grocer will never get back the eye he risked. That's the way women are, always the same type for the love command and for the most global project of all, against which environmental pollution and world peace are nothing: marriage. They all want it. Women and marriage, that's the perfect combination, especially in the country, where there aren't many distractions and you soon get enough of them. Marriage follows. It's not possible for a woman to say 'thanks, but no thanks'. The grocer will have to buy his bananas somewhere else and deliver them somewhere else, the door is shut to him. He hasn't got the faintest idea to whom this door is opened, but it must be to someone. He hasn't seen the woman behind it for weeks now. In the end the niece in Krems will get something she hadn't been expecting, and she'll get it after the aunt's end. It won't have paid off, that the grocer so decently delivered food to the old woman in his car. Others were quicker and there already. The neighbours, too, like to munch along, leftovers, too. They stare at the garbage. The things she throws away, they can still be used! People steal from one another, first out of conviction, then out of love. First they introduce themselves as neighbours and immediately transform themselves into friends, that is, greedy beasts, just as in our dear Balkans, which we meanwhile know better than our own living room, where the place appears on our screens at least four times a day, where neighbours were still neighbours but didn't stay that way. Our own neighbours spur on their apocalyptic steeds, so that this shoving, splashing, dripping flood of old men and women is directed into the bed, which stands in the bedroom, where often the TV doesn't come in. If one doesn't proceed carefully, it may be that one goes under and pleasantly anaesthetised by Anafranil suffocates in one's own shit. Stealing isn't so easy, often it's hard work, otherwise we'd all be doing it.

The two Janischs, we're agreed on that, want to get either immediately or a little later a whole house or several houses for nothing, that's all they've got: nothing. In fact the desired pieces of real estate are to be added to the ones the Janischs already own. They'll first have to change the gears of a number of women, I'm afraid. One starts up in first gear, one comes to a stop with the last. That must have been another serious tailgate crash. Just a moment, the police are coming right now! And it will always have been our own fault. The officer of the Country Police takes it all down in his notebook and takes photographs at regular intervals. To save costs the rural police posts are not fully manned. Often officers have to be borrowed, who are easily distracted. You ask, how quickly this or another woman can be swept off her feet? You do have to sleep with her, and then you have to skim off her cream. In the country there are still some who feel guilty about extra-marital intercourse, so then one just promises them marital intercourse, there are just a few obstacles of flesh, blood and bones to be cleared out of the way. Just you don't be getting on your high horse, there are a couple more in front of you! They also have to get a cock inserted, how many times a day do you think one can manage that, we're not so young ourselves any more. The lady has to be on probation for at least a year and in that time only gets to hold and look at it, after all we need to hold onto the contents, so that another doesn't get suspicious. A brisk confession in between, and everything's all right again.

It all depends a little on the fullness of the hair, on the character and whatever else there is under the bonnet or in the wallet, not just on the properties. Until the little sweetie's horse power, poor thing, is exhausted. Women are sometimes already grateful for the fact that they still have their gearbox at all, when life's bustle, laughter, shouts slowly begin to ebb away. So, for a while at least, one simply has to attend to their equipment, when on duty one always has to drop by briefly in the car as if by chance on routes and detours one has thought up, everything all right, madam? Earlier I had a very bad feeling, but at least it was one. I haven't had one for a long time. Well, someone rang the bell earlier. We'll track him down, if you'll just let me in now, I'm a public servant and can safely be used at any time like a paper napkin! Don't be embarrassed, you can eat with your fingers if you like. Careful, my cock jumps out just at the sight of you, look how it's dripping, perhaps I'd go away from your carpet, but your vinyl flooring is damned hard, but I know something harder, do you see it here and now? Of course things would go better, if we would proceed to the bedroom right away. In the outer room I only put in a brief appearance, but in the bedroom I pull the whole thing out, don't worry, it won't stand around looking puzzled or get a piston rub at the wrong moment, just because you're too dry inside, it'll always do the business, no matter where, I know it. It'll get going just as soon as it sees you, it'll stand up in the room just like a man in a uniform and pull down every little thing, what was I going to say before? Now we'll just pull down the panties (oh yes, please, do keep going!) What, you want to get on top of me? The public makes demands on us, but not as much as you! Well, do as you please, I'll stay cool, but I would like to be on the mattress, doesn't matter if you haven't tidied up, I'll tidy up inside you! In any case, now you're going to get the absolute, which you've been longing for all this time, it's pretty long, but would go in your handbag if need be, if it could go at all. Yes, women are often modest, because they had a hard life. But you've never seen something as smart as me, have you? And it's fun with me, too, I'm no child of sorrow, I'm a child of jokes and laughter. I don't mind if you already undress in the outer room, in public we'd better not be on first name terms, I'll just close the door and prepare myself for the sight of you without your underwear, that can take a while, what you will have bought them just for me? Well, I'm honoured! Then leave them on, for all I care, it doesn't matter, anyway I understand you as well as I understand my hunger and thirst or my desire for houses, yours above all, at whose door I still have to knock, if I want to come in. Didn't you report a hungry marten with a sweet tooth in your hallway to us yesterday, madam, oh, it wasn't you, then it must be a mistake or the badger from next door in among your blackcurrants. Such a big smelly beast! Take a look at my little fellow, he's been waiting all this time for you, I'm holding him very firmly now, so that you can stroke him, otherwise he'll run away from you again. You can look at this nice magazine first, that I've brought with me, you can choose the position you'd like. No it's not a garden centre catalogue. Whatever you like, he'll do it for you. I won't stop him, the little lad. You can bet your life on that, whatever's left of it. Really I'm due a decent pension, for all the stuff I stick into a woman. You hammer and plane away, and then what comes out is always the same. It only looks different, smaller somehow, it seems to me.

And all the stupid excuses, so that the colleague on patrol doesn't notice what's going on. Both their hearts, his and Janisch's, beat. They roll along slow or fast. Attention is paid to the younger officer, for a short time they are a pair. One arm brushes the other, while people cheerfully drive off, because this one time their misdemeanours have been disregarded. The hairs on his colleague's arm briefly stand up on end, then flatten again, please don't brush against me again Kurt, or if you do, then unintentionally. But now the patrol is already driving somewhere else. The colleague, a young family man, supposes nothing and of course supposes something and first of all he has to be wearisomely bound into the Sport and Skittles Club of the Country Police to shut his mouth, but not by placing one's mouth on his. Then the mouth would really wake up. Yes, all that is on earth, I love you and more or something like it, then when your mouth kisses me, it's not so difficult...

Well. Let me tell you. Unfortunately one has to talk to women a lot, but quite differently, so that they become erotically inflamed. Naturally desires must not remain secret (nothing at all will ever remain secret!), because then they cannot be fulfilled as secret desires later on. It's talking that makes a person independent, so he can ask other people the way and then go off in another direction after all. Talking is also the hobby of many women. Odd, when they sit down, they surely don't do it to be quiet. So let's give them a reason to cry out! Wonderful, how it tears the words from their mouths! But it's better if one manages to put it in beforehand, into this mouth, which otherwise always goes on talking. No one needs to give it a leg up, it has a permit, it can make demands, and it does so at length. Well and good, let's just get started and stick the cock in, where her tongue is. Like a lollipop to suck, then at least they're quiet, women, because with all their social worker standards, which they're so keen on, they don't want to hurt a man. Wait a minute, I can still hear moaning, it's passing across a contorted face like clouds across a storm-lashed landscape. Sadly a country policeman doesn't earn much and still has a wife at home, from whom he has wearisomely drifted apart. At any rate they've still got the talking in front of them, while their hand reaches out to a trouser fly. Women can describe places of interest, torture themselves for weeks just for the sake of a moment, wait for years for the next one, be consoled and put off; when at last a brash erection stands ready for the both desired and heedless, headless performance, then all waiting that was in vain, because a human being flowers like a poplar and goes out like a cigarette stub: is forgotten. One simply has to understand women, everything depends on that, everything is dependent on that. Politicians have to do it, too, of course, if only with words, as men we'll perhaps manage it better with actions, something new for once, and all our actions are now really the last thing. A true act of love, if one meanwhile had more and better things to do. Sometimes even jogging has to be dropped. Then the country policeman takes his own car, it's for a good cause, this lady in the side street next to the local kindergarten has got the itch again today, I have a gut feeling about it, what, it's three weeks since she got it the last time? I would never have thought that it's already so long ago, time to give her a good going over again. What she wants, is for her stomach to be pushed down onto the mattress and to be opened up fast, intended for immediate use, because she has long been open to everything, but only rarely has the opportunity to get well oiled when she does open up. So that the creaking of the hinges (the secret drawer isn't pulled out so often!) doesn't sound so loud. There are little children next door, a whole crowd of them!

Basically everything can be done with women, it's as if they had done something wrong and wanted to be punished. And whatever has never been done with them, that's what they want to do more than anything else. That goes as much against the grain with men, as sitting down at a piano and not being able to play. But it has to be, the pleasant comes with the useful, cheek comes with a certain behaviour, a rebuke never comes, because one doesn't even wait for it. One simply does it first. Afterwards it's done, and one isn't prepared to discuss it with the next woman, although she will likewise want to know all about it, whatever. With women, not even the obvious comes of its own accord, it first has to be explained and shown to them, once they've been surprised by a firm grip of breasts and sex organs. Oh, but that wouldn't have been necessary! I'm obedient, even without you bringing me these pralines, you can get them here in the Merkur Super Market, to which people hurry from afar with winged feet, I'm sure for less than what you paid for them. But after a while, they already know in advance what to expect and open up already wearing the transparent dressing gown they got by mail order, or without it. With a little training even the age doesn't matter, even if one would prefer to train something younger. But the commonplace ones are at least modest in their requirements.

All of this costs men like Kurt Janisch time and money, in return they can deposit their worn-out furniture and exchange it for a three-piece suite, if they're lucky; please, there's still plenty of room inside me, the children are outside or have already left home, I'm happy to hold the little back room open for you, so that it's not too much trouble. I'll also make a little room out of myself, if that's what's wanted, just for you, well, what do you say to that? I'm enthusiastic, because your spare room, in fact the whole apartment, is exactly what I've wanted for a long time. Now let's give it all a good scrub, agreed?

Those actions, however, to which one turns, when one has nothing to say, and a woman doesn't want to sign something precipitately without having read it, bring in even more time (when the woman is finally dead) and money, a good investment. It doesn't happen without an effort on the part of the policeman and his son, who, although still young, is already infinitely versatile. A man of many faces, a multi-Janus head, pumped up with synthetic vitamins, so that one doesn't see his features all that clearly any more, yes, that's the sort of head the young man has on his shoulders. Just take a look at him, if anyone is capable of finding favour, then he is. The son is also very good with his hands and can do any amount of other work, apart from installing wiring. His father, however, comes first for him, and his father goes over dead bodies, which when they were alive, had been a side-dish for his meat. Why then do the policeman and his son have nothing but debts? Why have they lost everything that they already had? I don't know. The father can advise us, the father can judge us and save us, so that we can always keep an eye on what's ours. I don't actually believe, that it's the first time in the history of the Country Police force, that one of its representatives will have done such good business with kind-hearted death, who only fetches his own, never strangers. Death fetches those he has already marked. In that he is like the forester. Normally these public servants trained in the use of firearms only shoot their families, and even then only when it is necessary, because the latter wanted to run away. Afterwards at any rate they're left with the houses and the ground. But then they only have their little upper storey to themselves, and that's precisely what they take a shot at. If they survive it and haven't put themselves away at the same time, then later on they shoot themselves in the head.

Nonono, that's it, these two men have specialised in death. And the assets of death are a department store's worth of things, which no longer need to be bought, because they're part of the inheritance. And something like that happens right in front of our eyes, in the countryside, not far from a small town buzzing with excitement and risk and possibilities for sport and play, where everyone knows everyone else from the tennis court or the law court, if after a game, as so often, an argument has started, coarse, and with lots of words of abuse, where one belongs with one's acquaintances. Until one finds better ones. The district is bounded by its abrupt end. After that there's only the motorway left and the motorway right. The small town is like a pond, with water flowing in at one end and out at the other again. To leave this district behind is an achievement like crossing a river without horsepower. Curtains are lit up punctually, glances are exchanged, one gets worse glances for better ones or the other way round, that's business too, and no one does anything about it. The locals can certainly take, but only rarely do they take it any further.

Sooner or later all human beings are dead, that is their common fate. On the other hand it's not like in the city, where sometimes one doesn't notice right away, when someone has died. More often than you would think, the doctor writing out the certificate is the only one still to get a look at you, so why make yourself pretty?, and in a city apartment block who would tell you what's happened to a travelling salesman, whose post is piled up to the top of the letter box? What has happened to a gentleman like that, where is his keeper and where on earth is there a keeper, who would protect one? Policemen always know where something's become vacant, their jobs didn't fall into their laps, they had a talent for it and like to set themselves down in a ready-made nest, from which like the cuckoo they expel others whoosh, now we're all tied together and have to loosen a bond again and undo a knot. Death is man's fate, sadly there are all too many men before that. You can always rely on the police! But who really knows something about these barking keepers of the law, whose behaviour amounts to impudence and at whom one is nevertheless not allowed to laugh out loud, otherwise one's for it, and can reckon on a clip round the ears at least? One only has to step in as overbearingly as possible with one's inquiries, the Country Police Force, which knows everything, knows that; and in almost every second house there's a woman all alone, longing to let in anyone at all, if he only did come at last, then there would be two of us at least, and death perhaps comes along later, too. Then it gets really cosy. Before one can even promise the woman some-thing (inspection of wiring, unblocking the drain, looking for the missing pet etc.), something nestles youdidntseeathing into the hollow of one's hand, a head with soft hair, and you shoot out with, whether she would like to be taken from the front or back. The chatting rushes down the wires, it's not called foreplay yet, but that's still to come, and it's irksome because the neighbour-hood might hear. Then one looks at the woman, candidate for intercourse, everything all right? Is the hole closing up again or is it still wide open like a screaming mouth, because it's no longer used to being nailed, thrown down carelessly and not even decently stopped up? The head only learns to think, to whom the apartment and the furniture actually belong when it's been almost cracked open. You belong to me now, says the country policeman in an ear, not quite in his right mind when he said it, but only one person hears it, you can always deny it. Do you have any objection? No heart is heartfelt, when it has broken into a guarded house, and then one wishes for another body part, that can stand up to more. Women are so ruled by their physical urges, you can't believe it. The things that occur to them and all the places they want to do it, you would have to have a map in your head like a Cruise Missile, to have ideas like that; in the bath tub or on the kitchen table, that's still OK, but on the floor in the cru-cifix corner, good Lord, but it's cramped and dusty, God didn't want us to fuck around at His feet like worms, which he formed, like all of us, out of the dust, and he can't even get a good look, because he's nailed so tight up there! And how you get rid of it all again, that's a problem, too. Kitchen roll is the solution, but there's some who use sponges stiff with dirt or scraps of cloth from the kitchen sink. Sometimes, as soon as one comes in, the cleaning things are already looking invitingly at one from the place where the woman would like to be forced open, doctors sometimes cover up the instruments, women always display them brazenly and without embarrassment. Everything. They've got. Death succeeds in making us dumbfounded. That's only where the women start, because their mounting is unlimited, best of all they would like a golden ring. Love allows them to take in so much. But for the time being death is still stronger. Let's wait and see how things turn out.

Hair everywhere, even sticking to the palm of the dead woman's hand with traces of blood, I would say, these are the remains, steeped in synthetic hair dyes and permanent waves, of a human being of the female gender, and this female was allowed to see and experience a great deal before she died. Perhaps the telephone expert and his policeman father have a built-in war vent, well, I think they both like to get into fights, but have to restrain themselves a bit in public, one as a servant of the state, the other as a salaried employee. But it has to come out some-where, the beast, and in a woman it usually has too little space to run around. Afterwards one puts in an extra run. There are some with whom one is even hungrier afterwards, you embrace, you give each other a good licking, but the pupils are already flicker-ing restlessly over a head, which is practising inexcusable behaviour and is perhaps even a little embarrassed about what it's doing, glances after all precede a human being. They're already wagging their tail, before anyone can pull out the appropriate white stick. By the way. Am I looking too serious now? Oh no, that's the last thing I wanted! Good and hard into the woolly hair every time, which can't really check the blows. Take a look, quick, at the past, there you could see a serious man, likewise the head of a family, bellowing without any inhibition at living people, who would now have been almost dead, had their way of driving had consequences, because they did something wrong in traffic, well-well, car drivers in the days when they were still somebody and films were made about them, always the car drivers! Sometimes the cyclists, too, who, however, are already kicked enough by merely existing. Lonely women, well-groomed, but no longer young, they snatch at everything that moves and wears trousers, which after all they do themselves. But that's not enough for them, and they sometimes get given an extra titbit, meat, which they had given up reckoning on, and which now draws them into its reckoning. Hmm, is the apartment completely paid off? A very well groomed woman is already going to the hairdresser for the second time this week and having her nails painted fine as silk, something like that gets noticed; better than a poet could say it, her body says with these signs, that it is full of longing and at last knows, who for.

There next follows an imperious knocking during the round around the junction by the savings bank, that's where the chemist is, and we live right above it, and the next moment the door has to be opened naked, although there's hardly been time to dress, in order to provocatively cover all the curves, which are required nowadays. If need be oil has to be applied to their form after bathing or they have to be remoulded in the event of an accident. It doesn't really matter, when even engines get tweaked and whole chassis are lowered. Today the cheerful colours again glow from face, hands and toenails, it's quite a sight. We, too, are someone, we always said that at the top of our voices, until we were nothing and no one any more and no one was thinking of us any more.

A country policeman observes himself, how and whom he hits with his ball-point and his block. He has a feeling for how one could get this woman to proclaim her satisfaction with loud panting and groaning. With a woman with whom he's clicked, he first of all steps aside a little and permits himself expressions which are unambiguous, and only two days later the lady, although the situation was so unambiguous and the telephone number unambiguously changed owners, is walking restlessly back and forward between the windows, smelling under her arm pit to make sure it still smells of scent and rubbing herself with lotions. He must come today, otherwise at this time we would already be sitting on the train to Vienna, to visit an old friend! It's on her mind from one moment to the next, she can't help thinking her life might not yet be at an end, because someone still wants into her end, whoever it is. Death comes soon enough. An address is taken down, where the country policeman also takes down the car numbers and their fines, we'll take time to look at that in the next few days. Wherever there is a small chamber, it can be opened up. Above all the single, disappointed ladies in their middle years immediately give the key to themselves to anyone, without looking at him closely, they know: If someone opens them up, there's not much going on inside any more, but through determined sweeping out, something, which the woman herself does not even know yet, could be whirled up inside her and turned into something magnificent. This gentleman is experienced and is in practice, even if not in household matters, but if one could get a house for it, then one gladly does it. Then one even embraces a wooden shed and rubs oneself against it, until it weeps resinous tears. What does he see in me, when he's so attractive, that he could see even more of in younger, more beautiful women? Why not in fact? Why not in fact me? Come right in with the inquiry, here's the waste paper basket in the hall along with the little bunch of herbs and the little clip board, where we can make a note of our shopping!

In other cases, since the car driver wants to please the police, one only has to hold out one's hand, and already the notes come flying in one after the other. In return the driving licence is allowed to stay at home. Signal discs can be raised and people directed by merely pointing, almost like a murderer. Simply unique on earth. It's the best job in the world. Let's adopt an inquisitive expression and put on spectacles as well! Take a look: The grandfather is still saluting in the photograph, which he'll probably never get out of now, just as he never got out of this area when he was alive, look, how well he does it, in the photo, yes, the gentleman on the left, not the one on the right, that's the king, well, does time stand still? No. No one keeps still. But now, let's get away, into the open air! As if grandad had known, that his picture is being taken, but of course he will have known that, we can see it now, we see him in the ice cream chill of the moment, the concentrated gaze of obedience, sweetened, enhanced!, that's him, grandad, look, here, in front of the king, he's standing to attention in front of the monarch, whom he'll never get to know any better, as we know today, although it might have been interesting, who knows which person would have something to say to which other, unfortunately often in a foreign language? No one knows. I believe, that this sentence, although I wrote it myself, is not right. I for example have nothing to say faced with the figures I create, bring on the stock phrases and some more, and another and another, until they squirm beneath me with pain or perhaps also because they've too little space. They should never have pulled out this language nerve without an anaesthetic! The king doesn't look like anyone one knows. A king is always somone one will not get to know. He may be kind-hearted, conscientious, whereas others don't even need a conscience. They can't afford it, and we can't afford anything cheaper either. A slim man in a dark suit, the king, always stay properly in the picture, no he doesn't need that, he's already in too many pictures!, and in his day, in the 1970s, was often and with pleasure pictured beside his slim Latin-looking wife in the magazines of the ladies' hairdressing salon of the village. A good place in which to make an impression on the fancies of women, who like to fancy themselves, especially when they sit on these white upholstered chairs and think it makes them more beautiful, and to implant longings in rose-pink or petunia pink. Those that fancy themselves are even easier to get, who quietly fancy themselves and look down on others, but secretly, when they're all alone, then they tolerate no moderation, and their bodies run immoderately out of control if someone caps one of their thin little stalks, with which they desperately cling to their property. And which puts them into the horizontal posit-ion for life, which they can lose at any time. But by then they will have lost themselves long ago and no longer know who they are and how much they still have in the bank. Not as much as before.

In a ladies' hairdressing salon a country policeman would be even more conspicuous than a king, unless a customer had parked her car wrongly, then all eyes are on her and her hairstyle, a semi-finished product. The country policeman would be generous but just. He arranges a meeting and prepares to obscure the evidence, so that behind the blinds he can fulfil all secret desires, including those which are not kept secret at all. Instead they force themselves upon him like inquisitive dogs, which are immediately sent away again without the stiff retriever stick they're panting for, chased away, because they are so wet and unappetising that one hardly wants to lie down beside them. But there is a stately home to be given away and one says very softly: come! And then he comes. If the women don't get a king for the bedside table, where the magazines with all the colour pictures lie, perhaps they'll get the servant of the state, who has to be there for the king at all times. Paper: doesn't blush. In the photograph the king is altogether relaxed and casual and friendly. I would say, this woman is freshly permed, but unrelaxed, if I would dare say so and had not forbidden myself to constantly look down from my high horse at what I've made up. The father of the country policeman could still be alive today, the way he looked then. Here lives always come along twice or even many times over. They stand next to one another like houses, one the same as the other, but that doesn't affect me. The lives match one another like clothes, but often they don't match the person to whom they were handed out. They are mostly uneventful, as if too much life had to be distributed among too few people, of whom each receives more than enough of one and the same fate, of which we now carefully pick up the pieces, having had a smashing time. The mother of the present country policeman, for example, it's as if there was another one of her and then another, as if most of the women here were like her, I still know at least one or other of them and can offer them to you to make your choice. But I already know, you'll choose something else, but then at least the side-dish will be right. How enthusiastically she used to look at these pictures, Frau Janisch, as if inwardly elevated, incidentally at exactly the same hairdresser on the main square, but then the chairs were green and harder. Later Frau Janisch even bought the magazine, so that she, too, would have something to leave her family. That was when she could still walk upright. Let's act as if it were today: So she looks and looks again, as if the king along with her husband could vanish into thin air before she can even show them off, and all that while her hair is being wrapped around thin rods, oiled and then heated up, the very fine roast, smelled long before it's ready (and again every time one's hair is washed! All of life is chemistry and smells accordingly...), and she tries to jut out of her dress, the country policeman's wife, as if it were made of exactly the same dotted silk as that of the queen and not for example done in an anonymous workshop under the backcombed hair, which please must look exactly the same as her majesty's in the photo. Unfortunately that's not possible. Not even we poets can do that. Instead of which the person looking for advice is handed a wire hair net for her head and something completely imperishable and incomparable in trevira, nylon and other artificial fibres. Not bad either, made for all eternity, unless one sets fire to it, but that's just it: different! Eternity doesn't want it and gives it back cheap, since already used. There's nothing to be done. This queen was a model for many women of the time and unleashed imitative impulses precisely because she was not beautiful, just as we are all not beautiful. But, she too, a very well-groomed and smart woman, there's nothing you can say to that. No criticism on our side is necessary here. Anyone who hasn't got beauty in their account needs clothes and hairdresser all the more badly, in order to be able to imitate beauty as successfully as possible, before one hits the street in this new dress and there immediately shrinks again with all one's shortcomings. On the contrary, often one even has to add something, house and property. No grounds to take in guests as well, whom one then has to feed one's own flesh, because there's nothing else in the house. I personally know one, two widows and single women approaching retirement, who succeeded in going much further in their public appearance than had ever been foreseen for them. And then they were still overtaken by younger women. At the last moment. I strike the gong. Boing. Time's up. Every time is up some time. I've often said it and I'll often say it again, because it's so unjust that time passes, but I always have to stay here. It lasts just as long as one lives, because one's own life is the measure of time. Here comes the next one that is no longer one's own. So already in the course of one's own life it must be taken hold of determinedly. That's as clear and transparent as the soup, which people have dished up once again today behind their freshly cleaned windows. Who's going to eat it all?

Today there's once again something lurking behind the responsibilities and reports of the country policeman - I can't yet quite see what - when he pulls the drunks from the pub tables, hits them, examines his victims briefly and superficially, because you don't see the internal bleeding, and then calls the ambulance, because of course the victim bashed himself and his not very full head. The victim says nothing, because he is unconscious, and doesn't have much to say anyway, when he is conscious. You're just not allowed to kill anyone, that would be the condition that's agreed verbally, one's only allowed to put his head together with his ears and the vital nose and the absolutely essential mouth in a plastic bag, in which breathing is impossible. That is its nature. A smoked sausage is also allowed to stop its breath, we've got nothing against that, I assure you, that's its business entirely. No one else's. Talk about the miscellaneous brutalities of this country police district has got as far as the county town, where it's mentioned with a laugh and a particular, knowing expression. Nothing can ever be proved. Although killing involves a profound emotion, an inner importance which allows one utterly to forget oneself, because one has thrown oneself entirely upon another human being. Just ask a murderer, he won't tell you! That one was allowed to kill, above all: one could do it, for that women think you unique, because otherwise they don't know anyone up to it. They like to crowd round the violent criminals, the country policeman knows that, he once arrested one, they didn't even let him put on his shoes, after he had shot his wife with a revolver and seriously wounded his adolescent son. But something like that, to get someone like that, is like a win in the lottery, even if not the big prize, because in the country people enjoy killing, they practise on animals after all, but quietly, there are houses, you find five bodies early in the morning and don't know why. These people don't get much variety (the examining magistrate, when informed, that the culprit has a firearm and was able to make use of it, immediately passed on this infernal information, he already knew his man's number from other cases, the latter was never just a number and had among other things also fired on the Kobra special duty unit of the Country Police force. It's not healthy). Mostly the murderer does end up in prison and is defused, his family is disconnected, the murderer however has not been devalued as a result, along with his tormented heart, which he now displays openly. Indeed, I see: Some women are already writing him beautiful love letters. The country policeman has had them weeping and wailing in front of his duty desk two or three times, the women, while he, nervous, because he's got too few fingers had typed up a report. Some perpetrators do nothing but cry, the whole time, but they never ever express regret. Perhaps this house provider, in whose little home this perpetrator will soon, in about fifteen years, be sitting at table on parole, will give him a helping hand. He will pitch in, he promises her, he will crush his conscience in his bare hands, till the juice runs out. The only silly thing is that he was caught. Then at the trial, with his final words, the murderer apologised as kindly, as good-naturedly as possible to his victim, but by then the victim was long buried and no longer heard anything. That was an interesting man, one should try to learn from him. From others one can only learn, that there are no longer any hidden Nazi printing plates in Lake Toplitz and one can drown if one looks for them nevertheless. Yet the area around the lake is to be cordoned off as a prohibited area. The Country Police can do that. Using an underwater TV camera, it's possible, with a bit of luck, to find another corpse after three or four years. Like the eighteen-year-old schoolgirl, unfortunately as a skeleton, in the forest, or the apprentice who wasn't even sixteen yet, unfortunately in shallow water and hence still intact, in the lake, in the lake. We're sure to come back to it.

The country policeman would never apologise, why does one make something of oneself? The slim ones, who have worked hard for their figure, go a step further, and climb up the mountains every day or climb the walls at home, because one man, one man in particular, hasn't called them. The country policeman only has to take advantage of the opportunity, because in their own car everyone makes a mistake once; anyone who believes no one has seen him is making a mistake. Women like to be conquered by the country policeman. For a long time they've been regretfully gazing after their disappearing good looks, which now, without having asked beforehand, another, younger woman has taken, wearing them quite without inhibition, as if they belonged to her. Something has just appeared to me, I think it was the Virgin Mary, but unfortunately I was someone quite different. Oh dear, now because of it I've run over this stop sign, which has been planted here for twenty years. Because I turned round to look at my rival. Every woman forgets herself sometimes. Besides there isn't much, of which one should take note. One should never let a man, even a murderer, off the leash, once one has caught him, and one has to hold the end of the leash very tightly. That's why in general women like murderers of women so much. Because they have specialised in women. They look at the walls in prison and during this time can't be looking at other women. But there are certainly other reasons. For the time being at any rate they're harmless, the murderers. After someone has unscrewed their fuse and they're in custody. Now they have all the time and leisure in the world to look for cosy women pen pals, who will soon turn up to see them in person, because they think they've been invited. The conduct of the detained culprit, who cannot practise his profession at present, will then be pure fun, the way a lamb likes to have fun with a wolf. Thank God I'm not responsible for these women. They in turn are responsible for their children, whom the murderer can kill at any time, if he wants to and has the opportunity, because he will have got that fatal parole. It would have been better if he hadn't got it. But it was so nice, nicer than anything! I and this woman, we swear, the next time he wouldn't have done it any more. As it is, he has unfortunately won a free game with the knife again, it's your fault, Mr Prison Chaplain and Mrs Prison Governor and Mr Prison Psychiatrist. I would never have expected it of this completely cured murderer! The man has always been an exception. Women don't much like to see the murderer out of doors. The temptations would be too great there. Good thing that the man is inside here now. A thirteen-year-old has just reached out for the light switch, a long smeared trail of blood leads directly to the floor, where he will be stabbed more than twenty times. But the mother would rather weep for the killer than her boy, that way the weeping makes her happier. After all, she has more children, all exactly like this one, if in different age groups. One hardly notices, if one is missing. The murderer is shot trying to escape, because he wanted to kill a nun in a chapel as well. They got the wrong man, the woman who loved him now weeps inconsolably. I could still have children, but I'll never ever have such a man again. There are so few like him, and that's exactly why I liked him so much. There's a popular belief, that someone has to be imprisoned, so that at least he pays attention from inside his cage. He has nothing else to give, so we'd better just forgive him. But we digress to these touch-me-not flowers, who absolutely want to be broken, and fate alone would not have managed it for fifty years. I ask you, what did the man actually do? Seventeen years ago he chopped up a young woman teacher with a knife, nothing more, there are more women teachers than there are murderers, who are a rare timid kind of wild beast, and still really wild. Not something that eats from the trough and shyly rolls its eyes, where the other troughs stand in the forest, beside the pool, or in the cellar next to the keep-fit equipment. To demonstrate his long-standing non-aggressive gentle nature, in prison the man preferred to wear ladies' tights, perhaps so that in future he is better able to put himself in the position of women, this gentleman, who is dead now. If he has relatives, who believe in him and who are fond of him, then unfortunately it's my turn.

The women stick out in their fragrant soft-rinsed wool, as if they were the main thing and had nothing but success with men, when they, nicely garnished with pullovers, t-shirts and scarf, success guaranteed, serve themselves up free of charge. In fact they are at best the dessert, if there's still room for it in the gentleman's stomach. That's something they don't know. Why do they feed the murderers like that? In their place at table I wouldn't have done it, I would rather have bought myself a dog, given how grateful animals are, more grateful than a man we know. I don't understand any of it. I imagine: Murderers exert a gentle hypnosis, some investigate and analyse their future victim for months. They take the trouble to attach concrete rings to them, and sink ring and victim in the nearest river. A human being is only cotton wool, a vacuum. If he's lucky the murderer gets a new notion of the essence of human beings, an advantage for him, which we writers will find difficult to catch up with. They are sand, human beings, there are as many as there are grains of sand on the shore. Well, I don't know... Hardly has he killed someone, than new victims come running up, they even come shooting over from neighbouring countries (there are whores in Vienna, Lower Austria, Burgenland, the Czech Republic and California, and everywhere they are throttled in a singular way with their own underwear. Mr U., a man with whom I personally have corresponded on human and political questions, prompted it and, when he saw that he was the only man within a considerable radius and women were nothing but dirt, well then he took care of them himself, affronted by their glances, because they weren't aristocrats, who would have made a better match for him. How could I have known that? Nevertheless, he didn't charm my soul, in contrast to the souls of others). Here comes another one, I can hardly follow her, she's twenty years older than young Mr L., a quite different case, an envious type, who's a bodybuilder today and in this way has at last created an entirely new body for himself, has become another in the truest sense of the word, so Mr L., exactly, he shot his cousin, girlfriend and her mummy full in the face with his pump-action gun, but they didn't need their faces after that anyway. Mr L. couldn't build himself a new face, he's only grown older, as we all have. Where will it end? And now here comes a woman from Germany, who could be a substitute mother for the culprit, but would rather be his only lover, because there aren't so many places, where there are no possibilities of comparison, and here she has found just such a place. It's the prison, it's the special penitentiary for almost broken lawbreakers. That's how the women imagine it: for once a man whom it's worth lifting up to themselves! And then careful you don't drop him! I fear you'll rupture yourself like that. First of all, however, thoroughly martyred by the culprit's ability to stay cool. How one longs for the rare tender moments, when the core mantle melts and the sweet centre of marzipan and nougat is revealed: highly explosive, I can tell you! Try a Mozartkugel, you'll soon see the difference. At least this motherly woman, with whom truth to tell the young man finds it a bit dull sometimes, is still alive. A close shave, he's still inside, safe inside. Basically this woman never talks about anything except herself, and the one listening to her can for his part talk to no one else, apart from ninety-five other women pen pals, about whom, however, the woman knows nothing. The murderer only wants to get out, which surprises no one, who knows the culprit a bit and the women who are always visiting him. Outside he would be safe from them. Only this woman, still talking about herself, wants to go in the opposite direction, pushing against the crowds at the desk, and even here inside, behind bars which mean the world, be seen by this wild young man, a figure, who is at stake and goes on risking his stake and perhaps if possible be touched by his hands and admired as someone, whom one has never even seen before and yet has always known. What does that mean? That means, the woman will become the outside. A place for which she is not destined, unless she were really presentable. She's from Bottrop, in the Ruhr, and has taken up residence in Austria for the time being, in order to trump younger women, abandoning everything, even her home town, where she was an executive secretary, that was just a town, which never made free with her hot glances. That was her last trick, now she hasn't got any more. I swear I'm never going to mention the woman again! She was an example of nothing at all. So, now I've taken my revenge on her, only I don't know what for. The prisoner pockets all the profit. They all like to get close to him, the dear ladies of the Lord, whom they have chosen all on their own (whereas e.g. God was already there before, always already there, from the beginning). Even if the lord and master is twenty, thirty years younger, then they really storm the prisons. They literally board them with their freshly painted talons, which would break like glass if firmly gripped. Not in order to resolve to be better people and likewise to improve the culprit, but to be for him, who hasn't got a choice, first mother, then lover and then: everything else as well. After getting to know him better. Of course. Mother is altogether the best thing of all (women don't seem to know that, because they obstinately don't want to be mothers). At least not until their head is cut off and displayed in the window of their little lingerie boutique. As long as there are inquisitive people in the world, they'll stop in front of shop windows and believe in love, which would be even more beautiful in this pretty lace combination, I could imagine. And then that! A decapitated head right in the middle! Incidentally do you have any idea, why matricides so often cut off their mothers' heads afterwards? They could also cut open the stomachs and pull out the wombs from which they, the sons, came, and give them a close inspection for once, couldn't they? I don't understand it. They could be content with the killing itself, but they go to the trouble of sawing off the head like Salome, who didn't, however, have to get her own fingers dirty. Sometimes they even stick the Gorgon in the blender, if they have one, which only demonstrates their lack of technical talent. They've never had the opportunity to study, otherwise they would have known that. But wait, back to the beginning, this one has studied at university, economics (but didn't have a clue about solid-state physics!) now he's doing it again, I've heard, studying. Fortunately he's quite healthy again, it's been at least a year since the murder. But I feel so happy for him, that he's out again and now he can until further notice (until he has a girlfriend who looks like his mama) be built up again and find out how far he can get with boldness. Into the newspaper! Oh, that would be nice, to get as far as that!

Yes. They will take murderers home, where after only a few days the latter will kill the woman's children, one at least, as we already said, unfortunately we've always said everything already and made no bones about it, we had no bone to pick. They do something like that, the murderers, because they don't want to start a new life and if they do, then alone or with someone else. But never with those, whom they already have. Perhaps their souls want to become human beings, but reason wants something else, it wants, what we all want, but don't dare do. We should all hate corporeal life, but only this country policeman, among others whom I do not know, really does hate it. One just doesn't notice at first, because he sometimes jokes and laughs and sings songs to the accordion.

Since it never comes, one will always think love is somewhere else, chase after it and oneself soon turn from hunter to hunted. Well, go on, you too can bring a murderer into your own home, or you can at least correspond with him beforehand, so that the anticipation is all the greater, e.g. this knife-killer, who likes to wear ladies' tights so much, you'll have plenty of them in your wardrobe! No, not him, he's already dead! Later on the thirteen-year-old son would only have masturbated onto the tights anyway, thinks the country policeman, who has followed the case in the newspapers and on TV; he himself has certainly heard of such sensational cases, but he has hardly ever experienced any himself. He fills a post, which fits him very well. Not bad, the cap, and the revolver in its holster. Great. Looks really smart. The culprit would hardly be out again, thinks the country policeman gloat-ingly, before he would smack this woman in the face again, who's standing there whimpering in front of his typewriter because of some petty pub brawler, who put her in hospital for three weeks, and is begging for a permit to visit him. But her tormenter will never let her write the novel of his life! Well yes, at any rate not on my typewriter. No way! There will soon be PCs purchased, which can store even more in their memory, about which women can then be reminded if need be, when they stand in front of one again with a smashed face. Yet there was no right of return. The perpetrator will write the novel of his life, in which he would rely more on reality than on dreams, himself. In order to become famous. Women are worse, without having been really bad, they age early and like to neglect themselves, unless they get attention. Then they blossom and smile dreamily. For that (to get attention!) they would do anything, they would even kneel in front of the American president and take his penis with all its secret charac-teristics, which haven't even been shown on television, in their mouths. We won't need a bed for that, although we will unfortu-nately need a judge, and the judge is the whole nation. That would be something, everyone looking at me! I would be able to put up with that, no problem! Something that every murderer is, really every one: ambitious and attention-seeking. If they were allowed to go home, they would immediately sit down at a piano, even if they couldn't play at all, just so that people would listen to them.

One really would have to arrest men and lock them up, in order to be able to protect them from women, thinks the country policeman, who knows it all or at least has heard of it recently or seen it somewhere. He will draw his conclusions from that. We catch them, the women, act as if we worshipped them, thinks the country policeman. Why not the other way round? Why should they not adore us, in this particular case me? It can't be so hard. What does that mean? I could manage it, couldn't I? So, now life is for once really being challenged, it's no game any more, and one declares oneself the victor. One would have to intercept the eligible women before they get murdered, thinks the country policeman. First of all we'll send tact off on a long journey, basically women don't like anything like that, they want to be taken hard and anyway we've got enough juice to score in the big road battles between pedestrian precinct, sports centre and shopping centre or get us to the industrial suburbs where the formerly flourishing nationalised industries are on their knees and trying to crawl away, but are stopped by a ball and chain held tight by the trades unions from undertaking a flight of capital abroad. The unemployed will then just have to see how they can market themselves day after day. Lack of tact but not lack of talent is all that a murderer needs. And we've certainly got that, if we look at ourselves in the right light in the mirror! The curious may stand around at the scene of the accident, the country policeman climbs over the ribbon and is at last free free free. The lake is still. There's a woman already, who's involved in the accident, she owns her home, and she is likewise free, even if not in sexual matters. A freedom, however, which she doesn't appreciate, she would much rather be in the custody of a man and not be responsible for it. And that one over there, she even has a whole detached house to herself, although she's only a single person. She's screaming, screaming, screaming at present, as only such citizens scream, who haven't had an interlocutor for a long time now. Aha. She has the nerve just to roar away like that. In the past she's always behaved with restraint, but now she's straining to let it out. Now she's letting go. This heart demands precision, is it really just her that's meant, her alone, the woman, the only one, or are there rivals? Anyone who wants to get to the country policeman, must knock first, but is often sent away again by his colleagues. We are none of us poor, and we don't like to be shown the door.

One has to know the secret of how to get a good grip on women. One doesn't absolutely have to be a doctor, in order to slit people open, but it would be better if one were, if one wants to find the serpent in the stomach, which once led us astray, the evil one, where else should it be: as a man one would like to be doctor, psychiatrist, surgeon and anaesthetist all at once. Even if one had nothing else to do it with, but this fairly long, powerful organ, the scalpel, which doesn't have to take time twisting and scraping, when it wants to get in, it's not a spiral drill after all. The drill imposes itself, without even glancing once or twice up an empty dead end in case anyone is coming down it at the wrong moment. Courage grows with appetite. The screaming woman beside her car which has got a dent in its tin roof, suddenly falls silent and stares at the man in a uniform, as if she were looking at a live man for the first time. The mascara is running down her more than fifty-year-old face, it doesn't really matter. The face shouldn't stand for so much food, because it looks a little puffy, but that doesn't matter either. Down below, on the valley side of the lake shore, beside the woman and the country policeman, the landscape spreads out alongside the highway. The landslide has finally been cleared away, also the hair, which strangely enough they found in it, these thick tufts of hair, no one could work out what they were doing there. Ultimately it makes no difference, who or what one embraces, the important thing is that one can grab hold of it, when the time comes.

There are lights on in some houses, where widows and other single persons are living. Their faces are like unentered rooms, which are waiting for someone to switch on the light, so that they don't have to do it themselves any more. Their organs roar. If need be, they would even commit a murder themselves, if only someone would at last come to them. Some unfortunately are shaken by the tree of life before their time. To ensure that their passionate feelings don't perish unused, they get into their cars and drive off in order to get to know someone. To be finally brought in as harvest, by the traffic or its guardians. Don't get killed and don't drive too fast. Just don't make a mistake now! Fifty years with a clean record are soon used up! Someone simply has to make this country policeman rich, otherwise the needle will stick. No sooner does one lay one's hand on a woman's neck or throat as gently as a hypnotist, than they throw back their heads like horses, bare their teeth and get so wet, that foam squirts from every hole. No one sees them fantasising about vanished love. Everyone sees them longing for a new one, and here it comes. What a good thing, that I got into my car. Oh you pale-coloured Japanese mid-range car, which was seen at the scene of the crime! The tongue is displayed in the open mouth and wants to be bludgeoned by another tongue, where's the limit? The lips still want to linger at the place it all happened and exchange further caresses, as if it was just like a Mills & Boon novel; tin for gold chains and rings and bracelets, just as gold was given for iron, where's the limit? Where does a body have limits anyway? This longing: women who desperately observe their own state, size up a distance, but cannot get back to dry land again unaided, in order to reach a more pleasant state. Marriage later not excluded. As if they couldn't let themselves out, because they're the only thing they have. But why then give it away so greedily? They can hardly wait to thrust themselves forward in the most complete way, to give themselves up to a stranger's hands, without a female assistant animal keeper on TV having tested the fences of the little house, the barred windows of the apartment (so that the animal cannot fall out onto us), in which they, the people are to land, usually not very gently. No matter where they come down, whether a soft or hard landing, the important thing is, we come, have a little slime rubbed into us, have the Kleenex to hand and hold the stalk tight, before the bloom of budding affection has shrivelled again. Before it even rose properly. Everything as usual. Precaution is better than after-care, e.g. after a cancer operation. A big opportunity, authoritative entrance, the gun, a uniform which announces the master, because it runs ahead of him with a calibre of approx. 9mm like the obedience which one knows how to produce in a woman. Strange, thato others have such problems with it! The curtains with their curtain rail-lubricant (unfortunately he always has to leave, pilots always have to come down again, too) are torn aside, the neck is stretched in order to gaze after him, as he disappears down an alley beside the drug store, without looking back. And yet one had embellished one's pink and bluish gleaming interior, which can only be reached though a narrow passageway, but that's the way he, the only one, will come, so nicely with folds, in order to give it a new look, but there was no need for that, one discovered. You, you're fantastic, one clearly heard that, it's only three weeks ago, and one heard it from a mouth above a square jaw, and meanwhile a hand leafed around below and sometimes also climbs higher, where it pinched, scratched and practised slapping the flesh, just great. Was it true, what one felt then? Afterwards they don't rightly know, are already greedy again, the street door only has to slam shut, and so want to have it again and again, in order afterwards to consider everything in peace and quiet. Is ready cash, jewellery, ownership of real estate available? That, in turn, is more important to the man, and a bath tub now would be nice too, muses the country policeman, who has made himself dirty and furthermore would like to get rid of the smell of perfume. His wife isn't waiting at home to get a smell of the man, because she wouldn't dare do that. This man now belongs to me alone, I can do what I like with him, thinks the victim, for as long as she can still think. For as long as she is still all there. Another man is meanwhile already dead, inside him are the drugs Anafranil and Euglucol, they lower the blood sugar level and improve the mood, but it's no use now. The criminal was female and turned to unfair pharmaceuticals. An athlete doesn't need anything like that. The woman is often like someone dead anyway, because she does not know, when and how she should move during sex. The murderer gets on top of her and drives around the place as he pleases, a ghost driver, who's never changed direction. A spook. He's driving around with the dead woman in his car, he's even got on top of her, imagine that! He's filled his car with corpses he's picked up for himself, which he'd rather not make a noise about, they're sleeping so wonderfully beneath and behind him, just don't wake the dead! The murderer can awaken a feeling. He himself must be cold. He dare not be modest.

Kurt Janisch (I always find it embarrassing, to name names, don't you think so too? It sounds so silly, but how else should one speak to people?), the country policeman, always already feels the juicy colours all around him when he wakes up in the morning, but they don't mean a thing to him. But it immediately drives him out into the front garden, where the flowers bloom and promise something more, that is, a woman whom one can pick up with flowers. The country policeman likes to wander amidst the greenery of the rural hills and mountains, where even people are allowed to live, although there's not much room for them there. The people are enclosed by the mountains, like a child by his cot. Without fail they settle in the valleys, right up to the hills, where holiday homes have to take leave of the world, when the landslide comes, and everyone throws themselves at everyone else, because the holiday makers want to play away. The sleep of the country policeman is like the paths through the mountains. There are many of them.

Why does it occur to me now: Yesterday Kurt Janisch dreamed of a pair of bears, who were once young, a yellowed photo shows them in their young days, they had been intended for a nature reserve in the area, quite near, but then installed in a bear-pit instead and nevertheless delighted the tourists for years, even behind bars. Now the two bears have died at a great age following a long serious illness, one right after the other. That's how one knows that time is passing, when the photos curl at the edges and turn yellow. Death pushes itself imperceptibly over life, the photos of the happy young bears are overlaid by the old tired animals with mangy fur. Oh, the soft hair of human beings, why does it move me so? Their trees grow heavenwards, but the country policeman, the squad commander, comes and cuts them down, if they threaten to harm his superiors. Yes, sir, we also conduct security operations, and our dogs recently received yellow blankets for their assignments, so that they're seen immediately and they don't cover any strange dog with impunity, the brutes, the good dogs, along with their good noses. The Dobermans are sick too often. The Belgian shepherd dogs can take a bit more. It's only the poor bears which are dead now.

2.

There lies the gravel pit, a stagnant stretch of water which, like every other, spreads before us forever flat beneath the surface pressure exerted by God, dark and yet open, an opaque quantity. Oh, if only the ecological balance of the water in it had not been upset! Hence, sadly, the lake is not a dark jewel encircled by mountains, which sometimes throw off their nerves, the water varicose veins in the rock and cast them down their own besotted slopes, man and his misdeeds are to blame, yes, yes, the landslides - everything slips down the slopes over their hips, the mountain shorts, the earthen covering, this sodden, doused greenery, which can no longer hold on there. Unfortunately it rained so much this spring. Tracks were buried, on which cars were parked oh dear. People can no longer leave their holiday destinations and are left sitting in the locals' trap, the latter have to scale the heights of their best manners, in order to bear the visitors for so long. In the winter they had already practised killing by avalanche, the locals and their native snow, that triune son of water. (Meanwhile the water has assumed another form again.) This living play of nature finishes off everything in a trice. And right away here comes a whole concrete wall of snow, this popular, but inconspic-uous (once arrived, it simply lies around everywhere) piece of sports equipment, that falls down to earth around the clock and no one, apart from the athletes, really pays attention, unless they haven't got winter tyres fitted yet. And this snow is suddenly like stone, like concrete, which has a stomach ache and thus must empty itself over everything. We, too, have to watch it on TV, even though we're more interested in the little football. The lake then. One essential detail's missing, that is, there's no life in it. The trout go strolling in the River Mürz, they avoid the storage lake, they already die before that, hooked by an angler or from the power station sludge, if the sluice is opened too quickly, I've already mentioned it somewhere else. I still don't entirely understand the mechanism, but whatever it is, the fish die in their hundreds. It happens in a flash. In every kind of rock and in every kind of terrain there are suitable basins or cavities, into which water fits, but then again its composition doesn't suit the fishes. They would have said something about problems beforehand, if they could have spoken.

Why is it that just this stretch of water has swallowed so much and what, that caused it so to lose its balance? The water really has to be fed a great deal of unhealthy food, to get so fat. If we start with a nutrient supply of 10 mg per annum, but then increase the amount by two per cent per annum, then the lake has a nervous breakdown, because it believes it will have to cope with even more, and has long since lost its appetite. But at the moment I can't see what nutrition it got at all, yes, in fact what is it subsisting on? Who set the cycle in motion, until something sat up, had a good stretch and then got up and left without making its bed? Nowhere do I see food for the lake, this is not at all an area of extensive agriculture, it is an area of extensive leisure use. If anything, then leisure should lose its balance, not this lake.

The afternoon shadows fall very early across the water, crouching in its tub. It has not been formed by tectonics, volcanic action, erosion or accumulation, rather, someone simply blew a very big hole in the ground, so that he could throw the rubble from road-building into it, and then someone else had another idea and preferred to fill the tub with water. You see, other bodies of water are even produced by the wind, this nothing in the air, ice, too, can melt and thereby make water. This water, however, was poured out, but without a food chain, no, that was not added (that is, the consumers and producers within this biocoenosis don't come and go, they simply remain, but see for yourself:) there are two, three rowing boats lying there, you can pay at the inn on the other side of the highway, where you will also be handed the paddles that go with them. And then look into the water just once, no one will stop you, but the species garnishing underwater doesn't lie next to juicy fish bodies, snails, microorganisms, this side-dish, rather, is never anything but weeds, weeds, weeds, simply green stuff, you can see that with the naked eye, macrophytes, vegetable organisms; your voice will sound as if muffled by a park of living plant creatures, should you take the plunge, the tongues of foliage will caress you like the branches of trees, but if I were you I would think twice before going in there. If you can't swim, have a last photo of yourself taken beforehand! Well, this water does not look like water at all. Just the way it clutches at your throat, if you want to do some water sports nevertheless! This water is simply not as close to nature as you. Even if you avoid it and lean over the side of the boat, the impression you get is of jelly, gelatine, ton upon ton of water plants, nodes, rhizomes, I ask myself how can they even aspire to photosynthesis, if light cannot penetrate the water at all? Look at the snapped off twig floating over there. It is already half submerged, as if it were petrified and too heavy for the water, which treats it severely and swiftly draws it down. These plants, they shouldn't really be here at all, and in healthier water they wouldn't be, at least not in such gigantic quantities. Did the nasty climate do it? Did something rise up which climbed to the surface, odd given the youth of this stretch of water, whose chemical properties suggest something much older? Upper layer not very permeable, eh? Of special significance to the dynamics of the depth ground water due to extended stay below the surface? What, no depth ground water at all? The tasteless juice simply poured in from above and then the hose thrown away?

There's a boat floating on the water at the moment, as love floats around in humans and makes no progress nor gets beyond itself. It's even possible to get out of any village, after all. The boat has sought out its humans and now glides forth without splishing or splashing, it is no longer surprised at anything, for it is used to this water, which just seems to have this special density, a different specific gravity from normal water. It is almost as if it were solid, which would be the opposite of water, a copy from an original water block, but they'll never manage to get the original quite like that again, what did I really mean by that? It doesn't matter, I'd rather not say, because I would need pages for that, which I will certainly miss in my life, that is, the nicer back pages. So it's simply water, but it doesn't look like it and doesn't feel like it. If you want to swim, you're better off driving to Kapellen, which has got a pond for swimming, I'm telling you, it's friendliness personified, with its caravans, its squealing children taking off into the blue sky with their water wings, everywhere the multicoloured joys of discovery. OK, it's still too early in the year for swimming, the water is far too cold. Whereas I would say to the lake e.g. it can hardly be discovered, because it's so hard to get there, in order to discover it. It doesn't impose itself, this almost black filling, which was supposed to set a water cycle in motion, yet even precipitation does not visibly appear to strike it. As if there were a brake on its fall, as onto a sponge. It's simply a dark surface next to the highway, just before the bypass, where at last, since a couple of years ago, there's no need to brake any more. I also brake for animals, says this car, which cannot do anything on its own. They first took the material for the road away from the ground and then gave back cheap water in return. Even you wouldn't put up with that. Imagine you've got a corridor, where you could put up cupboards, and instead all of a sudden the full bathtub comes towards you and buries you under its watery hollowness. The bus drives a little way into the village, but the old B road then continues unhurriedly on foot, the bus turns round again, it has to pay attention to the federal highway. Now one can send five-year-olds to the grocer's, they could at most be run over by a pushchair. And here's the little bus shelter, crudely rustic, as if knocked together from gingerbread, not unlike a feeding rack for game, so that it's not so conspicuous in the landscape, a piece of furniture, yet in the open air, but then again not a piece of garden furniture; I wouldn't go so far as to sit myself down comfortably there, under the inquisitive glances of the neighbouring residents, and hold my face to the sun. Doesn't matter, it wouldn't make the face any better. The little house with its little bench is more a piece of working furniture, which takes in people for a limited period, principally learner drivers, apprentices and old people, who have no car and have to go to the surrounding towns, on one side as far as Mariazell, on the other to Mürzzuschlag, I haven't been able to free myself of this area for ages which, like myself, is inconspicuousness personified, but yet also a fetter nevertheless. It sticks to me like I would myself to a beloved person, if I had one and a suitable opportunity.

The question is, how is it possible to describe such a water landscape, like that of the lake, without really knowing its language? I am wary of the innocuousness with which this stretch of water appears before the public, but it doesn't do me any good, it acts as if it could not disturb its own surface, and it really doesn't disturb me. This numbly paralysed, yielding nothingness, into which the skilful oars dip, yet on touching the surface their skilfulness at once deserts them, they become clumsy, shy away from dipping in again, which nevertheless could take them further, well I don't understand it. As if they would get goose pimples from it, they can hardly move in this aspic, in this gelatine, cannot turn, want to come to a standstill and submit to the always ice cold water cake, in which they're stuck like the gateau knife, guided by the clumsy hand of an invisible, noisy peasant bride and groom - the women, chrysalises, sticking out of tons of petticoats, beneath which simultaneously clayey, clumping feet emerge and will deal out kicks. Yet even these will be smothered in the thick reed beds of the shore, and the foot in the shoe breaks while green trees try to caress its pain. But the water won't allow that. It won't have anything nicer to tell you than I, that's for sure! Why did they put water of all things in this gravel hollow? Even this water here drowns in itself without a single cry. This stretch of water is not a dynamic member of the environmental movement, it is a piece of water standing there absolutely silent and stupid.

On the other side of the road, as if shielded from every terror by a beautiful pair of hands: the inn, adorned with a geranium dirndl blouse and the garden that goes along with it, so friendly! From here the path to the lake seems further than it is, it is a path from the light into the dark, cold, damp, where it's such an effort to draw breath, as if one had to buy it specially; and children's pleas for a boat trip are almost always refused. I would say and I'll repeat it again and again, because perhaps then one can imagine something altogether definite: The water is dark green to black, at most green, at least black. The hair of the vegetation moves beneath the surface, dead undergrowth is dragged along, the green drowned weeds yield to an invisible current, the expanse lies open there and yet displays no kind of openness at all. On the side opposite the inn a rocky slope rises up, the young birches, larches, firs, the maple on this steep shore (no setting posts, although it would have been sensible to put them up, so that the whole thing doesn't one day slip down into the water without knowing what to expect, stupid and usually unconscious, but first of all fundamentally evil, just the way nature is) cannot be reflected. But really, why not? Because that side is simply always in the shade. This lake is not in the sunlight zone, that is its and the tourists' misfortune, yet the trees on the slope really should be able to reflect themselves. Why don't they? Why are they so lazy? Cut into the rock a little path, on which ramblers are often to be seen. They can't escape us, the song goes like this: forwards or backwards or be forgotten. These people are not walking around in the opaque world of the rich. Often they're families with small children, who cannot be accommodated in a hotel, because they would immediately tear it down. But usually they're pensioners, the evening of whose life grants them the full TV programme, because they don't have to get up early in the morning. The few boarding houses here are really good value, the food is good, too, and is locally grown, yes indeed, this landscape has been vigorously cultivated, more abundant organic joy has been wrung from it, so that the naturally fertilised fruit and veg., the specially produced animal shit is coming out of its ears, does not have to be bought as an extra. The animals themselves are available, too, bred on the farm, and they are killed here, a maximum of six at a time, in the little district abattoir. It's not like in the big slaughterhouses, where ten Poles pitilessly hack at a living thing, break it down, for, measured by their own life, the animals here have a super time, and anyway most of it is all the same to man or beast. The main thing is to eat one's fill once more beforehand, before the knife slips into the hand and out of it again, stick it in, under the skin and into the flesh heave ho! Do you have the talent to be happy? Then on no account waste it here!

Look, there go two people again, no, three, in hiking clothes and climbing boots, equipped with sticks, walking on this narrow little path, on which if need be one could even walk in high heels, because the terrain presents no difficulties at all. But professionally kitted out for the unrefined mountains, it's just more fun and doesn't even cost much more. These are people who would dress appropriately and comfortably even in their coffin (so that they can frequently turn round in it), yet nevertheless economically for heaven, so as to be let in at all. They look down on the lake, which swallows up the sun, as if a life-long eclipse prevailed there, and think the dark expanse is like a country road at night, on which one encounters someone. Others would prefer not to encounter anyone. I can understand that, I would probably be one of the latter. So, now the people are gone again, because I can't see them any more. The water is so cold, if one pulled it out of its dripping bed, one would immediately throw it back again, hardly taking a second look at what one had caught hold of. This water would never fall to the surface of the earth as precipitation, it would rather precipitate downright dejection in someone who for at least a week had been hoping for better weather. Coldness pure and simple, in peculiarly amorphous form. If the water had any agility, it would clamber out of here of its own accord. The whole thing isn't very deep, but the creepers, the hussies, would simply pull one down to the bottom, a place which I would rather not imagine. It must be indescribably muddy, dark, icy, dreary there, the point, as it were, at which the body of water is unconscious, but nevertheless unceasingly, with a part of its memory, which has not been regulated by the Alpine Convention, which encourages the harmful substances not to be unloaded here, with a part, which is lying in wait, presumably lying in wait for its own terrible awakening. Not even on its surface have I ever seen ducks, it would rip the fat from their rump, and they would be drawn below the surface quacking wretchedly, that's how I imagine it, because I love animals and wouldn't want them to have unpleasant experiences. Well, obviously they wouldn't like that either. It seems to me, that they never alight on this stretch of water, which appears to be stiff with fright, because it has been poured out here and not over there, where it would get the whole sun, on the other side of the road, where the inn is, too, and even there, no matter how sunny it is, it grows cool early, because of the mountains all around, and cardigans and jackets are taken out. There the ducks are then on the plates. A little jetty, but what for? If no one walks along it. Well, who could have known that beforehand, when assiduous voices were ordered and oars handed out and perseverance practised, when losses were made during the early months. Sometimes one sees and hears children here, who suddenly fall silent, however, and stare at the water, which is so different from what they had been promised, a face which on closer inspection turns out to be a hideous grimace, a web, in which one will become entangled. Not the place for cheerfully coloured bathing suits, beach balls, inflatable animals, rubber dinghies; none of that is granted this lake, there's no change in it and so it doesn't make for a change. It cannot put on any surging robes of foam, because this metal water can neither bestir itself nor be stirred. It seems to me too simple to blame the absence of any of the sun's rays. The tanning studios, at any rate, have any amount of them, but human beings don't get any better as a result. Only such people go there, to lie down in the wonderfully gleaming coffins, who themselves want at least to change the colour of their skin. They secretly suspect, after all, that they must always remain the way they are created. Whoever ends up in the water here - no thanks, as Franz Fuchs, the bomb maker and quadruple gipsy murderer from Gralla, that's forty miles from here, would say loud and clear, so that he can thereby spare himself the well-deserved trial and enjoy the time in peace and quiet in his cell. He can't shout louder than his bombs. I can't hear him anyway, and now he's dead as well. He hanged himself. This water is soaked in itself, that sounds paradoxical, but it's true, so far as anything can be true. It is, so to speak, water twice over and for that reason solid again, no small success for an element that is eager to learn and would like to continue its education, although granted only limited opportunities to do so. With a bit of effort one can always make more of oneself, but at the same time always keep one's feet on the ground, which is nearly always horizontal. The spirit-level, which does not want to stand and only measures what's lying down, knows that, too, oh dear, that's not right, one can also measure the perpendicular with it. I think this water has an acid temper (but can also be alkaline), because no one is exactly scrambling to be a suitable partner for it, in play and sport and fun. It's rejected, so it retires offended to its room. Even the mother of this water, a rather low, newly built retaining wall, from where I'm standing it's on my right, on which the usual small plants are not yet growing, wild birch shoots, small willows, grass together with dandelions, any amount of wild fennel and coltsfoot and cow-parsnip (or is that the same thing?), is only allowed after repeated knocking to enter this water, in which terrible things are evidently produced and which in the shape of tough untearable creepers and drifting plants and algae destroy all other life. Only lifeless life is permitted here. Who with his wings parts the heavens for me? And here we have the first candidates for the room, crows, they're just everywhere, but not on the shore of this stretch of water. Hence nothing else is allowed to live here either. An enormous insignificance - and who can bear that? What on earth is to be discovered in something like that? Perhaps there are, after all, three thousand different varieties of aquatic plants in there, but I don't know them, verticillate, indestructible life, therefore, I wouldn't want to have to count them, the species, then I would have to bend over this water or spontaneously, thoughtlessly completely give myself up to it, and I've never done something like that before.

Oh, how nice, the sun is just taking a final brief walk on the steep shore! So brief, that the darkness, with which I am to be punished immediately afterwards, seems even darker to me. Beyond the lake the windows of the inn flare up for a moment, so it must be about five o'clock, the time at which the sun, at this time of year, graceless as a sleeping infant, but it just doesn't know any better, stands up, pays and begins to leave the garden of the inn, a beginning which also already leaves one behind. Most are in any case sitting inside, because after all it is still very cool outside. It's no different for the highway, which is pleased to make the acquaintance, even if only fleetingly, of the vehicle tyres; briefly they snuggle up, could be friends, and then they're gone again, next please, so that rubber can rub off and rub out. They always leave just a whiff of themselves behind, the tyres, or somebody dead, they get right on top, dead animals, too, cats, snakes, hedge-hogs, hares, even deer and stags, which are then hurled to the edge of the road and left lying on the verge, left for the ants and worms to eat. Soon the sun will be gone completely. Wind rises. The water in the lake (here I am, as I see, tireless in my urge to describe!) is hardly ruffled, where are they, the graceful waves, they could certainly be a bit more full of themselves. Are they stiff with fear? Fallen silent at the sight of themselves, because they have no tender, sweet face, which they could raise to look at and assess one another? I would so like to know more about the inn, but I would not so much like to see the kitchen before I eat, and still less afterwards. Trippers are always strolling past it, cyclists are flashing signals in the sun with the mysterious, rare metals of which their sports equipment is made, their backsides cannot arouse any desires for assessment, they flash by too quickly and are gone again. What else? Over there's the path to the Alpine springs (fifteen minutes by bike, on foot it all depends), which were enclosed for the Vienna Mountain Spring Water Supply, a sight which would be worth visiting, but which one can no longer see. Before enclosure it was a nice destination for an excursion, now unfortunately the water always stays at home and, in accor-dance with its demands, the home is built of stone and concrete and what do I know, ceramic pipes?, and like everything that's always sitting at home, no longer interesting to the beholder. One can hear it frothing, one can hear it murmuring or whatever it does, but here, too, one no longer sees any reflection, no bubbling merriness, no little clouds of foam spraying rainbow mist, no cheerful rushing over stones, no roaring gushing forth from the earth, there's no sitting in a concrete home and throwing foam around. The water is located, properly enclosed, inside a pipe, and in the city it ends up in our glasses and pots, why then do I feel that something's not right? I would be the first to complain, if instead I had to knock back the ground water from the Mitterndorfer bore with all its nutritious nitrates!

Well. The families are slowly setting out for home. Small

children are stuffed into pushchairs, hands are shaken, parking places found and, to the patter of spattering gravel, abandoned again, whatever's alive, which is anyway only held together with difficulty, is finally pulling away in different directions. Those who are allowed to stay together tie themselves into little bundles of rods, which will soon hit out at one another again, they can hardly wait, the couples, the passers-by, the relatives sort each other out and lie down voluntarily on their jigsaw underlays, where they are to be properly fitted together along with their often quite unusual hobbies. Swimming, tennis, skiing, rambling. They have looked at the area or even live entirely in it and hence only have short distances to go, usually by bike, in order to get back home. But the bikes of the natives, whose customs consist in always being customers for something the vacationers already have, these bone-shaker bikes are different. They are plain objects, which don't trumpet any kind of sporting ambitions, they can't keep up anyway. The mountain bikes and their jolly owners in their jolly clothing, they're like the fingers of a hand being moved, one moves and the others join in. They are many and quick, to us whom they leave standing they say farewell even before they've seen us. What should the people here begin, when they began to look for stuff like that in the department store in the county town, at first among the special offers? But the children of the villagers have steadfastly cut imitations of racing bikes out of their parents' living bodies and are beaten for it (more often than the city children), because so much has been spent on them. The bodies on the adults' bikes are wrapped up in exemplary manner, sometimes still even in a dirndl, clean, although ever more frequently one sees shorts and jogging pants on the bodies of mountain folk. Undignified times, to what do you drive your occupants and why do you drive them on, when there is no place to which they could drive? But don't be deceived, even if I constantly attempt such deceptions, so as to make things simpler for myself, many also drive to distant lands, to places e.g. where I've never been. I, however, have really never been anywhere yet, not because some sins or other could wrap themselves around me there, but because I'd rather sin at home, where God even announces the weather to me in advance on TV, slowly, so that I can write it down, in case it's worth the proper guilt. Sinning is enough, there's no need for surprises as well.

So the children are decked out with spoils, which their relatives have forced on them or which they have cadged for themselves. If someone has lost his self-control with them, then their bawling can be heard as far away as the lake, but no further, the lake is the limit. It swallows everything. I've already said so, but it's on my mind nevertheless in a curiously insistent way: Usually children like to gather on the shores of bodies of water, they splash about, splash each other, pick up small stones and throw them at one anothers' heads, get onto air beds or air beds which have disguised themselves as animals and, as if spellbound, they stare into the distance, where such animals sometimes sink without a sound, or where boats have fled as the only way to get away from them, in order to do a few exercises on the waves. They beg to go out in a boat, the children, best of all in a pedal boat, which can never ever capsize, there are three of them here, but they don't look as if they're ever used. Some water is sloshing about in them, cloudy, muddy, sluggish, how did it get there? It's too little for a leak, for the free and easy games of boisterous water fanatics too much. The boats are definitely neglected, I can see that, but why maintain and look after them, if no one wants to go in them? Presumably it squeaks, when one, what do you call it, the thing you step on, like when you play the harmonium, it's not a bellows, it'll be a kind of plastic paddlewheel or something like it, so when one operates these things, and the boat moves jerkily and haltingly forward, how about greasing the bearings for once? There's even a steering wheel and one can imagine oneself at the helm of a speedboat, in which one could have an accident. That has already happened to world-famous people, spouses, fathers. One can put the fear of death into younger siblings with malicious words, if one pretends that the boat is certain to sink now, because it's not going to stay upright much longer, luckily I can swim, but you can't, tough. These are all things one can talk about, but no one talks about them here, it would be superfluous. One doesn't talk about things which normally can only be written, but neither are the people who live here in life's good books. They'd rather pay on credit. The children in the inn's beer garden sometimes walk the few yards over to the slide and the swing, with which at any rate they can catapult themselves straight onto the compost heap - where the hens are scratching and the cucumbers and pumpkins, too, are still only in their infancy - if they're skilful enough and want to drive their parents to commercial TV and then to the washing machine, but they always come back pretty quickly. They've had more than enough of such parents, pressed flat, brightly coloured and always cheerful, who are incessantly washing, know them better than their own, who don't have much time for it, but then they don't need any with these washing powders and liquids, it all happens in the twinkling of an eye, just like that. The TV is also nearby, it's in the kitchen-living room. Perhaps the parents have only forbidden their children to cross the main road by themselves, because they would have to do that to reach the lake. No, not a chance, I'm sticking to it, there's something that I simply don't understand about this mighty lake, well, it's not really so big, in fact it's rather small, compared to Lake Baikal, but it isn't what it was either. The parents could go along, and they would certainly not be so hard-hearted as to refuse the children the boat trip, it's very cheap and in the course of time has even become a little cheaper. There's a solution to everything, though I personally don't know one for the lake, it's a mineral solution, but no one knows the details. Not a nice sight, the lake. At first everyone was pleased, that now there's something like that here too, so mysterious and beautiful, so splendid, that'll attract the tourists and does them a constant service and sometimes a last honour - but then its health began to fail, and suddenly no one was pleased any more. And why does no one pour in the tried and tested good algicides? Conjecture: then the algae would certainly be finished, but the lake would have to swallow the weed killer as well, when it was already unable to hold anything because of its weak stomach: the water would remain deader than dead. Even artificial aeration, if we could afford it, would only produce short-term success, because once the water begins to breathe, then it wants to keep on breathing more and more, until it believes it's a human being. The water is so presumptuous, there's nothing to be done. That's why it's better to leave it to its imbalance, isn't it? If the lake's dead, we can make a new one beside it, exactly, right beside it, no, over there's better. Now what does that look like? Many will be against it. And further upriver there's the big dam for the local electricity plant, nothing's happening there any more. The water has to work and has no time for fun and games. And we're not going to blast another hole in the world just for fun, are we?

Strange for a piece of water, which induces most people almost involuntarily to come and look, since it could cause one difficulties of every kind, I need only think of the landslides and floods which last week we could keep track of in every detail on our screens and now still of the broken off roadside, after the catastrophes for their part had tracked down whole villages and car parks and were even successfully after a whole inn, gulp, in which the beds were already waiting patiently, almost unprofitably, like open savings bank books, because the season was about to begin. So one thing follows another. But one could also think of sporting variety, when one sees the water, one could get out, take the surfboard from the roof of the car, and we're already there. We do exactly the same with the roads and the wheels, we make ourselves masters of our sports equipment, and nature is slowly getting nervous as a result, it gets us in its sights, takes careful aim, its finger is already itching on the trigger, but because we move so fast, it's constantly losing us. Lucky for us, but ultimately it is we who always have to be moving on. Well, but now, unfortunately, it has found us after all, nature. Every corner, every patch of this piece of water has left something deep down in the mountain and now cannot find its way back. It's possible that something has been catapulted from the red iron-bearing rock of Styria that did not want to be filled up again, because it would like to enjoy the view itself for once, and if it had to be filled up, then not with water, but with wine or beer please, don't take it so seriously! We'll just bore a completely new hole in a completely different place, to tunnel under the whole Semmering, but there, too, the water that was there before, and has older rights, is already coming towards us. It doesn't encourage us to stay, and right away there are some who now no longer want the hole. Water in the rock, next time if you please just leave it out, God! Just put the water in this pan, we can do with it there! The nature conservationists play their jolly comedians' roles, and at some point they, too, will disappear from the surface of the earth, beneath which everything will be churned up again by animals, laboriously, they're so small, they're so small.

So no caressing or scolding voices reach us from this piece of water, I would even prefer the nagging of a father, the complaints of an overworked mother, the whining of a child whose face has been smacked to this eerie soul of the water, these eyes of the water, which stare at me, these lips of the water, which want to devour me, well, they'll be taking on a bit much there! I weigh nine and a half stone now.

It's dark now and has grown even colder, the grit left over from winter rises in a cloud when someone drives over it, and it's no longer enough for anyone to be present, he would like to get into the warmth of kitchens and pub rooms. People have come out of the open air and fled into the enclosure of their families as if they had no other shelter. Food is dished up, the skates and skateboards and climbing boots have to stay outside or in the cellar. With choice listlessness the fathers cut a piece from the roast, which, a last desperate remedy, is supposed to animate them again, supported by an almighty double glass of wine, a miracle that they don't lose all hope. Nature, which treats us so sternly, also takes a break. That's what we call everything that has to stay outside, and nature has been baked into a block of darkness, cold, mountain wind, mountain stream and regularity (yesyes, the plants in their predetermined vegetation units, one can almost set one's clock by them!) and eaten by us and other animals. That successful sampler nature, what could I not describe now, if I reassembled old descriptions, no matter what, it always sounds good, doesn't it? Come right in, you cute comparison of mountain lake with diamond set among the mountains, how well I know you, just lie down there! no, but not on my toes! The strawberry slopes and the river squadrons of fish, the thicket of the pine plantation, where all the lower branches have unfortunately died off, mutants donated by the tourist board, so that the excursionists are better able to see the mushrooms on the ground, but they aren't there any more either, because they've been suffocated under eighteen inches of needles like Salome under the shields of the soldiers. Also probably an experience with far-reaching consequences, but not something I would want. By the lake meanwhile, because we are not in it, we do not see the following: the surface level, that is, where the water level runs in its trough, the wood piles, because none were driven into the earth to strengthen the shore, instead this shore is lovelessly made up of boulders, dumped down just as they were blasted out of the rock after the soil flesh had been picked clean; a screen of reeds has at least been placed in front of it, or it has itself taken the trouble to get here, a walking wood and further: the stone's throw, that's just these quarry stones, a ton weight some of them, spilled down and crudely dressed, which the reed bank with its green pencil bodies masks. What lives under the water? Let's take a look. Nothing lives under the water any more. No need to pour in anything else that's dead!

With a terrified expression, as if in the middle of the darkness he were also seeing the end of the world before him, a single figure (male, 54) stands on the shore. All remaining figures in the area have withdrawn to personally protect the species in front of the programme Austria Today or even to maintain the species, no matter, in any case into their little houses. Until now, so it seems to me, the figure has proceeded in a very purposeful manner, unlike nature, which takes what it can get and gives whatever it has. Only giving and taking are one and the same thing with it. This time the figure has set itself the goal of not looking its deeds in the face, I'm telling you that, because I already know everything about the figure. That's the nice thing about my job. The man has wrapped his deed, not very carefully, because he was in such a hurry, in a green plastic sheet of the kind that are used to cover the freshly hewn wounds of building sites, so that no water can ruin the damp, expensive concrete, but the things are never quite watertight. And in any case now the opposite of what it is usually supposed to do is being demanded of the tarpaulin: Water, please, come on in! The packet is supposed to get heavy very quickly, not like the earth which is supposed to get very light for one. As far as colour and shape are concerned, it is impossible to tell what the packet contains. It doesn't appear to be anything big, but it's not small either. So, now you know exactly as much as I do, that is, everything, but that's entirely thanks to me: because I've attached a couple of pennants, bells, horns and flashing lights to this packet, so that now really everyone knows what's inside. But how else should one say it in a proudly inflated life's work, which one would like to trot ahead of and impetuously toss the feathers in the headdress before the wind does so and there's nothing more one can do about it. At all events one should be able to say it better, much better. The package is heavy. The man has quite a job shoving, pushing and pulling. The water is at last supposed to do its destructive work on the parcel or it can do whatever it likes, just eat away, for all I care, it really makes no difference to this man here either. I think his behaviour is so unutterably fearless, as if he wanted, indeed dearly wished: This package should be found again as soon as possible! But then why is he hiding it at all? He could put it down right next to the highway, the effect would be the same. No. Modern tyrants who have long ago won the right of self-determination for themselves and their refuse, compete relentlessly to dump rubbish there. So perhaps the effect would have been the opposite, since no one ever clears anything away. The package could still be lying there in three years' time. It wouldn't be down to us. Why is the man not smiling full of anticipation? Inside the plastic sheet there, I'm saying so, although there's no need at all to emphasise it, there's a nice piece of body, belonging to a woman. Just a moment, I'll take another look, that's right, it's not a man, it's exactly what I've thought up. A woman. A man would be heavier. One would need accomplices and a cheeky little river, which after one was finished with the body, would carry it away. I once knew someone personally, who with someone else drowned someone in a real river. The cock of the man, whom you see here, is still erect, it's like that nearly all the time, fantastic!, almost like a skier at the bend, which threatens to carry him off the track, but he counteracts it, so his cock stands up straight to the end and refuses to get any smaller, what else is the man going to do with it? He's already done everything with it that was possible. It was no use. He even tried to build on it, but this foundation might perhaps give way unexpectedly and on the way down to the cellar one might at least once briefly have to look a human being in the face instead of the arse or the breasts or the legs. For which one would first of all have had to find the necessary peace and quiet. No one should be there to observe one scaring oneself to death. The hearts of women are often of a cheerful spaciousness, so that it is also possible to go into reverse in them, if one wants to get away again, yet in a car, which is often the most important thing in a relationship, even inserted as obligatory by senior citizens in their Lonely Hearts adverts, one never quite gets there, it always has to stay outside unfortunately, the car, unless one is in the woods, then one has to park first; but hardly has this man stolen into one of these hearts, which he has been looking for, than he is completely indifferent, even cold again, forever unimpressed by sights or events. Beauty does not touch him, because everything he finds beautiful, absolutely must be dead. How I could have laughed about him, if only I had wanted to! I could have been afraid. This man rarely laughs. If he ever looks in the mirror, it's as if he can't remember what he looks like, perhaps because he longs for nothing so much as material goods, so that as if as punishment he first of all has to visualise himself. And in his greed for property he then forgets himself, sometimes quite suddenly, but he never forgets what he wants. If asked, he replies, correctly, even intelligently, indeed quick-wittedly, then again obligingly, smiles, the question even stays in his brain for a while, so that he can look at it very carefully or change his mind before giving an answer or evading it. Perhaps he can after all draw some advantage from the ever-repeated question of his wife about eternal values - life or death, kitchen bench or chairs, couch or easy chairs - please, Kurt! Perhaps he'll finally say something, he has already been asked so many times (well, we don't have a digger to clear the old kitchen furniture away, that's expensive, more than new stuff!). So that for once his dark soul, like ours after the cinema, which was the last time it came to life, may rise up and stretch its legs. Even plants feel more than he does, I swear to you, e.g. they respond to music, as it says in this magazine which this man's wife, who grows flowers, brought home yesterday, pure waste of money. There's much that he does quite correctly, some things are also wrong, he sleeps, he gets up, an overgrown child, that has learned nothing yet, not even children's tricks, but he doesn't pick up on stories or songs at most on instructions for use and building plans and bank statements, which show him, that his money unfortunately has been recently withdrawn and the rent for the last three months is still owed. I see something there, it's true, but don't say anything yet for the time being, something about his work, which he does really well, even if always with one foot on the wrong side of the law, which in his job is very practical (you get to know villains and part-time villains) and is actually quite usual. Nothing that went beyond the everyday duties. He is, what he is, no, he lacks something. He completely lacks a whole dimension, that is, the dimension, that there are other people apart from himself. It's as if you knew what time it is, but not which year, which month, which day, these are units, which even if strange, distasteful, have our life terms in their hands. We request them to be considerate. They are superior units, which can indeed be made a little more refined by the addition of the spice of life, but we can't quite get rid of the bitter taste. The man is completely normal, as far as I can see, but he speaks as if with a child's voice roaring out from deep inside, and always only to himself (long ago, as a child, he had still felt something, it had been nice then, everything OK with his scooter, his bike, his ball, the sweets, over a hundred times, such a spoiled, a pretty child, no little Mister Guilty or Mister Ugly, quite the opposite! Golden haired. Good as gold, to get used to the inevitable, that is: gold makes the world go around), whose vocabulary, however, is very limited. It doesn't matter, the man always knows, what he wants to say to himself. Or, let's see the picture, where have I put it, oh yes, there it is: as if it were a paper cut-out, onto which one can clip his clothes, uniform, jeans, the good suit for his own funeral, the braided grey Styrian suit for Sundays or the Country Police Carnival Ball, the track-suit for nothing, but no one has ever thought that one can also pin feelings to people or that the sweetheart can carefully pin her eyes, but she's not going to be doing any sewing again, is she? Shouldn't her dear eyes open at all any more? This man doesn't have room, it doesn't matter what for. He needs space, it doesn't matter where. He wouldn't know, on whom he should waste anything. Odd, that people are never suspicious of him and, on the contrary, often immediately expose their innermost secrets to him, perhaps because they suspect that otherwise he would be gone again, before they can even take their clothes off, lie down on the couch and display themselves to him without anything on. I correct myself: He does have dreams, the man, they are, however, nailed to one or more houses or owner-occupied apartments and so not at all times freely disposable. Well, one house, a little house, he already has, his wife brought it into the marriage, that's also why he keeps the wife who belongs to it, despite the cost. Ah yes, I see, other houses have now come more within his reach, his son e.g. pays a small life annuity for his, smaller than the life of a certain old woman her body meanwhile almost wasted away because of alcohol. Fortunately the person will die, but the walls within which she hid away will still stand.

But then again there's no doing without bodies, precisely the most decayed, frail cling surprisingly fiercely to life; this man lets nothing rest, he always wants more without letting go of a thing again, now everything has to turn out for the best. There he stands, steady as a mountain rock (sadly he has less and less time for the mountains, they often come last now. Besides there's no building land up there, only wasteland struck by rocks), stands outside the shops which sell only the cheapest lines, outside the inn, where the teetotaller and sportsman drinks no more than a Fanta or a soda pop, into which he then, under the table, pours his schnapps (which he never pays for either, because he has always entered as a figure of authority). We are dealing with that mysterious continuation of ourselves to which everything falls, because it belongs there, like gravity, at the bus stop, where the car driver doesn't take the bus, but prefers to take someone else instead, before darkness falls, which he penetrates with a pocket lamp, but only if it is absolutely necessary. Batteries cost money, too. And here he knows the way at any time, even in the dark, every stone on it and every protected plantation of fir trees, on which he himself need protect nothing and no one, when he sits down in the middle of the spread table of a woman.

What's coming down from the heights there? It's them, it's always them, the mountaineers, the hikers with their own or other women. But of course it's always a matter of where you're standing. Who touches a meadow full of flowers with his feet, and yet the meadow remains untouched? Unbelievable, that there's such and such a number of women, particularly ever since they've been driving around in cars just as much as men and can also turn up in a different place from where they are at home. They are drawn out into town and country, into the county town and onto the country road, and that they are so different from one another is likewise unbelievable. And then they stoop to this man, they've hardly clapped eyes on him and they're on the ropes, he cuts them down or not, in his hands they soon gleam like polished pieces of furniture. Yes, indeed, and afterwards they are alone and been taken for a ride, with the itch, but not sewn up, I can already see that from this distance. There have been a good five of them in the last two years. Not all that many, I know, but it takes time to look after them, because nowadays they demand quality in order to be satisfied. It's not enough for them to rub up against the wall of house, which is badly plastered or turning damp, the house should also belong to them, after they've been saving themselves so long for the right man. They don't let their cars do something like that either. That they wipe their dirty tyres on someone or that someone takes the liberty of doing such a thing with them. Cars also belong to many women. Many cars belong to women. Thus one becomes a vessel, they probably thought, once they had chosen this car in their favourite colour and even had to wait for it. One spreads out, the bed for that already there. It's recently been specially acquired, together with an orthopaedic mattress, for a very special person, who will lie down, where no one has lain down before. And one already knows all that in advance, after talking to him just once, on the dusty road, where one showed him the driving licence and the vehicle documents, and he was such a wonderful, unique man, one never saw one like him before, and one knew: He's the One! And why? asks the shop assistant at Billa, with whom, since moving here to the country a couple of years ago, one occasionally has a bit of a heart to heart, next to toothpaste, soap and detergents. I don't know. That's the answer. The rather stocky, but muscular-looking, dark-blond police officer is considered to be a loner, a reputation which he has never really resisted. A man who hides his feelings behind a robust manner, but who can also show small weaknesses. How sweet of him! He effortlessly overcame the barriers, with which I have protected myself until now, says this woman to the supermarket cashier, who doesn't understand her and who would at last like to go home. But hardly has anything so wonderful happened to one, than one is immediately buried again, and that is the disadvantage with lonely people, by miles of worries and suspicion, as if one were the landscape itself, which is idly waiting for what will be inflicted on it in the shape of mudslips, avalanches and rockfalls. One finds oneself in the water, instead of being water, which can travel anywhere, but unfortunately on one condition: downhill only! So it's better to stay at home, so as not to miss the telephone ringing, or you just take the telephone with you, which can play Bach's D Minor Organ Toccata, which it's been taught. After that you only have to wait for your number to be called.

Then miracles happen, an angel enters and with his wings cuts in pieces what divides two people, and it will come, it will come!, for example the best-loved miracle, which is no miracle at all, for a human being is as if made for love. But that is deceptive, often a human being only looks as if he is. On the contrary, God never does well by the good, and they, although they, too, love and want to stay, fall apart even more quickly than the rest of us with our ordinary joyless life, and later on one doesn't recognise them again, the good people, when the seams of their genitals come apart and the sawdust pours out, which once lent them a bit of shape at least. Even wood would have been affected by such an experience, the glue would have fallen from it. Because no one reassembles these tender lovers, who wish only to forget themselves in love, and this time reinforces them right from the start with some plywood, so that they can at last stand up by themselves and can stay up a little longer in this position. Afterwards, nevertheless, a human being is never the same again, even after just an hour. Take a look, I'll show you: This miracle happened to the woman there, and to the one over there, too, I think, and over there there are five together, but the miracle caused that one a lot of trouble, this self-absorbed, retiring, quiet, shy woman, would you recognise her as someone who moved to the country, because people in the city who got close to her, which she had always invited, hurt her, mostly without wanting to or knowing it? This woman is too sensitive, she's already paralysed with fear and I've caught it, too. At this moment the man opposite her is devoting himself entirely to his career as a lover. He has already made some progress, and has got just as far as the little café, where they know him and so where he doesn't like to go at all. But this time he didn't want to contradict the woman's provincial loneliness, the relationship is still too new, the woman is already touchy enough, so he let her have her way: to show herself in public with the man! At last! She gets a lot out of that. And so there they sit side by side. On the other hand something like that has never ever happened to the man before, but in the daily tabloid he can read up where it leads: to love. In sequence. Until marriage. Until death. The country policeman's wife reads whole novelettes about it, from start to finish. The man holds his own in his hard job, which one can carry out with a dog and/or motor bike, but one can only bring the dog along in the car, or it has to be left behind altogether. The man holds his own in the atmosphere, the climate that goes along with it, and which until recently was purely man's business. Whether it rains or snows or whether the sun shines, it doesn't matter, the men made it, complains one or other woman to no one in particular. The man is quite different in this respect, usually doesn't even know what she's talking about, at this little café table, someone who gave up her career, but who had such a good income in the city and out of fear of disappointment again and again avoided close ties, as she declares, as she already declares, because again and again she was: abandoned, abandoned like a stone in the road. That's how the sad Carinthian song goes, but I don't know the rest of the words. I should know them, because soon the whole world will be Carinthia, and then there will be terrible punishments for anyone who doesn't know these beautiful songs by heart. Well, why does she come here, the woman, where no one needs her. He needs her so! He's not interested in what she says. He's interested in what she has. He goes to open up the millionairess, but no, it's not millions, let's make a rough calculation back and forward: it never works out. What one needs is only her property, but she's still using it herself, and even if only to start out from it, to explore the area, its rare Alpine flora and fauna through books and then to cuddle up all the more cosily on the couch with a glass of wine and a book. No, Kurt, today I don't need you, today I want to be quite alone for once, but call me, definitely. If he doesn't call, she goes off the deep end. While we're on its beauty, this area would never get adequate attention, if it were not beautiful. Otherwise no one would bother about it, apart from the scantily dressed tourists, who get everywhere, and to whom the woman for her part feels superior (among the tourists there are also some who are overloaded with clothing, they just have no sense of proportion). In the man's cheerful disposition there is in principle no room for any woman, which he doesn't say. But for a house of course, always, even though in the nature of things it would be much larger: A house of one's own, somewhere to feel at home. Charm is already lying ready on the plate, today it has to stand in for butter. It'll manage that. This woman would be much smaller and manageable than the house, she could prove that, if the country policeman would only take a proper look at her, from top to bottom. And in the house there would at last be enough room for his expansiveness, his mountain bike and his hobbies, which are a waste of time. He should rather spend his time with her: Yes, take a look at that, I would describe him like that, too, before allowing myself to be hit. He isn't capacious, but expansive, not in the sense that there is truly anything cheerful about him, but clean and empty. The furniture has been pushed against the walls, so that his body can more easily be encouraged to carry out the much, thank you, practised movements, which should cause the furnishings no more damage than absolutely necessary. When things have got that far, one wants to have them along with the house. At most the bed will collapse at some point. One sees a person standing in front of one, and then suddenly it's a woman. One sees her waving her arms about, shouting, weeping, saying please please, because he wants to leave so early again today. One can see her performing tricks, in order to seduce him, now she's even getting up on her hind legs. She threatens him. Funny, we're already at home with her again. Earlier she calmly made coffee, although earlier we've already drunk some in the café and are now eagerly waiting for the sniffing course in matters of tenderness and trust, which had been promised us and for which we have already put down a payment: Two people who can't stand one another, but don't let go of one another either. For various reasons. In time they will learn to fly and take flight, because there's no other way they can get away from one another. One of them at least has to go, so that the other can stay. But why all the work at the stove, if the woman in the end - she doesn't quite know yet, how to offer herself up completely, she would rather offer food and drink - throws a hot cupful in his face, why all the cooking and raging about so little? Why such a devil of a temper? And now she has to wipe up the coffee again alone and spoon up the soup alone. It really wasn't necessary to throw things around with people who haven't done anything at all. After this noisy scene, the woman, unappeased, but well brought up, is allowed to cook a less solid meal, this time something exotic with pineapple slices and spices, which were brought here specially from the Naschmarkt in Vienna, would you like that, Kurt?, no he doesn't know it and doesn't want to know it. Now this time he doesn't want to, he would rather practise his power of attraction. Please please, eat something, then there's dessert, then I personally will get carried away with you! Stop, now she has a good idea, she will offer the man, who has already rejected her offer and who preferred to consume his nourishment in the disguise of sausages and fried egg at lunchtime at home with mama, his meal in a completely new, unprecedented way. He will be so happy that he will be unable to control himself, like a spring which would be worthy of control, but meanwhile still has to wait for such a thing. And so she's going to serve his food, you won't believe it, well, then again it's not so original either: wearing exclusively the new, expensive lingerie she bought just for him at Palmer's in town. Is that not a brilliant idea for her brilliant appearance? Is that not a change for his eyes, which on the grey roads have had to see much worse things, often also stirred, beaten or whisked with blood? What else can I serve up? Her entrance, which she should have rehearsed earlier, so as not to have induced this dreadful laughter in the man, which will appear here from now on at irregular intervals, would have persuaded him, if he had wanted to believe his eyes. After one had listened to one's inner voice, one could spread a little of the food on one's own body, with its juices, so that it can be licked off. For no other reason. A woman doesn't dream of anything like that, she's read something like it on some enclosed instruction sheet, and ever since she believes in the ability of her body, modern, confident, financially independent as she is, to stand up to all physical demands (others have to unreel many miles of threads of fate every day for that), no matter what else one sticks in her mouth, sometimes even a clenched fist, ouch.

Then suddenly she wakes up, as e.g. today, sleepwalker that she has been, blind as she has been, on the stairs. A little blood is coming from her vagina. What has he stuck in there this time, bigger than a slap in the face, smaller than a tractor? Perhaps the neck of the beer bottle? What was it? And her clothes have trickled down the steps right beside her, in the wrong sequence, some are missing altogether. Furthermore the door is now locked from the inside, didn't I say that before? did I forget it? Well well, who's in the flat now, in the house which both belong to her, the ground floor, too, of course and the cellar with sauna and wine racks and skis and hobby equipment? The woman sees herself kneeling completely naked in her misfortune at her own front door, a torn bit of clothing, which has soaked up something, clutched to her breast, her eye pressed to the keyhole. Is he really inside with someone else or is my eyesight making a mistake, has it got it wrong or is it suffering from strain?, with one as young as that, has he had the nerve to do something like that with her?, and really in my own home? I've got the essentials right in front of me and cannot deny it, but neither can I talk about it. I think, the man doesn't know how far he can go with the woman. Well, not that far anyway! But he gets going nevertheless. He would, however, prefer to take a fast car. Her role will be as front-seat passenger.

The woman thinks: It simply can't be true, that right now, at this very moment, he's blowing his trumpet into such a young girl, she's no more than a child, it can't be - this instrument belongs to me alone, only to me. Although I hardly know how to hold it. But with me it's certainly in good hands, in better hands, because I've already heard many famous orchestras or eaten them out of the tin and waved the baton along in person, leaning back comfortably in my easy chair, because I didn't forgo the planned dream course of studies and nevertheless completed the piano course as well and took a special exam at the end, I'd like to see another woman do that. Others again claim to have seen me pretend to play a piano concerto by Beethoven, but Alfred Brendel was lying on the silvery gleaming windshield wiper and was moving diligently and fluently in time. People lie. It cannot be, that this man is already rejecting me, before he's even had time to depend on me. Perhaps he doesn't know what he's got in me and that these and similar wounds he beats into me can mark someone for life. They don't draw a nice picture of me. I would like to have a nicer one. I imagine, that I have kept persistent suitors at a distance, but not him, the one and only! For whom I have waited fifty years.

But not him. I would never do that to him. Before he even knew, how nice everything could be for both of us, he would already have turned me down? No, it can't be. Perhaps instead I'll be allowed to crawl around on the floor in front of him tomorrow. So that he finally understands that he could also enter my ever open door, from above and from the front and from both sides, they're my good sides, because I've only just fallen in love with him, hark, what enters from outside? Now of all times. No one, I hope. No one must see me like this, naked, bleeding and my clothes all mucky. I hope it's not a colleague of his, from the same station, who's come without being called. Screams outside? That's right, it's me who's screaming, what, it's supposed to be me? That doesn't sound good. It sounds like someone who wanted to cut him short and instead, presumably in a rage, but why?, was thrown out onto the stairs, where it's cold. The body that goes along with it will surely keep, in this cold. It was boiled down long ago and imprisoned in a special little glass house, a dear little Snow White in a glass coffin, where unfortunately everyone can see it. That and more than that, more than a coffin, that last little house, also provides clothing for women. We don't need a man for that at all.

This woman here is, I think, greedy for property, whom property, however, was always refused, so silly, and who is now on her feet again, making for the hall window, perhaps she can get into the apartment again that way. But first she would have to go outside for a moment, where everyone would stare at her. Let him come. She's not going to come now specially. He'll see. He should take her and not the other, who hasn't even finished her training as an apprentice clerical worker. The woman has that on good authority. In place of all my property, he's not going to let himself be palmed off with something else, cheaper, thinks the woman, and certainly not someone who's hardly more than a child. He'll prefer a real woman. That's her offer, she can let it stand, we could also make a smaller one, which would not stand so well.

We could live in an attic room and be beside ourselves with happiness, although there wouldn't be much space: happiness, because the room was holding us so tight, that we couldn't fall down, I'm so in love, what happiness, that there's you and me at the same time. There's no room here at all. I've got more than one room, I've got a whole house, where we can make ourselves at home. It's bound to go wrong. Someone who is forced to give, is poorer than someone who gives of their own free will. Hopefully this night will soon come to an end and I can stop this pointless work of thumping and kicking the door. His hard knees together with the track-suit bottoms - the pattern docsn't match, but the knees match him very well, once the trousers are gone. And then, and then, pointing at my body, no, not showing the door, I've done that all too often, although we haven't known each other long at all, but shyly (which is not highly regarded, everyone should immediately point to what he has, and what his speciality is, and what he has to offer. I imagine it, as demonstrated by Jesus, pointing to his bleeding heart, often with the smart accessory of a crown of thorns plus two, three drops of blood as additional hint: Things are already going downhill!) pointing to where this stupid door is placed anyway, that is, in my house!, and where it is out of place to simply come breezing in with another woman, particularly one who's so much younger. So, now all limbs are present and correct, a body as hiding place is present, too, no longer brand new, but a bit of all right. In the dark there's no problem. Doesn't he see that. I'm so in love. Likewise there's a suggestion in the eyes, but there's no clear or distinct image in the hall mirror. Why does man always only appreciate in women, how the bodies open their mouths wide and scream scream scream. I still have to cure him of that. It'll turn out all right in the end. He can't stand it. He puts his hands over his ears. But he can't strike a single right note, even one, for instance while he's eating. He's not musical. Actually he's bad-mannered and coarse. No one brought him up properly. Evidently he can't hear these screams either. Or pretends that he couldn't. He only sees screams, if people let them drop out of their mouths in front of him, but they don't bother him, their screams. Usually people stand right in front of him and around him, but never behind him, because the country policeman always wants to keep an eye on them. Some are desperate, point at their burnt relatives in small cars and weep a bucketful. The roads are nothing but a bloodbath, a bloody brood, as if people had been born only to be ripped apart on the roads again. In the past admission was charged for that and there were no roads at all. He's tough. Everything that comes from this woman: He will ignore it, simply because he doesn't see her, if he doesn't want to see her. He's got to change a bit there, she thinks. It'll turn out all right in the end. He has seen too much, and if he hadn't seen too much - this woman would in any case have been too much for him. All her doors are wide open all the time, doesn't she notice there's a draught, she really should shut them. Does the country policeman feel something like fear creeping up on him? The man has known for a long time, what in her case is behind them, he doesn't have to break in, although he hasn't known the woman long at all. In fact he knows in his sleep the location of all the household furnishings, which are supposed to serve human beings for their convenience and which instead wind around their limbs like nooses, until they've been paid off. I think they will be kept open for ever, these doors, in their frame of a scratchy hair shirt, that barely covers them, so that they are not right away recognised as doors on opening, the first time the bell is rung. It is as if they had never been shut, doors, yes, there's a lot I could say about that; a man is, if I have to swear on oath, a man first of all (that's not the only thing here, which I haven't said myself. Real live people once said things like that and still say them, if they're allowed to, word of honour), not one of the many there have been in his life so far, has ever expressed the wish to regard this man as a friendly, family being. Here, in this place, no one has had to leave grammar school early, because no one went there. Here, in this place no one has gone without studying, to be satisfied in some other way, for which no money and no position is needed. The positions can all be invented, or here, in the magazine, there are some, too, it's always the same ones, only the people have to change. With illustrations and photographs. In any case, here every woman has tried after a while to get rid of the man again as soon as possible, just as one is always relieved, when the relations go at last and have let one off this time even though they urgently needed a new sweater. One knows them all too well. They are like oneself, only different.

So here, on the cold stairs, a former foreign correspondence clerk and business translator and part-time pianist from the formerly big bad wild city, holds her head in her hands and blubbers. She knows, in how many languages one can plead and in what tones, she knows many of them, but she should also know, that tones are no use, if there's someone who doesn't want to hear and feel or has no receiver for them, not even in a dental filling with detector capabilities. This woman simply cannot be understood. That's the way it is. It's all no use. The question, which we have meanwhile almost forgotten, although it's often been put, goes: Why is the door to the apartment suddenly shut, locked from inside, just where the key is in the lock? And why doesn't the spare key open it up? Because you can't get it in? No. Because it's outside the house under the door mat, where we can't get at it. Anyway, it wouldn't open up at all, if a colleague is sticking in the lock on the other side. Can't it be put more simply? Well, I can't do it. And why is the woman still waiting and has now forced her body to wait with her? For whom is she doing it? Let us free the body from its constraints and let us be quite frank ourselves: Of course I understand, that the beloved man can't go home to where his wife is with the girl, after all I've read enough novels about that and similar unpleasant matters. Please, come and visit me and bring me something nice, that's what I said to him, almost cheeky, wasn't I?, after he had examined my documents on the country road, as if he had personally picked up copies of the laws and brought them with him, in order to throw the book at people. It was all as if carved in stone. He had thought for a long time beneath his crash helmet. As far as I was concerned he could right away have taken a cane in one hand and my arse in the other, because I really had behaved very badly on the road, it's true (disregarded right of way of the country road, but really nothing came along, from any direction, and the one who did come, I didn't even glance at). The country policeman hesitated, stared at me, as if his eyes were halters, oh yes, that's how a relationship begins, even if only to one's own body, but which one didn't have beforehand either. And then he gripped my arm, he gripped me by the arm. In an intense conversation with me he absent-mindedly held my upper arm with one hand. But then I was already waiting for the other hand, so please, when is it finally going to come? So I said, what you can bring me, when you come to visit me, that is above all, you! Yes, always remain yourself. I think you're good the way you are. You are the man of my dreams. Tall, strong, blond, blue-eyed and you look like a Viking, only a little smaller. You have a powerful erotic effect on me. In addition you are the tower of strength I have always longed for, exactly, that's what it says here and as far as I'm concerned it can stay. How lucky, that I picked you up on the road first of all, then accepted my punishment, and, already with a firm date with you, on the spot, where I stood with lowered eyes, which were right below my modern short haircut in Caucasian blonde, so already with a date arranged, met you again in an outdoor restaurant in the county town, quite by chance as far as the other customers were concerned and so also found you at last, for my part for ever. So, I catch my breath a little, now I want to decide my price per cubic metre. It's to be expected that I set the tone, after all I've seen almost the whole world and understood most of it, too. But I didn't expect that you would pay no attention at all to my tones. You brought a measuring tape with you, what's that for. It's high time to mark out the remaining space, it's the space that I need, before your arse can touch my oak trunk (the bed is made of that precisely without any use of iron the healthiest thing possible and brand new and no nails!) for the first time. Why don't you follow me. Further occasions are to follow, until I start feeling better. One last spark of reason has stayed with me, now it arouses my anger, a smouldering fire develops, which eats away my views and opinions at breakneck speed. I know, I know, I should keep up with all the fresh cut flower girls, this year's harvest, hardly out of their leading strings, but I can't do it. You're already a grandfather. Valentine's Day is already definitely past for this year, on which you didn't bring me any flowers. Perhaps there's nothing like experience? Well, perhaps like mine. When it comes to women any amount of experience can in five minutes effortlessly be cancelled out by youth. Yet you're not so young yourself any more. On the other hand: If I want something, then a whole peace studies research institute could not get me out of a war with myself, which I would start immediately. I can fight, bloody hell, are you talking to me, then you'll soon see. I shouldn't love him, this man, but I do. So time passes. It's the bloody truth. No letter, no postcard, no phone call, no divorce, no decision at all, no engagement, there's nothing without him, only the naked, grinning nothingness of death, and that comes ever closer instead of keeping its distance. But I still have a lot of time, perhaps the best of times. Statistically speaking at my age the safe distance from death is 38 years or perhaps a little less. I beg to be allowed to write to him, but his wife has never seen a letter which someone might have written to him, except the bank. His wife, suspicious that some repayment date had been missed again, would immediately tear open the letter and disembowel it. And if I press him, then he just goes, he really did go once before, that is, he knows how to play the game. Disillusionment will come to me and stay. I want to come myself a few times before that and go again, in order to make things cosy once again where I am. Now more than ever. So who am I.

I mean well by myself, if I love him, but, for me at least, there's a limit to everything. He simply stays away, after I have asked him to be allowed to be his wife one day. My panic leads to ever greater states of exhaustion. After three weeks he comes again, at a loss I try to teach him English or French(!), which he may find useful in future, when foreign women drivers would like to ask him something. But he just wants to have a pleasant rest, without thinking, can only be induced to make the most essential movement, down to his fly, which he can do in his sleep, like a young dog, except a dog doesn't need one. I think it is this combination of sleepiness and alertness, which attracts me so much to him, as if an innocent, unselfconscious writer were repeatedly to force himself to write me dirty letters. Apart from the physical he does absolutely nothing here, the man, no repairs, although in my house there is a constant lack of physical energies, to carry such things out. But then he does listen to me, when it's almost too late, when I tell him, as if I were the only girl in the world, and then he always grips my arm or my shoulder or my hips and looks at me, and I allow myself to be carried away again. Until the tide goes out again, because I never ask questions nor ever question anything else and have already lent him money again. I don't ask him anything either. Ask a stupid question and the postmaster of love replies: host not known. I run hot and cold by turns, if he reaches out to me in a particular way, which I could describe, if it were not indescribably beautiful. The next day my description would already be askew as worn-down heels, because then he would do something quite different that I hadn't expected, and which would be much more beautiful. He is sometimes tender and attentive, for which I've been waiting for weeks, but then I'm over-nervous and have to take a sedative. But when he grabs my arm, he could immediately apply to make someone my guardian, it doesn't matter who, I would let him right away. Another time, if he feels like it, my hero drags me by the hair, bleached by colouring and anyway no longer of the strongest, through the apartment, although it should be the turn of my poor arm to be gently held. That's how we always begin. As we go on. One day this man completely tears the gusset of my trousers, although I'm feeling in need of some tenderness and sweetness, and plays around quite roughly with me down there. I fit in entirely with what he wants, but in doing so I at least want my dignity as a human being to be respected. If he doesn't grab me I immediately long for violations. I prefer it the other way, but I don't dare say so, otherwise he'll want a side-dish as well. It all takes place while one, as I do, trusts in love, as all people must. One should rub oneself well with lotion beforehand, otherwise one will burn in this sun. Sometimes he's like a naughty child, he burrows around in my female organism, in which all my organs, I hope, will keep their place into old age, but one can never know in advance. Hanging loose, gaping quietly and bobbing against each other, please, may I present my organs to you, they are entitled to everything, even to take your driving licence or to fill up an organ donor form, so when he's there, I can't even say it - with him they stand up right away, the organs, without even knowing what's wanted of them, they at any rate are ready. Maybe I'm not yet, who's asking me. Like every child in school used to do when called out, when a teacher still had authority, there they stand. Like the number one. They're already gaping and they've hardly been touched by him, only by him, the lips of my vulva, although I already wanted to slam them shut behind me, but before the world, these little trap-doors with their very own feelings. They only feel something with this man. I don't understand them. I don't understand why. I don't understand myself either. Nevertheless: At least my body is talking to me again, a good thing, that it's not too late yet, a good thing that you have to remain silent while reading. Please tell that to your radio and the other pieces of equipment as well, phew, they're already quite exhausted, it would be a good idea for them, too! How precipitate of the man to go now, when he's only just come, he hasn't even looked at me properly yet. Apart from my hole he hasn't seen much of me yet, the eternal cave tourist. And if he had thought a bit longer, he would perhaps have had something quite different to say to me, than what he actually did say. Drain in the bathroom, hot water tap in the kitchen, there's something wrong with the boiler, too, there's something wrong with all of them, there's something wrong with me as well, which would be worth investigating or leaving alone. I have my longing. I'm sure he could repair everything, DIY is his hobby. He doesn't do it. First of all I'm supposed to sign the whole house over to him, then we'll see. That's asking a bit much, don't you think, but I don't have any children and won't have any now. I'm alone.

So, now I wrap it in a riddle, why am I nevertheless so content, even happy, if he's just nearby and sticks just one single finger, silently, to still me, to please himself, but of course to please me a little, too, am I wrong?, in my cunt, like a dummy in a baby's mouth, only that shouldn't be shaken about so much, otherwise the baby's head will fall off. But that he should, hardly has he halfway finished doing that and I want more, much more, am even thinking of getting into a proper rage again, but that he should in all my beauty, onto which only a couple of days ago he vaguely squirted, without even looking what and whom he was hitting, that today he simply, earlier he was still quite tender, that the very next moment, he would throw me out the door and down the stairs, that I've really never experienced. The man's got some nerve. I can hardly believe it, and I've never even heard of a similar case. I was not prepared for that. My expression has completely gone off the rails, and I am utterly shocked. All the rails rose up to embrace him, and then this. Not even a serious accident. Only a derailment. Now he's gone. No, I hope he's still there, the brute, the wonderful man, and lets me watch him through the door with a minor, that is, he doesn't even let me do that, although it would hurt me very much. Does he want to make me even more jealous? I hope he'll come again tomorrow, at least, my heart that's your's, em, his heart that's mine, and let me wash his shirt, after he's, for a change, discharged himself onto it (he just doesn't leave his juice inside me, he seems to fundamentally, stubbornly avoid that. There my driving licence was evidently enough for him to see, that I would like to do the driving. I still have to cure myself of that. Says the loving woman, who has met someone marvellous. Yet I would so like to leave the driving to him. But the car, my car, I would like to drive that) and had to put on a clean shirt, the uniform shirt. Although he's still there now, I'm already hoping, that tomorrow we'll be all alone together again. He'll discuss everything with me in peace and quiet. Even an animal has more rights, am I not right? But an animal doesn't have any panties to take off, and that's half the fun. What is left of me for me, since no one will relieve me of myself? He has to go on duty. The policemen have taken care to organise who relieves whom a long time in advance. Then it's the turn of the next shift, who immediately keep the motorised public company and have to put up with a great deal of unpleasantness. But they never take pity on the vanquished.

Well well. Suddenly my country policeman is standing in the door, I missed that somehow. Because he opened it, the door, just like that. Done. Now you two girls can get dressed again. That's how fast it happens. The country policeman says something like that or thinks it, because he doesn't even have to say it. I'll take a look beside you both, he says, in case there's something lying there, and I'll ignore you, because I never find anything there. Does someone still want to suck up my tongue, right down to the back of the throat, just the way you like it, but it really hurts me? My tongue would really belong down your throat, it would fit you better than me, my poor, spoilt tongue. That's what you think, both of you, don't you? I would be glad, if someone at last took my organs away from me, because I'm sick and tired of them. But you want to hand yours over to me, and then I'll have a double set. Then I'll be saddled with them. The country policeman thinks: I'm not unburdened. I'm depressed. Have the funny feeling, that rational control over myself could fail at any moment, and then something happens, which afterwards I won't be able to remember any more. Is it not also an act of cannibalism, by you two against me, this continual lady-orgasm donation, which I'm supposed to present you with, and you simply lie back and wait for it? Why do you so much love to belong to a master, and why are you surprised at the risk, which no insurance company has informed you about, of then burning up like a matchstick? (Has anyone, who called him, ever heard him talk like that? This man says nothing most of the time, some believe he can't speak at all, this suitor, who likes to eat roast pork. But already the pullover, that his Penelope has knitted him, doesn't suit him. Fate, don't you have an extra thread, and I don't like the colour either, but the woman thinks: Now he knows, that I've been thinking of him!) There is hardly a coarser, more brutal man, unless he gets drunk, as ever quietly and steadily. Then he becomes almost polite. Then he almost appears refined, but even then he plays according to his own time, which he beats, always into a stranger's flesh, with an industriously rhythmical hand. Yet sometimes, rarely, speech just pours out of him, as with many noticeably tac-iturn men: an almost feminine quality of Self Dissolution, as if there were a chance of a scene to be played between his whis-pered, casual obscenities, if he doesn't release them quickly enough from their body prison, so that they can become repeat offenders and earn a little more punishment on the side.

So he opens the door. He opens his mouth, and between his lips and mine there is violence once again, observes the woman at the same moment as its happening, but it's too late: He then sets me down, cursorily wipes himself off himself, and the beads of sweat are trickling from the corners of his mouth and his temples, look, there are more drops on his forehead and the sides of his nose. He doesn't really need the fear he sometimes feels, but it finds him nevertheless, again and again, very easily. It was only me he once told, already very drunk, that he was afraid of being eaten alive by the women. He doesn't like kissing, and I've drawn my conclusions from that: I must protect him. If necessary, from himself. It's a pity I actually have to tell him that. He doesn't need to be afraid at least when he's with me, to get excited, I told him, with me he doesn't need to be afraid at all. Now that I know him, I'm not afraid either. He means something different. Women should be afraid of him. It's wonderful, how wrong he is. How many people are there, who don't want anything of themselves to remain? Not many, I think. Most want something to remain behind, even if only the lightheartedness with which they sat down behind the wheel of their car or their achievements in art, hard work and industry. I don't want to say anything about shame, others will speak all the louder about it. Shame would like to remain, too, please, it wants to write about itself, it wants to state something. But that's rather unusual, after all. Its owner, however, already wants to rise from the tavern table, the food's finished now. He wants to go and look for other private parts apart from mine. Aha. I'm translating the country policeman's words into civilian language: One simply has handle you and lick you clean uninterruptedly, he says. You women can't leave a man in peace. You do everything for it, you turn yourselves into my instrument for it. Or you turn yourselves into another instrument, if I claim to like and play that better: into humming violin notes. I've still got to teach you the flute notes. What, you stick big ban- knotes, which you'll later miss, into the thongs of the strippers, whom you went to see with your girlfriends, for a change just for women, snigger yell! So you've forgotten yourselves twice already? What's that stripper group called? The somethings. No, not the Kennedys. And the shrieking, always the dreadful shriek- ing, when more of you are together, and which I nevertheless consider to be an expression of the remotest loneliness. Where else could you make so much noise than in nothingness, or no, the opposite rather. Women. Your weakness is: You can't be, like me, alone with yourselves. I can't imagine another reason, why you want someone like me, of all people. The next moment you're already raising the sort of cry I hate, and then to object, when we men want to go away from you. Because you think, we're not coming back; shrieking yet again, shrieking, however, which this time, fortunately for me, is coming out of the other end of your body and so cannot tear apart the small chambers of my ears. It all depends, however, on which end of yours I'm bending over.

The country policeman knows the word instrument from the local brass band, which practices in the fire station. That's why I'm completely justified in using it here, otherwise things would-n't have worked out so well, otherwise I would have had to make do with something like wood and chopping or with branch and sawing off what you're sitting on. Or I would have had to write down an obscenity, which I would not have liked to do. Baron Prinzhorn of the FPÖ, I'm telling you: The Personal columns are constantly playing with these words, which mean something dif-ferent from what they say, why don't they just come out and say it? Why don't you just say what you want, Mr Prinzhorn? Take possession of the whole country and fuck it?, well, the recipient of these words is a kind of child, fortunately a mature one, who doesn't know how big the building blocks are, which he has kicked out from the toy quarry, which he got as a present for his birth-day. Even someone wrapped up in himself can say it to the deceased or the disappeared, and once again no one will listen to anyone else. I could carry on for days, keeping quiet among these people, thinks the woman, about as long as the period of his faulty development originally lasted, which probably already built up in his childhood, as a teach yourself psychology book I bought for 340 schillings in the bookshop and already consulted in the metro tells me, OK, I'm making an estimate: it'll last perhaps until he's seventy, after that the hormones slowly go somewhere else, or run out or don't run at all any more. He knows no mercy, not with anyone, this man. He is a disciple of himself so to speak, who only rarely has grounds to break out in justified rejoicing, for example with such exclamations as: I am the undisputed master over your sensitive organs, which at this point I would describe as quite acceptable, but nothing special. That goes for both of you, Gerti and Gabi, and I've got lots of opportunities to make comparisons and many other opportunities, too, more than I can make use of. It's all no use, it always ends in the grave. As with my mama. It ends up as an object, more or less as I feel my own body, which can break out under me at any time, if I don't open my flies fast enough. That's why it works so well. Because I just manage to control it, it's a worthy opponent, my body, even for myself it is: unpredictable. I prefer to look for a solid foundation for it, before anything dreadful happens and my statue topples over, which I have blasted away from myself. So that I cannot be sucked in by the emptiness around me. I always have to run away, but property could just hold me. That's the best thing to stop me falling into this pit full of snakes, which are baled out in buckets, and they're all hanging out over the sides. That is the pitfall, of which I dream so often. No idea, who dug it for me. Since I dream about it - was it me perhaps? Perhaps the dead snakes embody a superabundance of property, which has been confiscated. But there's a hole in the bucket, all the muck is running out at the bottom, and only the snakes are left and show me paradise, but I'm supposed to plant the fruit trees that go with it myself, if you please. Or I find a person, who already has some: One can never have enough property, because we're always striving after what's most difficult, that's man's fate, and best of all we would like to leave the rest of them to their fate, to take from them what they've got as well. So, women, I can play on you like no one else. I lay down everything, when, where and how often. I'm the best you've ever had, and there'll never be another either. I'm very conscious of my qualities, I always say: I am the sorcerer not the apprentice.

Now the country policeman has to go back to Gabi again, who is sometimes bothered by the lack of desires of a child who already has everything. But today it has to be me, thinks the man. What am I to her? Perhaps the rascal with the dimples in his flesh, which she wants to bite into all the time. And she's allowed to move around all by herself under me. I would even like to watch her doing it. So. Now we're over and done with it again. Gabi has to go, her mother's always waiting in the evening with the meal. For sure. That's OK. She's already leaving, Gerti. Look, she's already going out the door and grudges you every glance, but then in a little while, you can have my little guy again, the carefree one, he's already puckering his lips and whistling something for you, although he's really tired, by God. Don't worry, he'll be waiting for you again, but not now, perhaps not even today. Please be patient. I'm not so young any more. OK, then today. Later. I promise. Possibly much later. Worries and annoyance are things the fellow avoids, whom I have allowed to grow, as you seem to believe, especially for you, so he avoids worries and annoyance like a whole political party, he confided that in me earlier, before getting a good spit at Gabi, the bad boy. Oh yes. So for that you congratulate Gabi. For going. Don't be so mean. And you don't congratulate me? When I've been working most of the time! Is that not worth anything? Have you found your voice again? And that's what you needed it for, for you to scream at me like that? Just you wait! I'm coming right back and then I'm going to give you a good knocking with the carpet beater. I put it next to mine earlier, your voice, you voluntarily turned it over to me, I didn't need mine either. Exactly. I had it, your voice, you gave it to me, there was no need for you to scream for it so much outside. What, I was moaning, too? Why should I have been moaning? I can well believe you, when you say that this is your house, I've now heard it at least five hundred and seventy times. I do know it. The house wouldn't have anything to say, if it could speak. It would appeal more to me. And it wouldn't make so much noise if it did.

Well, if you really still want it now, then you want it, there's nothing to be done. Although I explicitly said later, but you don't listen, do you, you don't want to listen, you want to feel: Before I admit that I'm beaten, I'll give you another good scrubbing. The only thing we haven't had a go at yet is your cellar. Your cellar vault, which you proclaimed was your greatest treasure. Exercise never does any harm, that's why I went for a drive after all. I'm going to teach you some patience, because soon I'm going to let you wait again for hours, for days. Just because I happened to meet Gabi on the way, perhaps she was even waiting for me, I can't help that. So. Suddenly she was standing beside my car as if she'd fallen from the sky, once again, I didn't hear her coming, she was standing there, as she does nearly every morning, when she makes a show of going to the bus stop and then disappears with me, and she absolutely wanted me to give her a lift. And I was there. I can't help that. It was the wrong time. It wasn't her turn. What can I do. Oh yes, I know, what you like best. Take a look at what I've got between my fingers, it's all wet, apart from some pain, about which I can only be surprised that it's there, because I can hardly feel anything. I'm always astonished: What you've got down there, as with a young girl, is still surrounded by a very thick bush. The bush is very cute and exciting, even if not to me, but it has one advantage. That's where I would most like to hide, if I could. I imagine hidden behind it is something intricate, something bigger, tremendous, a building site, a not properly cemented hole, which I'm afraid of falling into. I'm always glad when I come out again, after I've let the hole brush against my lips. If it wasn't for the house, which closes over me like two legs every time, and I'm safe. In the end it wasn't worth getting undressed. I look at you: You were already undressed before. Your risk. Why are you always tearing off your clothes as soon as you see me? And something else, are you trying to belittle me with your pet name? It would be so much simpler, if you just kept your clothes on. Nothing to be done. You'll have to keep your paws apart in front of your sex, if you want me to drop in for a visit. Perhaps I'll get back to you later. I'm not looking you in the face now, I'm looking a bit further down. I'm telling you half the truth now: It's your house, for which I'm paying this full price, but I wouldn't go any higher. Well, maybe a bit higher. Pair skating with me doesn't work, even with someone who was more frivolous than you. It doesn't work. I'm too fast for you, every day I have to cope in the traffic, which is itself fast. It would also happen without me. I am too often somewhere else. I want to get away from myself, before I'm even properly with myself. How I would also like to be away from you, but I don't dare stay away altogether. Your house can't run after me. Only you can do that. Not until I'm dead will my organs not be put to use in you women. Then you'll finally be quiet. Then I'll be quiet too. It frightens me, that right away your hands have to start fumbling over me, just when I would like to live cosily inside me and enjoy myself. You are at once rash and idle. Looking alone is no longer enough for you, since you've discovered your bodies. Now you want to confiscate other bodies as well. No idea, who put that in your heads. You only are, because I am. Aha. As if you were women doctors, doctoring around on me, donating fluids to me, but which always undermine me, and instead draw a kind of basic foodstuff from me, which you use for something or other, which you brew up against me in your pots and pans. I dissolve in your hands, as you desire, but no, not really desire, you want to have me quickly to hand again the next time, but, imagine, that's exactly what I want. That's what I want myself! I want to be away. You only want to be carried away. But I really want to be away! I have a certain attachment to this unpleasant situation, which I always end up in: to be pinched, patted and finally torn in little pieces by your hands and then swept up. As a result, curiously, my appetite grows to its full size and promptly returns to you. As if I immediately wanted to be eradicated. Disappearance, beautiful compulsion to disappear! You're always just screaming: here, here again and again! Present! As a woman! Present purely as woman! This place is occupied! By me! Yours by you sisters! Mine by me! Take a look at your stomach, Gerti, you're not going to get rid of it any more by running, although running together would be not bad, we could be together, but wouldn't have to be. We would keep a minimum distance from one another. Your figure has problems with its figure. Look at yourself and your hips, they shouldn't be there, they should be closer to you, they could easily come two inches closer together. So Gerti, do you want nothing

at all, or do you at least want the finger, which really should be
more than enough? You can say it out loud. Tell me loud and
clear, if that's what you want! Quiet. Now I'm talking. And I'm
talking as a woman. I would like to say something, too, for once,
given that I've got to write the whole time, because saying the
unsayable is part of it, part of all the opening eyes wide and licking lips and throwing back hair, with which we women want to
tell men something, always the same thing, and they already know
it. Because they're too tired to guess what we want and it would
be too expensive for them to pay someone else to find out. We
women always want the same thing. And then we want it once
again.

There is a kind of woman who, evidently out of spite, can take
quite a lot of punishment and is even less merciful in handing it
out. One cannot turn one's back on her, otherwise she hardens
herself and knocks one down along with herself. And if that does-
n't work, she summons up her arguments to help her. But this
woman is and remains soft and yielding. She melts away. Or is she
hard in order to offend someone? Her water is populated by
lower organisms, and she tolerates even those, the little tri-
chomonads, which she has also already got from the country
policeman. Otherwise presents from him come only very rarely.
Her doctor has prescribed something for them, but you have to
treat your partner at the same time. He refuses. He doesn't want
any prescription, it's his job to prescribe the rules. He has no
symptoms. Mr Janisch, you have to take something like this seriously. Otherwise your whole gang of women would always catch
the same thing from you and you would catch it again from them,
if you didn't have it already, haha. The country policeman does-
n't feel anything. He must be sort of primitive, or something?
Does he feel anything at all? Does he have to be scattered around
with his motor cycle first? Does his lower jaw have to be torn off?
The woman points out, it could also cause him harm later on, if
he's already infected now and will inevitably pass it back to her,

no sooner has she been cured by the drugs, but he hasn't. Rubbish, there's nothing that harms me. I'm an animal. Take the soft bits out of women, and then one has to take the rest away from them as well. This woman here doesn't just have her gate wide open, she's even put up a sign, where there's really none needed, especially if she looks at one as if she had the eternal bliss, which God alone promises, and he had to let himself be nailed good and proper for it; so the woman has learned this bliss in this man hardly had he come in off the street. Because she's fallen for someone even before the door slammed shut. The country policeman is sometimes so angry he could kill this woman. There she takes her proud claim on him out for walkies through the whole village. At the time when he had just met her, it had gone like this: She stood in front of him, as if fallen from the sky, in the road, embarrassed, sweating a little, because she was in such a rush, even though the car had done all the work, by the driver's door of her car, ready, from now on, to make a happy face at the sight of him, the country policeman, not to take her eyes off him even under the greatest strain, and at the same time draw out his cock, its outlines ever more evident down there, before her inner eye, so that it should jump into her hand with the one sentence, I love you. Meanwhile all this time it was only with a considerable effort that the country policeman could stop himself hitting her in the face. The text with which he had wooed her stood written in raised letters on the country policeman's trousers (there was no price tag. Price list on request from the shop). Now he's supposed to give it to her again every day, preferably several times. With the organ, that this dear red, somewhat sweaty face has, and which she likes so much that she doesn't want to let go of it any more. For the man she has ripened into a whole co-operative house building society, this woman, who's got housing available for life. But ownership would be better. She's still deaf in that ear, but she's already turning her head in his direction. There would then follow conversion of the property, and for that everything else will be laid down right away without asking, do you want furniture, please, go ahead. Do you want me to be laid down as well, with pleasure. That's the best opportunity to lie back there's ever been. You'll only get this house if you take the carpet and all the fittings as well, as a present. The other way around you lose everything, and things will turn very quiet around you, because you'll have to spend the night in the open. Only when the other wild beasts come will you hear anything, but it will be too late. Quite without foundation the man fears something like that, every day, and the bank reminds him of it as well, dies irae. The simplicity of his behaviour and its single-mindedness is probably indebted to his bank debts. Why does she have to run into one everywhere, this woman, when she gets hot. Why does one immediately have to show up for her, for this demanding lady, who then ends up taking what she can get, no matter what, however often she denies it and says, she wants more. Much more can be expected from her. But once she's been turned on, it's impossible to turn her off in time, she's already boiling over with love and desire for this wonderful man, a nice gesture, don't you think?

Then I can just stay at home and let mummy cook me a goulash, what's all the fuss about. At home I can have whatever I want made, but you women, who want to be implacable and not forgive anything, one has to read your desires in your eyes, before one doesn't fulfil them and nails you once again, until one's buried under the planks of one's coffin. In a very similar situation, as already mentioned, Jesus was exhibited on the cross in Gallery Golgotha, do you know where that is? Yet I've known you women inside out for a long time, almost like God. Always the same thing. I'd rather masturbate, and I've been doing it since Wednesday. Since that day I've discovered a completely new method for it in my daily hours of sleeplessness. I confess, sometimes I can't shove my organ into you at any price, I can't do it. I'm afraid of this operation every time, I admit it, but sometimes the fear gets too big. Thanks to my job I have access to terrible pictures of crushed, or alternatively burnt people, who originally were also highly thought of by someone, I assume, but have now involuntarily had to give up their shape. I think I'm not the only one who secretly likes such pictures, and every morning I can't help taking in their dear, delicate scent. Perhaps something will turn up. That's a good day for me then. I would like to tenderly stroke the tattered skin, the mashed bodies. I'm telling you, at the end my mother was so ill (said the country policeman to the woman, who was framed by her car door, a few weeks earlier, to a woman, who already after three minutes ardently wished to be married to him. One can take language courses, however she wouldn't put this man behind her for a long time yet, she knows. He's only a village policeman after all, he'll naturally feel flattered by her interest, and so on, everything designated, labelled and put aside), my mama was so ill, you've never seen anything like it. A couple of weeks later the woman is already equating him with God and is herself sick with love, because he can't protect her from herself. She clings to herself, as a drowned person does the water. It's no use. He can make use of her as he wants. Everything you've ever read about organs is combined in these road traffic victims, though unfortunately it's the wrong ones, that is, the organs would be right, but the places they have taken up are the wrong ones. Have they been flung onto the asphalt road surface, just for me to give them the hard shoulder? I'm only asking, because I like them so much. Bloody mush. People are muck. For that the man has become an idol to this woman, not man in general, but this one alone, whom she loves. It's a form of glorification, as in the church, of subjection in every area, which she certainly enjoys like a good old red wine, but which is becoming increasingly dangerous. Where do the glass splinters in the mouth and in the hand suddenly come from? Something like that only turns out well if a relationship has to stand up to the tides for at least twenty years, so that one can picture the human ocean, which God has in principle forbidden. His picture alone shall be lawful. He alone shall pass judgement. But come the day, someone else will inevitably come along, and there are plenty of other women. If the relationship doesn't last, then the one who gives up totally is finished and ceases to exist. Or a new relationship comes along, which lasts until one gives up the ghost. Listen to your doctor or pharmacist or read the leaflet once again, but properly this time, before you order something unsuitable!

The country policeman, however, knows yet other bodies. He can imagine them at any time, if he wants. They readily pass his lips. He talks as if he had already forgiven himself for everything, but for what? Women don't know how dangerous he really is, and if they did know, they would only steer all the more impetuously towards his powerful, somewhat thickset body cliffs, throw themselves forward, until their little boat breaks against a resistance they haven't seen, because it was buried down below under the women's foam. They would want to introduce him to their women friends, this man, even to their mothers, even if the latter had moved to Majorca or Bali or if they didn't have any at all any more. But the country policeman obstructs her and him undertaking anything with others, and in particular he obstructs it with this woman and with Gabi. With these two. They are his problem children. He's very secretive. You nevertheless always leave feeling satisfied, the country policeman consoles his female clients, after they, often also on Sunday afternoon, when he's supposedly at the alcoholics' practice meeting of the volunteer fire brigade, have come freshly washed and appetisingly tender, warm, with a floury dusting from their underwear, onto the table without a stitch, their hands in front of their breasts (how curious, that they always make this gesture, they only do it with the country policeman, involuntarily, as if he could catch sight of something. When after all he knows their innermost selves. At some point something does seem to have made them suspicious), and then climbed down from the kitchen table or the settee again. And I'm the one who always has to stand, no, I'm not the meal, says the country policeman Jesus to his ardent admirers Mary and Martha and to his penitents Mary Magdalene etc. and to his people in general, enclosed as he is in his little box, the halo flowing round him (no, his name is not suddenly: our Jörg, as one says in this country, only because he's so adored). I am always the one who eats, and here you're welcome is my body, take and eat, you too, no idea, why you're so crazy for it. I don't see anything special about it. I say insolently to this woman, who can be glad that I've come at all and say something, even if it were only to utterly trustingly confide in her, she won't do it for less: Gabi, for example, have you ever taken a closer look at her? 16, t-shirt and jeans and a jacket with a shawl collar and black ankle boots, she doesn't need more than that to look seductive. Why do you always daub so much red on your lips, Gerti? Do you think it's nice? I for one don't like it. These rags in which you drape yourself, so that one doesn't look so closely at what's underneath, really, they don't bother me at all. But they don't do you any good either. They come off anyway, they're the first thing to come off with you lot, and fast too, because you know in what order you put them on. The only time you're faster is when you're shopping for new clothes and shoes. I'm absolutely sure, that Gabi, she loves me, don't you think, Gerti? She's so juicy, one would like to eat her right out of the wrapper. Meanwhile you're waiting out on the stairs, Gerti, I'm not saying that because I'm annoyed, it's just more convenient: It's best if you wait on the stairs down to the cellar. It will cool you off a bit. It'll do you good. I know, I know, the stairs belong to you. But no one will disturb you there, you like to be left undisturbed, don't you.

Love doesn't pull down barriers, as is often said, it builds them up, so that behind them people learn to wait and are not always pointlessly kicking the iron banisters. Of course you're my main course, Gerti, always, always, don't worry, it's with you and only with you, that table silver and table underwear are lying around and getting bored, so all alone. We don't like to invite guests. And your house encloses only the two of us, and also, if desired, your whole property with a friendly little gesture, come on in!, a house without a guardian and fortunately also without an inheritor. I herewith apply for the job, for which this house has invited applications. One can knock at the door, who's coming in? The bodies wander around in crowds, sometimes I'd like to open them up and for once have a good look at what's inside. But the Lord above always helps me at the last moment, and restrains me or maybe not, depending on whether he's at home or not (and whom on the occasion of my last moment I nevertheless would rather not want to have at my side, after I've had to see so many last moments on the roads. Well, in that state, half burnt up in a Honda Civic, I would not like to be seen by someone, even God himself!), and smashes e.g. this VW Golf full slap-bang against this truck there, on the left in the picture. It would be interesting to look at the open flesh under a microscope, all the cute little bacteria, how they all swarm around there after only a very short time. At some point the flesh is so broken up that it won't go any smaller. One cuts it into slices and places these under the microscope. One travels far away with the bodies, they have, a long way from anywhere, even from me, an accident with the car or the plane and have to eat people, if they have nothing else. That's my favourite fantasy. No, Gerti, you're no obstacle to that, no way. I won't have to cut my fingers on your panties, your knickers have always mysteriously disappeared beforehand. I would rather die than be without house and shelter. I want to be the guardian of everything, that's my duty, that's why I chose the job of policeman. So I rub my hands smooth, spit diligently into them, and again and again, as if it were the first time, force my way into you, best of all through the back door, then I don't have to cover your face with a towel. I prefer this entrance, which is really an exit, even if making headway there is more of an effort. I'm meanwhile thinking about something quite different. You can't have noticed that at all. Why then are you already screeching like that, when the skewer hasn't even got there yet, to roar his commands? It doesn't matter. At least I can't get lost inside you, because your house, my most urgent need, is always all around us, playing, presumably out of boredom, with its dear twisting stairway, which you've polished so nicely with beeswax, yes, the banister, too, standing around looking dumb is the hobby of this house. After all, apart from you, there's no one to whom it belongs. You already cleared away the marks of the previous owner years ago, in the belief no one else would be coming along this way. The house was once old, now it's new. A gem of a house. All around only people who don't know the area. Well. I'm there now and write out a notification of an offence and place myself right next to it. Behind my fly I calmly trace out, because it's what you want, my cock, do you see it? It's like a statue, but not of the Mother of God, is it? I would rather show it to someone else. You look lovely, I lie, despite your age. I think you are arrogant. Well, not now any more. Don't shout in my ear like that, you don't have to put on an act for me, I'll ram you anyway, until I'm finished, no matter what and in what pitch you shout, and at the last moment I pull it out again, no idea why, the cuckoo pops out of the clock, too, and doesn't know the time, which it shouts out for hours, I mean every hour. You can also twist round under me, to look me in the face as best you can, although you're lying on your stomach, and you can go on shouting if you like, as much as you want. No, no one's coming, whom you could have called. At most someone passing the house, who knows you, will be surprised. He hasn't been invited to this engagement party, and your friends and relatives, I hope there aren't any now, haven't been asked to come for that reason. I imagine I'm the only one to come and wolf myself down in a kind of mincer. I alone should exist, and I, too, would like to disappear, but always only in me, not in you, you can believe me. I now know you inside out. I wouldn't like to stay there any longer than necessary. You look out from your elevated financial situation. I would like to keep that situation by the way. I've already checked the basic conditions in the land register, whether it might be possible, yes, everything belongs to you, no mortgages, and so, for obvious reasons, I shall go on leafing through you for a bit. It's interesting. I only enjoy what I can see, because I don't feel anything. For example, your new wallpaper. I like it and it can stay, it's quiet and it keeps quiet at least. Luckily I don't have to feel it, just see it.

The man naturally never talks out loud about such things, he talks, as has been said, very little, but I believe that's what he thinks, quietly, that's the best way of thinking, only TV hasn't understood that yet and gives us sound as well, so that forever sweet toothed we can pile a glob of whipped cream and another and another on top of reality, before at last we get really stuck in. We're going to regret it at some point, when we're feeling sick. Well well, so he wants to get lost inside himself, Kurt Janisch, not in someone else, because something like that would make him afraid? But I don't see much of that yet. Perhaps in the end he even wants to digest himself? Perhaps that's how he likes to imagine it. Then he would have to part with the least of all, is perhaps what he thinks. Why then is he always falling on others, for no fault of theirs. That's how cannibals always start. First they want to eat themselves, and then it's always others after all, whom they get a taste for. And when taste has got going, e.g. on an excursion into the TV or a video, then if need be they get to work on the bodies themselves and that as large as life. And already, often of necessity, shit and natural bubbly are flowing out of these bodies, sometimes out of fear, that one day one might have to pay for it instead of being currency. I've got the exact figures here. The man says very long-windedly and nothing is said in reply: Think of me as the unhappiest and at the same time as the happiest person, if you have to detain me here. And how else should I (yes, me!) express it, than with these few diffident sentences, out of which I might almost have built a conversation between us, but only almost. I would have made a little crib, if I hadn't run out of nails. The bank isn't giving me any credit at all any more, quite the reverse, the bank wants me to pay back the old loans, and all of them at once as well. Later, like his thoughts, which can never sit still long enough for them to be properly thought through to the end, perhaps by chance, perhaps through planning, this man will avoid prison, because he won't be recognised for what he is. He's meanwhile, but sometimes by the quickest route, heading straight for personal bankruptcy. Or not. I alone know everything, because I have executed it specially in water-colours, is that not unbearably watered down?, so help me. Or is that exactly how it happened. So I'll help you, too, even though I don't know you at all, with my word, which like a go-cart I slide under your uncertainty, into which, after all, I've steered you, and already this man, through the music of his words, can make contact with me, with us, and you can complain all you like about boredom, while you're reading this, but please not to me. With this problem I'm definitely not standing right behind you. Not behind myself either. I'm not standing anywhere. I, too, would prefer to be doing something else apart from always reading.

Other people are even blown up by a laugh. But here real dynamite is contained in the owner of an extensive muscle mass that is still to be climbed. Who can do it. Who wants to do it. No one knows much about him. I'm the only one at the moment, who's saying he's explosive. And, for all his dangerousness, it's a plain rod that this extreme walker plants in the ground of womankind, yet this rod is a tough one. Basically the man wouldn't need the miracle stick, he always finds his way wherever he goes and a suitable pace as well. He can still walk well alone. The fuse can burn, there can be an explosion, rubble flying up, just ask the manmade lake here at the entrance to the village, which didn't make itself either, what that's like! One wants to be left in peace, is even perhaps a little ashamed, that waves several feet high foam up around one, the underwater embankments, the gently waving pubic hair of the lake drifts upwards like a furry shoe thrown down for a woolly cuddly toy - one has something between one's teeth, which one laboriously has to pull out again, one slurps the rich content of a mellow slime, which perhaps consists of nutrients, perhaps not, but basically one doesn't want to eat any of it, one would prefer to spit it out, let it nourish someone else! A sermon on the mount will be preached now. There are too many who want to eat, and they remove the basis of the man's existence, and one woman or another is supposed to give it back to him: If this man goes and doesn't come back, I'm going to die off inside like a whole region, which has absorbed too much nitrate and phosphate, thinks the woman. He can do anything with me, but he shouldn't do it. This flesh, for example, is so cold, brrr!, because for half an hour it had to lie naked on the steps down to the cellar and almost spend the winter there, you exaggerate. The sun can't yet properly penetrate the walls of the house, but no, it only seemed as long as winter to the woman, it wasn't longer than half an hour, at the outside. Perhaps this Gabi girl also has a life's dream, it doesn't, however, consist in giving a country policeman valuable gifts, but in receiving these gifts herself. Will you buy me this, will you buy me that, that's what it's like with Gabi non-stop. What am I going to buy it with. It doesn't matter. The young ones at any rate are still supple, you've hardly pulled them out of the wrapper and they're already jumping into your mouth. Their bodies still deceive themselves all too often in their addressees, they don't read the sender's address and the small print, they don't have any experience and then the wailing and the weeping start up again. They're hardly more than children, who see us again and likewise want to go to the café, in front of everyone! on Saturday afternoon! They all want to. How will mummy, how will both mummies, how will the cuddly toys, who have stayed at home, respond to that? If we only knew. Days go by. Weeks go by. His rare visits. Time passes differently for young people. The old save themselves all that, because it doesn't do any good. They learned how to save in harder times, and where do they find themselves now. Nowhere. In no-man's land. They don't know that the hardest times have just begun. This young woman must surely see, that a different recipient is marked on this body, which at this moment falls on her, like a wolf, who has at last found the leg of lamb in the fridge. And the second body we see here is likewise mad about the man, and unfortunately about the same one, and unfortunately it had to stay outside, the body. Nothing to be done. At least the body out there wasn't tied to the banisters. All one can still look forward to is loneliness and isolation and illusions. And one can get self-doubt and submission for it, say our entertainment experts with their pouting lips, isn't that so, Mrs famous sex adviser Senger, you too, in your little newspaper column, where you've been imprisoned for safety's sake, just in case you want to say it to us in person. No doubt someone is about to leave again, although he's only just come, and who will that be? Right, that'll be Kurt Janisch. How dreadful for these two women, each in her way matchless, that they have to experience something like that. And that's why unfortunately they can't set us an example. They don't give anything. They might perhaps have a lot to give us, but they don't do it, they prefer to give it to someone else. But they don't want to go either. The confusion, which often prevails in very young people, who look at one covetously, because basically they would much rather have the latest computer game or the latest pair of flared trousers bought for them, is that confusion at all, is it not single-mindedness? They are as ignorant as they are greedy, these young people, but mostly they look cheerful, in the hope that then they are more likely to get it. I can't say anything about that, I don't know what they do at which time. I don't know what they do at the same time. This confusion among young people, therefore, is often the result, as one can read here and everywhere else, of too many families having been destroyed, because the daddy, ever more frequently also the mummy, has cleared off, and that's what exactly the same newspaper tells me, in the shape of a quiet different figure, however, it's the authoritative figure of a priest called Paterno, whom I already listened to yesterday, but then his voice said something quite different and his hand wrote something quite different. But the most amusing and friendliest thing, just like the saddest and most frightful one are often unfortunately the most terrible nonsense, even though this newspaper has already said it one way or another. At least the other way here has not done so. It gave away a guglhupf recipe, hmmm, that turned out well again! Oh, if only they had occurred to me sooner, these pieces of information for the information bulletin of the school of life, sooner than to Mrs Gerti Senger and the priest August Paterno, before I was able to start a new page! Then I would have also been able to write them down here, these pieces of information. So they're still written down, but written down somewhere else.

There's someone who's earning nothing but blows from life and wants to be given a beating for it as well! In the case of this young woman, whom we've mentioned, the normal breakdown with the help of oxygen is sometimes simply not possible, as in the case of this lake, which we've also mentioned. Surely one should at least be able to breathe by oneself. Can you hear the wheezing? That funny sound? She's got asthma, Gabi, I diagnose with my razor-sharp mind, because I've heard that sound somewhere before, and once I had it myself, half my family has had it, and she can also get an attack at any time, Gabi, if she gets so upset. The man has just explained to her, from tomorrow he can't drive her to work in his car any more, because his wife has found out. A lie, because his wife wouldn't care, she has her garden and her needlework and her soaps on TV. A necessary lie, because the other woman, Gerti, would care, if she ever did find out. But she knows already, Mr Janisch! But she shouldn't care, because she couldn't do anything about it. If she does talk to him about it, he takes offence and asserts: a man needs that, because he's different from a woman. He has already paid her in advance for everything, with his penis, which in a man never lies. By which it often doesn't do its owner a good turn, I think to myself. Gerti should be satisfied and leave him in peace. She would pay for her own presents, many times over, I think to myself once again, for example, this little bouquet of early Alpine gentian in merciless blue, which the man, unwillingly, because what is all this beauty good for, one can't buy anything with it, has picked on the mountain. To Gerti the bouquet is priceless, but she will nevertheless try to cough up something for it. And now it seems as if Gabi wants to get him into trouble, I'm telling mummy, I'm not quite sixteen yet: she's picked the wrong guy! It's legal for the woman, for the man and for another man it won't be legal until later on, that's how nature planned it, and that's also the way the laws of mankind planned it, which have imitated nature and which are then surprised, when people now yield and go astray, instead of the laws. So from tomorrow it's finished, Gabi, and you take the bus or the train again in the morning. I've had enough. If you ask me, that's too heavy-handed an explanation for a girl, who likes to be taken to the disco in the next village by her official boyfriend and then simply disappears. Pop! When she needs oxygen so badly. That's why she's out of the house. She says, the oxygen was outside, where she got it. What has her father, whom she no longer has, her mother is divorced, to do with it? Her father has nothing to do with it. He would just order her to stay at home period. So here's Gabi lying about on the floor and throwing her head from side to side and trying to breathe out. What to do, she's completely out of it, and one can't just tie her to the carpet, so that she calms down and just keeps breathing in. Come on, Gerti, give me a hand! Well Kurt, that really is asking too much of me. So much youth, that's far too much of a good thing, and there's not enough air in here, I think, because none of it can be broken down again by bacteria or fungi quickly enough. Take her outside immediately, take her home, can't you hear! That's how it is with nature, with foresight it cultivates its own pests, but they, too, are nature's children and help her diligently in her work.

How easily an accident can happen, and one is called as a policeman, but is on the spot as a human being, when one somehow tries to hold still such a head, whipping from side to side, so that it doesn't just fall off. It's banging from side to side like a bulging garden hose that's out of control, but there must be a leak somewhere, there's such a funny gurgling in her throat, above the collar bone. All this fuss from the hose. Just because no one is holding it firmly. Whoever doesn't want to hear, has to feel. When they're listening, people are quiet so they don't miss anything. When it comes to love, they then let out what they've previously seen and taken in of strangers, who just for them have laid themselves down on a strip of celluloid or whatever, it's magnetic at any rate, in order to produce that eternity, which lust supposedly desires. Some people would rather have change. Eternity. Everyone thinks that about a photo, but it's rather easily inflammable. Which one is oneself, too! You wouldn't believe it. We'll immediately send it to an Austrian Lonely Hearts magazine, the photo, the tape, perhaps they'll take it, perhaps they know who we are. I hope not, because we are the FPÖ candidates for the town council of Ternitz or Gloggnitz, somewhere over there anyway. How they must suffer, when they're alone, these people, and no one is recording them! Ecstatic glances, smiling mouths, agitated poses, which were supposed to have been exciting, yes. I would not like to be immodest and I would not like to be to blame for anything either. The older people, expanding a bit, they stay quiet at least and if at all embrace one in despair, because they can't get anything else, in a vice of two thighs, yes one is oneself the sugar cube between them, the man just manages to put up with something like that if need be. He's learned to be a worker. He's an amateur bricklayer, amateur joiner and amateur villa owner. Whatever one's doing, one can think of something else at the same time, he says, best of all to think, how nice it'll be when whatever one's doing is finished and the freshly painted or stripped and repainted door has slammed shut behind one and one is: inside, inside at last. Yes, he would like that. Because no one in this world understands, that one would like to lock the door behind one and the world, so that there's no one any more, not even oneself any more. And for that one absolutely must have the following: a house and home of one's own. No one should get in. Only you, sweet Jesus, uncomfortably fastened to the cross, so that you don't make any mess either. There's nothing that can be locked up so completely, as something that belongs to one. There's no one that can be locked out so completely as other people, above all, those who think marriage, this prison, is the greatest proof of the love of a man for a woman and the other way round, exactly, so when are we getting married, when are you getting divorced? One thing after another, but in the right order please. The marriage, so this woman hopes, will stabilise our relationship, which not even a cellar would do for a gloomy tall office block, when an earthquake measuring 7.9 on the Richter scale comes along. You can judge. But first there comes the executive. I hope it's not the executioner coming. Even if it sounds macabre to you, that ultimately I only want to die, although in busy traffic I have to be helpful, energetic and quick in my reactions and fulfil modern demands, WHY. Asks the country policeman, who is also at his wit's end. Why should Gerti's love of Kurt Janisch be so different from the unhappy relationship with someone or other? No idea, as far as I'm concerned.

So do you hear this unholy racket now or don't you? At the moment it's taking hold of the whole household, where there's even a piano which has to be handled every day, so that it doesn't fall ill, this grand from the city apartment, which here squeezes desperately into a corner and still occupies almost the whole room, while its tone sinks down to its boots even standing in the corner, because the climate here is harsh and simply too damp. That's the first thing we'll sell. The living room: where CDs and arts programmes, indeed the whole universe, are eagerly monitored and preserved, because nothing in this world remains a secret. What you hear is bestial howling, howling of a harmless, masterless penitent, who doesn't know whom she should touch and for which master she should do penance, and she doesn't even have a veronica to wipe her eyes. So much sand has been sprinkled on them. Her eyes run and run. But nevertheless she's already waiting for the next sin, in order to commit it immediately, as a precaution before someone else does it. The man is worth it, but earlier he was inside the whole time, with another woman, with a much younger woman. But the woman long ago wanted to suffer under his whip of flesh again, and he wasn't within reach. Can't be reached at present. Try again later! How disappointing. It's pointless trying to call someone else. If one longs for someone, he should come in person. But the country policeman we're talking about has now, much later that day, actually the next, if one calls the day night, when he left the house of the wailing, weeping woman, who seems to be foaming in her own soap opera, arrived in the coldest place possible at the moment outside of a deep freeze: the shore of the lake.

It took him a while, driving with difficulty across stones and through undergrowth, to get there.

He couldn't have acted any differently, he tells himself. He once again feels quite the master of the district, but somehow it doesn't cheer him up. He doesn't care at all, whether the water gives up its booty or keeps it. First of all the water gets its packet, nicely packaged at any rate, earlier the country policeman had to go especially to an out of the way tool shed to fetch the tarpaulin, actually he's already been driving around with it in the boot for a couple of days, what for? (Question as to premeditation: Did he himself put it there with intent, in case he would need it at some point?) Let's go on, then we'll have it behind us all the more quickly. Then the water can chew at the package for a bit or a bit longer, and see whether it likes the taste. It can open its jaws to draw breath, at the same time spitting out the human roll with the plastic cover, then snap at it again, or it can also keep the meat roll of course. Is it meat at all, or flesh? Everyone's always so nice to flesh, if it looks nice and is pretty in the right places, perhaps even transparent?, at least just barely covered in transparent motives, so that nevertheless a bit pops out of the wrapping which is scooped out in exactly the right places, and has been placed there for that very reason. So that one suspects what anyone can anyway see at a hundred yards. But it's important to the man, that something more comes of it. The flesh is only the means, the mean value is the money and the highest value is a plot of land with a house on it. For that the country policeman carries out duties, of which he has deprived the community, because instead of directing the course of traffic he has been having intercourse himself, one of my tiredest jokes, I know, but I'm happy that I've found it, I had been looking for it. I know, I know, you've heard it all before. But consider this: There are nevertheless unbelievably few of you worldwide. The man, however, would do quite different things than I would (or than would occur to me), so that his desire for belongings is fulfilled. Two legs spread, for him alone, just like that, and a whole house puts in an appearance right in the middle. So this man puts himself down as an advance, but in the same breath demands himself back again, because himself is all he has to invest. But perhaps he needs himself again later, for something else. The country is supposed to be safe, because the existing small stations of the Country Police are not being closed down, which have made and still make a valuable contribution to that.

Here's the charming, manmade, inner Alpine lake again, it's always getting into the picture, when we don't want it to. But this time there's a special reason for it to turn up, we had almost lost sight of it, because it's already so dark; it's not exactly soil protection, that nature and landscape pastoral care have done to it, but neither are they to blame for what has happened to the water. Nor is it because of prevention of air pollution and waste disposal, no, wait, perhaps it is because of waste disposal, because right now I can see, how some kind of waste or whatever it is, at any rate someone wants to get rid of it, is being put into the water there. One wouldn't keep watching mere household refuse so long, out into the barely rising, gently rippling waves, the lake can also toss the roulade around a little, play with it, we'll see if we can't get the wrapping open later, it should be a snip. The man has tied it up well, made double knots, attached something to weigh it down and removed it again, because it could perhaps be traced back to him. He surely doesn't seriously believe that all that will work as permanent medication against the reappearance of the packet! Water can do a lot of things, but one thing it can't do: digest all the things thrown into it. Cyanide from a gold mine into the Danube, from its tributary the Tisza! A gigantic dying is just starting, and you can watch it live, you're still alive at least! The poison speaks for an hour, and the fish would have to swallow it for fifty years, if they weren't dead now. Or shall we leave it wrapped up for a while yet, this death role, which someone is playing here? No turbulent river current is playing with it, and the lake is too dull to embark on a proper scrap with a completely motionless, tied up body. So, now even the most stupid reader knows what's in there, because unfortunately I couldn't keep it to myself any more. How does one do that, say something by not saying it? I fear everyone has known it all the time, from the beginning of time, even if not all of it through me. And the Austr. Food Standards Code does not lay down what people and their inland waters are supposed to eat. It only states what they're not supposed to eat. Meat is of course excepted, otherwise the whole of Austria, which subsists on meat and alcohol, would go on strike together with its mountains and lakes. This country always wants a little bit more of what there is, it doesn't matter what, at any rate always more than it can take. Cannibal country. And we like ourselves best, when we are well disposed to ourselves, because we've been well behaved, that is our spice, in which once again we want to let the others stew, until they're really hot for us. Perhaps, also, because no one can change the thousand schilling note for the taxi for them, not even the bank. Whenever the bank is really supposed to do something, it can be guaranteed not to, it would rather pester us with demands. And what the inland waters are supposed to eat instead, that's written down here, please read it immediately, although it undoubtedly doesn't particularly inte-rest you: at least two hundred years of biodynamic, organic and ecological farming, in order to recover from its own toxins again. Everything should always be healthy. You, too, should start immediately by eating healthier food. Finally, I've attached a number of signal lamps, reflectors and coloured adhesive strips to my poetic art, so that if all else fails you'll hear all the bells ringing at once, until you're almost deaf. It'll turn into a wonderful chorus, once I've given the cue. And with the words meat or flesh I've provided an additional hint, superfluous of course, I didn't need to say it at all (at least when a heavy object is dropped into the water, then it's not hard to know who or what is meant), and now it's all no longer art, a pity, really.

But then again, the dumping of wrapped perishable objects is not entirely without risk, if only one man is available to do the job. I have a suspicion that otherwise, and ever more frequently, illegal waste is dumped from this point on the shore, because I've several times seen trucks with their lights out parked by the upper bay, where it's easier to drive up to the edge, and where one can also see more easily. There are no fish here who would like to turn themselves into sharks on a special course, to first of all eat out the eyes and then the soft parts of their catch. There won't have to be a long search for missing persons, because one will soon know and see on photos, that someone has gone missing and is now unfortunately going to be found in a terrible state. It really would be better for this young woman if she were in the middle of the ocean, with forty pounds of cement round her ankles. A father recently even inflicted ten pounds on his child, a little girl, and a beautiful, cool, merry river, whose secondary movements immediately rocked and pushed the child around, although it soon made no difference to the child with all the foam in her lungs and upper respiratory tracts and all the cement attached to her bound feet. Tomorrow the mother and the boyfriend of a young missing person will from the start have been convinced that something must have happened. They'll have some copies of the most recent photographs of the missing person made by a photographer they know and go with it themselves from house to house, into the shops, into the inn opposite the bus stop and into the bus stop and show it, the photo. They will stop cars on the road and ask the occupants whether they haven't seen the missing person, a certain Gabriele Fluch. Finally they will have had just enough time to stick a kind of wanted poster of the missing person to the electricity masts along the route she usually travelled to her apprenticeship, but the adhesive will not even be dry behind the ears yet, when the packet, not a day too soon, will have been found in the lake. All without any success in life, on a day like any other, life rented an extra room, in order to do something extra in peace and quiet, which it usually never does.

It's all basically a world one can keep track of, one can see as far as one's sight allows, that is, differently in the case of each person, and some can see right through bodies, because there's nothing there that could interest them. How copiously this water spreads its wings, how generously proportioned is its space, how assiduously it has increased its biomass and the detritus, so that its need for oxygen has grown exponentially, it's got nothing else to do the livelong day, because it has already killed everything in itself. Is that not a nice symbol for this man here, who is facing fairly critical times, because he would like to digest himself and make himself disappear and instead always has to be hunting and chasing himself, in order then to find out which of his hobbies could keep him alive a little longer? Which ones it definitely isn't, he already knows. And as if there had to be a last straw on top of everything else, now something dead has been added to all the lifelessness in the debris of his life, a daughter from a good home in the village (with a single mother), that's what I've been told at least, but it's not quite right, I think, a present time that was pretty as a picture, and then this human sausage plops into the water, just like that, without the least grace it may have possessed while still alive. The longer I look at this face, the more certain I am:

The disappearance of this girl is no problem at all, because she's available reproduced so many times. She has made herself up to look like all the others, in the shop she even chose thick rubber mats as shoe soles, so that the adjoining legs look approx. four inches longer, and from tomorrow her face, which wanted to smile out of magazines, will instead be fixed to the masts a hundred times over. So wherever one looks, this girl exists so many times over that she has simultaneously gone and stayed here!, a whole photo wallpaper has been made out of the young woman. This sweet little mouse, as the poet says, exists so often, even if in another, foreign shape, nothing else has any room any more between her and her pictures, which all: don't show her!, all photos, which had previously nodded to her, and were immediately cut out of a colour magazine with the weapons of a woman, a small pair of scissors. No, these are, rather, weapons, which are such, that woman (whoa!) doesn't even need them, there would be nothing for them to do. That's why one doesn't need to be in the pictures in person, one can also let oneself be represented there by other women; I've seen it myself, this nothingness, all the photos as if from the magazine and from the other magazine, I had the time to glance at it, that was enough for me, and I learned something from it. Down, into the water, always just down, and then not again: down. Once is enough. It works the first time, while the photos really always have a considerable effect each time we look at them, unless of course we were in them ourselves.

If it were up to him, the man would row out specially in the boat and there, where it's deep, further out, where the lake snacks on the tree shadows from the steep shore, heave his food parcel in its own snack pack into the water. But there are no oars in the boat, and one can't very well run around the village with a pair of replacement oars, what would that look like. Alone is the night, it always does everything alone, that's why no one offers to help it. The night is the night, that's its attitude. One sees nothing. No street lighting by the lake. No light during sex, that's lucky, because we haven't specially washed our feet, they're quite black between the toes. And the pedal boat, it has a key, even if not for an ignition, otherwise it would be a motor boat, we don't have one available. The man can't get far enough out on the water with his meat (his catch). Yet the killing of his prey cost him as little effort as a cigarette, the end of which burns one's fingers a little and which one quickly stubs out; we see, no, of course, we don't see, it's dark, you don't have any choice, you simply have to believe me, so look at an embrace, which for months has been usual between the two, in the car, in the front seats, while a cock which has been brought along for the purpose is already standing there upright and expectant. One hand stays on the steering wheel, one head is shoved under an armpit, nestles into that damp, cosy hollow, oh how deceptive, as if it wanted to hide away in a cupboard. Long, thick hair, generously heaped with tips from Brigitte on how to shine, but a nut-sized amount is sufficient, spreads out on an arm, a living mass, as one says, everything as usual, otherwise no one would have made the effort, to prepare memories of it, and then to hang them out to dry on a TV screen or a poster, where everyone can see them, models for everyone, for the next time. Then one can do it oneself. There's no such thing. Yet another of those, who behave exactly the same as always, after having read several how-to books, about exactly how not to do it, better a smart short hairstyle, your hairdresser deserves that once a month, than an unkempt flowing mane!, so one of them will unfortunately do it nevertheless just as usual, in the hope of being acknowledged as a good, languishing, eager woman in love. But today she's in trouble, when really it's the man who should be: Does he have someone new? No, daddy, that's not allowed. He can't do that. The capacity to act will be taken out of her hands, since the young woman, Gabi's her name, to the accompaniment of laments, accusations and pleas and already precipitately giving herself up, without any address marked, or what is to happen to the body in the event of death (although one might be able to get something for oneself nevertheless, if one were smart and already donated one's corpse to pathology beforehand), pulls down a zip and takes out a cock, as so often now, it's been going on like this for many weeks. The skill is in doing it again and again, but differently each time. Someone who is easily bored would never manage it. Thanks, the pleasure's mine, says the penis, so now I have to pass into a stranger's hands again, I've hardly had time to get used to the previous pair, and my owner is also somewhat in need of a routine, I would say, run away, if you ever catch sight of him in the distance! No one listens to me. I find it rather unpleasant. They always find me, feels a not very pitiable piece of meat in addition to some more pleasant feelings, which are now beginning, have your ticket ready and fall to your knees in front of the bouncer, please, on your knees now, this moment! Gabi's groping, often clumsy fingers are unerring, as if the country policeman's cock had a lighthouse beacon, or a flashing warning light, so that one can avoid it in time (no man is an island, he stands above everything, he is an aeroplane or at least in an aeroplane) and not grab it right away, without first pausing and thinking, or if thinking is at all desired, to think about the rubber for insulation purposes. And then perhaps at some point you produce a short circuit, well, you know where the country policeman lives, if you want to phone him there. Women. If this man happens to be somewhere else, they immediately become suspicious, because the country policeman has gone out and couldn't leave a single contact number. For example this house, in front of which he's standing once again, he would absolutely like to have it. And if he had to fight for it, with the clumsy and also somewhat too sensitive weapons of the flesh, then it can't be helped. Flesh. This house belongs to a woman. Its façade already has a sceptical expression, when the country policeman enters. We certainly can't fool this house. This house is already made. In the house a commodity wants its eyelids to glitter and present itself with the eyelash flutter of a new striped sun-blind. She has rubbed herself all over with something, the woman who lives here, but she didn't have to make the effort for the sake of this man. He overlooks everything that has no value, nor does he have to ask for patience or look for some peace and quiet, before someone comes up to him, on his own stairs, likewise made of the best, well hung meat, that no longer longs for anything, except to be released from its place of custody and to get away again. Then I would be, says the meat in its own voice, which we like to listen to, and its owner, to whom someone or other will also listen, then the two of them, the flesh and him, would at last be at one with themselves: alone. They, too.

No grave should be made of me, thinks country policeman Kurt Janisch. That would be the worst thing for me. To end up in a small container. No. Preferably in a large one!

The girl on the other hand. Her body still belongs to her, passing its time like a song bird, hopping from branch to branch, until she hits the ground below, but by then she has long ceased to have herself in her hand. So please, what's she getting up to now, she's banged into something with her pointed tits, which she can keep for all I care and whose production in the nearby district hospital is still evident. The man cannot even take Gabi properly in hand for his almost dreamy, yet precisely directed hand manipulations, she slips through his fingers every time, which doesn't, however, annoy him very much. But it would certainly be no big problem for him. Standing on the shore as life-saver of a small child or a car, he would like that better. He would jump into the waters without hesitation. His penis nods, when it's squeezed, but also of its own accord. How the girl has to laugh, when she sees that. She asks especially for this movement, which he wrests from an implacable life and from a body which is deaf to entreaties. Women are mud and that holds onto everything. Slime. Something can be drawn out, a sledge, a wheelbarrow, and before one can pull the cart out of the dirt, it's already disappeared again. The mud has it. Only occasionally, during a thunderstorm, do women voluntarily part with something, rushing in fear out of their emergency accommodation with their families, which they must be ready to leave at any time. For once the mud has time to spread, calmly and deliberately, I mean with deliberation. Then there come the women, a whole flood, stir everything up, themselves most of all, because they are so in love, and then they lose themselves, in their own mud, because their partner has suddenly gone, for no reason. What, already? So soon? That's a gloomy prospect! We can't see any reason! Perhaps the mountain will come after all? For the time being its stones are coming down. It can take a while before it comes itself.

I don't know, there's something different about the girl this time, the country policeman is still thinking, as her blissful gaze at him is suddenly as if extinguished. So. Yet another veil over her pupils. Finished. The man's peace of mind is gone. Now he has thrown the older woman, in whom he places some hopes, out of her own living room, just because of the girl. She had become quite unbearable with her constant demands for more, without even knowing everything she's got. She doesn't even have all her wits about her, one is always missing. She should for once go and rub her gusset herself, with her own hands, so she sees what that's like. But when she's supposed to wank off in front of him, then it only makes her all the greedier for him, precisely because he wants to watch her. It is one of many variants of the heightening of pleasure, all of which she would like to get to know later at her leisure. Eager for knowledge she listed them all, the variations on her flesh. She even gives the man orders, because she's waited so long for it. She has a right. He'll take that from her. He has a method for that. He's already dreading it. He knows: As soon as he opens his shop, she's already running in, and he's the one who's supposed to be directing the traffic. He hardly has time to start his engine, and she's already trying to throttle it. He thinks, she wants nothing else except to feel number one in his books. Can't she hear her expiry date, even if she can't read it? Doesn't she hear, on the other side of the door, the moaning of an adolescent still under sweet sixteen? Well, that's a different tune, isn't it? As fresh as a folk song, as resolute as the federal anthem, but one doesn't know the words. All the notes the older woman has mastered, the man knew long ago. Because he reads them from her red, sweating, enraptured, blissful face, which she puts on when she sees him. And the tune she strikes up underneath him is false, he thinks it is even deliberately faked. It is a strange whimpering, which begins to turn into an almost practised groaning, hardly has he touched her. He wouldn't have believed it, if he hadn't heard it with his own ears. This woman doesn't have any more devotees than her house. In reality an unpropertied property-owner, that's what she is, who believes she resides in the realm of the untrue but beautiful. That's love. Jealousy upsets whole goods trains, it upsets me too, but the goods are what count. Get your doll out of my house and do it this minute. Oh no. I'm sorry, I didn't mean to be so rude, please, don't leave me. I didn't want to order you to do something, which could be terribly painful for you, but even more so for me. I haven't once doubted your love or entertained the least suspicion, even if behind this door you're ramming this little girl into my ground. I love and sacrifice, and I don't draw back from that, because I see that you could never deceive or exploit me. Go now and get rid off her! Before anything else happens.

Such blubbing or something like it, often heard, often seen on the display, but never read, heard or copied, now emerges from the handfuls of hair flowing down, which gently drape a glans which has already turned blue. We are in the car again, which is standing there, something else is standing too, only the heater is running. Afterwards the man will have to pick strands of hair from his mouth, pull them like fishbones between his teeth, which right away, you never know where you have to be first, it's like the homebound traffic jam at the junction with the Federal Highway to Mariazell, on a weekday at five, so which he'll need, to feign kisses, which would actually have turned into angry bites, if the tongue had only joined in. But it has taken cover in time, sticking to the side of his mouth, so that nothing happens to it; he's already dreading, even before he opens his mouth to let in her aquatic bird of passage, one of many, and in addition all the flaps and nozzles of flesh, all of it, all the flesh won from impenetrable swamps! As if it's disappeared. He must force it, the tongue, well now, somewhat belatedly, it is joining in our aerobics exercise after all, after it had briefly withdrawn behind the barrier of the teeth for a rest. The tongue would fit very easily at the edge of the lake, but it is the slow-flowing rivers of a woman which are squeezed out through the sweet fingers of love. Juice shop. Have your glass ready nevertheless, you won't get anything else. If you place this glass on a tea light, the light will never flicker and go out. Because it cannot get away.

We are now on a parking lot, which isn't one at all. It is, fresh-water life-forms can confirm it at any time, almost a bog, thick, juicy fennel stalks everywhere, though not until summer, now fresh weeds are just beginning to grow rampant and swamp the place, foul, stagnant, vegetable, right next to it the winter refuges of birds, it doesn't matter which. The vegetation is not yet fully developed, that's still to come. Rome wasn't built in a day either, but on swamp-land nevertheless. We just have to watch that the wheels don't sink in, so that we can get away from here again, but there's plenty of brushwood, it can be put under the wheels if need be. So that we have the necessary friction and the peace and quiet for a young woman called Gabi, who at this moment is like-wise rather naughty, to pull a face and give this man a blow job. She has mastered that like an older woman, but she hasn't mas-tered herself. That's something they can all do, women: be bad, until one has to smack them on their raised bums, yes, turn it round to me, whispers the man in her ear, at least she didn't suf-focate earlier on, Gabi. She's recovered again. A reason to be cheerful, but only one of many. So now she's ended up here, on this human island anchored in the lake, swamp island, this is exactly where, later on, it's already settled, he has to open up the salty face down there once again and give it a good licking, she won't give him any peace until then. Otherwise he'll drive straight back to the other one after all. Earlier we didn't get to where we wanted, she stopped us right to the end, the other one. Swamps only exist where there is very high precipitation, but Gabi is still very wet, from what, from that. Please, just let me drive Gabi home at least, the country policeman said a couple of minutes ago to Gerti, let me, I'll just quickly drive her home, and then I'll come straight back to you. I'll take her away, and come back as quickly as possible, right away, but you'll have to give me ten minutes, a quarter of an hour, you'll get something in return. No, nothing will get in the way, not this time, it did other times, but nothing will get in the way today, I promise you. For today, even I've had enough. I know: you haven't. This man may have enough, yes, even of himself. Nevertheless best of all he likes to do it with himself, which he conceals from all the people close to him: For him that is the equality on which our civilisation is based - to avoid as far as possible being measured against others! He reflects, condemned to making advances: all the women, and so many all alone!, but most of all he is attached to himself and his dreams. They are all dreams of bodies, and they are sometimes even better than the dreams of houses. It is a pleasure at last to have people in front of one, and without the small difference between one another and what they have between their legs, that's not so very important in his opinion. He's had enough of women, he's never fed up with property, but the bodies, they befall him and overwhelm him. Nor does he see anyone he knows in front of him, but faceless people in indeterminate positions. How nice. Children, whether boys or girls, get their chance just like adults. The age of the children is unimportant, they can be almost sixteen like Gabi, they can also be infants, it doesn't matter which month. And they all open up just for him, like suns.

So what am I doing here, right, I'm describing one side of the culprit (you can meanwhile take the others. I haven't properly addressed them yet), from which really the return match should now come, normally in the shape of squeezing, pinching of nipples and kissing somewhere or other, the sort of thing one does, as often as possible please, in the case of this man, I fear there's unfortunately too much biting as well, that's the most important thing for him, he could have been recognised by that. It's always the same with lust, people let themselves go, but every tiny change immediately confuses them, and they want to go home again. There is much that distracts them again, their projectiles, even if the change was specially marked in the book of life, even before one opened it: The victims believe nevertheless, they're not loved any more, if something is done a little bit differently from usual. From whom did they learn it? This young woman here is lying ready on her knees in the car, the floor of which is very clean, you'd hardly believe it, and her jeans are losing hardly any fluff either, they are the most popular brand there is. Because of it the forensic experts will in days to come sweat blood rather than analyse it. So, a couple of bars back: His game, the man's game, now an almost furtive gentle groping, as if he didn't know where this body is, which is where it always is, on the passenger seat, already half on the floor, with its head in his lap, that's how simple the language of bodies is, everyone understands it without words, so with her head in the man's lap: this young woman, already a lover, grazing by the shore, lost, even before she could find herself. As usual the man has spread his legs a little and half turned towards her, as not even God, the Creator, would, because he would never allow his picture to be taken in such a position, he's surely got the right to his image, except no one bothers about it, including his agent, the priest, he's more interested in little boys, and Jesus is just too old (but how else should we find out if he's really man enough to torment us, this Lord God?), heavens, where will it end. Now I've lost the thread myself, the first set goes to you. You can have it, if you like. So, back to the position again:

The man, is that clear?, the woman: facing him, her pelvis thrust forward, and the crown cork, with which the penis is sealed, so that it's not exploding all the time, possibly in one's own face, it's in the likewise wide open mouth of a woman, now, say it finally, so: a slight pressure on, how shall I explain it, well the carotid artery divides at a certain point in the throat, yes, there, into two parts, and between them there's a ganglion, and that's important, you should never squeeze it, that is on both sides at the same time, left and right, because otherwise you die or someone dies because of you in seconds, please don't alarm the player, he's almost ready now, and he's squeezing with his strong fingers, which are familiar with signal discs, measuring tapes, laser guns, even an ordinary gun, from above, as if by chance, it could accordingly also have been an accident, if one had no clue about the anatomy of the throat, because one was always concerned with other parts of the female anatomy, where it's wetter and more interesting (where there's water, there's life!), but the man knows this spot, and he altogether knows more about bodies than about anything else, and has attended all the obligatory first aid courses, some even voluntarily, to get on in his profession, which already go beyond first aid and are almost second aid, I mean the spot on the delicate stem of the neck and then also the spot in the fir plantation, he knows them very well, in the young corn which grows right up to the shore in the almost muddy ground, not where during the day people like to say, let's go for a little walk, the spot is deeper in the dark, hairstyle-spoiling forest, and the other spot, the one on the body, this proud article, which is available either completely free of charge or is anyway always too expensive for people like us, when we're standing in the perfume department, in order to camouflage it at least, well the body, naturally it likes to put its best goods on display, but that doesn't mean that one can just stick one's hand in and take them. In short: The aforementioned spot is accordingly a little to the side, is easily accessible and the man has strong fingers, which would not, however, have been at all necessary. You and I, we would have managed it, too, if we had known where and known how, to squeeze the nerve spot between the carotid branches, I will find out what it's called, but the doctor, who's supposed to tell me, is still busy with something else. You'll find out right away, as soon as I've found out. At any rate now you know, where you shouldn't grab, even if you don't know what it's called. It can't do any harm, if as a precaution you get an expert to show you the spot, so that you avoid it in future. So, no, not again: There's a spot, you shouldn't even try to reach out for it. It's like a door, which you shouldn't open, and now everyone's dying to do it, aren't they? People are allowed to see everything and grasp at everything and they grasp nothing, but just there: really please don't. What, did the man first bang the girl's head against the door handle? No, I didn't see the man bang the girl's head against the door handle. But I'm always the last person to find out about anything. Something on a sunken path through a forest, in the middle of Austria, has, without visible injury, gently, as if by chance, gone slack, the trees only stand up all the straighter, to stand out all the better from the human beings and to display toughness, which not everyone of us manages.

And now she's being cleared away, the girl, together with her name and her actions. Tidied up, wrapped up and removed from the earth and dispatched to the water, where she has already arrived. All that needs to be done is to open the cistern and give the float valve a shake, then it'll flow again and flush away everything that we had intended for the water.

3.

Roses, tulips, carnations, all three wither; but not all at once, because they don't all grow at the same time. Carnations don't grow at all, one can only buy them at the florist. The flowers, how pretty they are, they don't covet property, a little patch of earth is plenty for them, they don't even know that others, less sedentary, covet property that is not their own. They live, and other flowers live next door, for our delight. Shush, they're listening to us! Being quiet, perhaps we, too, can learn new possibilities of existence from them: is it better to be snapped or to be right away completely broken off? But also how to show off and spread oneself around. All their high spirits: nothing self-important! The front garden blooms and is carefully weeded, as if with a pair of eyebrow tweezers, Mrs Janisch does that, and she does it on her knees, in order not to fall into the pit, which she doesn't see, but about which she knows: It's over there, somewhere, not far away, dug just for her. Perhaps by her rather selfish husband? No, probably not. She nevertheless seems quite crazy about her beautiful garden, perhaps that's why she begrudges alien plants any association with her own native ones, which she has so laboriously tamed. An attack of immodesty, that's what one calls weeds. The garden is the kingdom of Mrs Janisch, whereas her husband is on the look-out for other kingdoms; right now in the kitchen-living room he's bending over an architect's plan, which doesn't belong to him, and neither unfortunately does the house that goes with it. In this plan, as in every plan, including God's, a kitchen is marked in, it's as if people always wanted the same thing and that really means: themselves, except bigger and better please, so that from time to time one can also cook. How on earth did the country policeman get hold of this plan so quickly?, after all he's not responsible for the land registry but for catastrophes. E.g. when the mountain comes calling, first of all in small amounts, in rockfalls, then later perhaps the whole thing breaks off, is that because of the old mine, of the many very old mines underneath? The whole country is completely hollow inside! And then all the people in the environs of the mountain, which also wants to move, but has no plan for doing it, have to leave their houses, which they built so laboriously with neighbourly help, which is what they call the black economy round here. Saved decades for something and now this! The mountain casts an enigmatic glance at us, and whoever he throws a glance at, he follows it up with more, to add some weight to his glance. Who's talking down there? It's only us. So I, the mountain, will make you disappear now. The valley, which was likewise undermined by passages, doesn't want to be left behind and threatens that first there will be one subsidence, and then plugs will certainly soon form, and the water trickling through will become less and less. And then, says the valley bottom, grinning from every crevice, I'll really get going. Because, thanks to the high drop, this plug cannot be expected to hold for long. That is why, says the valley, and it grows ever louder, because it has to be heard above its own howling of subterranean winds, that is why it cannot be concluded, that because the first water and mud subsidence, which will then have occurred, will come to a standstill, that, should one attempt to pump off water underground and put up wooden partitions, that because of that anything would have been effectively sealed off, far from it. Not a trace. You see. That's exactly what will be left of the people down there.

Mr Janisch would prefer to move into one of the houses that are already there, then he would have two of them, his son would also have his (not quite, the old woman, to whom it belongs, is still alive, please don't forget to bring her no flowers! Not until her funeral will some be handed to her, from the garden naturally, what do we have one for), Mr Janisch jun. wants to do some rebuilding then, but that can wait. There's still another person living inside, a person one can't simply take out of it like jam out of the jar. The people here owe the mountain countless unpleasant hours, and as far as dirty tricks are concerned it is in constant competition with the lake. The lake gets something tipped into it which doesn't agree with it, the mountain has thrown off its magic wood and has become a threat to people, settlements and buildings; it is a wood with an excellent effect on public welfare, so let us set up a welfare committee, not to cut it down, but to keep out the water and the stones and to break off dolomite and other nonsense, but this wood has not kept its promise. It didn't keep the stones to itself, it would certainly have been a feat, since there are so many. And below it, too, there are shocking scenes taking place, a house slips into the depths, and nothing but the balconies with their floral decorations are peeping out, we're enchanted by them, so much beauty in such a small space! It's just being photographed now, before it disappears. Look, the tree up there, it's interesting, too: Its root fibres reach desperately into the air, will they manage to catch hold of the piece of earth that's sledging down to the valley there, but already the whole tree itself is toppling over, and in the air in which its root ropes are waving around it won't even catch a midge, in the air there's no support any more.

Nice and warm today, but the days are still rather short. It'll come. They're already stretching their limbs. Spring awakens. A girl's room in an attic is empty. The whole business, the dream-heavy feelings behind drawn curtains, at the edge of a precipice, is not the routine case, which it will appear to be for a couple of days, it is not a case at all yet. A young woman is missing, it is assumed she has not been able to resist the wide world, the district capital, yes, the one with the big hospital, in which people die of cancer, which they were unable to show to a doctor of their choice in time - people never have time for the essentials, and if they do, then they wouldn't know which ones and which kind - it is assumed, therefore, the young woman has presumably been unable to resist the world beyond the village and simply hasn't come home for a night. Didn't feel like it. A vanished young beauty, a lost light. Don't panic, beauty is untouchable, just try to catch hold of this beautiful swan, then you'll soon see! Beauty is untouchable, it's for our eyes only, so that we all get something from it, not only the gentlemen who climb over marble cliffs, in order to get to know Naomi Campbell or Cindy Crawford personally. Gabi Fluchs will pop up unexpectedly, but she will be most urgently awaited by her mother and her boyfriend. She can be here at any moment. We'll start waiting now. So, early in the morning her mother waits with the familiar comfort of a cup of white coffee and a sandwich with either sausage or cheese, usually with both. Then, as every day, the daughter is supposed to catch the bus, the stop can be seen from the living room window of the detached house, or the train, but the daughter doesn't see why her mother always has to be gazing after her as she does so. Plants bloom in these troughs, too, and reach out cheekily to the shiny windows, until they can get a hold and look into the room, but why then do they so persistently and stupidly turn their heads away to the other side, to the flashing sun? Perhaps they looked too deeply into the window glass? Why do we not want to see what is evident and would interest us; what forces us to constantly incline our heads to the other side? On the other side are the people who should be our models, beautiful and good humoured. And we are here.

The sun entices us out there. What, the Wörthersee is somewhere else altogether? It can't be! We don't believe it! Well, it
doesn't matter, stranger, we'll just drive there. How good it feels,
the sun shower. Do we, too, have to find out something, that to
know would certainly not make us feel so good? We have to see,
we won't give up, what others want to obscure: They use sweet
smiling cats' faces for that, or stylised portraits of dogs, stuck to
the windows of cars, and for this purpose alone: to keep off some
of the light, to stop the glare. Early in the morning Gabi always
thought she looked so pretty in front of the shiny bathroom mirror, and she was, too, remembers her mother. Getting up ten
minutes early to put on make-up, that will perhaps get her one
hour's pleasure, later, again and again, but not until later (that's
the point of pleasure, that one can't consume it right away, first
pay at the checkout of the drug store!), and yet she always smiles
herself into a good mood again in the mirror, our Gabi, who's an
apprentice in a big building materials company. All of it without
success. She's hardly started. But the sun has already risen for her,
no one can be brighter than it, and the thousand pieces, that the
atom has ordered for itself, in order to enter into competition with
them, nothing can be brighter than this sun, except sometimes a
human face, which in the end one still doesn't like, for one reason
or another. But one is too dazzled to notice. So we'll just leave the
face to the one it belongs to. It won't suit him either, it didn't even
suit Socialism, which took it off right away and put the old one
on again. Then Socialism was content again for a few years with
what it was familiar with.

So, how can we help up to its feet this ground, which is just
rushing down towards us, down the mountain flank, and
promptly landing on its nose, not on ours please? This nice, com-
radely mountain - also a face which has fallen and no one wants
to help up. The mountain has dropped its mask. Now it already
looks different from how it did a little while ago, when it was still
whole. Perhaps houses will even have to be evacuated? Watch out,

that could mean loss of homeland and lead to critical situations! I wish I could plan an early warning system, but would need help, so that the life of these people here could be maintained to the same high standards they are used to, inclusive of deep freeze cabinet, into which at least one whole deer would fit if it were foolish enough to go into it. And also inclusive of a glazed conservatory, in which things could very well be a bit more exotic, if we had been sent the appropriate catalogue, which we ordered on the phone.

The mountain remains unpredictable, again and again it throws off its debris, which has grown too heavy for it, it has to relieve itself. Last year's avalanche alone, thank you very much, it need not have been so generous, that first the slope slips down, and then all the rock follows. Austria. Just as during the holidays visitors have been getting to know it from above, so for centuries and millennia, mines have been getting to know it from below, at every level. The country's top side and its underside are well trodden. The country exists as positive and negative, depending on where one finds oneself, at the moment unfortunately we hear more about the negative. Why do I always only see the negative, I am admonished. I don't know either. Perhaps I don't know the country well enough, so as to be able to do justice to its good sides. One can be shut up inside the mountain, no I wouldn't like to get to know this country from the inside at all, the outside is already enough for me. We have mining to thank for all that, for being so hollow. You probably think, the doors always open when you hammer on them with your fist? A mistake. Right now you're sitting in the mine cage at the bottom, and while up above the rubble is breaking away from the mountain and howling and raging the mud is coming to visit, you yourself are smashed to pieces down there, and no one will ever see you again. Someone should have taken care of it, the mountain, shielded it from human beings, instead it turned into a shield somewhat full of holes for them. The thunderstorm came, a thundering and roaring as if from a thousand express trains arose, yes, exactly, as if, let's say, rather: five hundred trains are pulling out at the same time. Ordinary mortals were frightened to death, and the rest did then really die, it's true, you can read it up in many other places, if you don't believe me. I think of the big hit, that God had with these dead, who will be in the papers for years, but he wasn't on target. The mountain wouldn't have helped me, nor anyone else either. No one helped it, although it was put in our care, and what did we do to it? We hollowed it out completely, disembowelled and made what do I know out of its innards. This and many another mountains have been ground down into baby powder, is that not unbelievable. The big doesn't remain big, it is as if it's made for whatever's small. We've already said a lot, perhaps too much, about the water, but we will no doubt be able to say a great deal more about it, when one day it's finished with you. Nature is as romantic as a human being, both want to have a nice experience and can, too, but a human being moves in a larger radius. This missing girl, Gabi, likewise had no end of care, but you see how deceptive such protection can be; you'll understand when the storm comes and you're left standing in the rain with nothing to shield you. All right, all right, I will stop, but not yet.

Gabi is gone, like a part, almost a whole horn of this mountain. Nature adapts to human beings, or is it the other way round? Just try some time to meet a mountain, after all, the tourist brochure explicitly demands it of you! The mountain won't avoid you, but the human being, in this case you, certainly will. Or the mountain's removed from the pitch, where it was only tolerated on the sidelines, in smart, glittering wrapping, as a cheerleader and everyone jumps for joy at it and at its commands, when the team underground in the display mine wants a boost. Someone squeezes his button accordion and there's an incredibly loud bang. Every girl with a boyfriend among the players is already happy in advance, we simply must win, we must! And we, every one of us friends of the mountains, shake arms and legs, to be harvested as ripe fruit by our charges, when the time comes. The mountain's coming. We can do nothing at all about that, except conduct a conversation with it.

What fashionable shoes Gabi bought herself only last week from the birthday money she got in advance! She would even want to be buried in them, even if the layers of the soles have turned out a bit heavy, even clumsy-looking compared with the remainder that is built up on top of them. The mountain, full of understanding, thinks so too. The layers down below have become too heavy for it, and what does it throw off? It throws off its upper storey, which is not to blame in the least. A very independent girl, our Gabi, sensible. The new shoes are gone, they still haven't turned up, perhaps because they're too heavy. She also has a boyfriend, who is now at a loss. Although she's only sixteen, with a discount, because she won't be for another two months, she's already had a steady boyfriend for a long time, he's very nice, I think, perhaps a little boring and pedantic for his age. At least he's not one of the inconsiderate, insolent kind, equipped with fashionable sunglasses and ugly haircuts and hooded sweatshirts. He has drawn up a life plan and is sticking to it, whereas the others only have a goal in life, with nothing in between as to how they want to achieve it: No, I'm being unjust, the goal is the fast car and the beautiful house and several beautiful women. Of all the other treasures one only needs one of each, oh if one only had it already!, apart from money, there can never be enough of that. So I'm slandering young people, because I'm no longer one of them myself, and everybody remarks on it. But I'm generalising again, people are incredibly different, and life is an altogether far too dirty business, particularly if, like me, one doesn't want to get one's hands dirty. Money, that really interests us, but work, no. You will permit me to look at the carefully devised map of New York, as I write this. I would like to go there and as fast as possible! This lad believes of himself, it's only natural, that's he's got something to offer and looks attractive, both of which are quite true, only he doesn't dress well, nor does he come from far away, where for instance Father Christmas is kept in store until his big appearance, but he ranks, even among the youth of the village, among the also rans: not an outsider, but someone, nevertheless, on whom one would not place any money, even if one stood to win a lot. Let's wait and see, it'll look different in a couple of years, then he'll be earning a good wage and be able to afford a bit. After all he's getting a good training, even as shampoo and water are running fraternally down the sides of his car. Gabi will then have to run through questions for his exam. One would virtually have to drive across the border to find another little place where there was a similarly ambitious young man. And she lets him get away, our Gabi, when she doesn't even have to keep the door shut herself, she doesn't have to do anything with her friend, just be there, and yet last night she nevertheless didn't turn up at his house, although yesterday as every day he could have been a good influence on her. He is, I can't repeat it often enough, a quiet, hard-working lad, and has never believed what was said about his girlfriend, all made up by her friends, it's said. It can't be true, there, behind the lipstick, inside there's supposed to have dwelt an insatiable appetite, for what, she had everything, didn't she? Feet are made for walking, and the younger they are, the further they'll go, what's the point of this unequivocal remark, if one's still unable to move? It's as if one's nailed to the spot. If we had been apart for any length of time, then it would have been something else, says the schoolboy with his own car. If I'm sitting next to her, I'm always good to her. The room in Gabi's parents' house, that too, I can only repeat: really pretty, cuddly toys, magazine photos without warmth and pity, that this pretty girl nevertheless was unable to get enough points for the amateur model competition. She sent in the photo quite in vain, our Gabi, a narrow miss is still a miss. But now it really does come in useful, the nice photo, which a photographer, who really knows what he's doing, took of her. Because her mother and her boyfriend don't, not exactly, carve it into the wood, but they stick it to the power masts between the house and the next village, and they go even further. Over here, closer, a little bit closer, yes, in the house, you see the room of an innocent girl. Her father already moved out years ago and is living with another woman, three villages on, towards Mariazell. Now that's a woman!, I'm telling you, she's a home-loving creature, gentle, yet as if from another planet, on which people are put together differently from here, exotic and unforced, because one can't force her to do anything; parts of the hands of the second wife of Gabi's father have developed almost into flippers. The fingers have grown together as far as the penultimate digit, it looks strange, but occurs frequently in this district, in which even the valleys have it off with each other, because there are so few of them and they find nothing else to play with except for their own boulders, their own debris, their own bodies. The mountains play with themselves, and sometimes they play with people, if they can catch some. No, don't look the other way! I'd like to continue with my descriptions, but this time something quite different, not far away. I, a pole-vaulter, but one who doesn't like to increase her pace, have for many years been cautiously courting this district with all too many words, and what does it give me in return? My characters evidently want me to fail myself, yet I always fail because of them. Let's see, if this time a whole lot come at once to finish me off! What do I see? This district only gives up pictures of itself, pictures which I've had to have made myself. But I'm going to stop soon.

Far, on the other hand, far away from me, something soft, like food, if you insist, I can have it prepared for you immediately: Whatever's lying there, it's not a boat, but we wouldn't need a boat now either, perhaps a shopping trolley. The morning smiles, it hasn't read the newspaper yet. The mother, a cigarette bobbing nervously in the corner of her mouth, talks on the phone to her daughter's boyfriend. Both display growing disquiet: If it were really true, that Gabi has gone away, which is what it looks like? Consider the good mood, which disappeared the moment that these two people almost simultaneously picked up the phone, fortunately not the same one, but they wanted to talk to one another. What good does it do? Talking is like walking up and down on a small island. It's soon over again, because one has noticed that one can't get anywhere by talking. So does technology intervene ever more frequently in life, we didn't teach it to be constantly ringing as the signal for a good conversation, which we value more this time, because it costs something, indeed technology intervenes in the shape of Elise or Mozart's Jupiter Symphony, yes, I've heard them myself. And it spits us out again, pale and shocked, ready for the presentiment of a telephone bill. It's printed here: It must be right, we are dust! Except dust cannot rise up against such an injustice, that we are supposed to pay just for talking. Unless one were to blow into it with one's own breath, which we wanted to use for this talking, until we all turn blue, our consciousness expands and we see things that aren't there. The dust is in our bad books, it's fled: under the furniture, the carpet, our feet. Who has given technology the right to spread news, which is then perhaps not even true? Communications technology has done it, this revolution, somebody had to do it. It won't be anything important. Again it won't be this telephone with Gabi on the other end because she had a breakdown; with whom she had the breakdown, that's secondary for now, the main thing is, she's still alive. Come home, Gabi, all is forgiven, forwards and no forgetting, and how can we forget something, that we don't even know yet. Perhaps Gabi spent the night with a girlfriend, which one could it be? She never told much at home, probably there wasn't much worth telling about, not a trace of problems. Let's ask her former schoolmates, one is by chance, no, not by chance, employed by the same company, likewise in the office. Commercial training, that lends a feeling of dignity in the face of a society in which only property counts, then at least one knows, who has it and why, and so one also learns exactly why one doesn't have any oneself. The uninformed have it much easier in this respect than the already affluent. The uninformed, whom one can also call the unscrupulous, they don't back the banks, they get on the backs of people and suck them dry. Well thanks, it wasn't much, but now I need another one, one for the road, I hardly felt the last one, it was just enough, that's all. The sick can even threaten the sick, and people like to say, this society is sick. No idea what's wrong with it. Usually not much. Why pay interest? It's possible to get by without it. It's also possible to get by without the nominal wage or whatever it's called, which one has, before some people or other deduct such and such an amount from what one never had in the first place. If one had something, it's bound to have been less afterwards, but less is sometimes more! No, not this time. Until suddenly the mountain comes down to hit us, and to check whether it can be true, that it got twelve head of people, as punishment, because it's been completely hollowed out inside. Because of the mine, which did not fertilise (but nevertheless fed many), but rather did the opposite: This mountain, thanks to the mining, which undermined it (see job description!), this mountain is hereby wound up. The mountain is closed. No, you cannot take your animals with you, they stay, yes, the pigs, too. The mountain has to eat something after all. He doesn't forever want to be the loser and is now bringing in his harvest, and taking it down to the valley, where it was never allowed to go before, although the inn is there. You'd be better off getting yourself to safety as quickly as possible, the mountain is heavier than you are! Take only the essentials, your savings bank book, cheque card, documents, cash and the photos of relatives, so that one knows what they used to look like, since now one has to move in with them, be thrown together with them in a heap, a pack, and get along, which one's never done before. And that for so long, until the relatives, after life's long journey, which we have to squash into three weeks, will have aged prematurely and look almost unrecognisable. The boat is full, no, not this one. There's no one in it. Plants don't need to absorb any complex chemical combinations such as vitamins or amino acids, which are a must for human beings. In human beings the chemistry has to be right, otherwise they can't produce the glue for their bodies, to enrich their bases and to attract sexual partners with interferon, I mean, with pheromones. By and large people simply want to be rich, they don't want anything more than that. Women, on the other hand, want love, for that more than a dozen chemical elements are required, which then don't work, because one has swallowed too much of all of them. Not even a simple cake could succeed like that. Women in general, they often want to live in a monoculture, that is always allow just one person to cultivate their little field, and so it's always only the same thing that grows there, and that's never enough for the chosen one. Or he doesn't want it, he feels cramped, he wants something else, from someone else. Oh all right, here you have the other thing, luckily we had it in stock. On the other hand, there's also the woman. Isn't she as pretty as a picture? Yes. Impossible to touch her. One particular person would be enough for her, but she can't find him. She thinks this one good and this one, but he doesn't want to. We women waver still, uncertain, which one we should pick. I'll let out the secret: It absolutely must be Mr Right. No one else will do. That can't be so hard, in the lottery you have to get six right at once. And not one number less in the weekly last judgement, the draw on Saturday afternoon. With people the choice is infinitely large, there must be someone there for you, surely? Well, just take him, it doesn't matter, does it, if you become unhappy one way or another, your kind isn't dying out, believe you me. The loins of the foreigners from the Balkans not least will make sure of that, says the former Federal Chancellor. Let's hope he's right. It can't be healthy, to have thousands of possibilities, and only one of them is suitable. The train has departed, no one tells us that over the loudspeaker, a scarf pressed to their face, otherwise one would recognise it and its voice, which in reality, however, belong to a certain Mrs Chris Lohner, present a thousand times over, one can hear her in all the railway stations of the land. But who hears us? Other objections? Good, I object: A fresh plot contains everything, all the nutrients, in sufficient amounts, and if there's a house on it, that's a whole lot more. Very desirable. Before it slips into the hole. It's only a question of time and company-family planning, whether a new mine is opened up right next door, a new hole is dug, oh no, too near the surface once again, we're in any case already reproaching ourselves, for having exposed the people here to such danger, so that we could almost bite their feet from below. There are also voices now, a little a-cappella chorus, which says, the terminal moraine, a peripheral disturbance, has caved in and caused the catastrophe, which was in the making for millions of years even before a drill came anywhere near the mountain. Yes, miners, time also has its questions, although it already knows all the answers. It knows what it means, when something goes simultaneously forwards and backwards, because time is nailed down in space and instead people always have to travel around so much. It knows what it means, when, the moraine misbehaving, huge quantities of water and mud flow into the underground workings of a mine and crush the people there like flies in amber, unfortunately without making them less perishable. The process is a different one. Amber is like a tin can. Mud is, well, just dirt, not made for people to stay in, unless voluntarily, nose up, to check if there's a little air present, which has usually clothed one so wonderfully well.

Earlier it was quite a different day wasn't it, could I have got the date wrong? Gabi's boyfriend washed his car, while Gabi watched him. She was not allowed for example to get up and go away or do something else, after all one doesn't see something so interesting every day, today is an opportunity for a whole car to be soaped and then get a decent shower. Usually it's something reserved for living people. If I sit next to you, I'm very close to you, thinks Gabi's boyfriend about her, who knows her much more closely than that, but otherwise always likes to have her close, and dips in the sponge once again, tirelessly. Only he who knows longing, knows what we suffer, when we see a faster car. But at least ours has to glitter and flash, even without wanting to take a turning. The Governor of Carinthia, Mr Haider, has a real Porsche, but unfortunately it's not here in Styria, where feelings have to put in an appearance in person, in order to overwhelm one. People don't keep their feelings to themselves, but importune others with them.

The mountain does something quite similar. If a person is hollowed out inside, one often doesn't notice it right away, with the mountain one also only notices when ton-weight bits of debris are buzzing about one's ears like flies, or one starts to fly oneself, when one's hardly learned to walk. One's feet slip out from under one, together with every good ground, which is why the mountain should have remained where it was. It stood perfectly well there. It didn't bother anyone, at least not me. More silent than silence, the mountain didn't say a word, except when the trippers fluttered around its slopes, but now it seems to want company and comes right into our dreary house, immediately going off with it as its new chum. Whoever wants to, can leave, I already said so, but not: to the mountain. It can leave, too, as it pleases, or did we give it cause to? We would never have suspected it beforehand, otherwise we would have left it in peace. But where has Gabi gone today, who, in principle, likes to go out, not always with her steady boyfriend, but usually nevertheless, and if not with him, then he feels second best. Admittedly then he's got his car, which is neat and tidy, but he has to sit in it alone. Where did Gabi always get to, when no one saw her? Quite an amount of time, if we add it all up. She can't have disappeared into another dimension and have returned to us unrecognisable, our Gabi, no, she can't have. She has disappeared, trust me on this point at least, even if I once claimed something else. The disco is a temptation, and outside, in the dark, one has to watch out, in case someone grabs the crack between one's legs, someone who is so drunk that he can no longer tell top from bottom, never mind. The woman wants to be free to dispose of herself, so she doesn't let him. And yet, even on the borders of consciousness, the drunk does find a certain spot, always, he whacks the woman on the head, at the same time ridding her of itchy vermin, that's his calling. Him of all people. He's the best thing that could happen to her, he thinks, if he examines himself and her without prejudice. If he's already on the spot, he might as well kill her, because she could have recognised him, who, apart from her, would begrudge him the pleasure. Everything is pleasure, says the television, and this woman in any case loved her figure and her hairstyle more than any human being. But ultimately she was made and nourished for just one man, whom by chance she has already found. Am I not right? This boyfriend is exactly right for her. In future her mother will forbid Gabi to go out without saying where she's going, she must tell her or her boyfriend, that's what she resolves in the course of this very nervously eaten breakfast, in which she pays attention not only to her stomach but also to her inner mother's voice. Later she'll cycle to her shift, sew brassières in a factory, which lies in no-man's land, or already on enemy territory (the conflicting emotions of women, child or work, enmity or servitude, fried eggs or scrambled eggs. It is certainly hard to decide. Fried or scrambled, one wouldn't like to be either, but that's something for the television, where people pour out their being and then don't want to wipe it up afterwards. They wouldn't even have any time to do so, because someone is already sobbing and throwing their arms around one's neck and begging for forgiveness in front of millions of people for something or nothing at all. Well. We're already in the picture. It isn't reality, in it we would still feel the hand that tears us from this life, whereas on TV one just sees everything, it doesn't hurt) between two small towns, a small town and a village to be precise. In the latter there's only a bus stop, nothing else that could attract people, who in turn should attract other people with foundation garments, corsets and bras. Things like that always come in useful, so that humankind doesn't die out, because that's what women got their bodies for, usually square-built like a honeycomb, and the bees have finally gone. How does one put a shape into a body again? The last but one model can be had at giveaway prices and so already sold out. No, we don't have your cup size. Perhaps you can roll around the floor, until you're flat, then cup B will fit you. But this line is also finished, I've just noticed. Ask again in half an hour. So now women are supposed to worry about the underfloor protection, no, the floor protection, as well, so that their body parts can be decently presented. We've got several sizes on offer and recently even in-between sizes. Until the very new sizes arrive and the cutting out machines have been converted. Throughout Europe people are now to be remeasured, because their bodies have changed in recent years. That encourages me, like many writers I'm all too hasty in considering the business of creation as settled, and wanted to devote myself to it in peace and quiet. And now I have to look at it anew again! What a bore. The women working here aren't the dregs, on the contrary, this is sought after, well paid work, plenty of overtime. Mummy is a business and looks at her children. Why are her children so beautiful? Because they are who they've always been, only earlier they didn't know, that one can make oneself beautiful, they believed that beauty is not something made, but something one receives from nature. That would be fine, we would then only have to persuade nature to come over here as well and do its work on us. But it doesn't do it. No wonder, that its stones smash us to pieces, if we give it such insoluble tasks: Making people and then making them beautiful on top of that. Everyone else has to go to the perfume department, so why do we make such a fuss. In every small-town self-service drugstore you can find more beauty than a film star can use up in a lifetime. Nature tries to settle down, but it can't always be the setting for a diamond ring of at least half a carat.

Our Gabi doesn't rely on nature, she has seen too many mean tricks played by nature in this district, without much sweat, but costing us a great deal of sweat. Gabi has accumulated a whole collection of eye shadows, mascaras, foundations and lipsticks, nowadays it's pure stupidity and ignorance, if four-year-olds don't

paint their fingernails, but they do it because there's always someone else who has started, and so they do it, too: keeping pace with
us and our relaxed behaviour. There's always someone else, but
one doesn't like to acknowledge them. After all, that's why we go
to nursery, to remain forever young and still look the same later
on. Until the undeferrable duties come, which take up so much
time, that we don't have time when we need it. So they don't do
like the swallows, who instead industriously build their homes
against old stable walls. So they really have not stolen their
homes, the poor industrious little birds. The work they have to put
in. Children can go where they want, madame, and your child is
already almost sweet sixteen, for the Country Police a case like
any other, in fact not a case at all yet, just wait another one or two
days, we know all about it, a young runaway, an item in the local
edition of the newspaper, of interest only to the inhabitants of
this village or the neighbouring villages. Even in the county town
not everyone knows the sweet name of your little place, and you
really want to know for certain? Where your daughter is? For the
rest of us a quite different calibre of person evades the cameras,
photographic agencies and educational institutions, for example
Princess Caroline with her newborn daughter from Vöcklabruck
Hospital. They escape just like that, a source of concern or of
fun, depending on what's in demand at the time: No, I'm mistaken, it's always for fun, yes, we do something, and we do it
properly from the start, two or more together at a time. It's well
known where they all come from, they are children of the country, of the country disco, where around midnight the sons of the
carpenters (and joiners) and the daughters who are at last going
to see some drilling, get undressed and show each other their juicy
organic pork fillets (hand-reared! No need to stand on the grill
and fall through, it's better on the new beige fitted carpet!),
because they know what they want: big city life, without having to
go there. There are no distinctions at all any more, as far as enter-
tainments are concerned, it's big and beautiful everywhere where
we are, wherever we are. It would be a great help to us, if we

could be everywhere at the same time. And here it is already, your entertainment! They nevertheless feel, I don't know why, constrained and want to get away from here as quickly as possible, and wherever they end up, they get nothing for themselves, the children of the villages, nothing, that someone else hasn't got already. And there's even a legitimate claim on nothing, and it is inevitably made, when even just the first pink nipple flares up in the stroboscopic techno light and immediately fades away in a wet mouth. Chunk chunk chunk hammer the bass lines. And the sons of the Alps carefully filled up to the permitted measure pull their height of fashion trousers, which have already penetrated the most remote mountain valley, but not by themselves, they were too slack for that, there always had to be someone inside them, whom one doesn't know, down below the hips, open, belt buckle! Open up! Where is thy sting, I mean: your tongue? Show what you've got under there! and they show cocks and tits as God made them, mostly not very carefully, once again there were too many people working in the shop, who wanted to grab some for themselves, in the branch of a gigantic megastore. Right, God, you won't get any thanks for this fourteen-year-old already having droopy tits like full vacuum cleaner bags, to make up for that everything else about her is rounded and bulging, oh no, now she's puking at my feet, and now someone's falling down right into the puke, in a moment he's going to drive off again in his car, relieved. My opinion is, it would have been better if God had put in some overtime and created something better. Something beautiful like mountain, valley, a lion and a Jaguar car and a lake and the like and so much music besides, rather too much than too little, always, no, not this lake, don't claim someone else's glory for yourself, someone else made the lake, but as far as I'm concerned, You, God, could have done it much more often. But the lake was made by men, but I don't like them either any more, says God, after all these years they're no longer up to date. They're not the right size any more, and they don't look right either. I'll go and get the new magazine, so that I can do it better. The difference is really not so great, I do believe, that on this point I really am right this time. The people in town and country are becoming more alike at terrific speed, in some countries there is no country any more, people read the same magazines, and they all wear the same things, there are just two companies, which make all the stuff, and soon there'll just be one, which assumes so many names. It is human fate, I've now forgotten what, and some wear it earlier than others, so then it's also over and done with earlier or out of fashion. What counts ultimately is always only all the fine, good flesh, which, since one can't eat it, is again and again and then once more thrown onto the counters in the bars and is downgraded and dressed down, if it doesn't measure up to our ideas. Even the lingerie factory is more generous to us women, who need something different from a man. The bodies have been puffed up in various places by a sensation-seeking press, which shows no consideration for feelings, and feelings just are the spice of bodies. Afterwards at any rate one should take the taxi home, that's healthier for everyone, particularly for the taxi driver.

There go a middle-aged woman, who once gave birth to Gabi, a cheerful teenager, that's exactly what she is, like all the others, a young person, who preferred to be with someone else, no matter who it was, rather than alone, and a young lad, who at the moment is still going to a technical secondary school, hopping from electricity pole to electricity pole (when they've gone rotten, they're butchered and new ones are planted, then new men, whom the country still needed, clamber about on them like squirrels, a Mr Janisch jun. among them, he too already the father of a schoolboy, young as he is. A final squirt of milk, milked from a jolly evening in the dance hall, and after that: intermission, then close-down and curtains), and both together are sticking up notices, which show Gabi's face, a black-and-white photocopy of an original star photo, yes indeed, that's what it was selected for, but was unfortunately returned by the addressee, and now everyone can read it, whether he wants to or not. These photos can't be avoided. It's afternoon, the sun is already decently warm. The drawing pins bore zealously into the tarred wood of the poles, which bear it patiently and with heads held high. At last they are important, not just for light and telephone calls (both essential to a tragedy! In a good light something even worse could happen, and one would see everything quite clearly and certainly immediately pass it on. So we've got everything here, when on TV a man would like to make up with his girlfriend and both of them cry cry cry so loudly, that there's almost not enough power for it). Gabi's mother and her boyfriend knew right away: Something's not right. Our Gabi doesn't simply disappear like that, without telling us where she wanted to disappear to. Life is a crime story, it's unbelievable, all the things that can happen to a person, mostly it's little things, but that's just what one has to have an eye for, because at a second glance people are completely uninteresting. Well, not to me, I live off their diversity, which makes for more work, however. I'm not allowed to declare anyone boring, and if I do, then I have to explain at length why. And why do these two, mother and future son-in-law, have such a bad feeling? Already early this morning. They walk along the route which Gabi usually takes, whether by bus or on her bicycle, even stop car drivers and ask them. The pair of them will end up going on foot to the county town, where the building firm, Gabi's master, is spread out under the vault of heaven on the greenfield sites, which border all our towns, even the least among them, yes, those above all! Only there do the customer and employee car parks cost nothing, because the ground didn't cost anything anyway. Why stand there at all? Dusty road, paper-strewn hard shoulder for dead animals, I don't want to write everything down again and again, that happens here, but I must. From time to time a wreck is towed away. Injured people have to be cleared away, too, they can't simply be left lying there. They leave their blood there, part of it, and the modesty of their possessions, the half-open handbag, keys, well-worn purse, little lucky charm attached, a little teddy bear, at least it's still alive. Yes, when one drives a car, one has to rely on looking, always straight ahead, but also look in the rear-view mirror from time to time, please don't forget!, and one should trust one's eyes, when a truck comes round the bend doing sixty, it means it!, when it comes up from behind, big as ten water buffalo, and takes one on its horns, before one's even heard it snorting. The country roads here are blood roads, and the landscape is the circulation. That's why we're always going round in circles and not getting anywhere, because we couldn't read the map.

Now the flowers go on flowering. No one takes them for a walk without killing them first. But dear hands are already waiting and are held open, perhaps there's a new piece of jewellery as a bonus. She never said anything to me about problems, says Gabi's boyfriend to the Country Police, who would rather follow new paths in traffic surveillance than implacably pursue people on their old well-beaten trails, right into their most intimate spheres. One has to catch them in good time, before they go missing or have been so squashed on the road that they can't even be recognised any more. At the moment local traffic sections are being set up step by step in individual districts which were equipped with the necessary equipment - including unmarked cars! Yes, indeed, just you watch out, something that looks just like you and your familiar little boat through life, which you get into punctually early every morning, in order to bring it to life with a divine spark and a whiff of petrol from the atomiser, careful: a rapacious wolf in a BMW can be hiding there! Since 1991 completely new possibilities also arise from the possible use of laser guns to measure speed. There's one already, who flashes and is not God. It can't be, protest immediately! What do you need a light for, you know very well that you were driving too fast. Big Chief Nimble Forefinger also doesn't need much more than this one finger for the camera gun to achieve a convincing (and lasting, there's a photo as a memento!) success, and the target is always you. So why the gun, we can easily make a rough estimate, that one was doing sixty. No no, it's not so simple nowadays. It was doing seventy-five. The gadget made such an effort. We want to know exactly, and the legality of all measures of criminal prosecution, which were admissible until now, also remain effective when the new police security law comes into force, so pull yourself together! A pretty throat, a pretty pharynx are soon squeezed tight or torn open, with no other tool but the mysterious eye, which finds the area, which death particularly likes to visit for a picnic for two, even if only for a couple of seconds, but that's enough for him. Yes, this is a good place to live, thinks death, this flesh is still new or as good as new. It wasn't expecting me, well, so I'm coming unannounced, and no one knows anything about it. So I can easily come again, since no one saw me the first time. The next time perhaps I'll even come in broad daylight, which I don't need to be afraid of. I wasn't caught the first time, although police patrols with two officers each were in the area providing minimum cover! Luckily death, which was informed in person, knows where each patrol is poking around: I'm afraid of no one and always do the right thing, he says, or he can do it another way - whatever I do, it's always right, I am my own court of last resort, so there's no right of appeal, there's no higher court. I see, how anxiety takes hold of you. You're asking yourself, why does something exist, with which there can be no bargaining, you even bargain in the electrical shop and in the builder's yard, even with the country policemen!, and really do get a lot of things cheaper than you'd thought, just think of your new garden grill, the demonstration piece, on which the demonstrations left no trace. Me, you'll even get for free, but in return, I make everything you bought beforehand completely worthless. So it's better if you don't buy it at all, you're better off buying a candle, a few schillings, it'll be worth it, to someone, just to you! Well, who will do you this good turn, I don't see anyone who would do it. Please have a bit more fun, while you still can, so that you get to know even more people, who will take care of something like that for you. But unfortunately people never listen when they're having fun, even if you bawl in their ear, they're having so much fun.

A way of speaking that's meanwhile out of date, this passage should in any case be deleted, I think, but then the whole thing will be too short. The cries of passion, this bawling, with which the genitals, our subjects, distend, as if they were frogs and were now being pumped up even further, almost as much as their own-ers already are, well, we still have mastery over our bodies, don't we?, so these cries should be adjusted to contemporary usage, isn't that so? So e.g. you can easily dispense with the meaningless courtesy of having to address a country policeman as officer. And then when he forces his cock, lovelessly pulled out of the trouser leaves wrapped around him, between your legs, sweeping aside with his hands the troublesome thighs, and drags you, preferably even before you've grasped who this is, into the bushes, hitting you on the back of the head, so that you are involuntarily forced to lower it and keep your mouth shut, because you can't yet speak German well, the language of our country, the country police-man's thoughts are already somewhere quite different, with someone who stands as solid as a building and isn't thrashing about all the time like you, then, then it's quite all right to call him by his first name and say Kurt to him, where on earth is he? Where on earth are we? Perhaps you haven't even met him yet? That's just too bad. Then you can also go alone into the booth with him, and not to cast your vote, which I wouldn't do if I were you.

4.

Grand, wild water, you fall with little head held high, even if you've already been tamed! Here, where you're just foaming, you haven't even been chlorinated yet for your domestic users, who in the city stand under the shower and want to drink you as well (but they prefer to drink something better, stronger). You tumble down from the slopes of the High Alps, which is where we are now, to get away from us and do something useful, perhaps also undertake something entertaining, one thing at a time, work first, then pleasure, cool and clear, free to your home. The limestone High Alps of Lower Austria and Styria can fall down without you as far as I'm concerned, they wouldn't know what to do with you, but no, that's not quite right, it wasn't here, but right next door: A whole lake together with the shoreside trees disappeared in the limestone mountain range! One gulp and gone, as if the lake couldn't get along by itself, as if it wanted to belong to someone else, to the mountain, a big lake, yes, it made progress, only in a backward facing direction, inside, away from the astonished visitors. And it took away all the gawking trees standing around as well, so that nothing would be missing in its subterranean mountain dungeon. The visitors were left behind. You sweet water you, you are gathered up by the steep forest roads, the inclines, the plastic slopes, the rocks, at first you look enchanting, transparent, glittering, then you turn to mud, become soil, while we, along with you fall into the bottomless limestone pits, but only into the little ones. Here there are no dolinas, which could eat up whole lakes. You have to go further south for that. Water: you come, yes, this, too, along with all the soil into the houses of the area, in order to take a look at what you've been missing, when you decided to remain wild. But they upset your plans there (and you had a sparkling water as well, didn't you? Yes. I ordered it, but it didn't come), when they contained you and sent you down the pipes, with no message except purity itself, for which you first had to be caught and held tight. How pleased they were at first, to have got hold of you in the middle of the alpine pastures, you're always trying to run away. But soon you've become a plain fact, which one can also eat, if one still can't grab hold of it; so of course you were contained, so that, even if very diluted, like all truths here, you could be believed nevertheless.

Here, at the start of the snow line, and soon he will spiral even higher up the mountain, a man in a brightly coloured track-suit is racing along, as if he were flowing himself, a shadow on stones, away from the eyes of the world. If you ask me: No one will very easily outdistance him, after seven kilometres he's still running quite easily. That's typical again: A restless man, who can hardly keep his secrets locked up inside his skin, to make up for that his clothes are a good fit, and they fit him like a second skin. His vigorous ambition, I like it. Yet he is not one of those who want something good in the world. A spirit, who's always negative, except when he sometimes says yes. Fine. His constant dissatisfaction, I like that too. So I put him together for myself and now pass judgment on the result. To each his own. What would satisfy him, now that I don't like so much. So I pass judgement, and my judgement is harsh. He constantly wants to get something for nothing, even if it's a whole house, I certainly believe that. I merely hope, the one he has intended for subjugation, whoever it is, will play along, when the time comes. He's made a contact, which will be important for his future, and he's not going to let go of it again: Something big can come of it: The obedient oppress the submissive. Neither side will get anywhere. This man would even pit himself against the water, if he could find it, but the water has finally been shut up down below, it is itself a very large place, and it flows away, whereas the man is looking for his limits. Nobody is going to show them to him. Wait a minute, now I see the boundaries, they're made of steel, look like railings, and they are transportable. He didn't set them down himself, the country policeman, his colleagues in the capital did that, in front of parliament, to protect the demonstration-free area which the representatives of the people have raised up against the people, in order to show the latter: You're not part of us, but don't worry, we'll represent you anyway. The country policeman's commanding officer announces to this mercenary, so often late for duty, in bitter words, that overtime can no longer be paid, because the regional government doesn't have any money left over for it, and Mr Janisch receives these bad tidings with apparent subservience. Another house less, in three hundred years at the earliest he will have one less. I like that too. The fact that he can accept that. In other respects the man definitely has to be tamed, but no one can do that to his desires. He would need support, because he can't find them, his own limits, and goes unhurriedly onto the wrong track of his being. Well, he won't find the water either any more, we've put that under the earth. The earth a pair of lips that has received it. The man in his persistent angry darkness would not want to lay himself down in that. The water is already there, no place is reserved for him anywhere. The ground even swallows up houses, think of Lassing Mine, which disappeared, and the consequences! The house, almost all of it slipped inside the earth, you can still partly see (the part that's poking out of the pit), if the people living round about let you, you can even see the window boxes usual in the area together with their colourful inhabitants, whose heads are meanwhile sadly drooping. You can still see the very tops of the furniture pieces, dear guests, toys, junk, stuff accumulated over time, but once again no one has time to water the flowers. To do that one would have to leap thirty feet and be able to breathe in mud. The locals don't want any people who find catastrophes beautiful, but now they have a place themselves, to which visitors can travel at any time, just to take a look. And they wouldn't even find this place by themselves, they would have to look at the map and ask the locals, because there, where there is supposed to be something, nothingness has stopped over, to be drunk down eternally at the break of dawn. Only in a more solid house could he feel safe in the long term, thinks the man, despite everything that can happen to houses and that can also happen to one with people. We don't need to make any allowances for people who have disappeared, we won't see them again. Right now the country policeman is planning an extra storeroom in the cellar, under the stairs. If he takes something away here and instead builds something over there, a radically rustic cellar room, for example (the bones of the deceased could easily decorate the walls), then it'll work out all right, and even if it were a hollow space, a nothing, which also needs walls, of course, otherwise it wouldn't be nothing, otherwise the whole house wouldn't exist, which is itself a hollow space and only, like the clearing in the forest, becomes one by acquiring limits, consisting of itself, we place an order for them in wood or stone, and then we sit down inside and make ourselves comfortable. Could that be due to the fact that this man in his intimidating loneliness has long ago: lost his limits and would like to meet someone, who points them out to him again? And this time they should enclose a larger area than before, please. We would be happy, if we could see his face, the face of the country policeman, for once, and not only have it described. Or is he himself the drawer of limits, is there something about himself he wants to forget? What does he need, so that he no longer hides his light under a bushel, but can forever cast it across a well-furnished room? If the room remains quiet, the light will always strike him right between the eyes and then fall on the Persian carpet, just where the cigarette burnt a hole. After all, we got the carpet so cheaply because of the hole. We, however, with our sense of legitimacy, don't have to go so far at all, to find our limits. They are frightful, luckily they are as a consequence watched over by armed guards. It's enough, if we run for three hours, till our tongue is hanging out. But for the half-naked marathon man five hours aren't enough either, then we, he and I, read the newspaper, which doesn't want strangers to cross our borders, unless they book hotel rooms or find, somewhat cheaper, shelter on our farms together with the animals. This last three-quarters of a line, but only that, not one letter more, I can't afford to give anything away, I dedicate to the poor man from Sri Lanka, who yesterday was fished out of the Danube at Hainburg, as the sole survivor, the remaining fugitives capsized with their rubber dinghy and drowned and have disappeared. Heat-seeking cameras have been specially developed, to keep the borders under surveillance. People who are looking for shelter can be identified in the view-finder, even when they're lying flat on the ground. On these human carpets, at least they don't have any burn holes, because in this case we've burnt the whole carpet, we practise our fawning manners, which we require for those strangers, who are to be stroked, slaughtered and gutted. The rest get a good smack around the face and are then eaten by our dear rivers, so they don't cause us any extra work. So here no one slips on carpets of human flesh any more, people are now enclosed like our springs and thrown into grated refuse containers. And then if they throw a fit, a lid gets shoved on top as well. We once again know everything that we forgot about humanity, when we looked at animals and they looked back at us. And we know even more, when we have looked at these strangers through these heat-seeking cameras and they haven't looked at us, because they don't have such cameras. Indeed. Even when they're lying flat on the ground, the strangers, we can still see them: Aha, so there it is, our own, sole border, we'll find it all right, once we have moved it. At least when our partner plays around, we'll certainly be able to show him our limit then.

The country policeman, whom we actually wanted to describe, before we slunk off behind a tree, has a special watch just for running and a pulse rate gauge and a solo gauge that cost a lot of money, oh no, that's not true, they're presents from a woman! With that he could feed one of these poor souls for a week, if he's keen on watches, and knows how to prepare them. The country policeman is informed about that, and his information is very modest: Once the water was still here, right below me. He knew his way around this geo-information system, this hiker and sportsman. This man of the law, his own law of course. Soil, water, forest were indispensable, like him they have an extremely complex range of duties and must not be mistaken, as to what they should do when. Now unfortunately we've lost nature; when we were looking for it, it was a handy opportunity to set things right at the same time. The water belongs in the ground, the forest belongs on the ground, the water doesn't belong on top of the ground, and the forest doesn't belong in the water, otherwise the water overflows, I mean, comes over us. I constantly have to make such decisions with respect to politics, economics and extraction techniques, with very far-reaching consequences, when I want to say something about nature. There's no other way of putting it, because nature doesn't exist any more, so why should it suddenly come back? Just so that I can look at it a bit more closely this time? Nature is the opposite of something, that has something to say to us, although it very often pleases us. That's why we now have to express it somehow, so that everything really does come out. At present nature is nowhere to be seen. Please hand me your efficient planning and decision-making outline, on this basis I shall then be able to write something entirely new about nature, should you in all seriousness expect that of me.

As a child the country policeman sometimes cycled along the stream down in the valley with his father, while the water comfortingly bubbled up from the depths, only just arrived from the mountain heights, and still with the vigour of its origins fairly high up hopped over the stones, its own work, because all water comes out of itself, so it belongs to itself and no one else, and so we have stolen and used it, haven't we? or not? And the son also walked around with his father, I can still remember it myself. His father was friendly, sometimes even kind and protective like a hut up in the Alps, unlike the weather house, one never knows where one is with it, sometimes the girl is outside, then the boy, and it's impossible to decide, which of the two one likes better. There comes the nice thought, that one of them sits down on one's face with their naked buttocks, the legs hanging left and right over one's ears like a pair of cherries, and then sometimes one thinks involuntarily: rather the boy. There's more to him. Perhaps the character of the father, also a country policeman, was a bit lacking in colour. If we're talking about water: To the son the father appeared dull, as if nothing recognisable could be reflected in him, as if his feelings had been impoverished under the pressure of his advancement and the constant performance of his duty, with which the former small farmer's son had to prove himself. Although everything was always there for the son when he needed it, it works like this: Sometimes pay no attention to the child, then again be strict with him, which is only fair, since for a long time one ignores the child, whom one was raising up, until then it falls down the cellar stairs. Keep a close eye on the child, if possible frequently step on his toes, so that his legs grow heavy. That will do him a great deal of good, because he will be able to recognise at an early age the difference in his father's behaviour, in accordance with the Domestic Animal Husbandry Index. Behaviour is fair to animals, if the following points have been addressed: possibility of movement, ground conditions, social contact, hutch or coop climate (air! light! God!) and intensity of care (teacher! cane! stone! scissors!). Points are awarded, and the score should really be higher than 25, if the child is to sit the test and his elders, who, as the word says, are older, are to pass it. As he walks past, the father nods absent-mindedly to you, so, he's not going to hit you, at least not for the next ten minutes. Perhaps he'll hit your mother, because he likes doing that more, but not you. Not yet, this time. Perhaps again the next time. Let's just wait and see. The father has died meanwhile, of cancer. Wasn't he still there, only yesterday, when he had his son read the signs of the shops in town as a reading exercise? The lad looks at what's displayed in the window, then he says the name of the shop. Wrong. But if one can't see it, it doesn't exist, does it? Even forests, though not of course those with a primary welfare function, because they are supposed to protect us, ward off dangers by crushing people, settlements and buildings, which did not comply with official provisions or prohibitions, to pulp. Yes, they come down in person, the forests, if they've got into a rage. Who would have thought it of them? They're not sorry to make you suffer, when your house was standing on this spot just a moment ago! Was the father not nice to his son, who almost jumped as high as the father's parting, when the latter deliberately stood on the boy's toes? The son should please raise his feet when he's walking! Not shuffle along like that on the gravel of the inn garden. When after all one only comes here once a month as a treat. If you think that's nice, then you might just as well regard the struggling bushes in my front garden as embellishments.

The father did well by his son, yet it was always as if he remained in a dazzling, far-off other place, blurred, and that's the way it should be. The child should look gratefully at a photograph of the father to discover his whereabouts: We've moved. New address - Row 14, plot 9. Then we don't need the child for one or two years, because his father is with God. It would be an unheard of event to be able to climb up a ladder for a piece of cheesecake or some other effeminate confection, for a man that's normally a trifling task, a trivial matter. By that I mean to say no more than, and why didn't I say it right away: Every child wants to admire his father, no matter for what, but one doesn't even get business support, no matter for what. The mother has to take care of the rest, that's more than I or anyone else could otherwise ever forget. In the case which unfortunately we have to deal with here (because it won't become healthy of its own accord, now I'll just try a root treatment), the mother was a secret red wine drinker, like so many women in this area. Where the waters don't simply briskly come marching along, but are always plunging down, as I already said, it's not so easy to catch hold of them, then there the wine is allowed to flow freely. The cheapest kind. So, we'll just keep this double measure in the kitchen bench, and then sit down. If we need it and can still stand up, we've got it right away, we just have to raise the lid. Surely our mother will still be capable of rifling her own supplies! The cupboard is big and full enough, particularly if one's seeing double, to open up, so that the whole wine in its bottle-green dress, like a lizard, can slip into her hands and in a flowing movement disappear into a mouth, always the same one. What distinguishes the mother-son relationship? A close relationship would be distinguished by warm-heartedness, understanding and other positive aspects, if such a relationship could be established. Now I have to step back a little, because ignorant as I am I only know about mother-daughter relations, and they, too, are not exactly caressed by the rising sun. At any rate they don't give me rosy cheeks. As a side-dish for everything, except unfortunately all too rarely above us: the sky of an indescribable blue, with sharply defined clouds moving across it and reflected in open, dragonfly-like, gleaming window leaves. A moment ago maternal nodding off drew streaks across the panes, although it's some years ago; stop, there's someone still moving there! I don't believe it! Mummy, you've wet yourself and made your botty dirty, while you were bedridden, says her son more or less to himself. He had meant not to think about it. To really look for something like it, he hadn't meant to do that either. And, because he seems to need to, he continues: I hope life will one day carry me on to someone who's worth it, someone who is at least as precious as the beautiful women coming from nowhere in the l'Oréal adverts. Then again some women are not like mummy. They are more like climbing plants, which cover the wall of a house, hopefully their own, and if one only asks them firmly enough and fertilises them decently, then they yield a crop, and I stand underneath and catch all the fruit, thinks the country policeman.

His father had then removed his mother's soiled underwear, he had shaken his mother out of her panties like refuse out of a bag, the chicken bones are sticking out in all directions - the bag can be used again, not the refuse. Stop, the other way round, away with the urine, the shit, and as always everything that stinks is between the legs. Can they not find another resting place, those two, which would let us, at their centre, be cosily all human, because there at least we would be allowed to be so? That's how it was. And then his mother got clipped round the ears again because she was constantly shitting herself. The flourishing of this woman, the wife of a police colonel, don't forget, seems for an eternity before her actual end to have consisted of dying, and unfortunately God/father, very much against his will, should have put an end much earlier to the lying there in bed above me. You try living on a dunghill and doing exercises at the same time! No one in the village suspected anything of the drinking campaign of the country policeman's mother against herself. Or everyone knew it, because they all do it themselves, and if they haven't got the time for it, their closest family members have to do it for them. I know nothing, but say it anyway. I can still see her now, forcing her tiny great-grandson to get into the pedal boat with her, yes exactly, Patrick, I've just remembered his name again: all alone with his bawling great-granny, screeching abuse, who at this moment also starts to rock the boat like mad. Something terrible could have happened, on another, deeper lake, Lake Erlauf, which would have hardly felt this little burden, but swallowed it nevertheless, it hardly bears thinking about, so I'll spare myself the thought, too. Nothing happened, did it: An elderly woman, a child, and how quickly they're gone again! Yes, this stretch of water, this favourite place close to the Mariazell Mother of God, where one can learn sailing and even diving, wanted to do something itself for once and swallow a little boat as well as a whole lot of pee. It's surrounded by the High Alps and the high mountain springs, and in return it's allowed to eat something from time to time, I just made that up, and the lake would perhaps contradict me, if it could. After the victims had been recovered, the lake would still look beautiful in the newspaper photo, twinkle playfully at us and immediately tempt new strangers, who are supposed to become friends.

In between, however, she always really pulled herself together, she tried to at least, the mother of Kurt Janisch, I have to admit that, one has to be fair. And that's something God would never be; on the desolate plain, in the deep fir forest, on the mountain peaks and in the valley bottoms they all drink, why only the men? No, the women do it, too, but one wouldn't so readily believe it of them. Well. Ever since, all these years, Kurt, the son, wants to build his own paradise, for safety's sake here on earth. It's true that one can save oneself from awkward situations by swimming, assuming one can and just happens to be in the water, yes, swimming, if you have to, but one can't get very far ahead on life's hard path with it. And only what one does oneself is a job well done. In principle he's always been a teetotaller, the country policeman. But once doesn't count, and so this principle should no longer apply to him. And when it happened, that another well-known local drinker chum (yes indeed, in the school of life she sat right next to the mother of Kurt Janisch, take a look, there in the last row but one! And the other rows are almost all occupied by her friends) in the final stages of a liver value-decline lent out her house for a life annuity, and did so to a Mr Ernst Janisch, whom she knew personally - I really can't remember ever having heard a single cry for help from her since her fiancé failed to return from the last war, and that really is very long ago. So country police- man Kurt Janisch, who helped this crooked deal along a bit on the quiet, stuffed his son together with the latter's little clan, three people in total, into this old lady's padded envelope of a house, stuffed them in with a woman who, stamping like a whole herd of animals, walked and still walks, night after night, and anywhere in the house, whenever she happened to think it necessary to control all kinds of evil living creatures, and does so right up to the pres- ent day, yes indeed, she's still alive, she just keeps going! Is it getting too complicated for you with all these old ladies? Don't worry! If you know one, you know them all. Their husbands hammered away, till their hearts came to a stop, and the wives boozed, till their reason came to a stop, because it had trickled out of them. In any case no further inquiries may be made about the life annuitant, so that she doesn't end up in a home and her own home at the last moment ends up in the hands of strangers. But the creatures she's looking for always reliably disappear as soon as they've been caught, that is, of course, only when the old dear pours water, flour, sugar or fat or whatever onto the glowing cooker. Only the spilled and buried memories should never be awoken, those we gladly abandon each time to the fire, when they rise up and want to cook something, an ancient passion, for example, which has long ago ceased to be true. Fire gets rid of everything quickly and cleanly, even things which are not there at all. Only our relatives should stay a while, although only in our memory, and then the worms and maggots, who are allowed to gnaw the bones in peace in the endless mine underground, get them. The relatives in their friendly earthen shell, into which they have been thrown, are somehow not quite as dead as all those burnt almost without trace, don't you think? I think that's the way Christ wanted it, and then he founded our state, so that the peo- ple there can be dead while they're still living, which makes him especially happy, all things, all people belong to him, before and after. They already want to have their death in life. Jesus believes, it's all a performance just for him alone, what a fabulous event! In fact there's only one who's truly and madly for him, an archbishop by the name of Krenn. God promises eternal life, and of course the people here go on living every day, as if it were for ever. That's why they've stashed their savings bank books. Well done. Soon they'll all have to bear names, the dear books, nothing at all can be done anonymously any more. Well done. That too.

The men in the country policeman's family, including the half portion, our Patrick, are on top of it, no flies on them. They still remember all the fun and games from great-granny, but of course when she joined the family the son's wife naturally first had to get used to creatures appearing to a person outside of wood, meadow and TV, real beasts, that aren't there at all. But they weren't on TV yesterday either, so where are they coming from. In future I'll say nothing about great-grandson Patrick, one less!, because he's already got headphones in his ears, a TV tuned in to space channel in front of his eyes and the door locked. Soon he's going to hear, know and understand better music, and follow it, until the car, in which he's allowed to take a lift, will have wrapped itself around a roadside tree. Today sadly he's still too young for that. To accompany all that the old lady wears, in all the abundance of her house, a not exactly impressive negligee. She doesn't need to. Because only in a house is one really protected, outside it one can go for a walk naked and be chased back inside again, for arms and legs and the rest aren't nice enough to be presented to the public; only for the price of a house does one voluntarily face such a sight. So, the rolling thunder, the piercing flash of lighting are on no account allowed to drive in here and stay, as if this were their garage. That is, if one has a lightning conductor, which one should please no longer connect to the water pipe, I don't know why either. It's not allowed.

Now at last it's today again, that's how I want it. Can't you hear?, now one only feels the water's soft approach, like that of the mother, who delivers a blow unexpectedly, while one still has one's hand in her purse or one's own fly, a game that one really wanted to play all by oneself; yes, the water's almost noiseless soles, they absolutely don't need to be the latest model from the shop window, with bold streamlining letting fly, they're always on the move, tirelessly!, the main thing is, downhill, but it doesn't see the light of day any more, the water. It remains hidden from our eyes. There are also tiny offsprings, for the hikers and their water bottles, clumsily feeding into little metal pipes, under which was shoved, lovelessly and with no sense of proportion, a hollowed-out trunk of unprecedented ugliness. Tired trickling, two little corpses, wood and spring, which flow into one another and into the bottles or straight into mouths. Let us not be a fearful band, let us be strong, proud, yes of course, it's my pleasure, right away!, whom one must involuntarily follow, as this animal, a fox, follows the call of the wild. But one cannot also expect the animal to clean up its wilderness itself. That or something like it is what the country policeman's daughter-in-law might be thinking, as she scrubs the hotplate and screws the nappies tight around the old woman, so that the woman doesn't immediately pull them off again. There's a strong smell of burning, of urine and of shit, the dear old sisters whom we know already, they're my favourite relatives. As proof of his inability to do small and unimportant things, the man presents his wife as his partner, who is supposed, if you please, to deal with all of that quickly and odour-free, what else is she and the drugstore there for. The partner should already consider what and how much we're going to have later on, namely the whole little house, plus land, that's how it's put down in the good books at the notary in town, and in the beginning was the word, fortunately not mine, you should be thankful for that. Now that would have been something! Now I've characterised love, I think, as well as I could, love, in which women always think they have to do all the talking. I've got nothing more to say about it now. This time, in a solemn ceremony, I'm going to skip all that sighing and complaining, that goes along with love and that

I bought especially, no one else is going to give me a break. I'd prefer if something as complicated as love doesn't come near me again, let it come to the beautiful and the young. It's only fifteen years or so since it called, please, not again!, I've got nothing in the house. What I know about it really is enough, and it'll be enough for you, too, if you stretch out your arms, to ward off the brutes, whom no one has cut down to size yet (or who have come to nothing), who want to enter you at the wrong end, from art, from piano playing, from the CD player. I and another woman were always so hard working and then that happened. Now we're both older than then, when we were young. Who wants to blame someone, if first he wants a house, to get to know himself and find out what he's actually capable of, of murder, of roughcasting walls, of sanding down floors, of painting kitchen cupboards or putting up new wallpaper. As if one had to shake bones instead of plums from a fruit tree, which is theoretically and practically impossible, so day after day one has to exert oneself in vain, before finally reaping the fruits of one's actions. But one mustn't go too close either, otherwise it falls on one's head. But one has to go up close nevertheless, otherwise one doesn't get anything. Property is the only thing that counts, we are so happy that we got to know it in good time, and that, even if not entirely of its own accord, it has promised to stay with us. But we do have to feed it decently. Property, I know, I know: There are some who don't like the food, and they want to go away again, or the neighbourhood doesn't suit them. Sometimes we lose our heads at the mere sight of property, we're quite beside ourselves, how beautiful this house is and the one over there, too, we'd like it even more, and soon we ourselves don't count any more, we only count it, PROPERTY.

But now swiftly to the other side, to the opposing party, who wants to be loved for her own sake. That's her hobby. What does she tell us, the lady, who plays the piano, and is serious about it? This is what she says: My love, you can nail a mirror to the wall over there, if you like, in the middle of the furniture, which you will additionally choose with premeditation. But please don't go! You can nail the whole house to yourself, but please don't go! I would otherwise have to prepare myself to become lonely. My affection would have to change to disaffection, and it wouldn't like to do that. All my life savings are in this house, I accumulated them, so that I can make myself comfortable one day, when I am no longer young. Now the time has come. I have personally and laboriously raised the house, first when breaking it in and then at the topping-out ceremony, hasn't it turned out well? What am I pleading for now? I'm pleading, don't go! Take the house, but you: stay! At least give me the address, where the house will be put up, once you have taken it! Because I have one or more cata-strophic relationships with one or more awful men behind me, and now I want to be unruly one last time, thank you, and sin-cerely beg you, don't go! Otherwise I've got nothing else left. You can also sell my dear porcelain dolls I've been collecting for years, some of them presents from my old piano teacher, I must call her again some time, but I don't feel like it, I only feel for you, so you can sell all the dear things, if you like, because, as you've been say-ing for a long time, they only take up space, which afterwards you will make up with me. If only you stay here, by my side, you're surely not a man who's afraid of relationships? No, that won't be you, because in this magazine it says that it would express itself quite differently, and you never express yourself at all. You surely won't be the kind of man who admits to having made mistakes and talks about a shared future, without there being one? No, that won't be you either. If you like, it's all right by me if you break through that inviting wall over there, it seems, just like me, to have virtually invited you to do so, it seems, like me, to be calling to you: I would like nothing more than to cave in, and if I survive that, I would like to marry you, and then I'll be so happy, that on the other hand I could die. We lonely people also like to flee into seclusion, but we are then so happy when, like refugees, we are allowed to come out again, even if only to go to prison. You can smash a hole in the wall with the sledge-hammer, if you want, even if then the hole doesn't lead anywhere, do it do it, just to love me even more. You'll never understand me, but you must not forget me nevertheless, and you can knock down the wall over there right away as well, I don't mind, you don't even need to ask me, if you want to do it, please do it. Knocked out by the effect on my poor wall, I'll sit there but not for long. Soon I would want to come again, like a child to the heavenly Father, to whom all children are allowed to come first of all, so that He can give them His Kingdom. And you are also very welcome to build a conservatory made of thermoglass onto the garden front, but then, however, one won't be able to get into the cellar any more, because the steps would also have to be walled up. So you'll have to think that over and look at the plan once again, but instead you can break through a door at the rear, by which you'll be able to come straight into the house. You will, however, be unable to reach the ground floor from the cellar, because you have got rid of the proper door. Where on earth is the architect's plan, I can definitively prove to you that I'm right, only I can't find the plan now, what does it matter, who needs it, why do we have to go down to the cellar, and what do we need plans for, we're already fulfilling them before we have them. After all, we found each other without any plan. At a crossroads, quite naturally. Simple and natural.

Please don't go! Don't go! Something like that crossed my mind, as soon as you arrived. I would otherwise have been dismissed too humiliatingly, if you had gone away. Without giving me the reason. Tell me why! I open my mouth to my few remaining women friends, and then, after long streams of tears, oh no, now some have got onto this leaf, that fell from no tree, it is, rather, part of what was once tree, I shut up again. I open myself up, in order to experience something, and then I close myself again. It's all a boundless realm, but not my realm, it is the realm of thunder and cries, of the roaring foam and of the clouds falling like atomic mushrooms, no: rising clouds beneath which the camouflaged lover can proceed resolutely against his enemy (likewise a lover, like him!) and claim to have been sent straight from heaven to his partner, with an incomplete address, however, and there's something not quite right about the partner either as things stand. But the missing part of the address was completed by the Santa Claus Post Office, why then is what I do and say not so well received? In short, this vast realm is the realm of converted detached and apartment houses. So that people will at last be happy, they should now all rise simultaneously from their places, to look for their very own way, and then they after all just go home, where they can do it with each other in peace and quiet or with somebody quite different or have to wait, until someone calls up who would like to do it with them. Never mind. They'll always need a house for that, a house keeps its value. A body decays. There are many with whom it rankles, that they don't yet own this or another home. Love and passion can bear simply everything, but they can't get along together.

The headwaters of the mountain spring water cover 600 square kilometres, I call that almost boundless. A lover like this man is not, a lover like she is, should learn, it's the best way to start, that if one wants to be happy there are always boundaries, even if at the moment they still seem to be far away, and that one shouldn't cross them, if one really isn't the water in person. Otherwise sooner or later one ends up in the swamp, which the water, however, has also made, when it had nothing more useful to do. Now such nimble, pleasant creatures live on this treeless terrain, pleasant!, because they are so small and one usually doesn't have to see them, the plants alone, sweet grasses, reeds, sedges (what is that? Please write to me without delay, if you know!), bulrushes and cat's tail to gnaw at, I tell you: a paradise! All these plants are rooted in water-logged soils or at least ones that are flooded from time to time. Have I promised you too much, when I promised there would be something happening there? Take a look at all of it at your leisure. You can nevertheless not turn into water or only with very very great difficulty, but I can understand, that is what you want now. You can only become dust for the time being, if you like. You don't have to thank me, I've saved you something there, everything that comes in between, you know. At best, if one is brave enough, one can melt at the sight of another person. What, not the thing for you either? You're more someone for processed cheese slices in the handy tear strip pack? If you were fluid at last, then many of these creatures would frisk around beside and in you, you would see them at last. You could become a place to spend the winter! What do you say to snow geese and other water-dependent birds of passage? Or would you rather be a breeding ground? Herons, coots, cormorants? You would never be alone again, I can whisper that to you, but you won't hear me. These creatures always cry so loudly. It would be a preparatory exercise, a little bit of a change, to be as sweet as this Claudia Schiffer (you, who in time to come will step in here, there won't be many of you, but I have to tell you that she's the only woman in the world who during this period of time will not be covered up by the rain of self-hatred), liked by everyone, if I only knew how it's done. But even more I'd like to know how one manages to look like that. Watch the snow, when the sun kisses it, it disappears for sure, but how good it feels at the same time! I'm telling you, it feels like it's in clover! That's exactly how you have to do it. Forget yourself! Only a short time ago, you thought you satisfied yourself, not some pictures or other, what picture should human beings present, after sport has finally finished with them? There you sat, pedalled away, hopped in a sack, ran as if new born, fresh off the treadmill and the rowing machine, and you grew hotter, grew tired, careless, aha, you've forgotten to turn off the stove in the sauna and to bring those legs together, that belong together. You brought others together. What, in your health club there's a guy standing there at the juice bar and giving you a wave? Unbelievable. His BMW is already waiting outside? It's incredible. Then you must be under twenty-five or live near the city boundary, so that, if he had come from out of town, it wouldn't take him too far out of his way to drive you home. And exactly there, in the fitness shop, but which is really a people gallery, this exciting man has just turned up, long hair, naked to the waist, short trousers, an isometric drink is dangling from his waistband or it's sticking out of his back pocket, and there you've found a man, whom you now have to listen to attentively, a figure bathed in light, and yet to a great extent innocent when it comes to his appearance! That's just what I don't understand! Hard to believe. Well, I don't know what his limit is in weights. Someone to whom you have to listen attentively, whether you want to or not, and although he doesn't even want to talk to you. As he does so, his eyes roam restlessly around the room, looking for something better. Never really paying attention. Oh dear. A considerable degree of harmony between two people, a good strike rate, everything is just right. But then: He made my thoughts go completely in the wrong direction, a woman says to me now. But I'm not listening to her either. What am I saying. I'm telling you, each time one duly heats oneself up again for life, even if all the vitamins have meanwhile unfortunately been killed off by the frequent reheating. There we sit in all our cause and effect, desperately embracing the other, as if he had ever been even a little hot for one; it's embarrassing for me to say so, but at the moment I find the water and his homes much more wonderful than your feeling, which you wrote to me about yesterday, and which, as I see with some disappointment, is smaller than you made out to me, because you're still alive; at any rate this feeling is certainly smaller than your apartment. How otherwise, in all its protectedness, could it survive next to you? That's what you would like, isn't it? To be protected. The big one. You won't do it for less. How on earth did this man hit upon me, this woman asks herself and the one over there, too. She is afraid of being completely alone, because everyone has turned away from her, and above all, she's afraid of having lost a terrible amount of strength with the man, before she will even have got him. Kurt Janisch. If he were human, he would feel sorry, that the woman would give up years of her life on the spot for him, because she believes that when he appears, the heavens open: One gets in, but one doesn't get out again. He only wants her house, after all, yet how small it is beside her feelings! But he doesn't know that yet. And when he does know, it'll be too late. How frail is man, high up on his population equivalent, which he produces, calculated from the daily accrual of commercial and industrial waste water, which largely does not concern him, and his domestic waste water (dishes, baths etc.), which certainly does concern him. Why does one not simply go to sleep and dream? I don't know, but thank you very much for showing me this possibility. What is so wretched about me, that I can only be used for writing? But still, I'm well out of it, compared to you. Because such a quantity of feeling can't be described at all. So no one is going to reproach me, if I can't do it either. Like many other colleagues, one would have to make do with water, if one wanted to work that out. Fire is OK, too, but it eats up too much, too quickly. It leaves nothing behind. Water leaves more, it has brought so much along, principally trees, boulders, mud etc. Love, please, you take over! Otherwise I have to do that as well. Well then, I'll jump right in feet first, because I never look where I'm going anyway, sweet mistress of language that I am, it loves me at least, now where's she got to? I can't even hold on to it. Puke. Retch. Here are a couple of names with which I would like to do that too. You can think up the names yourself, one of them could well be yours.

So far so good. Without pumping, therefore, the water drops through brick conduits and galleries to the city, where it is forced into the bunker, I mean the reservoir. We've given our promise, but the reservoir has to keep it, without reservation. How should we talk about someone who kills out of love, himself or others or no one at all, or for some other reason, which I, because I have to speak, jump after, like an angler with his net, when his catch threatens to slip off the hook and escape. We shouldn't allow ourselves to be carried along by happiness, rather by the air under an aeroplane or of course by our dear water, please, there it is already, fulfilling its duties, answering the call of nature which it itself is. Water, of which I ceaselessly talk and sing, that glittering whirling mass, which after a few lines is already so close to our hearts, furthermore water has more solid props than our feelings. Our feelings say, if you really love me, then you will do that and that and that as well. No talking back.

Without much pumping of the heart and puffing, the fit country policeman, at the moment not on duty, otherwise he wouldn't be here, continues to set his sinewy legs in front of him, always one after the other, and the forward body always goes a little way ahead, uphill, where one's feet never like to rush ahead. They can't, because the body doesn't want it, it has its own sense of rhythm. Every person has to follow his own body after all, which is his guiding star in the darkness. He appears on his own stage, the country policeman, but he's so quick that he's hardly appeared before he's disappeared again and has turned up somewhere else, two feet, two and a half feet, three feet further on, not much further, hurrying, almost involuntarily, as if this subterranean water was carrying him away on its shoulders. That it can do so, we know, indeed, this very water here, in this catchment prison, which rumbles underground and once fumed and foamed above ground, when someone threw something in, which didn't belong there. Nevertheless, it was immediately carried away by the tireless force of nature, constantly making unscheduled reappearances, and when we see it, it's as if it had never been gone at all. We always only see it for brief periods of time. Now one only sees, built into the rock, the water's little house, in which it, unfortunately enslaved, yet full of energy, romps around and which it wants to get out off, no not out, it wants, as always, to go downhill, otherwise we would need a pump. And we humans have exploited this quality of plunging water, as we exploit everyone and everything, that we lay our hands on. Now it has a reason to perform its duty, soon it will admire on TV the plates and cups of the good-looking neighbour, which were washed up with it plus a very special liquid, blessed be its name. One spent so long persuading it, yes, still the water, of its usefulness, and now it really does believe in it and, in order to make a career for itself, abstains from loud roaring, rushing and foaming. These three words are good, I think, we'll hold on to them as long as we can and then recycle them when possible. We mustn't repeat them too often, otherwise we'll be reproached with that, too. And if we say, it's intended to make all the hard things we have to experience go down smoothly, that it's for an inner creature, that in a certain way also has quite a hard time of it, because every time it wants to kill, it gets a pailful over the head or the turned up garden hose in the face, then once again no one believes us.

For his age, but then again he isn't so old, he's in the prime of life, Kurt Janisch is in very good condition. After all he trains to stay that way, he's already done his stretches today, he usually does that at home, in front of the mirror in his parents' bedroom, perhaps to check whether he's still there in the mirror which is firmly fitted into the wardrobe which already belonged to his parents. There has to be a mirror in every house, and if it's too small for our height, then a bigger one simply has to be put in. Strange, such a good-looking man, married, R.C., and then he doesn't like to do his stretches in public, although people would like looking at him, no one would be biased against him. At home, there he likes to look at himself, sometimes endlessly it seems; so where does this aversion to the unknown, but even more to the people he knows, come from? He always does his running in more out of the way places, which he all knows in his sleep, he grew up here, after all. Glances turn to follow him, involuntarily, of men and women, under the firs and pines and larches, often glances of strangers, who are on holiday here and among whom ill-humour because of the weather and the people, with whom one can't have a conversation, but who are fitter than oneself, who only has three weeks in the year to make a proper go of it, is at all times very much in fashion. But at a table with a decent mid-afternoon bacon snack and a large wine and a couple of glasses of rowan berry schnapps good sense soon evaporates and is replaced by senselessness. One can also knock it back at home with a roof over one's head, above all if one's a teetotaller, but, as already mentioned, the country policeman doesn't like the glances of strangers, which he easily takes to be disparaging. To him they're like slaps in the face, which really he should be dealing out, glances, which make his body inwardly devour itself as if of its own accord in a kind of shame, yes, that does occur to me, repeatedly: devour. It's really true, what the poet said: Shame always outlives one, no matter whether one's inclined to it or not, and inclination's always downhill anyway. There's someone who only wants to be away, cleared away, and yet does everything, in order to be there. Someone who wants to plant his house signs in the landscape like totem poles. They are supposed to stand and speak for him, because he doesn't like to do it himself, although women in particular are constantly demanding it of him. Their wish is that through speaking their interesting personality becomes even more interesting, that it will be interwoven as if by a glittering lurex ribbon. Something flashes, what is it? Oh, I see. It's the pullover, not the gold filling. They first want to go through many mouths, women, conduct amusing verbal skirmishes, but then again they want to be stilled, when e.g. someone takes the lips of their vulva in his mouth, sucks them briefly and then bites them as well, which wouldn't have been at all necessary, but one liked it nevertheless. Yes, please, once again, please, next week as well and the week after, until nothing more is left of us, that's just what makes it so especially good. That's love. The country policeman would now rather look for a roof, under which he would like to go up and downstairs. And the car, it stands on the parking place that goes along with it or in the garage. The country policeman has covered a large part of the garden in cement for his car, although his wife would have liked to grow flowers there too. Now only a teeny weeny patch is left for something so superfluous. The rest is paved over for eternity, even if the mother earth below has long been healthy again and would quite like to breathe again. So the country policeman's wife only has this narrow strip left for the flowers, but boy, there the double-blooming garden plants throng together, de luxe models only, it's something she has achieved by her obstinacy, the patch of garden is her hobby. At the garden centre the grower has all the plants looking three times as thick as they would normally be produced in nature, only in the garden catalogue do they turn out like that, creations of God, notorious for putting a gloss on things; I would not have thought that a civilian, who is not God, can bring forth such plants, but I see it's possible, nature really puts up with it. Yes, I could love such plants, but they only exist twice, once in the catalogue and once again in the front garden fragment here, so that people can see them, yes, that's part of it, what do you mean see?, but of course!, through the gaps between the fence posts or over them. A woman is different. A different woman would be different again. This woman wants her work to be admired, she is not the secretive type like her husband, quite the reverse. She's happy, that she can make a fuss about her garden, which her women friends admire, which, however, she is not allowed to have, she only has neighbours. Her husband doesn't like to see her gossiping with them, nor does he like to see what others see or have, precisely because they have it and he doesn't. He prefers to see, if it's true, that this woman is clinging to her possibility of existence, or whether perhaps she would let go, if one talked her into it. He doesn't want the consequences; he's so mistrustful, he doesn't even trust the sunbeams, which descend on his wife's garden like an army, one that doesn't destroy, but brings fruitfulness. Yes, that's where it rises, the dear sun, over there, go on, take a look, it's free, but put on tinted glasses first. Not a speck of weed between the larkspurs and the columbines, which both equally look as if it isn't really them. To me they look like rare orchids. How does the woman do it? She could win prizes, but she wouldn't be allowed to, unless they were paid out cash. This garden is like a wonderful silk cloth, preciously woven in the most marvellous colours, so beautiful, just fantastic. In front of it a solid gate, at the sight of which one would prefer to get lost, in order to be saved by it. Others would like to be transparent, so as to be able to ooze through the fence and have time to read the notices, which were stuck into the ground beside the plants, where on earth did Mrs Janisch buy them? With the husband nothing would be any use. Although: He's not really shy. It is as if his body were a language, which he himself has first of all laboriously to learn, while others already know it. There are others who sometimes even speak themselves as a foreign language, and then they don't understand themselves any more. But it doesn't bother them, because occasionally they like to find out something new about themselves, and regret that it will never be in the papers. They say to themselves: How could I have married this or that woman. They wake up between the legs of someone, whom they've only just met, these brave people. Today they are in charge. Yes indeed, these decent, hardworking and competent people have become a power in the land nowadays and I wouldn't like to get in their way, if I were you (I think I might be able to do it!), unless you were sitting in a shiny Jaguar, like the one which the new Minister of Justice would like, and I would like too, gone all gone! The minister is already gone, too, and a new one took his place. The country is called: Austria. Get to know it properly or get lost! The country policeman at any rate always knows where, but not who, he is. Instead women want to get to know him better and even better. He wouldn't care, their building plan would be enough for him. Then nothing would be unfamiliar to him any more. Nothing would have to be fought against any more, one could offend everyone, and one wouldn't even make enemies. Everyone would be like us. Like us. The country policeman thinks little or a great deal, depending on whether it's necessary. But he doesn't say much, and if he does then his mouth moves as if held in place by a steel bracket, that's how greatly he restrains himself when speaking. He can hardly get his mouth open, not even for a greeting. Can it be, that women find something like that really so interesting? Because they don't listen properly to what he says, and in no time at all he can rise to be their hero (and not a zero, well it's a rhyme, if not a good one), because heroes never have to say anything and can just hit one in the gob? Perhaps. They know how to speak at any rate, that's something that women can already do, they don't need any previous knowledge for that. They manage it, even if they've never gone to the university of life, which one begrudged them, because they had one or more brothers, who in turn would have died in the hell of dissatisfaction, if they hadn't been allowed to study. They never finished it off. Studying. But look, this woman here managed it under her own steam. How peacefully she carried on her modest dealings for decades! Playing the piano, what do I know. She had already conquered heaven, before she showed up here, and brought heaven with her, to fit it into the jigsaw of the mountains, in exactly the right place, well, here it also has fresh air right down to those lying at the foot of the mountains as well, who all wear sturdy Goiserer boots, which, as the name suggests, come from Bad Goisern as do only a few of the chosen of this world. It's a small place, we can't all come from there. Only Little Jörg H., he can. Back to heaven. First, this woman had been looking for heaven for a long time, probably she mislaid it, but that's precisely what it isn't: a floor. And now, hardly has she found it, she has immediately invested it in a certain person. Unfortunately he, too, has meanwhile got lost, without the woman having noticed. This man and in a way world peace and in many ways music as well and reading: her hobby, these things had all been the stuff of her life. Now it is nothing but this man alone. Patience, I'm running too far ahead. I'm not going to reveal my whole army to you already, it stands on clay feet anyway, but not in China. What does patience mean, everyone's already gone to sleep. Why did I start sticking the twigs and flowers on it, which were caught by chance in my camouflage net? So that you wouldn't see everything at once, which you've seen coming, and now you've turned me off. A flick of the wrist was enough. Before I could get around to the business with the apprentice and Mürzzuschlag, and you could talk and smile about my many earlier remarks, which today I bitterly regret.

I hear music, it's like my wasted life, one hears it from far off, the music of life, and a moment later it's faded away again. I can't do any better unfortunately. At least be quiet when you get up, and go home, any book lying there will be able to do it better.

They often cling to him, women to the country policeman, like the members of a society which has a code of honour: stick at it! But he always makes a particular preselection, this man, before there's real fun and games with the women beneath the foaming clouds, before a thunderstorm, behind the dance floor, up on the rocky slope, where the last fruit trees are almost lost amidst the boulders and startled by the first frost shed their fruit, before it could ripen. The women who have left their cars on the windswept lower mountain car park (here there's a panoramic view, and further up another one, where in the wind the flags crackle) and threw themselves into the mountain wind, who crouch down among the dwarf pines to answer nature's call, except when they can hear someone, at the same time panting in fits and starts, because they're not used to such a gradient, in short, these women have become ripe for love, without yet having found the pleasure of harvest, which is what they themselves are, these red-cheeked commanders, who have lost their whole army, on their way ahead, doggedly, to the peak. They nod to every passing hiker, a little shyly, almost embarrassed, and no one notices that there's only one whom they mean, who has sent them a special summons for today. Now they want to comply with it, so that he can look important, which appears neither advisable nor necessary to me, because ultimately they will lose everything, instead of getting even one bouquet. There's no doubt about it, there's one man they particularly like, but they don't admit it, the women. He's a country policeman by profession. They shouldn't do it, commit themselves to this person's charge, of all people, and sign on the bottom line as well, so that they may be bound accordingly at any time, in an oath of disclosure, by which they swear, Jesus appeared to them and told them that they will certainly find happiness with this man. With him. They only have to renounce all others. Such men have already arrested mothers of small children at red lights and simply abandoned the children to the traffic and nothingness, the rattle of the salvoes of headlights on the wet asphalt. And if they throw themselves into his arms, although I've warned them, the women, then they should at least finish it before the glue is dry, but in his place now, the wall, on which they wanted to hang his picture, is vanished, simply gone. Their affection should turn to disaffection, I think, while they still have time. Unfortunately it's again and again enough for the women, that they're given a feeling, afterwards they can no longer tell, whom they showed it to. In any case, suddenly it was gone, who had it last? Unfortunately I can't remember that any more now. No matter, the relationship carries on, the tensions with the family also grow, one is called unstable and doesn't know why, because he's the one, as sure as night follows day. One doesn't doubt: a love and doesn't entertain: a suspicion. There is someone who reads her and doesn't even have to turn her over, because he already knew her inside out. One day it could be too late, how often have I written this sentence, and it's still good. It's indestructible, the sentence. Unfortunately, I always have to say, when it's too late. This time I can't say so yet, but I have a bad feeling. Well and good. Here's my clock, right in front of me. Writing, that's taking a sledge-hammer to crack a nut. Silly cows, women. All of them. Above all, the educated ones (at least I'm not one of them), as a man I once met who specialised in deceitful promises of marriage personally assured me. But they squander themselves precisely because they think it's all too late for them. Who would promise marriage, if he could also get on the train without it, and get away with other people's anonymous savings bank books, you see, and these are people for whom the train would even wait!

Not the other way round. Instead of women in their maturity beginning to save and to be economical. Every decent litre of wine knows that it improves with age and roughly how much it will cost. Do you know what a care home will take off you? You, and everything you own as well, and your children have to pay the rest, who will be up in arms, that they have to raise so much money. What, you didn't know that? One can't really say squander with respect to these women. They rashly expend themselves, but at the same time want to hold onto themselves and even pocket a juicy profit, because they've still got a couple of things to take care of in future, intimate care included. Things which they believe someone needs. First locked up then cared for by staff in white coats. That's what we needed.

The country policeman is always all ears for himself, he has nothing and no one else. He needs no one. Everyone gets what they deserve. But you say stubbornly, they're not getting what they deserve, just feel for a moment, or listen! Not even money is so self-seeking, that it could simultaneously expend and hold onto itself. It casts out a little beyond itself, what is it?, like a fishing-line, is that not a gold fish on the line, still as agile and amusing as in the old film of the same name?, never mind, whirring and unreeling itself it races across the countryside, this female self, yes, now I see that it's a proper self, which only in recent years, since there's been a special ministry for it, now unfortunately done away with, has been used to making decisions of its own, and was even encouraged to do so by the newspapers. And then it does catch on and decides in favour of one who's caught its eye, where it's an irritation and causes tears to flow, and bit by bit he destroys everything again. He doesn't even need an argument to do that. It's enough for him to be there. I'm fighting to get you, says the woman. No thanks, that would hardly have been necessary, says the man. He's someone who quietly makes his contacts: houses, property, gardens, apartments. He's not been very successful so far, but in a very short time he will perhaps nevertheless rise to be the hero of a whole fleet of houses. On his steamer, there he'll be admiral. Traces of blood in the stairwells? We'll wipe them away, what does it matter. Traces of sperm in pubic hair that belongs to a dead woman? Oh dear. We should have thought of that beforehand! It would have been a good idea, when we squeezed quite lightly on the nerve centre (situated at the bend of the river of the carotid arteries) of a desperate girl, what if we left behind usable DNA material, like the single hair in the case of the notorious pencil murder of St Pölten, which perfectly matched a particular person? No, because we no longer know how the hair found its way into the files. Since this time no intercourse took place, we needn't have any worries in that respect, this time only her mouth and his hand moved, slowly, over her throat. Several women have already disappeared in this area, I just wanted to say that, no one knows where they got to, a new age is starting, and once these women, too, made a new start, going somewhere, hitchhikers, mountain walkers from other countries, a widow, who lived alone, I've no idea where they all are now. Once a skeleton was found in the forest, which had a woman's stocking wrapped around its neck, a lot of it had been dragged off by animals, there was too little left for the forensic doctor. The hair on the skeleton's head, traces of it, like the faded colour of a lioness, no idea to whom the hair belonged. A human being is kept upright by energy, and in this case or another one, that has now been switched off. Wasn't hard at all. But before that, only three days before, then e.g. this desperate women, her head thrown back, had her cunt clamped round a cock, as if she never wanted to let it out again. What did it lead to? Ultimately it led out again. Such a feeling of love, she had really got hold of a mousetrap there, this young woman, the man under her couldn't get out of his car seat. He almost got into a panic. First she gently guided him into her, and then he thought he wasn't going to get out again. As if she wanted to clutch at a strange, quite new possibility of existence, that's how furiously that evening she threw herself on him, who is in reality inviolable, and sat herself on that thing, which as ever with him was standing straight up. No chance of resistance. The woman launched herself at him, pulled out his cock without further ado and used it as a guiding thread inside her. Yet when it was inside: yawning emptiness. Where can a person find his personality, if he doesn't have one, to fill the gap? Then strangers often have to fill the gap and pay a high price for doing so. And if these strangers don't want to pay, then one has to add on something oneself. You can die doing it! That is the law of pornography, even if one can't read: Out and in, and after a couple inches it's curtains again. It doesn't go any further. It could possibly go better. Every door can do it with me, every pencil in my breast pocket, so why shouldn't the two of them not manage it with one another? With the man it didn't perhaps happen quite voluntarily, he didn't have any great expectations, I think, but young flesh is a party, which cannot be so easily ignored, as when for example it puts in a noisy appearance, in crowds, for Mr Haider, and it wants to have music, too. Most, however, play their music against this gentleman and have fun that way. Later we wiped out the young woman's vagina with a rag from the boot, and this rag will surely have left behind fibre traces, we simply threw it into the bushes, but a couple of miles further on, no unfortunately we dropped it, where we happened to be standing, oh, if only we could remember! If only we hadn't been so lazy, to get rid of the rag, that would have been better, so that no impression of the indescribable stupidity of the wrongdoer would arise. There are already a whole number of Tempo handkerchiefs lying around there, which are quite stiff from everything they've already had to swallow in their lives. But the most important piece of evidence in this tangle of pubic hair would certainly be these stupid fibres. What use are they, when the cloth that goes along with them cannot be matched with a human being that goes with them? They are of use, when the sperm adhering to them can lead to an arrest, if, after mass screenings, it can be assigned to a particular man. And with the secretions, which are adhering right next to it, one can then also lay hands on the woman, who was firmly tied up in her plastic sheet, wait, no, we've got the woman, it's only her murderer we haven't got yet. Well, I think, they'll know immediately who the woman was, her photo is still pinned to the poles everywhere. Apart from which, everyone here knows her. The man, therefore, must go back to the scene of past pleasure, if possible even before shop-closing time and the body being found, and search the bushes. The rag has to be disposed of somewhat further away, and, who knows, perhaps there are older traces, on paper, which point to him, to manual use by the country policeman. It's no fun. The man will have to root around there in the dirt, pick up the rag and get rid of it. Otherwise his colleagues would take this rag to the laboratory. The man is tired. He's run out of juice.

No, not quite yet, I can hardly believe it: His cock is almost sticking out of his fly again like an inquisitive child, if he only thinks about it. About all the women and what it's done with them, and what it still wants to do. It seems to have liked it, it wants to know, what became of this girl, by whom it was mischievously, almost shamelessly handled. But it knows. This man is incorrigible, no efficient planning and decision-making structure applies to him when he follows his cock, which would like to harden and attach itself in someone, but doesn't have its own hook. At some point the women fall away, and then he falls out of them. Every night, as he falls asleep next to his wife, lonely and alone, he shakes his penis, his maypole, which is allowed to remain standing all year long, and there's still something hanging at the top, astonishing. To the man, it's as if this shaking passes over into his sleep, it must be so, because at some point there's peace, when sleep at last also condescends to catch sight of the tireless ones. Now we've painted such a nicely deviant pattern of behaviour on the wall. I can't bear to part from it. One can collect as much information about people as one likes, but the police, the investigators, see principally what they get their hands on, but never more than the surface. The rest is for the refuse collection. The police psychologist with his lopsided profile of the criminal really should go back to art school and produce a new one. The outcome of the search, the dead woman we've found, wait a moment, we don't have her yet, but we'll soon bring her in, yet the core fantasy, which triggers the killing, unfortunately we can't find that, because we don't know where at all we should look for it. This man is wild, but left to his own devices, others have a room with sport and hobby apparatus instead and are also content with that. It's no wonder that the psychologist can paint this room for us at any time, the room really needs it, too. Here's a man who since childhood has been engrossed above all else in his faeces, but understandably he doesn't make a show of it in public, he's not a dog after all, and so we can't observe him live. No camera would stay with it, and they are simply there always and everywhere. A pity, we've never seen anything like that. But soon we'll have a new TV programme instead, in which the murderers will be allowed to have their say. Then a childhood is marked by the death of an alcoholic mother, the interpretation is risky, however, since everyone here boozes, though not all with the same consequences, but the son's skin, stamped blue all over by this creeping death, will never be found again. Only slipperiness will be found and cold and rejection and hunger, but after something else, no idea what, and a sticky rag will be found, not, however, what was lying underneath it. The big roll of plastic will fit one woman like a glove, as if she had been poured into it. It seems the forest floor alone was under the unimmaculate cloth. Nothing else. You know, something terrible happened! And already the memory of a dead woman is linked to weeping which never ends, with fear of darkness, and right next door a woman has died again, not quite voluntarily, not of love, but nevertheless. It wasn't her fault, but she had become party to the invisible struggle of a furiously nail-biting consciousness against its owner, who is likewise a kind of anxiety-biter. He snaps, before there's even any need. So that later on nothing else can happen to him. The nipples and labia of several women know all about that, they can make a discordant song of it, but they don't necessarily sing it at the choral society, but off the marked piste, and so one knows nothing of the other. It seems to me that as a result this man I'm talking about is all the more concrete, also more alive to the women he meets. They think they know where they are with him, they have felt love's hot breath, the desire of hot teeth, and this crescent-shaped bite proves it to them, in case they've forgotten, my God, how it hurts now, earlier I didn't know yet that it was going to hurt so much, when I tenderly permitted, no, asked for it. Except these women appear to confuse the house of their body with something that is decidedly more permanent: solid stone or made of the more dainty insulation bricks. Not bad either. They can't compete with that. A matter of taste. So they have to hand over their little house oven-ready, so that it can be done up at last, so that washing can flutter outside, but not their washing, flutter as cheerily as a song, that can go round the world all by itself, one only needs to turn up the radio. One would rather be turned on oneself. The wounds have to be disinfected and cooled down with bags of ice. That's what happens when one holds the head of someone desperate to one's breast: Either he cries, until he gets terribly on one's nerves, or he right away bites you. Someone who owns nothing will at least be interested in their property, if in nothing else, think these women, and how gladly they would immediately like to give away themselves and all their property as well, so that they will very soon awake in the light, in the wonderful light of love, that pours from a person who has swallowed, no, not a pot plant, but a pocket lamp. And he is now her sun. For the man they would be the filling in the Swiss roll, so to speak, so light, so fine, with their property wrapped around them, and in which they have wrapped the man, hm, tasty! That's how they imagine it. Until the women no longer know where they are at all, and they suddenly have to dispatch themselves to a lawyer, to have it explained to them and to see who or what, if anything at all, comes back to them after a while, after, attested by a notary, they have surrendered their property to someone, who will not have been worth it. Doesn't matter, it was worth the property. Now

they are. No one. Alone. Now the lawyer is supposed to rescue
them, no no, that he can never do, the signature is already standing there and absent-mindedly filing his nails. Yes, anyone who
takes offence at the pleasures of others puts himself at the mercy
of a bad mood, my dear Mme Piano Teacher! And there it is
already, the rotten mood.

The country policeman knows how to treat women, my God.
This person, alone on the dusty road, in the window frame of a
rented apartment, she should really be quite herself in her yawning impatient disgruntlement, so, she's been stewing long enough
now, now the telephone really should be ringing. Oh it's you. How
nice. Where are you. The whole time she's been looking for herself, but actually for someone else, who understands her, and then
she'll know who she is. A ton of books with signposts right next to
her bed, where will we set them all up, and so now she's found
herself at last. No wonder that it took so long, because she has
found herself of all things in another, where she had not expected
herself to be at all. That's how one becomes important.
Ringadingding, now show me the golden ring, says the alarm
clock. Time to get up! High time! Life is here now and is about to
kick down your door. You've signed the request form for life at the
notary, Gerti, Andrea, Karin. Good. So. Now the women know
again what's supposed to be in their petition, worked out down to
the smallest detail, which they will soon withdraw again. It should
have worked one way and another, but it didn't work out. For
years there have been rumours, even in the county town, that one
time or another the country policeman is supposed to have tried
something on the side and then on the other side, but who's going
to check up on it, one doesn't check up on colleagues, even if one
doesn't really like them. He can't have had much success, if one
looks at his debts. Why does he have to buy so many plots of land,
he's already got one, his wife's. A name is mentioned, I don't
know which, and where a meeting could take place, at which this
name was mentioned. A rock is a resistance, which it's no effort to

climb. But the lack of resistance of these women, no, I don't believe it, they even leave their garden gate open, which is only two and half feet high anyway, just so that at last they can begin to love. Every day they are the latest special offers again, simply because they are something quite special. Anybody who didn't want to spend too much money would grab them right away. But what they promised at the beginning was already the end. As if love could not have climbed over, if it had really wanted to get in. The women have lost their appetite now. Today they have again summoned so much spirit out of the bottle, and now they want to be carried off on the spot. As a bloom is caressed by the sun, as softly, and the main thing is, as quickly. Best of all immediately. We have to beat the sun to it. It always goes away, just when the flower is feeling happiest. They want to look for food themselves, the women, an ancient male privilege. But they shouldn't do themselves harm, the silly things, whose personal best time so often appears to be achieved only in death, when one or two people stand around their bed and don't know what they're supposed to do. Yes, the sun shines, too, that's their aim, that's what they're working towards. The more strength the women put into their lives, the more strength they will lack later, in the care home in Majorca, where meanwhile of course their language, the language of money, would be spoken, if they had been able to keep any of it. Of the money. Their searching is like silently getting up and going home. But they stay a little longer, dust furniture, knick-knacks, pretty little somethings. All superfluous, it all slips through their fingers. But now they really don't need anything but love any more. Because they don't have anything else. I ask you: Do you need anything? And this was how you answered me. With finding oneself is how they answered me. They must have lost themselves somewhere, where can it have been, in order for them to be able to pull themselves triumphantly together and throw themselves into someone's jaws again. Some sauce, please. Why should we interfere with their goals? After thousands of years women in general have at last grown up and make their own choice from the menu, and they choose, well what, they choose themselves, and that in someone quite different, whom they don't really know at all. He's like me, they think, he's not like Walter or Gerhard, who meant nothing to me. Then they might as well have just held on to themselves. But this attitude will really never be able to tempt women into moving somewhat more prudently. But it isn't necessary, they know where their purses are kept. Here I can see all the more clearly, fearfully, that something is going to happen. I see it before my eyes, in my little workshop, where my work is being wrought now, and without any heat, I manage without warmth, it's all alone and so very small, I can't throw it into the fire yet. I have already hinted to what class of people this man belongs, that is, he belongs in no class at all, he belongs back in the kindergarten of humanity, where he, like us, should actually have been brought up, but his teacher was baffled by him, there sits a schoolboy and doesn't say anything, although he's been asked a question. A smack in the face, quickly, the way one chops wood, so that something comes out at last, but nothing comes out, only a creature briefly flutters up, because it has been disturbed, but it right away settles down again. The lad still refuses to learn, although we've advised him how he could do better, because we're sorry for him and add: Well, that's another fine mess, we really wouldn't like to know what's going to become of him. But now we know, whether we want to or not: a country policeman. A childhood memory suddenly rose and immediately fell again, we'll first have to digest this memory.

Now the country policeman walks briskly ahead of a woman, trotting lightly like a wolf, across the mats, where hayricks will soon stand. He can write more than just his name, he can draw something up, so that a notary can make a fair copy of it, whereas I have an unfinished manuscript on a screen in front of me, which glows it's true, but only illuminates a small part of my brain at once. The country policeman, however, has the overview and keeps it in mind, too. He always keeps everything. The name of this person counts more or less. That is, where it stands at the moment, on the promissory note he has issued, all he can do is keep his fingers crossed. But the man knows where he can get something. There's hope yet. If there isn't, then I could stop at last, you've said it. Don't you see it, this body I can see in front of me, I could almost take an interest in it myself, my eyes want to see something indecent, and my hands want to attack something indecent and play around with it, and then unfortunately I always want to say something unmentionable, how embarrassing, even if only for me. Not so fast, my room has to be tidied up first, I can't let anyone see it. Yes, this body, which we're going to keep running with, this arrow taut against the desolate sinews of the landscape, and he, he is supposed to have become the prize of this woman? No, personally I don't believe it. I thought it was she who had become the prize? One day she'll eventually wake up, and then bingo, but she doesn't win anything. At some point, one day it's payday, when the bank statements drop as deep as the unfathomable ocean, except with a balance one can fathom why it is so low at present. It won't be her day, thinks a woman, but her time will nevertheless have come. Then he'll get a divorce and marry her, in order to get the remainder from her as well. She believes it, she is imbued with this conviction. She wants to give him a very affectionate answer, very softly in his ear, for this party of her lifetime, but he isn't there. At last he'll listen to her for once. Yes, the time has come: Her answer isn't enough for him, it's not concrete enough for him, not adult. He tells her loudly. Do grow up. In a moment he'll be raging noisily on the street again, because the door will be locked, but not seriously. To the woman, it's as if he's always sending her back into the corner, although she even had years of musical instrument tuition and, perhaps out of revenge, even gave some herself. But she is unable to play this instrument. The greater her love for him, the smaller and more insignificant she feels. Often, when she catches sight of herself in a mirror or reflected in a shop window, she finds it impossible to grasp that he is with her and that it is her. I, another? Don't I hear pounding live beats as an accompaniment there? Please not! Do I have to listen to them as well, even though I only know the classical music of life, like the woman I'm talking about, and who likewise loves only classical music? Unfortunately it doesn't mean anything to the country policeman. In a self-analysis he would say, if he could: This woman is completely fascinated by me. I radiate an inner strength, which she has always longed for. How nice for me, it's a real gold mine. No, this man is like no other I know. Perhaps he's like the sea or the mountains, I know them too, but only superficially, the mountains a little better, one can at least build on them, if they don't throw themselves away first. Here building has been forbidden by the countryside commission and two hundred other organisations. One is only allowed to trample around on the mountain soil if one is a summer sportsman or a winter sportsman or an all-weather sportsman. The mountains simply belong to everyone. Only in heaven will we conquer them. The country policeman belongs to this educated and charming and attractive and active woman alone, as she hopes. She wants at last to find an inner home and shelter. That's crazy.

She can throw him alive into boiling water, for all I care, and jump in after him, and once he's heated up, eat him up inclusive of core and stalk, or whatever it is she wants to do with him. I've held her back long enough, in order to adopt her cause, let her gobble him up and in return present him with all the dishes and the house that goes with them. She will be digested by him and disappear, without trace. I can see that already. He turns to her, as he always does, it takes quite an effort on his part, he tends always to turn away from a person. As a child only bed-wetting, and he didn't really want that either, accompanied him for a long time, like an annoying pet that won't go away. Wait a minute, where has the woman got to now, she hasn't gone to make another coffee, has she? Doesn't she know what to do with her time? He quietly follows her and studies her like a schoolboy, as if she were a text, which one has to learn, in order to make the grade, and that is always property property property. The party he supports says so too, it tells its supporters that they clearly stand out from the others and deserve everything and more of what they have and still want. Except the members of parliament shouldn't earn more than 60,000 schillings a month, but that no longer applies now either. Property can become a nice hobby, but one has to train really hard with the tax office, in order to keep some of it. This man here should be properly acknowledged by me, as a student, main subject: Live, but don't let live. As student of the university of life, if you like, because he knows what matters, the quiet values. Property. Or have you ever heard a house speak, except through party noise and TV from an open window? What appears easiest to us, this man finds difficult: to be a human being, so say the poets, who have understood nothing, but want to talk all the time themselves. Well. The High Commission of Curtains is closed now, so that one doesn't notice right away that official business is being conducted here. This man, therefore, is a fellow student, but one who doesn't really want to learn anything, nothing, from nobody. That one can buy dolls in a sex shop, whose bodies look in a way unappetising, well, the head's OK, that while masturbating one can pull a plastic bag over one's head and tighten it at the throat, till one almost pops off, and then one pops up again, the bag abruptly, suddenly open!, please, don't forget that!, and there's our orgasm, which we once had and have missed for some time now, there it is again, stronger than ever before, stronger than with any woman, stronger than any arm. We had begun to believe we won't get one at all any more. But the shelves are full. Every poor man wants to be rich, that is just as natural a phenomenon as the fact that one can introduce all kinds of things into one's arsehole, both small and surprisingly large objects. That, however, one has to do with the other hand, one hand is supposed to tighten the bag. So one hand always knows what the other's doing.

He goes to the hairdresser once a month, the country police-man, to get a haircut, today is not that day. A conviction abruptly pervades him, unexpectedly, he then wanders through the territories of idleness, nothing, he wanders through the territories of his job, there he has often struck lucky. While driving, women make mistakes out of carelessness, absent-mindedness or incompetence, and already the country policeman has them by the skirt and doesn't let go again, if they're to his taste and he has got hold of their address. How quickly they consent and more as soon as he has unpacked them. It was the handy packaging, with the thread, pull here, which opens even the most buttoned-up. He stirs up a fire in them. The bodies can be thrown away, the heads one would keep, so that one can make sure that they don't talk incessantly, the women. They're real gold mines. They immediately offer him travelling expenses, gifts, then themselves, then the rest as well. In return they want to build on him. The same thing he has in mind with them. Except that he also wants to get hold of what they've already built. What appears difficult to us, to destroy someone and obtain a cement collar, in order to reliably sink the booty to the bottom, this man takes all that for granted, if you please. That's what he's there for, and he wants to put himself in every other place as well, which at the moment, unfortunately, is still occupied by another body: one or more rooms, in one or more houses. Squeezing into the bodies of strangers, that's good too, then only oneself is left over, a bird, which hoarsely, hoarsely crying, scrambles around on a corpse and doesn't know where the eyes are now, which it wanted to pick at first, so that the dead, with whatever senses, could no longer distinguish him. He wants to remain unobserved, the man. It didn't, unfortunately, work with his dead mother, he must still succeed. But then he would like to get into everywhere else as well, squeeze in, in order not to let go of himself, to be by himself and to stay that way, when he inflicts his wounds, of which others with small twitching body parts always die, after they have watched anxiously for a month, for years, what is to become of

this child. If someone looks at him like that, the country policeman would rather eat himself up, so that nothing, not even
himself, is left to be seen, only a house, another house and
another house, house-proud. Then at least he would be: gone.
What kind of man can he be? He is like an angel, with inner eyes,
no, not an angel looking backwards, in case someone is standing
behind him with a stone. His muscles and sinews don't understand either, why they are inserted into a thin but firm nylon skin,
which can contain simply every body shape, no matter where it
leads. But not for long. In a moment it will clutch a tuft of hair
again and pull everything attached to it to the ground. Exactly the
same thing will happen to this suit, there was a very similar one
in the adverts for holidays in Austria, encoded however, otherwise
no one would have put up with it, the suit - here we are shown the
population in the dress of the country, and all the things it gets up
to: Sport, please take over! But the whole population has been
locked up in its clothing, so that it can't get out and do any harm,
as so often, our population, oh dear, too late, now it's out, now it's
out - an endless mountain panorama in the background, which is
supposed to represent the boundlessness of this in fact rather
small plump land. We've meanwhile given up this goal again.
People don't want to visit us any more. But yesterday on TV they
showed us the new ski suits for the world championships, and we
were all annoyed at the way they looked; I saw nothing but shini-
ness and lightning flashes. My eyes were dazzled. In history:
boundless crimes. In the present: boundless pleasure on the high
crags, to which the paths lead, so that we can look down on the
others, paths on which we sportswomen and sportsmen can roll
or slide around. We are the party, which is the only one to let us
join. We are the party, which we have already joined, because: we
are who we are. And not anyone else.

The rumble of thunderstorms is approaching now. We are all
in the dark about ourselves, but to make up for that our conscience is clear again at last, it wouldn't have had a chance against

this weather anyway, which we didn't ask for, which was given to us as a present, and which now only harms us as far as the strangers are concerned, because today it's coming for the third day in a row, thunderstorms, rockfalls, hail, avalanches. Who will keep the children in the Alpenrose Pension occupied, until it's fine again? How wonderful, altogether elevating, after the mountains have risen up against us, when we are at last allowed to enter the mountain refuge, and the landlady hands us the strong hunter's punch, the parson's nose, the smoked ham rolls, while outside the world public walks past and ignores us, instead of dropping in. It's on its way quite without trousers, the world and its organs, without sweatshirt and even without walking shoes, we bought them all, we chose them from the catalogue. That's the way we like to see the world, naked, bare and dumb, so that we can again and again lead it up the garden path. We're somebody again, but which somebody? We are a European, fallen from heaven like the first sunbeams, which are now coming out at last, we have done so much and more to make it happen, that the foreigners will be happy and be our friends! But it was worthwhile. The civilised nations have taken to us again! Well, thank you very much!

He is otherwise something of a disrespectful man, the country policeman, and so he demands all the more respect from the young recruits. He doesn't care about anything, except this house, this one and that one too. I should explain that in greater detail now, but it's not necessary, because anyone can put himself in the same situation and immediately sign a savings agreement with a building society. But I don't know, there's something, it's better not to visit people like that, they always serve, perhaps because they're stingy, only themselves. That means that people who join up with them always have to live in reality and are not allowed to dream. Someone who one day falls in love with them is soon looking anxiously at them. Where have all the dreams gone? Such people can always hold onto themselves, even if they briefly give themselves away or rather: lend themselves out. It only looks as if they were expending themselves and spoiling others with their presence. We've got plenty of time, it only takes half an hour of my time, but not this one, to explain it to you in greater detail. You're yawning. You've heard it all before. I know. Even the country policeman's trainers are of the opinion, with respect to the rocky ground, which they briefly but firmly touch, that everything, on and over which they climb belongs to them. We take care of our homeland, and we like to keep it under control, and these are brand name shoes, even if I got them a little cheaper. Oh, a little herd of chamois, there are even two kids with them, how nice, about ten yards vertically below the gravel path. They don't crush anything at all under their hooves. How lightly these animals whose bodies appear so heavy jump from a rock on their thin little legs, we look enviously above our allied walking and trekking shoes at the same time trampling a couple of tufts of grass at the edge of the path, where a short time ago they were still found alive, so that the animals could eat them. High above, a pair of buzzards, crying loudly, so that the little animals can disappear in time, who still have to live off their winter fat, and are keeping themselves upright with their last reserves of energy. The district has become noticeably lonelier since the springs can no longer be marvelled at on the surface. We've been struck by that. For that reason, as well as for others, tourism has declined considerably, many have got alarmed about it, what's happened to our attractions? Where are the foreigners? Why don't they come? Are we being boycotted by our own guests? What have we dished up here? We've dished up the same as usual, haven't we, schnitzel, chicken, sugared pancakes. The mountain, which is one thing that doesn't consist of food, we're not the Land of Cockayne (or are we? or are we nothing else?), has been locked up long ago, but it can easily be unlocked. Like an envelope, which anyone can tear open, to read what message the landscape has and the one over there, too, the message is different for each person and so it's no problem to recall the messengers, our ambassadors. We are not to blame for anything. That's accompanied by loud music on the radio. And those who remain are already more elderly fellow citizens and prefer to walk around on the plain, look up in astonishment at the snow-covered peaks, take photographs and turn themselves into a reference work, which inns in the valley serve the freshest trout straight out of the stream. We'll go there afterwards and open the filler pipes. Come on in. All right, but here the path already goes up into the mountains, it's not my fault, it's better if you just stand still. Snow on the felling areas higher up in the forest, on these breaks between the trees, down which the avalanches raced with particular abundance this winter. It is now late spring (spring comes rather late here anyway) and still correspondingly cold. The noise of the inn died down long ago. Here, at least in the more low-lying parts, agriculture and forestry used to be carried on, but now an eternal water use ban has dawned. Further down there's a catchment basin, but you won't catch anything. It is the area, measured horizontally, which is bounded by watersheds, yes, shedding can hurt. In between there's the water, one hopes likewise permanently separated from us. Sports which are kind to nature are always welcome, but others not, absolutely no mountain bikes - strictly forbidden! This poet doesn't want them, and I don't either, but can't say it as nicely as he can, who would like to kill the poor cyclists, who would also just like to have fun. But running or walking, that's OK, isn't it? No, the poet has nothing against that. Although: Every step crushes approx. one thousand insects, a mighty spectacle, which is unfortunately also coming to an end, but only if one were as small as this ant here, there you are, its time is already up. That wouldn't be any good for us: being crushed underfoot. Nothing is grown here any more, here there is no chemical treatment for plants, and the plants of course look as one might expect, somehow wild, tousled, worse for wear, puny, don't you think, these are chance creations? They've got no breeding. Once they wouldn't have been allowed to proliferate here in such numbers and take away space that could have been used productively. To the country policeman, the thought that

something could not be useful is unbearable, and yet he involuntarily relaxes in this dramatic landscape, from which he has
learned, at least to appear wild and romantic when necessary.
Nature belongs to all of us. Too little always belongs to the country policeman. Nevertheless. There are some who say they have
observed that sometimes he also went here at night. Sometimes
he deliberately stands on every cluster of flowers, no, today he
doesn't want to pluck and pick up anything, not even edelweiss,
nature isn't that interesting after all, it's not an animal (put it this
way: An animal is nature, but nature is not an animal, providing
milk and eggs which we can use, and to be honest, nature doesn't
provide me with much either). It's called an eco-system, only Kurt
Janisch doesn't see how and where there's supposed to be some
kind of system at the bottom of it. To him nature is a green chaos,
like the party associated with it, and like the chaos in his brain;
and only his body, so that its performance improves, is worth
being first looked after and then honed, one thing at a time. From
such people we should learn to obey the state, without them need-
ing to waste any manners on us. When they kick down our doors
because we're black or have worked in the black economy, we're
harvested and only then cut, by the neighbours. A policeman is
always right.

It always makes sense to work at something, and mining has
had the sense, over the aeons, to throw the mountain bit by bit
into the depths, in seconds, if necessary, and even under the
mountain there are things happening, which are perhaps benefi-
cial to it, but certainly not to us. Because the mountain can in a
short time virtually liquefy itself deep inside, yes indeed, in the
depths, as if there were not already enough water there! So now
it also turns to mud, inside, and after that, watch out, it breaks
through. And it breaks through into neighbouring, already
packed, old worked out chambers, and sometimes, if they have
not been properly backfilled, these are particularly susceptible.
Who actually checked the consistency of the packing material,

of the concrete? No one? Well, then of course we'll need to call
the Country Police, to find that out, but not today and not this
country policeman, he won't be on duty. But one day, one day
some time, he too will try to find out, whether it's true that lean
concrete packing was used or not. Like all of us, he will need
experts to do that. The information won't be volunteered. A subsidence might perhaps have occurred if the chamber had been
properly packed, but not this catastrophic breakthrough, which
took people into the pit with their eyes wide open and afterwards
didn't let them out again even with their eyes shut. They're still
down there. Ten head of them. No, you won't get anything out
again, on the contrary, you're still in nature's debt and have to
pay. So: What interests the country policeman about women also
lies more below the waistline, which the more fearful don't even
dare cross with their eyes. The country policeman, once the
sunny credit side has been checked, always only looks there, an
area about which he has already collected further details on many
occasions, so that he knows his way around, if he ends up there
again. It's nicest in nice weather, this area, then one can at least
take a good look at the landscape, to see whether a couple of
death's heads look back and nod to the camera. All these fit to use
lives have been buttered into the landscape and then crushed by
the magma, well, by the shit, until they themselves have presumably become as soft as butter. Don't follow this mine to the
bottom, follow Kurt Janisch uphill, even if it's hard! Weighing
heavily on him, as on the management of the mine: economic
pressure. He must find success. He must. Failing which he must
go broke and be declared bankrupt. There we have the mine, and
there we have Mr Janisch's fly, they stand opposite one another
like two terrace restaurants by a lake competing for customers.
What will you do for me? You'll get from me! With fewer people
the mine had to produce as much as with many. It routinely had
to increase the tonnage. What must Kurt Janisch do now? Be at
the right place at the right time, have his arguments acknowledged and have the buildings and apartments of lonely women

valued. The Leoben Public Prosecutor's Office is waiting, at some point someone will stray into their side street. If the mountain doesn't come, then its prophet of property, Kurt Janisch, will come to us in the cramped building, and then at last we'll have him, we don't have any more room. Otherwise we have to come and get him. One hears rumours, these little liberties of the propertyless, but one hears nothing concrete. Welcome meanwhile to the Barbara shaft, where, however, there's nothing left to save.

In the mountain wind there's no question of forgetting. One can think things over very well while running, until the moment comes when one doesn't think at all any more and just keeps running, like a machine, like a politician who wants to make his mark, as if he wanted to have himself hewn in stone or at least have his picture taken, just as he has become through running. Now one's happy at last. One will outlast all others living, because one is so healthy. Now some forward thoughts turn up as well, yes, they get the better of us, but they aren't very good. One would never have credited oneself with such thoughts. The colours of this Janisch track-suit: copied from the professional athletes, whom millions look at, to see what's on their clothes and which is the right stuff, too. So that they can likewise load their life trolley with it (as if it weren't full enough already!), except now the colours just won't harmonise with nature. They have, however, been chosen for the sake of miles of arduous running exercises, these colours, so that at some later point, the frozen sportsman can nevertheless be found and given a decent burial. He stood out very well from the white of the snow, thanks to his track-suit. The mountain rescue team will see you better against the rock face, against which one day you will stick like a squashed fly, and if you have your mobile phone with you and its battery isn't flat, then nothing worse can happen to you, before the alpine rescue service's bill for recklessness and anarchy and the telephone bill land in your letter box. Then you'll bitterly regret everything. Then there's nothing to be done. Man in his eccentricity repeatedly gets into danger and has to be got out of it, so that everyone knows: He's back again. And on top of things. In sport people themselves have to be so much on top of things that they no longer need the mountain tops. But everything can also be quietly simulated in their very own personal fitness centre. These feet, made for walking, running or driving cars, now carry out one or two of these labours on the conveyor belt, which man should really wait upon, instead of it waiting upon him. Number three, the beloved car, which is by itself as strong as fifty pieces of fitness apparatus, unfortunately had to stay outside. One can always improve one's performance, if necessary. The country policeman, I think, seeks out solitude, not only to train there in peace, but principally to meet someone who will flatter him. Look, a woman in love, how nice, and she has already been affected by his behaviour, as I see. She staggers behind this person like someone with a fever or a mad person, in order then to be allowed to sit down on his cock. This woman wishes to allow, for the umpteenth time, a couple of parts of her body to be pulled out and entrusted to the cold mountain air. It is precisely those parts which this body table always laid with the best tableware has made available for this one man, to allow several tests to be carried out. What for. So that this man will once more be able to pass muster in the woman's eyes and senses. That's what for. She already knows that in advance. But the said parts will not remain free long either. A printer in a bank will later have stamped something, as proof that they are no longer worth anything. Because now the country policeman has the money. The body parts are all occupied. To make up for that we are now unemployed. The country policeman will have confidentially informed a woman on the telephone, he's driving past the farm, you know, knows anyway where the barrier is and where one unfortunately has to pay, and then up to the last car park before the path up to the summit. Yes, even a country policeman, although he's got ID, if he's not on duty, has to pay the toll, and then, Gerti, you climb a bit following the red markings, you know, as always up to the bench with a view, where we often used to sit. From there you simply go straight ahead, where there's no path at all any more. So then we'll follow the path, that belongs to us alone, right, where at most only the hunter is allowed to go, who is allowed to do everything, then continue to the right, as far as the point where you see the cross on the summit of the Windberg for the first time, you know, if one can see anything at all, because the fog comes down early, there anyway, you know, I expect, that you'll already have pulled off your panties or not put them on at all and opened your bra. Why. What for. We don't ask questions. Actually even the country policeman, even though he's got his mountain rescue certificate, shouldn't leave the marked paths without authorisation, except in an emergency, nor should he encourage others to do so, especially not someone who is not really certain on her feet, nowhere, not in life and not in death, but who would want to start an argument with him. He's born here and knows the area as well as he does his own trousers, which, as already mentioned, are skin tight and leave no room for mistakes. It's easier to get into the mountains than into these trousers. But the mountains can be treacherous, never underestimate them! Even if one knows them, they like to get up to their tricks, whenever they want. The country policeman doesn't believe in the legend, that if one kills a person they return as the lost, because death supposedly doesn't like it all, if one anticipates his plans. And the dead keep on coming until they are completely forgotten. Their ghosts meanwhile wait patiently at home, behind the barricade of the earthly, until they are informed that the time of being forgotten has drawn near. Young people (cf Gabi) are of course forgotten more quickly, there are soon too few who have known them, and they have other interests, there was in any case not enough time to really get to know Gabi. The way she really was. On the other hand it is of course outrageous: so young and perhaps already dead! Her characteristics were hardly clearly developed yet, moist walls, into which someone pushed his hands, fleetingly. The priest, should the unthinkable really be true, will have to lament an imaginative young life, which is now shut into a coffin, it's incomprehensible, inconceivable, that it could have happened, but the girlfriends will move away at some point or devote themselves to their own families. One surely shouldn't kill in full bloom, but in the bud it's perhaps not so bad, except for the one directly affected, who knows, if it would have come to anything. Oh Gabi, I think it's enough to drive one to despair. In this weather, with all the road accidents, the ghost drivers on the autobahn late at night... you could have died so many times already, it's a wonder you lasted as long as you did. But now it has happened, I fear. Perhaps the murderer is in some danger? One can never know. A stab of pain tightens my breast, but not for long, my breast wants to go on breathing, and it's best if people arrange to be free right away, if they find someone with whom they can stick their genitals together, again and again, until finally it holds.

A girl disappeared from a village, it will be days before it emerges where she's got to. Nature already knows, even if only a tiny part of it, and we are likewise a part of it, but a quite different one.

The country policeman races uphill through the wilderness. Even if you, too, find him good looking, then suppress this impulse on the spot. At present this man has other worries, because of an oil-smudged cloth on which there was something else as well, and that he already threw away days ago, into a bush. In the forest, which is itself beautiful, don't you recognise it? Yes, that one! Everyone likes to be in the forest, there's not such competition for light and space as in the water. There the pine trees have long ago crushed one another to death, their interlaced spindly little branches have formed a scratchy web, and their roots have sucked up all the water, which others would have needed much more. Underneath, dead needles inches deep. Not even mushrooms grow here any more. This wood should be vigorously thinned out. Nature puts everything they need at the plants' disposal, and they have the ability, which humankind doesn't have, of synthesising all the necessary compounds themselves: Please give me a dozen chemical elements, then I'll just produce myself, and then there'll finally be peace! Is what I unfortunately don't say. Is what the plant says to me. We're choosier, we aren't agricultural products, we only eat them. Who please will now reduce the acidity of this soil for me? No volunteers? I would need nitrogen, phosphorus, potassium. Not available either? What else have we got on offer, in order to enrich the soil? Protective enamel and a grinding machine? Can this woman still breathe in the knowledge that she didn't even put on her panties and already unhooked her bra in the car, in the car park, full of anticipation and in a breathless expectation, which almost made it difficult for her to walk, uphill as well? Her fingers trembled so badly, but she didn't need to be told twice, she understood properly the first time and hesitantly agreed to the unreasonable request. Someone who wants to set out on an arduous walk lasting for miles in her body shouldn't have to pay a toll a second time and then perhaps even have to lift up the barrier himself.

So there she steps out of the undergrowth, the woman, who hasn't often done something like it, still less in this condition. She steps forward as arranged with the man, she breaks clumsily, almost stumbling, careful! (over there is a vertical drop of at least one hundred and fifty to two hundred feet), out through the white channel between the boulders and the old glacial sand, which is lying around on the ground, and immediately tries to flit around the exotic beast, which is standing there scenting the air, as tenderly as an insect, and to pull out the yarn she has prepared for the net, and now the crochet needles, and stick the plug into the socket prepared for it and see what happens. She says what happiness is to her: that he's there now, as arranged. I love you so much. Miracles can't be more important than they are now, because they have already occurred and every hour new miracles arrive, which could perhaps make us even more happy, or right now, here comes a new miracle, this very moment, as arranged between us. But it's only the old one, wearing different clothes. The woman makes the man, whom she could persuade to meet her here and now, even if only briefly, for a moment, he hasn't said a word yet, but she has already said many, which I don't want to specially mention, the woman makes the man flinch with her words and appearance (he is not equipped to scratch her off the wall yet, behind which she has entrenched herself, but in a moment the whole thing will collapse, this silly wall between them), while she immediately, he hardly has time to raise his hand, pulls her blouse out of the yoke of the stylised dirndl skirt and pushes the loose bra up. Now it's only hanging by the straps, which really have nothing to do any more, under her chin, like a somewhat oddly cut collar, and then, didn't you see, then her heavy breasts, both of them, have fallen out underneath, past the open traditional dress, towards the ground. The woman has been warm all this time, for days now; yet as if out of embarrassment, to distract attention from herself by pointing at herself, she tumbles out of her container, meals would be astonished, for no other reason, than to be taken out and polished off. She already acts like a woman possessed in anticipation of pleasure still to come. There's no restraining her. So there she's already handing him her meat loaves for starters in her cupped hands and simultaneously instructing the man, even though her senses have yet to get used to such coarseness, but it's already bubbling out of her, she instructs him therefore to lift up her skirt, she doesn't have a free hand any more, and as arranged she isn't wearing any underwear. You see. That wasn't so hard, was it. Does he not first of all want to exhaustively probe her, before he comes into her and then, the obligatory part, as completion of the given theme, talk of his love, in her ear, into which he should gently blow, that's nicest, yes, he should declare his love, so that she can talk all the more exhaustively of her own? We can by now ask for that at least. We're paying for it, after all. Instead the man strikes her, almost affectionately, lightly on the side of the face and indicates with his other hand, he indicates a little roughly, to leave this path, on which she's standing, which isn't really there, however, it really isn't a path. The woman doesn't understand right away and is still acting as if she can't wait a moment longer and so, right here! wants to obtain the promised and longed for importance, under him, on him, between him and the void, floating in the air, sleeping on the earth, it doesn't matter, here and now, as we had agreed. Perhaps he could for once at least anticipate her and be the first to pull down his trousers please, but she doesn't say it out loud, that is definitely a fantasy of hers, which doesn't need to be interpreted. After all he could unfold her right here, on this little frequented path leading nowhere and penetrate her, no one else is coming, never, not at this time, which we agreed on, and when it's already beginning to get dark, and it's not a path anyway, at any rate not a public one. Down with you, on your knees, on the ground, I must, I must. I want to, too, but something else, wait, so, my breasts are already completely released, they can now, and with pleasure, fall against your hard male chest, and then you've got them ready to eat close to your mouth, if you want to take a bite out of them again; who doesn't dream of roast pigeons flying into his mouth or whatever it is one likes to eat, a pork cutlet perhaps, with cucumber salad. So, here I throw it down for you, as arranged, my whole heap of flesh, you can rearrange it with your hands until you know your way around, you don't have so much scope. You can let them hang down to the left and right of you, my fun bags, my dust bags, or I can give you a suck and blow, or you can bite very firmly again, as you did recently, it doesn't bother me so much any more, and that's what we firmly agreed; well and good, I shall now let my breasts fall and throw them to you, you'll instantly intercept them, right, it's good food for the hound in you, whom I've met one or two times already. It's no use running away now. But I only got used to it with a lot of whining, so quickly, I wouldn't have thought it of me, it likes to bite, if it's roused, the dog, what can one do, I know, I know. I'm happy that you still find me so attractive. But now I have both hands free and can pull the dress higher myself, up to my waist. But that's only possible if we lie down. Why are you wearing these silly jogging pants, you have to shove them down to your knees, so that you can at least move yourself a bit, are you doing it deliberately? We agreed beforehand, didn't we, so you could easily have worn another, more practical, more sober pair of trousers, e.g. the jeans, as usual. Oh, I see, the trousers are supposed to be camouflage, because you're supposedly going jogging, and anyway we still have to talk about something that happened yesterday evening. There's something we have to talk about, a sentence from one of our sentimental films, where the Alpine dairymaid has a sweet secret and is itching to get rid of it again in the forest. Something that I know. You know already. But not now. The god of love is standing beside us and will hit us on our naked bums, because at this distance it would be a pity to waste an arrow. He doesn't need the arrow for us anyway. We already love each other. Look, the skirt is gone now, it's no longer in your way, and I've already climbed halfway on top of you, you see, that's how I do it, I'll be on top in a second, done. You don't have to do anything any more. Except get a millionairess to appoint you her heir. The dirndl skirt and the breasts are staying firmly up, have you ever seen anything like it? kept there by their own gravity, we can forget about them, but down there, get a hold of that, it's already as wet as a whole lake, and look at the thick vegetation that's growing on it! Like dwarf pines, only with curls. You've been wanting to get in there all this time, Kurti, my Kurti, am I not right, or do you want something else? No. Nothing. Grab a hold, how wet my swamp down there is. That's all happened for you and because of you. That's what we agreed, didn't we? We can talk afterwards. So now she gets her second, now already considerably harder slap in the face, the woman, and at last starts, somewhat belatedly, to blubber again. As usual. The country policeman didn't even need to put a proper swing in it, and already she's wailing even louder, before she's caught by the second blow, which she didn't see coming, perhaps also because he really did pinch her nipples so hard, just as she had offered them to him. She had not thought that he would accept her offer. Her mistake. She comes a little to her senses again in her strident intoxication, which accelerated the importance as lover which she has assumed from zero to two hundred in a couple of seconds and then mounted to a frenzy. Then came the drop; having hit bottom, she at last listens to the man again, and allows herself, half-naked, the skirt already gathered up, almost dripping, not at all mistress of the situation any more, a hunted creature, who a short time before still thought herself a huntress and as if raised high on the shield of a Diana with menthol bottle plus bow and arrow, to be pushed and dragged behind a group of somewhat taller dwarf pines, it's really a whole dwarf pine wood. One wouldn't be hidden standing up, but for what we have in mind, one would at most be able to notice a slight movement in the bushes. There wouldn't have been more than that. Now at last the country policeman drops to the ground voluntarily and smoothly under the assault of the woman and her weight, which has increased somewhat in the course of the dull, uneventful years, as if he himself were ground, gives way and collapses under the force of an event, with which nature sensclessly, intelligible only to herself, babbles away to herself. And then the woman throws herself full length over him. She is so in love, she knows something like that is only available free or not at all or for a great deal of money. She of course will get it as a present. His cock is already standing there, well done, as if it had already been there before the man, first, from the very beginning. One can hardly get the elastic of the leggings over it, which one has to, so that there's a proper space for the explosion of two bodies. The woman has personally ordered everything for the table of her life and had it delivered to her house, as Sunday dinner. A call is enough, enter my house. The man no doubt can hardly wait to be introduced to her smallest room, and to have her served up nice and hot, a room which may be small, but a bit of all right, but you can get lost in it nevertheless, if you don't know your way around. Sometimes a man gets out of hand, if he has chosen the wrong kind of sport and doesn't know what he likes. Is that a moving pavement or is it a tiled floor, from which the blood can easily be wiped? The woman should at last show the country policeman what she wants, so that then he can do something quite different with his living, headstrong property. The woman is good at pointing, she was, among other things, a kind of piano teacher, and so this here is her stick with which one can go walking, walking, walking. Mrs Gerti, please show me at last with this pointer, what you want and where you want to go. You don't have to say it, but you should tell us nevertheless. Then we'll see our goal, but we don't have to see you. Who still has self-control? Nobody has any self-control any more. TV tells us that and shows it to us once again, if we haven't understood. Too late unfortunately. After eleven pm. Her body strikes a rougher note than is usual with this woman. This isn't a game. The country policeman hasn't really got his mind on it today, but he's making an effort because he has to. His mind is on another matter, which he goes over in peace and quiet when he's alone: In the communal shower, the men's bodies, nice people, to whom one doesn't have to be polite. Fine young bodies, in a bundle, one next to the other, all without clothes and simply unthinkable without their little man, at which one casts glances surreptitiously. Best of all the country policeman would like to carry them in his arms, their bodies dangling to right and left as if lifeless, what a wonderful, limp and yet heavy burden that would be for this man. Everything open and spread out, what there is, nicely prepared and presented by nature and borne as if on one's own body. Weapons. Beaming, he would be allowed to see every last thing, precisely everything that is forbidden! That most of all. He would help matters along with his hands, if he couldn't see far enough into the other bodies. What is a woman against that. She's dirty. A fish factory. It is neither necessary nor advisable to fit into a woman's body. Something of this body always clings to one, that can never be washed off. The country policeman secretly likes to look at pictures of naked young men, which he bought far from his place of residence, magazines, in which all the cocks seem to craftily eye him up, iridescent as snakes, with the bounce of steel springs. He thinks of these young men now, he knows each one by the first name printed under the photo. Perhaps the names aren't even true. One can hardly ring these men up. But no. That would not have been necessary at all, he gets his erection anyway, whether a woman lies here and offers herself or not, making an effort to be nice, but also passionate, if so desired. Both. One needs both and can do both. One would like nothing better than to tear her to shreds, this woman. Instead, decorated like a fighting cock, with its little red helmet, his cock enters Gerti, because that's what she wants, it would prefer to go somewhere else. And once it is standing erect, it can't do it fast enough, so that it's over and done with once again. Oh dear, already over? Please, here's the gate, where it always is, and as always it's as wide open as a barn door, and we eat human flesh like a horse. No music needed for resuscitation. The man can't bear to hear any more, he's already had to hear so much, for him the whole thing is a process without any adornment. This process can just go ahead and proceed. It'll be over all the more quickly. The man really has no grounds to care one way or the other, all he needs is the ground, he can throw the rest away. Doesn't Gerti have a Walkman there in her bag, on which earlier she could listen to Mozart as loud as can be? Immediately it flies out of the bag and down the rocks. We don't need it. Yes, only now does he notice, as the gadget is already in the air: She did indeed have one in her bag, and one of the earplugs was still in her ear from the climb, but she had already switched the thing off earlier. A pity, perhaps the chamois would have got some enjoyment out of it. The earplug is also pulled out of her, the gadget falls silently past the rock faces. The woman disregards it. She is still trying, through hectic squeezing, stroking, turning and pulling, to at last get the man to come onto her wavelength where they can swim away all alone, but together, the two of them, in the ether, in infinity, for as long as they want, today, however, only at the time we have agreed. It's OK, Kurt, if you've got the cash, Gerti. The lovers. After all they belong to one another at every other time, too, just as they wish. At all times. The woman has ceased to exist and lives only through him. The lips of her vulva are briefly raised, as agreed, he enters, and the lips close contentedly behind him. What was that noise, stop!, draws back for a moment and listens, darling, please don't stop, one listens with one's ears or the headphones and not with one's cock. This woman can never tolerate a distraction from herself and her subject, which is again herself. Her soul now buries itself puffing, panting, groaning in his. Earth flies up. We've managed it: The grave gapes open. The woman pulls his hand away from his own genitals, they're growing out of him, so there can't be any misunderstanding. He has to hurry up and get started, and then it should take a very long time and proceed tenderly. She shoves it in with her own hands, what has been held out to her in one hand, grips the rest of the man by the arse, shows her two rows of teeth, cries out and beats him rhythmically, if at first still somewhat cautiously, but soon more vigorously on the back, she's got a sense of rhythm, but it's her rhythm, not his. But it's precisely at this pace, hers, not his, that the man is immediately supposed to go on, but at the same time stay there and then: never go away again. Go away: no, he can't do that. I believe and see, that for their pleasure such people can sometimes behave as if they're crazy, this woman here, for example, but where the pleasure is supposed to lie I don't yet understand. I shall read it off myself and pass it on, if I find it. It exists, this spark of love, but one has to blow strongly on it and stick at it, so that the next time the spark doesn't go out with someone else. When one's in love, then everything is much more beautiful, but also more terrible, knows the woman, probably because a little bit of the spiritual is also involved, isn't it? No, it isn't! He will bring her a beautiful weakness, the man, but not until afterwards, when everything is quiet again and one can think and talk about everything and add oneself at will to what has been thought, at the places where one fits in. But only after it has gone on like that for a quarter of an hour, twenty minutes or as long as you like, a stiff cudgel thrashing the inside of her abdomen and at some point she has to cry out loud involuntarily with pain and pleasure, whether she wants to or not. She doesn't. And she mustn't. Otherwise it will occur to a hiker to see if anyone's there. In between he has to place his hand over her mouth, she'll chase away the animals and all the other sportsmen with her bawling, and chase them exactly in their direction. But we can't be doing with that now. There's no one there, darling. Everyone's getting ready to go to bed or has already done so. Doing something like that in the freedom of nature could become a habit with her, fears the man, who prefers to do it to her in her house. As caretaker, so to say, no, we don't say it like that. There he feels safe and protected, because it will soon belong to him. Here in the wilderness he almost feels afraid, no, not that, but he doesn't like it so much, one easily gets dirty, and that makes the woman at home suspicious. No, not really. This woman here is a burden. A pest. Today he would perhaps like to treat her somewhat more harshly and also take her from behind, which she doesn't like so much, so that she gets out of the habit of constantly ordering him around. This way, yes, this way, too, no, not from there, please not, I don't want that. Perhaps then at least she'll manage without him for a while, but not too long. Please not. Please not. You're not made of sugar, are you. Perhaps then at least she'll be quiet for a while. He goes at it a little more easily now, the man, he's got time. He'll convince her all right, after he's plumbed her arse a little at the entrance, where no one's keeping watch, that pain is not an expression, when someone is suffering. Because there is no expression for it. A scent is stuck in front of his nose, which he doesn't like so much. Now he's in the beautiful forest, he is master of the situation, no matter which, he turns Gerti roughly on her stomach and now he really gives her a chance to shout, but she's somewhat subdued. If she really wants to, then go ahead, she'll have good grounds. No, he would rather have the ground. From which mountain peak has he just come? He's only on his way there? What, hasn't she just asked him to stop again? What, already? He's hardly started. This way it's not quite as nice as usual, Kurti, this isn't the way I imagined it, another way it would be much nicer than usual. Wouldn't you rather like to come from the front, so that I can look at you lovingly as you're doing it? I like that especially, to look into your dear blue eyes. No. That I don't like so much. I prefer it another way. I like it like this and like this. Yet the man could now slowly and thoroughly subjugate a whole nation, and if it were up to him, he would do so at any time. No. He's not going to stop now. In half an hour it will already be pitch dark, and the newspapers would be unable to see the whole nation trembling before him. Someone unimportant, who becomes important, a big event as recently in Ischgl, where the snow turned hard as stone and rose up against the people, because they abused it for their own pleasure. Minus ten, and a terrific band stands behind the popular girl group, girls who can sing terribly loud, whoever they are. Next week it will be a world-famous boy group. We will no longer be able to read the newspaper and not know what is happening to us, when the snow turns into concrete and collects in a single place, where it doesn't belong at all. There's no kissing now. One can't call it rejoicing any more either, what the woman there is doing, who tried to throw her weight about, but there the man has already shoved her face into the dried up, pointed needles and gleefully rubbed her face in them, so that the decayed, rotting stuff presses into her mouth, nose and, ouch, into her eyes. He'll come to regret disdaining my genitals, she hopes, although he does love me, but I'll be able to convince him, he doesn't really know about these things yet, I'll persuade him to love and honour all of my genitals and always to support their unfolding. Coughing and spitting and with her bum involuntarily rearing up and twisting round, the body comes and thoughts go, until the man, with an almost careless blow to the small of the back, can once again control the spring sacrifice, which he has laid hold of there, finally on this occasion, and she lies motionless. She succumbs to her determination as woman, but she has determined place and time, something at least, no, nothing. She can hardly make so free now as to prescribe all the things he's supposed to do with her and above all: where. How long? As long as it suits me. But you don't suit me, you're too tight for me. The: please stop now, I can't any more, doesn't properly get out of her mouth any more, because her neck is firmly pinned to the ground as if by a vice and she can only occupy herself with agitated waiting and involuntary flinching and twisting round, because of constantly being pinched, and thrusting her bum, until he's finished at last. Soon a little blood flows. Well, she'll survive, at home we've got a good antiseptic cream for wounds, for use both externally and on the mucous membranes, since we've known this man, but it won't be quite as nice as we had agreed beforehand and as this woman had imagined it. No, this time, unfortunately, it didn't turn out to be as nice as recently, she's almost unconscious now, hey, wake up!, but the woman will, when she takes stock, much later, have been happy and content about so much affection and that at least he won't have killed her. Perhaps the next time. But a human being endures a great deal, I sometimes think: everything, but there are worse things than everything, and that is: when one doesn't get everything one wants. The terribly hard pinching of her buttocks wasn't very pleasant either, the woman registers, whose cash register rang and rang, because something was put into it, but without the man appearing to be at all aware of it. The woman counts up her takings - nothing there, how is that possible. Why does he do something like that? Presumably out of love and passion, neither of which could be controlled, and have swept their owner along like last summer's floods, but only half the street, they at least left the other half for next year, and next year the street still won't have been repaired. A fine weakness, in the local authority as among people, which is not to be confused with inactivity. But a new age has dawned meanwhile, don't you think? Do you know, for example, that age in which women determine what they want and when and where and how and why and above all: where they want to get to? Is there a secret compassion somewhere in him, thinks this woman, it must be there somewhere, mustn't it? Has it perhaps been half suffocated, because earlier she threw herself so intemperately and gracelessly on this man? But what should she do, if she simply can't control herself in his presence? What, you don't know the forest? I do know the forest, except not this one here, how shall I find my way out again? No, there is no secret compassion in this man, I say in his stead, not for anyone. But at least he takes his time with what he does, one has to admit that. However, for some people even time itself lasts too long. They wanted a condensed, abbreviated version of time, so that afterwards they can enjoy the infinity, the eternity of pleasure all the longer. At any rate the man has long ago ceased to be afraid of shit, I can assure you of that. He had to wipe it off his own mother often enough or scratch it off somewhere else or pick it off the floor. Would his penis stand up like that, if he didn't like to do all that and didn't like me at least a little, thinks the woman, just as with violent jerks she feels him discharge himself into her and after that fortunately quickly become smaller and slip out of her. No sound apart from loud panting and puffing. Well hello. Is he not pleased at his success, for which he had to struggle long beforehand with himself and with her? Is he not tired by now and would at last like to be a little tender? His grip around the woman's neck relaxes at any rate, with a sigh the man collapses into a loose bundle over her, unfortunately with his whole weight on her back. With that it's already certain that for a while, until he's had a breather, he will cement her breasts into the ground and her breathing will be considerably restricted. But she has enough breath, confidence and voice left over, in order quietly, but in detail, to declare the following, which she can't hold back, it simply has to come out, now is that supposed to be a question or not? Gabi is supposed to have disappeared, at least that's what I've heard. You see what happens. Didn't you take her straight home yesterday? I know, of course, where she was yesterday and with whom, and what should I do about that now? It serves you right, if she's run away from you, and now you only have me. Where did you drive her afterwards?

Why didn't you take her home immediately? You should really
know where she is. Will you go to see her again when she's back
and drive her to the office early every morning? Don't think that
I don't know! I've known it for a long time. Once I even followed
you in my car. Where is she now. Since she hasn't come home. I
know exactly, that you pick her up almost every day, early in the
morning. She tells everyone she takes the early bus or the train,
but almost every day she drives to work with you, that's what I've
heard. I've heard as a fact, no, as a rumour, she collects used tickets from her colleagues and hands them in for her travel expenses.
Her girlfriend says that, and another one, too. There's a few in the
village who know it. So if they check, she doesn't need anything
else. That's fraud, isn't it. Or worse. They'll surely immediately
notice, that the number codes on the tickets she's handed in were
bought at quite different stops or even for quite different journeys.
I've thought about it for a long time. How has the girl got the
nerve to do it. You saw her last. Or did you take her somewhere
afterwards? Ouch. Don't hit me again, don't ever hit me, and if
you do, then not in the face, I've got the impressions of your
hands and of the pine needles all over me, people will notice if I
have a black eye as well. No, personally I don't care, but I would
prefer if you didn't do it and would be satisfied with the love that
I give you. Yes. I love you. You love me too. Other people don't
know anything. They're not there at night, in my home, it's
impossible, no one can pretend as well as that! No one can. You
love me, too, I know it, I know it. In fact I don't even exist any
more, only you exist. I would like to talk to someone close to me
about all of that, but I have no one. You must love me, a little at
least, and one doesn't send what one loves to its ruin. Perhaps we
need more room for each of us, not only in our bodies, where
space is quite limited, as I noticed again earlier. We need more
room for the two of us. My house would be the solution. I agree
completely. Let's move in together. Please. I'll let you know immediately if I'm planning a change in this situation. But what should
I want to change? I want to change that you always return home

to your wife. I want you always to stay with me. Asked about my most intimate feelings, I reply, I would not want to change anything in this respect. I would want to have things exactly as they are now. Except that then you'll always be with me. Then I would not have to long for your presence, because I would constantly have it around me. And if I didn't have it once, then I would, warmly wrapped in the distance which there would briefly be between us, wait until you were with me again. Thanks for that. We have nothing to give away, but we'll be able to afford a bit. I can promise you that. That's more or less what I wanted to say and now I've said it. I long day and night for the sight of you. Look, how courteous nature is, it lets us go first, before night falls and one simply isn't noticed any more. And the ground opens and swallows one up.

5.

People would be very angry with me, if they knew that here I stick them into sausage casings and hang them up, exposed to every glance, but the trousers won't stay up without a body. The house door bangs shut. A young woman has been swallowed up by the earth, which, however, is no earth all. The earth is made of water, which is meanwhile playing somewhat listlessly with the body. There our Gabi is at present entering into a symbiosis of plants and creatures quite in harmony with the water, with each individual species separately. Oh, if only there were more choice! Because protection of this human-water community plays a key role, if people want to protect themselves and their species too, of course, but first of all themselves. In order to do that, they must, which is a lot of work, but necessary, so that humanity does not perish, protect all other species as well, because there just is this sensitive community basis, in which bogs, swamps, ponds and river meadows in particular are always very threatened. This young woman on the other hand is already dead, it's a first rate failure, if a life was already brought to an end so early. Who did what wrong? Who is the culprit? You know it, I know it, so why ask. One is only: young once, some stay young forever, because there is no later for them. They've saved themselves something there. In life they had a grim opponent, who in this case has won.

So the wanted posters with Gabi's modelling photo are stuck to the masts. The cars drive eagerly past, see the pieces of paper pinned there and brake abruptly and slow down with a screech, because their owners will have been curious, which will frequently have caused a headache for the vehicles behind. The remainder of their heads they can collect later at the hospital or from the breakdown service, where they will be handed over on production of the certificate of registration. A good thing, that we let a photographer into the house, now we've still got something left of this pretty girl. It's almost ugly in its pure beauty, her photo at least, and at the bottom a low neckline, the rift, which separates her from us older folk; when one sees that, one would like to have been a bit young oneself and then remained exactly that way. The neckline points to something, and not to this building materials firm in the county town, where Gabi was employed as a commercial apprentice. The company is invisibly stamped on it, although the photo rather signals idleness to the beholder, like most photos, don't you think? Perhaps it's because of the clothes, but the message of this photo is fake, the mouth is like one which would like to give a kiss, not one which would like to read lines on a computer printout, the expression on the photo is prettier. How good for this girl, that it was as if made to love and kiss. Gone. Are we in agreement, that the account can now be closed, inclusive of the owner? Not in agreement? Then you have to put her on the table, in newspaper format. In any case we assume your agreement and then automatically deduct everything from your account.

Gabi's mother wanders aimlessly around the house, helplessly, as if a picture had been taken of her as a sheep, it doesn't matter by whom, but had originally been intended as a prouder beast. Doesn't she also have a friend, in Germany, whom she would like to join? She is already taking off into a new life, the run-up lies right in front of her, shining in the sun, below it a promising frozen lake, in which she, that's for sure!, is going to land. The end of the glacier, its tongue, which oscillates or recedes, depending on the weather, glitters before her eyes; it doesn't look as if it's hard, where she's going to land. It looks quite like a glistening holiday paradise, but will most probably be, like many lakes, merely an accumulation of meltwater, that is, a vale of tears. But at the moment there's something of the judge about her, the mother, as she weighs up, what her daughter might have done, what has she got up to? Where is she? If one only knew where she is. She personally picked out this nice friend for Gabi, with whom she's even allowed to spend the night. What coded data can there be, to be filed and hidden in the computer? To be kept for later? Her mother knows all the data. After all, she entered it all herself. What of the more than 2,000 people to be questioned in months of work, by 20 police officers, who will be put onto the case? What can they find out! Why does one have to make a note of thousands of car numbers? Why has Gabi run away, if that's what she's done? Her boyfriend is still there and washing his car again. The automobile is already shining loud and strong. No, her boyfriend doesn't know anything more either. He comes to visit the mother straight after school, sits down at the kitchen table, as if he could just as well stand. Takes a cup of coffee as if he could just as well drink tea out of his Walkman. Talks about his girlfriend who has disappeared, as if she had never been there. Knows nothing, as if he could just as well have known something. She's uncomplicated and honest, are the words he has been taught at the technical college, when it's a matter of an electrical circuit, which admittedly would never open itself voluntarily, unless it's struck by lightning. But what is to be done, so that the circuit finally closes? We still have to practise that. At the moment the current is flowing in one direction, as if it could just as well flow in the other. The electrons are happy that they've got time off and no one is forcing them to do something they don't want to do, we can do it differently, but our trainer can't make us do it yet. As part of a team of fellow-students Gabi's boyfriend is just making an electronic door opener, but for the moment the door still remains locked, the circuit has not yet taken charge of the electrons, a circuit which would have the task of offering the electrons as little resistance as possible. That is also what our young people wish: no resistance to their plans! These electrons, the things they get up to with one another. No human being would have been able to think it up, but good use is made of it. They only want to follow their course, if at the end of it there is a room less crowded with themselves. Otherwise they'd rather just stay at home. Negatively charged, as they by nature are, they strive, unlike me, for the positive. One can take them as an example at all times (from Muffler/Eberich: Electronics for Children, vol. 276, p. 7, revised ed.). And at this moment an automatic door mechanism also seems to be closing heaven's door, which he thought was already within reach. His room in his parents' house, also the new little flat, on which there's already a down payment, is not going to be hoovered for a while, no small snack will be prepared any more, not a soul will vote him president of his world and cut articles he wants out of the motoring magazine and put them in a ring folder, nor will he very soon honour his heaven on earth, his punctual destination every Saturday night with a visit. Which he does not yet suspect. Gabi and another man? Impossible. There was no other man, and if there had been, then he would not be with her, because he wouldn't know her. That's just the gossip of jealous girlfriends. It doesn't count for much, because no one can account for it. There was nothing. Gabi was an open book to her friend, a window with its panes, so a suitable frame for him. That she could have been a first rate deceiver - if that were true, we couldn't imagine it, say mother and boyfriend unanimously. We always knew her every step, and when her boyfriend was washing his car, she sat or stood beside it and when it was summer showed a leg, when it was winter showed nothing, and when asked, said nothing special, but not nothing at all. She didn't know what she felt before she wanted it. Well yes, that she felt a bit cramped, we admit that. She wasn't so keen on the apartment which her mother had just started paying off, but her boyfriend was. The young man doesn't know what he felt, until he saw the picture of the new Ferrari and our Schumi in it like a cork. Gabi's features were usually like a marshalling yard, they moved, but it didn't go anywhere, anywhere further away, to the land of smiles. To Austria. Straight there. No. Always only back, no matter where to. Absence, although at home, a vessel placed on the table, which sometimes floats in the light, then again is plunged into darkness, as the tides ebb and flow. Wash me, but don't make me wet, and do it above the all-time high water level. Wait a minute, no water plants grow there any more, but there is nevertheless the desire, that a great deal of water should cover one's foot, and then even more, ever more. Everyone always just wants more, no matter of what. Whoever takes a risk, dies in it, particularly when the water level fluctuates according to the season. Quiet lies the lake, who lies in it? Deposits of mud, sand, debris and a girl, who is swamped by water, they lie in it, i.e., if the girl hasn't come to rest at too great a depth. In other words, in order for the readers in the training room between land and water to understand more easily: If it must be a book, then a good book! Our Gabi was a bit like that: You know where you're at. Well, I don't know. One can pick it up again and again, this book, and it's never boring, no matter where one opens it, but usually respectably in an Ikea double bed, which her boyfriend got as a present from his parents (yes, indeed, everyone has to contribute something, otherwise we would be nothing, otherwise we would be others), at all times with clean sheets for him and his girlfriend. Otherwise there was nothing. They have made a balanced use of their resources for the future, since they've not yet been squandered, because resources are fundamentally indispensable, but also cannot be multiplied, however. What I meant to say was: If there's a human being there, then he should also be left there, because when he's gone, no one can replace him. One can take another one, but this one, one exactly the same, will hardly be found again. Because one will find a lot to criticise in all the others, who are like him. My God, how are we supposed to fill the pages, if we can't even say the simplest thing simply! It's a complex field of activity, protecting and preserving human beings, and one can practise on nature from time to time. Of course that demands constant decision-making in many respects, which can have far-reaching consequences, but usually not, because it takes a hundred thousand years, until one person comes to the conclusion that he shouldn't have burned his old shoes in the stove, because they've been poisoning and destroying the environment the whole time. The person concerned should rather have warmed people up with a beautiful body and a dear face and a fast car and a fast-moving TV programme. Our Gabi had all that, and what good did it do her? None. As attractive as she was - none! no answer - in particular one can't miss this lovely photograph, hanging there, when one's waiting for the post bus, and many people, who have come too early, can't help but study the photo thoroughly, they've got nothing else to do, and the bus can't drive off in front of them, they're deliberately there too early. Although everyone knows Gabi in the flesh, they now stare at her photo for a quarter of an hour. How easy it is, to miss something, if one looks away for a moment. Although they all know Gabi well, at least to look at, she grew up here after all, on the photo she seems strange to them. There's something irresponsible, immodest about her, which appears forward. A completely different side is displayed here, which when she was alive one hadn't noticed. On the other hand such a look is altogether familiar from the magazines (the nude and her face, which she has too, at the top of my picture, and if not, then you're holding the newspaper the wrong way round or are looking at something that isn't a human being, on page five of the Kronen newspaper, but there should be a picture of a naked woman there, shouldn't there? My God, what's that, into whose face you're looking, is that a face at all?), and that on the photo Gabi is more undressed than dressed also seems normal to them, ever since they've had the TV screen, so for decades, in fact. There people do more than undress. They also completely undress their partners, and then they turn around, so that one can see inside them as well and: that they are really completely hollow and empty inside. One wouldn't have believed them beforehand. The bodies have meanwhile become so immodest as to thrust themselves forward everywhere, in order to be able to undress even more quickly. What fun! At Bauer Clothing every Monday the first five customers who arrive at the tills completely naked get a whole outfit to the value of 5,000 schillings - so you'd better hurry, you could really do with a complete retread! Some are overlooked unfortunately. Although they try to shout just as loud as the others. Such a pretty girl, our Gabi. Were one finally to find her, one would have to give her up again, and nobody would know. It takes a while to get going, after the usual waiting time, a routine search for a missing person, a certain country policeman also hears about it in the line of duty, but knows nothing, everything therefore, wants of himself to be able to take it seriously, hopes at least to feign seriousness, if necessary, but he doesn't quite manage it. He now puts on a sombre expression in front of his colleagues. He's asked, yes, like most of them he knew this Gabi at least to look at, his colleagues know that anyway, a pretty girl. Basically they know nothing. They don't know that Gabi is resting at the bottom of the lake, which is not very deep. Yes, thoughts are sometimes deep, but the reasons which cause someone to do something are often not. The country policeman is something like a tour guide, but only if there's enough in it for him. There he is, take a look at how, as if by accident, he rubs himself up against this younger colleague, stands, as if unintentionally, close behind him when they're undressing. His colleague has his shirt halfway over his head and can't see anything and can't resist, for a moment, which is over all too quickly, he is caught up in his clothes like a fish in a net, his arms are raised, his narrow hips are, well they're there and feature some red acne, I call something like that flesh, precisely in its imperfection. Such a pleasure to press the somewhat swollen cock as if unintentionally against the left hip of the younger man, so that it can follow the scent and can imagine a well-shaped body at least in outline.

We at any rate go back: routine search for a missing person. Computers go through their extensive collections of data and induce people who in reality have never met to come together, possibly fatally on screen. Where have all the sex offenders of the district got to? Here they are, they're already waiting in this machine, waiting to be consumed by the state, which of them have we released recently and which not, which child-murderers are being protected by the federal government again and inexorably pursued by our Jörg, for their whole lives, no, not by this federal government, by the other one. Who has not yet been put in prison for life and castrated and/or killed beforehand? There are a couple in this district, but it's not many, even including the well-known exhibitionists, who, at least in the early stage of their hobby, are harmless. We'll check up on them anyway, so we've got something to do before we go for something to eat or go off duty. But the girl will turn up again anyway, that's for sure. We'll make sure that it happens as quickly and unbureaucratically as possible and that she won't be altogether used up, the girl, when she is picked up, like a remark someone has made, quick before we forget it, before it has to withdraw and finally change completely, like the water in the lake. I see no sign of anything similar at the moment. I soothe my agitation about murderers; the environmental regulations will have to be kept to, no, we don't pee up against public trees and bushes, and nor do we pee in bus shelters or against the walls of other people's houses, this legal instrument, no idea which, serves to reduce regional disparities economically and ecologically, that is, at some point, some day, everything will be in proper order again in the plant and animal kingdom, and whatever doesn't belong to us: away with it, whatever does belong to us: bring it back immediately, we need it, quick march! Our Gabi is one of us, a native from the diversity of complex living creatures, no, from the complex diversity of all living creatures and animated nature. But we can't yet really imagine that she has already become part of inanimate nature, we need a picture of it. Where to get one, without stealing it. That a knockout of a girl has been knocked out of nature's plan, one of those in any case ultimately destined to be brace-wearing angels, yes, even they have to be given a helping hand, so that in the chorus or as soloists they look smart, well, knockouts: knocked out, but yet not so soon, hm, that the permanent balance between living creatures and dead and with it the ecosystem, is upset. So we don't want to have to imagine anything so horrible. Not this time. But the next time. Millions of living creatures may have disappeared, OK, we're completely used to that, but just one, that's not right, she should have someone to take along, let's see, who's still available. We always have e.g. harmful organisms on offer, and what are we going to do with them now? We make sure that the economic harm is kept to a minimum and that the harm to nature is likewise as far as possible kept to a minimum. We are careful with nature's household, but are not careful with our own household, for that we buy the new cleaner with antibacterial additive, that will kill 99 percent of all known bacteria for you, but that last one per cent, that's the problem. And because it feels it has a problem, something that can destroy more than it disturbs, it wants to let that out too at last, what are one's talents and abilities for, after all? As already said, one can destroy or create something. This one bacillus, this undesirable alien, which was left alive, can now multiply undisturbed, because it doesn't have any competition any more, and can make the most of its abilities. So we'll give this infant a nice new inflammation of the lungs, and this driving school pupil, who never washes his hands, a good dose of gastro-enteritis. Yesyes, chemical cleaning agents should basically only be used carefully and selectively where absolutely necessary, but preferably not at all. This individual girl, who did not remain alive, fell victim to a selectively acting murderer, who does not, however, want to be seen as such, only if it were absolutely necessary, because someone wants to see his ID (but his colleagues all know who he is! They buy watches and jewellery from him in a special grey area and think no more about it), and who was pursuing higher goals. No, I don't know all his goals. Information will be gratefully received. Ownership in itself is no grounds for complaint, unless someone wants to dispute it. That would then be grounds for an action for disturbance of posses- sion, who knows how that will end, it all depends on the lawyer. What if in spring the leaves slip out for a visit, and then someone tears them off. Will there then be no spring? Which property in any case are you talking about, for heaven's sake? There is one admittedly, but it doesn't belong to one yet. At this point in time the property is still hidden by a woman, who is now (if it were per- missible, I would say: She has pulled herself down over her eyes, so that passers-by don't recognise her immediately) loitering in her open house door and sulkily lowering her face, because once again a man has not come to the agreed rendezvous and has in any case probably frequently deceived her recently. The sex is right admittedly, it's the way she wants it and no other way, but preferably another way. But otherwise quite a lot is going badly, which we shall have to sort out. The worst version of the truth goes: This man cannot have loved her, because one does not send someone one loves to their ruin. Or does one? No, it can't be. Because whoever or whatever one loves, one always puts it in the refrigerator for a quick between-meals snack, if one's not hungry any more. Because after all, one doesn't want it to spoil and have to be thrown away. One stores the beloved person away, so that tomorrow and the day after tomorrow one can still eat of his wonderful body. Jesus. Oh, none of you were there in the nights! That's something I've often said. It can't be that he's been deceiv- ing me, for a long time, with a younger woman. If one were to ask: Which of us is older, how our polycolor-impregnated heads would sink! She had often wanted to leave him, the woman, but the idea immediately made her ill. She was thinking of making another choice soon, if she had one, thinks the woman in middle age and glances down a street, populated loudly but unharmoniously by women shopping, mothers with buggies and small children in wellington boots, so truly the grey main road is no harmonium. Time is short. And she in turn uses her elbows, the woman, she just isn't quite as young any more as she has made herself, because unfortunately only the dear lord God is allowed to make one. A man. Naturally. Rub things out in one's passport, who would do something like that! Dagmar Koller, wife of the former mayor of Vienna, will do it, but be caught.

In the meantime the need for action has become very urgent, but the last time someone else acted, who discovered her in her car at a crossroads, stopped and gutted her without even giving her local anaesthetic. Everything was taken out of her hands. Who could suspect it. We need something in writing. So sooner or later we go to the notary. The people who now want to act, no matter how and with what, they get first choice, and they choose someone they like. He tells the truth, is decent, sporty, clean and energetic and stands out from someone, whom they just don't like so much, although he, too, is decent, sporty, clean and energetic. But unfortunately one can't tell by looking at him. Fortunately only someone is chosen about whom you can tell everything by looking, above all, that he is steady on his feet, but he stands or sits even more steadily in his Porsche. The decent and able. The hard-working, too. What is their secret? I don't know, otherwise I would pass it on. Perhaps we want to be deceived, because we are constantly deceiving everyone, that is, if we get the opportunity. This woman for example has had herself sterilised, which she candidly confesses, although now she couldn't have any children anyway. She doesn't want children and has never wanted them, since she herself is a child and wants to be like a child for the man. Another child would always only have got in the way. The other, Gabi, herself hardly more than a child, also did nothing but get in the way. Which is the proof. Of what? For whom? No matter who it is, at the moment one sets the life and the soul of the party on him, and already he's off to the carnival at Villach or looks at it on TV and feels altogether at home in this country. Others live in the lake, no, you can't say that Mme Author, if someone is sleeping in a lake, that doesn't at all mean that they're living there. Didn't you see the rubber dinghy? It lives in an attic room with photos on the walls, baby animals and pictures of models, both of them public and private projects, it just depends who is making use of them and what he is exploiting them for. Exploitation is the main thing, in order to feel good oneself, simply fantastic. Every glittering snowflake tumbling down insensibly would say that of itself, while it's still in the air, it's looking forward to the soft landing, and then it's already melted. Not even a hot stone was needed.

The crucial detail, which no one saw, or everyone who paid no particular attention to it, was a car, which in the cold nights of the previous winter, before it went off in the direction of springalingaling, was parked nearly every morning very close to the bus stop. There was a high degree of probability that, waiting at the wheel, was the man who for more than six months secretly drove Gabi to work in the county town, and occasionally, when his own working hours permitted, also drove her back again. It's certain at least that more than half of the girl's journeys to work on this relatively short stretch were made with this unknown man, we won't even start on the other journeys, at night, mad with delight, otherwise we would sink to the ground at the thought of all the things these two got up to together and how they did it. Gabi must have deceived her mother and her boyfriend. Others she couldn't deceive, but they never said anything about it. No one knew about it, let's stick to the official version. Once in this sequence - if we stepped closer, then we would see more - Gabi's breath completely stopped coming, when perhaps she had been too much of a burden to the man, who after all only wanted to spoil her. That's not right. One does need a bit of it! It was

achieved through gentle pressure, because Gabi, spoiled by tenderness, became pretty naughty. The tongue, the larynx, the
carotid arteries, the lungs have been trained for public appear-
ances. If one denies it to them, because one wants to leave a
person entirely alone with their breath, then these two become
feeble in their ambition to maintain the functioning of the body.
They mock the rest of the body, call out to it: Without us you are
nothing and can do nothing. You can try if you like, you are at liberty to do that, but you will fall down, dear body, and rising up
will be possible only with great difficulty, or, if you are God, who
rises again, then that will become evident, at latest, at the moment
when the women roll away a stone and begin to weep and wail.
But if you are God, then you don't need us anyway. The oxygen
has been diverted from the brain, the brain surfaces have dried
up, the environmental conditions in the brain biotope have been
drastically altered. Anyone who believes species-rich life partner-
ships of thinking and thought would be more stable is right in
principle, but not always. A maximisation of the number of
thoughts should not absolutely be an aspiration in a project like
this, in case you're wondering why so few ideas are to be found
here, in this place. Then you just have to search! Apart from that
it is not absolutely necessary that there are many. More important
is: which, and also important is the analysis of my thoughts with
respect to the parts they play in my brain, because my brain gets
so easily bored and longs to instigate something new. And then
there would still remain to be decided which strategies with
respect to what I shall stuff into my brainbox would have to be
represented, so that they then represent me and that I in turn can
here decently represent and act as counsel for people living or
once living. The more diverse the TV films I empty into my upper
storey, the greater the number of species of organisms I will then
later be able to harvest from my tables and benches. I consume
dead stuff and make life out of it. I then have it well prepared.
One should also perhaps read the newspapers. Thanks, I'm
pleased to do it, it's always worthwhile. Here e.g. I've copied out

many pages, but I haven't joined them together yet. I'm always astonished how the natural things of life are revealed to me, but then I immediately slam the door shut again. It's a paper chase after facts, just you start, you won't, however, find anything any more, because I will have dismembered the bodies, and then I've poured the highly effective Andy Pandy drain cleaner, a British product, unfortunately no longer obtainable nowadays, on top. Now they're gone, like the two fried eggs earlier on. Oh no, now I've dropped the vague hints of one of Gabi's girlfriends, who one or two days ago looked thoughtfully up to the sky (she could never look as pretty as Gabi, that's why she's sprayed something around her, from a L'Oréal box, so that she can't be seen so clearly), and she said something nasty, which e.g. would not turn up in a story of the Virgin Mary. Now that the road is clear, this girl is groping around in her friend's life, hesitating as to what she can pick out of it, to make better use of it, a nice calm faithful husband, children, a home of their own, holiday, and then she drops a vague hint, pointing in a direction which is still hidden from our eyes. We see nothing. This hint will only be returned to later, when suddenly others will also point to it, like the sun, which shines back in the evening, before it finally lowers itself to the other half of the globe, where the soles of people's feet are already burning and they at last want the sun above their heads.

Which car then, learner driver? Fellow employee, please step forward and speak loudly and clearly into this microphone, so that our diligent officers can hear it! Well, I tell you, the lighting effect when Gabi came into the office, it was as if she was wearing diamonds, as if she was floating in the sun. One would have liked to squeeze her there and then, she wasn't a mother yet, but everything else, even Carnival Princess and Harvest Princess, so probably there was nothing else to come. I would really like to describe what a glow there would be in the folksy hut, around the beer and the music on the radio, where the regulars stare into their glasses which, dulled by the dishwasher, cannot give back a single ray. That by the way is why the regulars at their tables usually don't display a ray of hope or anything else. Such a pretty girl, our Gabi, as if she didn't belong to us. She laughed a lot, perhaps not quite so much at the end. And on the edge of the washstand in the Ladies lies an oblong case, containing lipstick, liner and mascara, which make her look even more beautiful, Gabi, a little ring with a rock crystal, a friendship ring from her boyfriend, is also there, when she gently lowers her head, looks nice, lets someone brush her hair from her shoulders and idly wastes a little time, which has been given by someone or other, oh if only everyone had as much time for themselves or they should take it, one would see the result. That's what's written up at the checkout in the Billa Market, where cleaning things for the times are on offer: eye shadow, moisturising creams, even pore cleansing strips. It's always supposed to go deep, although most people prefer shallowness and chatter away, as they buy a velvet hair band, that they would like to see this or that musical. Plants and animals are dependent on one another, and which eye shadow shade goes with a complexion, that also is dependent on both, which with a bit of good will could work very well together, if nature would only let them and would possibly accept cosmetic help. But it does! At all times. Please, come in and make my lumps and spots invisible! No matter what they want, we let the colours onto our skin, as we were advised, we also allow phosphates into our lakes and rivers, although we were explicitly advised against it. Gabi had a secret, so what, nature has its secrets too. Today nature is going out with this soil type, found at the edge of the lake. And tomorrow it will go out with another one. But with whom is Gabi going about, if not with the official boyfriend from the tech college? No one knows. No idea. But there is someone. No one knows how many manifestations of water there are on earth, but many would like to know, because wind-surfing, racing motor boats, sailing or swimming are their hobby. And no one is supposed to have known anything more about this young neighbour from right here amongst us? The wind treats the water cruelly, another hundred yards, and there's death waiting already and looking at his watch and tapping the ground with his scythe. Where on the other hand is Gabi, is the question some others are asking, who are also slowly getting anxious. Not many. Boyfriend and mother sit opposite one another and outbid one another in everyday normality, so that there are no silences. What else do they have to talk about with one another, apart from Gabi? The mother is meanwhile anyway thinking only about her friend in Germany, when will she be able to go again, what will he say about it, she'll soon be with him. They, the mother and Gabi's boyfriend, also outbid one another with Soletti pretzel sticks, which are always there. That makes things easy for me, otherwise I would have to think of something else. The boyfriend muses to himself how often his cock stands up straight at the sight of Gabi, although he hasn't even finished eating yet, and he was only halfway through the porn magazine; unfortunately she's not there now. She's probably pushed off, the house feels dead. An emptiness reigns, which today the young man can't fill with immature thoughts. Hardly has he entered the house than he is overcome by a strange shyness, he asks nature for once to leave his lust for his girlfriend right out of his thoughts today, but doesn't rightly know why. Thoughts are free. Today he wants to think about her tenderly, even demandingly, and the demands are supposed to end with a visit to the cinema in the county town, and beyond that for once there are to be no more demands. Will she once again grip his cock so firmly right above the balls as recently, and then slowly stroke upwards, to the very end, where she would grip even more tightly? She says it gives her the creeps, she doesn't like to look, but he's patient and can wait for her to do it again, and again and again, just as he has shown her. The main thing is that she lies there quietly and lets him enter her again and then moves her hips a little. A dream, I tell you! If you and I together were a house, we would collapse now. By nature Gabi is not very explosive, but a bottle of wine can do wonders. Earlier he briefly went up to her room, opened, has no idea why, the wardrobe, smelt the clothes, jingled a couple of thin gold armbands on the dressing table, he listened: nothing. The cupboard probably wants to go to sleep. Everything neat and tidy. Have you already spoken to the essence of absence today? No? Tell it, I'm looking for it! How quiet it is here. The approx. 2,000 cuddly toys are all happy as every day, at their own beauty and about how lovingly each and every one was chosen by their owner, one has to collect for years, that's why they're the only ones here looking really self-satisfied. Now the room could surely gradually dispense with the darkness in the corners, couldn't it? Everything's all right, isn't it? The technical college student opens the other wardrobe doors as well. As if Gabi would voluntarily sit down in the wardrobe for two days. The water balance of the earth continues to diligently wash out its cups, which are constantly being stolen, by people who are wasting water all the time, it's probably not their cup of tea. Oh dear, that doesn't work, and it's also a repetition. Forgive me, I often can't keep up with myself, at any rate so many landscapes depend on water, this most precious commodity, think of the Carinthian lakes and those of the Salzkammergut, where the rich have firmly and safely stashed themselves away and if they ever have to vote then always choose freedom and the Freedom Party. You can set your clock by them. The mother draws on a cigarette, already the fifteenth today, that will do her good and calm her down, if Gabi stays away much longer. The mother's bronchial tubes ask leave to speak, but we ignore them. Water, of which a human being is made up, so much so that one shouldn't put them in water after their death as well, water to water instead of dust to dust. Somehow superfluous, I think. Ground water research in the mother's lungs would say: enough is enough, in ten years at latest it will be possible to raise cancers here, but then we'll be dead and won't have to look at it any more. The mother is crying now and needs yet another handkerchief, because this one can't absorb and store much more. What should the ground or even my hard disk say, when I've served everything up so nicely and have explicitly let the earth know! Without the least twinge of conscience we expect them to put up with everything, how mean.

The people continue to walk along the paths and drive along the roads. Have they perhaps heard something about Gabi? Don't know her. A woman with a boring demeanour, I don't know which, steps out of her front door, and doesn't know either why she's doing that now. Of course she's heard the news, two days ago already; but she doesn't say anything about it, because no one asks her. She is still to a certain extent an outsider here, a stranger. A newcomer. This morning she again wants to be worshipped as the one and only, which she has always imagined as being more pleasant than it is. I've been telling her for years, but it doesn't do any good. Behind her rises her neat house, which would now like to stretch its legs, but instead by mistake kicks a person in the knees, who is now standing in front of it and is herself now placing both hands on her shoulders, so that her arms are crossed on her breast. As if the hands were using the shoulders as supports. From this moment this person has to stay in bed for three weeks. This woman had expected a bit more wildness from the man yesterday, at least as much as she had still got in the mountains two days ago, but since then the man has not shown his face for a whole day and a half. Another woman? Oh Jesus, what can I do, with whom can I do something now, there's no one there? This man believed, she loves gentleness, gentle advertising, for example, but his only model is the one for Palmer's lingerie, I think it's gentle enough, one can see the whole body almost to the heart; no reason to be envious, ladies, be glad that you're in the world at all! Would you really like anyone to read your thoughts? During the adverts this woman here often quickly prepares a small snack in the kitchen, in the summer she even makes chocolate ice herself! And when she comes back, the woman wants the wildness in this man immediately to be really wild. On the spot! She knows on which spot. She's sensitive there. On whose shoulder should she cry now? She has no one, and so begs the man to give her a family, so that she can once again say what's on her mind and get fucked for all it's worth. It's not worth much. But the man already has a wife at home. He can let her be, Gerti's home is nice anyway. His wife doesn't need him, the way this woman needs him. Today we'll make things nice and tomorrow, too. For that the woman loves and sacrifices, just as she learned to do as a child from the nuns at convent school for Jesus' sake. Or does she have to let this man go? If she doesn't do it, he will in any case run away from her sooner or later. She can't hold him. But if she now finds the strength, to let this man go back to his wife and family - he already has a grandson - then one day perhaps he will return to her voluntarily, at latest when all these people, every one of them, are dead, or not? But if she now finds the strength to open this jar of cocktail onions, then she will be blessed in that the rolls which she prepared for him earlier, with several hundred different kinds of sausage, will not taste as stale as recently. The sausage is off, that's for sure, it is perhaps out of sorts before it can be served, or is it only the woman's stomach? The rolls are so colourful and pretty again. You can't be too sure, we'll throw them away and buy new ones, we'll throw everything away and buy everything new. The woman doesn't feel like going to the grocer now, she might miss her beloved in these ten minutes. Let's just leave the sausage where it is and sprinkle paprika over it, not too much, otherwise his stomach will be as discontented as the sinners in hell, where things are also too hot for my taste, I'm already wet again. Except, please don't let him go back to Gabi again, that would be too much for this woman. If at least she weren't so young, Gabi. If she were at least older than the woman, but then again she wouldn't be Gabi, but someone else. Where is she then? Love is not only deep respect for the other from deep inside, it should also be able to be shown outwardly. It is invited to kindly make a bit more effort. Or is the man incapable of showing feelings? Would that not be a pity if disillusionment were to bring one down to earth every time? Three bottles of sparkling apricot wine from the Wachau, he likes that, it's nice and sweet. She'd rather have the sparkling wine without the apricot, but can't impose her better taste on him. Kurt is a complete pro. He phoned earlier. It's me. Drive immediately to our spot on the mountain. I'm coming too. Did you get that? Yes, of course, we were only there the day before yesterday, and all the times last summer, have you forgotten? The mountain wind is already howling with anger, that the woman is not willing to keep to this arrangement. What's wrong with her? What's she dawdling around the house for and waiting, although she should be somewhere quite different now? She's been summoned somewhere, this attractive figure. He is surely already on his way in his light walking shoes in the howling spring gale. Why isn't she on her way? Or does she have reasons? She won't be afraid? Curious. Usually she always does what he tells her to, and then her body immediately opens wide and pulls up all the blinds, even before it hears the certain steps that should be undertaken immediately. Exactly. I already hear the tearing of underwear like a terrible voice in me, perhaps I have a premonition. The house. The house is his goal, his one and only, she suspects, reads it from his face, even when he isn't there, in clear moments, when she's free to have them. But already she's doubting herself and her observations again. Such thoughts she has, for sure, but they don't feel right, and soon they disappear again, offended, as soon as he approaches and becomes more important than them, the thoughts, than everything else. Perhaps that's why he worries about the house and investigates it all down to the last detail, as if he wanted to make it have an orgasm. What do you want, this man is tender, he's potent, he fulfils the most secret desires of the house. New shutters? My pleasure, here you have them! The kitchen floor looks a bit dull and listless? We'll deal with that right away. The sheriff, which he is himself, is there at once. Compared to her house the woman almost feels small and unattractive. She watches the man as he investigates nooks and crannies. He could not draw the lips of her vulva apart more affectionately than these glass sliding doors in front of the bookcase with the classics. I can imagine. The man lies before her inner eye, crouching like an animal, looking up at her, and which she then allows to stand up and raise its head to her. Oh dear, it's looking in quite a different direction, the stupid beast. Was there not a noise, is the house door rattling, because it doesn't shut properly, I'll repair it tomorrow? At the feet of the beloved: no one, not one, so not the only one either. She will have to lay aside her dearest for today, in the hope of being able to pick him up again tomorrow, where she put him down. Why does she not set out for the mountain? It would do her good, get a bit of exercise. Today inexplicably she can't do it, although she's been having such wet thoughts the whole time, whenever she opens her brain-box in order to take out one of them, living, dripping, twisting, slippery and to greedily close her lips around it. Who can swallow all that? She can! This time exceptionally she's allowed to swallow everything, this time he allows her to. Otherwise not. But why didn't Gabi come home two days ago? Because that's what the woman heard from sources bubbling out of the ground every-where, there's no stopping them any more. These sources can't be channelled any more. Where is she then, Gabi, where is she? No idea. The last time he was still tender and attentive to the woman, his one and only love, because Gabi doesn't count, she can't even count to three, the mouse. The woman now wants him to fall upon her, to tear down and/or shove up her clothes, as so often, and with a good appetite sink his teeth into her cunt as into a well-filled sandwich, as so often; but then when he does it, it's not quite right either, because it's sore, the way he so thoroughly investi-gates and then sucks up her precipitations and evaporations, so that there is order in nature again. Order as in this house. Yes, we have several kinds of reproduction, vegetatively through budding, or, if you like, we can also do it another way: asexually through spores, but naturally two gametes can also merge sexually, luckily that doesn't lead to catastrophe every time, although nature always has a liking for catastrophes. And the woman always likes it, when he does something like that with her. It's her nature. What she doesn't like so much, is when he causes her body pain, bestows an unpleasant taste and an unpleasant smell to a dozen paper handkerchiefs or stuffs her filter with shit, instead of decently stoppering her. It's the same for her as with the algae: If the increase in quantity is too great, a thick, foul-smelling mass forms, as happened to the lake out there. The woman doesn't want to take it as her model, although she would like to be just as unfathomable. He should do it to her at least once a week, there should be that much in it for her, even if one is as busy as the man. We have the rest of the week off and can recover. If he didn't spread her with his hard fingers from time to time, she would absolutely miss it. Water! Please, we have limestone here. It lets everything through. He's the only one for her. He's the only one for her. Her nipples stiffen and stretch as if they wanted to pull a small cart. They really hurt, yet recently his behaviour towards her was sometimes rather bored and absent-minded, she has to admit, I agree with her. And why? Entirely because of Gabi. If he sees her, his eyes begin to glow, and he becomes totally randy. It's a natural phenomenon, which could always only be described, but rarely be seen. It mustn't happen any more, that he meets Gabi. Otherwise the house is off and he has to take the consequences. The woman isn't demanding after all, she's not even as demanding as the so-called indicator plants, if we're talking about nature, which make demands, unfortunately also often on us. With these types of plants their value as indicators is all the greater, the more specific the demands as plant type are. That can be used to investigate soil quality. No, it's better if his hands do it, what do I care about this indicator plant, it would only indicate that I'm not so young any more and that he doesn't like me as much as I would like, thinks the woman. She can only make demands because she owns a house, not because she herself is there too. Without her house she would have no value as an indicator. She would be a dial without a needle, she could never display her water level, her degree of moisture could never be judged, no one would be interested in it. Yesyes nature claims its rights, but only gets them after committed people have fought for them for at least fifty years. The water, which is now running out of the woman, indicates an imbalance, because the man, it appears to her, has not come for some time, but it's only two days ago, he's not stayed away so long before. Yes, he's often stayed away as long as that. Why has she forgotten that he wanted to meet her at their usual place? She should have left long ago. Funny. Something inside her says no. Now she would rather hang like a curtain at the window and look out, half hidden, to see if he's coming. How can he come, if he's already halfway up the mountain? When he was last here, he drove off with Gabi, the woman is quite certain of that, she saw it herself. He must have taken her straight home, so where is she? Did she go out again? On the way back he should really have briefly dropped by again, in order to see her and to be seen by her, to console, to placate, to fuck, what do I know, but he didn't turn up again. She only got this one phone call from him and then another one, which at the moment she's disregarding. Before he drove off - Gabi was already sitting in the passenger seat, weighed down by so much hair, that even before he started her head, exhausted, had sunk down to his lap, where no doubt his cock was standing up as if it never did anything else - she, the older woman, completely lost her self-control at this moment of threatened departure. As he was about to go (beforehand he tried the cellar door, to make sure it was still locked), pulling up his zip, which would soon come down again, she had clung to him, sobbed, begged, hoped, that he should at last see that there was something wrong with her, which he should repair, she loves him so much, she loves him so, which probably every child in the village could see, only he couldn't. Please come back! There should at last be an end to the nightmare with him and all the secrecy. But for it to come to an end, he would first of all have to come and properly and vigorously start from the beginning again. But he's evasive, and he expresses himself vaguely, when she demands a decision from him. But to demand a decision from him, he would first of all have to be there. But he doesn't come. He goes. She doesn't dare call him at home, because then his wife answers, blunt and stubborn as a Leopard tank, once it could at last be delivered to Turkey and at least two hundred people have thoroughly smashed each other's faces because of it. That night as Gabi was transported home, the woman didn't sleep a wink. Now, however, she's quite still, stands there just a little longer. If someone passes by, she pretends she's investigating something on the roughcast or the exterior window sill, perhaps dirt, mould fungus or loose plaster. She runs her finger over the wall as if she wanted to draw something. The house is all she has to offer, we shouldn't fool ourselves any longer, children big and small always want to get presents, that's what they have in common. She isn't squeamish when he hits her hard on the backside with the flat of his hand or with the ruler which is lying ready, on the contrary, in the meantime she really likes it, if not for long, she can't take it for long; it's impossible for two people to have a stronger contact with one another, of whom one is stronger than the other, otherwise the one would come out the other side of the other. It annoys the woman, that she somehow finds it exciting, when he forces himself into her from behind. Although she also fears it and resisted it for a long time. Until the muscles finally slacken, however, he has to hit her fairly hard and fairly long, often she can't sit properly for two or three days afterwards. On all sides women, including her, like to aim for the most basic experience, but when it comes, instead of enjoying it, one searches tirelessly for its origin in the past, all of which should also belong to one. Was he hit so much as a child? We immediately have to read one or more books, in order to understand it. The woman wants to understand and forgive everything about this man, otherwise all pleasure is gone. She's looking for a man who is ready and in a position to join up with her, to help her bear the burdens of life and naturally also to fulfil her sexual desires. Yes. Perhaps one should once again permit oneself the simple things, the love which every animal knows, but every animal, even ours, does not always recognise us and not exclusively as its master. When he has expended himself in her, the man goes home again each time, unless there are small repairs to carry out (she has often deliberately broken something, so that he stays longer!), as if he immediately had to look for himself somewhere else, to find himself. That's how she imagines it, because now she has already read one book and another about it. He goes jogging in the mountains. Already she's thinking: If only he's not looking for another! Anything, except that. Otherwise the woman does not begrudge him any pleasure, once she has at last fallen asleep in her own silence, in her own vapour and her lustre which she doesn't have. We shall certainly need a judge. The weak points of this woman will always serve us as starting point, because here we can begin with the control of her personality. The judge will do that, and he will be at a loss. But he will nevertheless have to pass judgement: She belongs to what is called the weaker sex. That's very practical, I think. One can buy the women ready seasoned and only has to shove them in the oven. So many are dead, even men, that it doesn't matter to us what happens to this one.

The country policeman's colleagues begin to go systematically from house to house asking questions. Who saw Gabriele Fluch for the last time? Not even that can be precisely established. Even late in the evening, even at night, the little detached house in which she lived is brightly lit up. Every window so bright, as if it wanted to invite everyone in, then Gabi will certainly be among the visitors, who constantly ring the bell, enter, without having properly wiped their shoes, and hold out magazines, to which we are supposed to subscribe, or thoughts about Christ, which we are allowed to enter. No she isn't here, Gabi. Everything has been searched. Her boyfriend has meanwhile gone home, he has to study for an exam. The mother will ring him immediately, if something happens. At his home his parents will do the same, if something happens. The family house of the Fluchs stands in a small group of the like-minded. Everyone knows everyone else but perhaps they don't want to know one another too well. Since the houses are all alike, the people want to be like everyone else too. Each is like the other and no one says anything about the other or to the other. It's an estate for workers, cheaply built in the sixties, but they've got everything inside, even running water, we were allowed to choose the wallpaper ourselves. It's just like life, in which the inclinations live, but if once they work against us, then no one objects to that either. They destroy us, no one weeps, but the result is quite respectable, because our house is still there after all. On this estate the people stick together, even without knowing each other particularly well, it's not even necessary. The inquiries lead nowhere. They are not yet very urgent, since at this point one still hopes that Gabi will come back home, talking and laughing, she doesn't hurt anyone, why should anyone hurt her. No one hurts her. Peace is strong and determined to reign. No one can make a stand against it, it pulverises even the longest war. A crippling passivity takes hold of people when peace reigns, don't give war a chance. Never again! Peace must immediately seize everything and take possession of it and its reign shall be endless and all-powerful, it is considered very practised, it can do that no bother!, the peace that gives orders, it is always very strict with us, stricter than war. That's how it should be, and we like to obey this stronger force, peace, its power is secure, its name be praised in all eternity, with brief interruptions. No, not in all eternity, the dead sleep there, and peace no longer needs to reign over them, they're already quiet. Of their own accord.

6.

Don't interrogate the face of a human being, it will tell you nothing, it will grimace or dissemble. The country policeman is partial to the darkness of night. The scene of a crime lures him again and again, and other places, which only a few people know, even if they were born here, also lure him. Whom does the country policeman disturb as he goes on his way? Only the bright feet of time, or is it someone else's feet?, which rush away ahead of him, into the darkness, at a rapid gallop, as if they wanted to laugh at the country policeman. For the victims of murder, nature is a bed, should they have to lie out in the open. But for the murderers, too, it's a made bed, which they are free to use, and for their killing business they cover it with seclusion, so that no one sees them, but one always has to reckon on something happening by chance. The car ploughs through the night, in the houses lights are still on, slide by as if they were ships, but it's the country policeman driving past. Soon from right and left the forest closes over him like giant folded hands over a head, full of desperation. The village has slipped away from Kurt Janisch, and with the village life slips away, too. It is often poisoned by neighbourly acts of revenge, but still, it's life. But also the houses, in which it takes place, they should all rightly belong to him, who himself represents what's right, here, if you please, he has the appropriate regulation gun, its barrel is just as dark as the night, not nickel-plated, not bright as this day, which as surviving dependent has remained behind with lowered head. So, now it reigns at last, for, let's say, at least another eight hours, pain and pleasure and pleasantries disappear together in the forest, snow hangs like a veil over the mountains, so thin that one can't even see it in the darkness. Today the woman didn't keep the meeting on the mountain, something like that has never happened before. A bad sign. Instead she constantly calls him at home and puts the phone down when his wife answers. She's slowly beginning to notice, but she doesn't think anything of it, because her husband has told her: Just you tidy up, and see that you don't forget anything, including under the beds. This revolver, a Glock, its 16 rounds lie properly in the magazine and concentrate on their big moment (it will come once and not be repeated!), surrounded by only a little metal and a great deal of polymer plastic, the butt fits easily into the hand, but it will not be so easy for someone to pull it out, at least that's what we hope. At the moment this weapon is just as relaxed as its owner, but inside it trembles towards an event, which will lend it importance. Night, transfigured night, let me be afraid at last! All right, all right. In the headlight cone a still winterblind embankment, spindly undergrowth, the stream only puts in an appearance right at the bottom, and will certainly work its way up during the summer, with gentle murmuring, at present inaudible because of car noise, a bit of car is already enough for a driver not to hear anything from outside. Here a passing place, right at the edge a stack of wood, a pile of shit, a bright eye, which a team of woodcutters left behind, is cut out of the landscape by the moving light, disappears again. On the left the slope drags itself up, covered in brushwood and dry, old grass, it will throw off its burden step by step, because it will soon be too heavy, the higher it goes, until it is empty, icy, pure rock, where only chamois can survive, will be able to rise up, alone, free and single; the individual branches of bushes point in the air, the birches over there have already missed their first leaf deployment, on the plain they're already diligently putting forth shoots. Further up there are perhaps even patches of snow, until there is only snow, we also still have to expect night frosts, a tasty dessert to follow the day that remained.

The road grants us the not to be underestimated pleasure of the blue, no the grey ribbon, which only thunderstorms are allowed to cut. The country policeman is on his way to the place, where he has already tidied up the bed of a murder victim several times, but he is repeatedly drawn there, just behind the village is the spot, soil cheated of plant growth, wasteland, but today the country policeman is driving further. Strangely enough he cannot remember whether he removed all evidence. Did he pick up the tissue or not. And if so, perhaps there's another one left over. He would also like to see if something was left lying at another spot, further away, where he also was with Gabi, which also has to be tidied up. He removed every piece of fluff, every scrap, but perhaps there are, left over from earlier intercourse, somewhere else, still a couple of stuck together paper handkerchiefs, which he now also wants to dispose of, better safe than sorry, he has a powerful torch, almost a searchlight, with him, the country policeman. Its beam will playfully leap after every thread, until he has caught up with and caught it. At this time, in this cold, no one will notice its hard, strong cone of light, still less down there, right by the river. One wrong move and the water puts one in its sack. It's as if the winter had returned, it has suddenly become so cold again. Over there the crouching back of a sawmill, a giant shadowy shape, there, too, the bridge (lovelessly poured of concrete, but completely suitable for heavy trucks) over which one can drive back and forward, the saws are silent, the lips, too, but the stream whispers, which usually one doesn't hear for all the squealing of the huge, rotating and wood-spitting metal bands. I say: Away with the stream! Down here at last, if you please: THE RIVER. In with the stream and off it goes. Thank you for your free appearance, but you're too big for me to describe, although I would be paid something for it, if I asked. At the moment I'm practising on the little things, though not with the modesty of some colleagues, e.g. a Mr K. whom I know personally, no, not the one you're thinking of. Once again, my God, what a coarse language one sometimes has to speak, if even animals and plants are to understand one: If one switches off the engine, one can hear it rushing, use another word, immediately, let's say: one hears it talking to itself, the river. So the stream has abruptly disappeared, and now the roaring river steps up to us, which had come strolling around a gentle left-hand bend, which it almost missed, and demands its quota of admiration. Now they are running along side by side the river and its embankment road, which has been leant against it, so that it looks halfway good, but the road stands there obstinately, stands firm against the river's desires to pull it down, to play with it, and only the inhabitants of the heights move, as fast as they can. To get away from it, because it is threatening to their tender feet or furs.

Dark alder thickets to the right, deep down below by the river, where one always finds them, I don't have to change much there. In addition there is now, a real rarity, a canapé on this road, on which there's hardly any traffic at night, an approaching car with a roof rack: Skis rest in their coffin-like box, funny, it looks like a cap for the car, and this box contains play, sport and fun in such a small space that it would be impossible to squeeze in people as well; how are they supposed to amuse themselves, when there's room for their apparatus, but not at all for them? The roof rack is practical in any case, I think, people can straight away be buried in it if they have an accident. The car shoots past and briefly finds itself on the fringes of a hail shower of contempt caused by the country policeman, who in any case feels contempt for everything that doesn't belong to him. No reason to get excited. So, it's gone, the fast car, like a wet poodle, but in truth it has remained master of the house, it was an S-Class Mercedes.

Despite everything the road is and remains dry. The eyes go
ahead, don't turn aside, here comes the turn-off we're looking for.
The crime didn't happen here, but here, as already suggested,
paper handkerchiefs from earlier unions could still be lying
around. If someone thought of examining these as well, then they
would have a scent, although a cold, dried up one. But we don't
quite know what modern forensic medicine is capable of.
Yesterday and the day before yesterday Kurt Janisch already
drove along the road at night to all the places where he's been
with a certain young woman, who disappeared, sleepwalkers
both, almost asleep in what they were doing, sometimes also calling to the other body: You can't do that, no, or can you? You can
do it better than that! Did we leave out any part of this body by
mistake? Then we'll attend to it the next time, till the first bit has
healed again. And if it can, the body then remains quite at liberty,
until one's home again, where another will without fail take an
interest in it. And where those already present there, who never
go for a walk, because they always have to patiently wait, want to
suck one dry again for the sake of this obliging service, even if
one has arrived back already completely empty and exhausted
and cannot possibly be used again today, except for washing the
car, where one has to do nothing else except to be and be there.
The car doesn't ask for anything more than that. Nature provides
the water. Past. Not a sound in the modern car, which glides more
than it drives along. Now just don't make a mistake with the
speed, don't attract the attention of a colleague (very unlikely!),
until one reaches the river bank and then at a particular spot has
to scramble down a fair bit, something only local people would
think of. The others, who don't know the area, would think it's a
vertical drop, and we're not going to break our necks just for
a fuck and we don't want to drown either. It's much cheaper
breaking one's neck on the road, without having done any sport
beforehand. Yes, there, about another two and half miles, that's
where the entry to the path by the river, hidden beneath branches, must point the way to an extinguished smile, to a

circling screaming, as if birds had come to visit and couldn't find the exit any more.

It can't be, do you see what I see?, in front there, on the road, a large dark mass, a heated mass, swiftly coming nearer, but with no glowing headlamps fixed to it, why on earth not. Nothing that could sprout wings and lift up into the air, and yet, how strange, that's exactly what it does do now, and there follows, fractions of seconds later, the soft impact of a body, which only just now came swinging along like a not quite full sack, which earlier, still in the forest, no one could beat, and which is now quickly and briskly drawn up from the road over the windscreen, the wedge-shaped profile of this modern Japanese car, as if by invisible strings, before immediately disappearing again. For another moment the night is darkened even further by the powerful bag of muscles, which like lightning and yet at the same time also ponderously (as if workers were bracing themselves sideways with ropes, grumbling and groaning, their feet pressed against the car body, in order to heave up, heave ho, their burden), slides up over the front part and the front window of the car as on a snow plough and has disappeared again, hardly has it appeared, so evidently the whole heavy mass was flung, almost dragged upwards, by the forward ploughing car and now already, like an unidentified flying object (but the moment that it happens, the country policeman knows what is happening), has risen above the car and landed on the road behind it. For the hundredth of a second the huge, already almost slack sack of fur and bones and horns hangs still and immobile above the vehicle like a strange, black moon, then it strives a little higher towards heaven, on a parabolic flight path, whose zenith (delta t), since the object, commensurate with the speed at which Kurt Janisch's car was travelling, will land 15 yards behind the Japanese car in the roadway, in exactly the middle of this stretch. While the bag of bones flies, it turns without grace a couple of times on its axis, a cumbersome comet, whose horned head, heavily burdened by the weight, points almost majestically in rapidly changing different directions, depending on the phase of the flight, and then lands on the road, the body, and is, for a moment at least, completely still. Quite unexpectedly Kurt Janisch's car was deprived of the momentum (M) which was necessary within the time (t) to lift the mass of a huge stag (m), a full-grown ten-pointer, for the killing of which the owner of the hunting ground up there had coughed up quite a sum, if the stag hadn't anyway had to cough its last, from ground level to the apex of its flight path (a), which was located behind the car, as well as to propel the stag in the direction of travel. The result was a drastic deceleration of the country policeman's car by several miles an hour. The car struck the stag above the fibula, or whatever it's called in this and similar animals, the bumper, therefore, caught one of the hurrying, swinging hind legs, losing contact with the ground, the hindquarters sagged away, down to the radiator, and off it went, off went the backwards flight, right over the car. At the corresponding moment in time Kurt Janisch was no longer driving very fast, he had already been approaching the turn-off down to the river and begun to look round, to see where he could park in the seclusion of undergrowth.

For a moment the stag had been caught between a number of force vectors, to which it had succumbed. As if gripped by impotent rage, something had lifted it up, shaken it like a fist, then catapulted it away, to immediately put an end to the nauseating aversion of the earth, which at last wants a little company, which stays for a while and doesn't immediately run off again. The earth prepares the whole meal. In return it has to pay with one head of population, it always has to pay. No, just a moment, not this time! The cars and the open trucks loaded with wood are always in such a hurry and leave the earth so quickly. Only the dead remain definitely, even if not quite voluntarily, with us, that's no fun for the road nor for us. The dead: so many! What happened to the rest? In maddened anger, in towering rage, the earth, in alliance with the country policeman, has flung the heavy animal in the air, apparently on a whim, like a crumpled, damp handkerchief, like one of those which the hunter and collector has originally gone to look for, and has simply thrown it away, the whole bundle of bones, without thinking any more about it. But only the earth itself has been struck, the grey road. The heap of meat has been thrown on its counter, now strip off the hide, divide up and sell the meat. Yet even as the animal, not visibly bleeding, turning somersaults, had plunged onto the roadway, the earth had evidently changed its mind, no we can't have such a good conversation with that one, who's interested in what a stag's interested in, acorns, hay, the backsides of hinds, well, and it now lets go the animal quite casually, the good earth. Let's just wait a bit for a human, there'll be one along shortly, at the moment the discos are still full of human tissue, skin, bones, hair, sinews, muscles and all in the revealing splendour of rave and hiphop clothing, sometimes one, sometimes the other, never too much, as far as the little honeys are concerned, our writing and TV-watching youth (up to the age of 50) will tell us, what exactly. Correct would be this answer: Tomorrow three girls aged between sixteen and twenty will supply the earth all the more plentifully with fresh flesh, so we'll let the game go for today, without eating it, while we remain here at the meat counter, the sausage stand of life, and stuff ourselves, till the grease is dripping from our chins. The animal is struggling up again, the forelegs are still kneeling, but the rear is already rising up, a hair-raising bleating noise, mixed with a kind of belling and groaning, listen, there it is again, what can that be, sounds like a siren. Fate is in such a bad mood that today it didn't even want to put together a decent carcass. The sound is quite close now. The stag stands unsteadily, still thrust forward by its own rage, to face the fate which it hadn't seen coming, after all it doesn't have any eyes at the back, but whatever has happened to it, it stands ready, its hooves lurching over the asphalt, to fight with whomever; fate, sluggish as it is, has not even reacted yet to this attack by the meat mass of this animal weighing hundreds of pounds, and already the animal wants to fight it. So, now, with some delay, fate is at last handed the stag's papers, a little late, as mentioned, there's no hurry, it'll not be shot until next year at the earliest, it is an older, but very beautiful beast, and in a year's time it will be still older, still more majestic, perhaps have fled from a younger rival, no, it's not sick, it is, touch wood, healthy, thanks for asking, and has by and large remained so. Now it's back on its feet, it could be king of any forest, its head lowered, swinging, no, the neck isn't broken either, this is the confirmation: Fate's documents are always correct, it knows everything about us. What's happened to the rest? Our brand new Minister of Social Affairs will ask you that in all seriousness.

Kurt Janisch has stopped, for a moment the car seems to him like a paper bag which has been filled with air and then burst. An animal has hit it a little too forcefully. The country policeman's heart hammers right up to his throat and into his leisure shirt. It's as if he is held tight by these two giant hands which clapped together above the car, as if they wanted to applaud him. The heavy impact of a living thing can produce such an effect in anyone, above all if one was not prepared for it, but one can also drive off with a feeling of indifference, until something even worse happens. Whatever was hit, torn, thrust aside, it has been thrown onto the road and is already lying behind Kurt Janisch. Where on earth did the car get the rage and the strength for that? It got them, this much-admired creature, brought up to kick, punch, shove, to show off and murder, from us. And another, animated creature now bleats and scrapes the asphalt, scratches the surface, drowned in itself, but nevertheless half on its legs again, gone head over heels, but on its hooves again and on course, one of the inhabitants of the night, to which it, too, wants to belong. What distant light could have drawn it? Here there is only the sparse illumination of the federal highways. The bridges are for people, on their way into the beyond, who wanted to have another drink or two beforehand for the long journey, who knows if we'll get anything on the way, so it's better if we first fill up with as much as the disco clothes will take, which should actually uncover us, a covering which unfortunately doesn't take very much, when a tree and the like or similar living thing gets in its way. The stag has hurried a little bit further up the wall of time in its eagerness, it has bounced off the pliant membrane which separates this world from the world on the other side, and which is permeable in only a few places, and has been catapulted back into the here and now, bounced back like a trumpet note, which was thrown back by a rock face, it was wedged in by the confinement of a road, which now returns it to nature. So. Nature is handed a present, for which it will certainly still find a use, because the hunter, too, is close to nature and deserves his pleasures. This stag will not escape him so easily. It will find it hard to get away. But still. Kurt Janisch reaches for his revolver, he'll have to shoot the animal, if he's seriously injured it. But that doesn't appear to be the case. The fall was far but not fatal. Only yesterday an express train tore up a whole flock of sheep not far from here, over forty dead animals, flung through the air like cottonwool balls, the good shepherd fallen asleep drunk somewhere, the dog in the field alone, not a hope. Now the shepherd has to bear joint responsibility for the whole loss, or don't you think he bears a responsibility, dear television audience, write and let us know what you think, it's your views that count. We will clarify the legal position and look thoughtful as we do so, and everyone will want to clarify it differently, I'll put a bet on that already. Kurt Janisch doesn't want to take part, he's thinking of his own legal consequences and resolves to pursue others, with his own law and rights, as the vultures do, and other birds of prey. Some take from the living, some from the dead. There are moments when one should smile, best of all at the camera, which is thrusting into one's face. This is not one of those moments. The stretch of road here is notorious. Per year approximately fifty or sixty red deer, mainly stags, they don't stay with their herd as they should, it seems to me, are mashed up. Do you hear the cries from the dreadful warmth of their pools of blood? Their carcasses are lying around everywhere, mostly on the hard shoulder (though not properly dressed). But often they also lie in the middle of the road, just wherever they've been tossed, not stirred, a few have even been stuck to the windscreen or were hanging over the bonnet like a fur stole, while no sun could be found in the dark night sky to wrap them in warmth a little longer, the dead animals. This whole landscape sometimes seems to consist of steaming blood and long-drawn-out cries. The cars conduct a campaign against life, which still continues at this very hour. Terrible things with wings, mostly crows and jackdaws, glide over it all, they come because they've been summoned to pick out eyes, they always have their tools with them. Crows can be quite wicked and spear the faces of the dead with their thorn beaks. This stag, however, will soon be eating and drinking again, though at the moment it's staggering around a bit, because it can't understand where it could have got so drunk, but it'll be all right. If no one comes from the opposite direction now, he'll manage to make it into the timber forest, yes, he's made it, up he goes. Down to the river would have been the wrong direction, then sooner or later he would have turned back frustrated, would have angrily reached the road, and a little later someone else would have got him and this time done the job properly. Fate never rings twice, one has to open the door the first time, it is too lazy to do so itself. The area is very abundant in game, and the spirits of every single person who lives here are completely different several times a day. Kurt Janisch's brother-in-law from Carinthia once related he had hit a pregnant hind, which had immediately expired beside his mudguard. That already doesn't sound good. Does this sound any better? The fawn spilled out of the hind's burst stomach and lay next to it, it had be personally killed by the driver with a stone, not a nice task, but what can one do in such a situation. No one, absolutely no one should suffer unnecessarily, that's certain. Because it would only have suffered, the fawn, so we put it out of its misery, with one foot still almost in the hot monster that brought us to this spot and yet only wanted to gobble its gas, at the next filling station, it wants to live, too, it's so nice and it took so long to choose it. What happened to the rest?

The engine, rapidly cooling in the cold night air, now ticks over quite gently, starting up again at last, listen, no, no sound of anything else here. Life was preserved and returned to the earth, thank you very much, but the address was wrong. Nevertheless the earth does not let go, once it has something. It sometimes lends one something, if one complains long enough. An abyss was briefly open and now it's closed again. The blinds are down. The ravens aren't coming, they're almost only to be found in the Tyrol. They don't fly so far. To make up for that they can speak. But at the moment they're offended, because they're constantly confused with crows. Kurt Janisch smiles for no reason, he's on a campaign, and to this end he advances into the field, to the dead river bank, where, beside the rushing river, the paper handkerchiefs sleep in their nest, which they've built for themselves, only from themselves, like the eternal Being. The keen eyes of Kurt Janisch inspect the ground, his watchful hands now grip the torch switched to function 2 (don't flash, we need a steady light, we're already nervous enough as it is!). His hands are still shaking a little. He bends down and crawls reluctantly into the undergrowth, illuminates the ground inch by inch. There's nothing more to be found there, only half-frozen mud, dirt, but who knows what a couple of rigorously deployed sensitive instruments in the forensic laboratory, in the sure hands of experts, would find? The senses of man should be more acute than the instruments he created, but they are not, otherwise one would not have specially had to invent them. Dark slope, do you surrender now or not, what you've pocketed? With the human herd, who trampled around today in the mountains and glided around on the pistes and cycled around in the forest, one can't collect everything they've left behind, that's impossible. Not even the Country Police will do that, so it doesn't matter. This country policeman at any rate is only still crawling around in order to be able to have a response

to the unpleasant reluctance in himself: I'm still looking, I'm looking, I can't help it if I don't find anything, just a moment, was it
more this way or more that way? I can't remember any more.
The bush over there a heap of needles, which prick unpleasantly
and aim for the eyes, like the crows, a small malicious army,
which, almost wiped out, has closed up, in order to offer final
determined resistance. No, we would never have crawled under
this bush, it would have torn our skins and tattooed it with weals,
instead of bringing skin together with skin. Gabi would anyway
have refused to crawl under there, her hair, her jeans, her new
jacket, bah, bah, double bah. The usual. Blubbering. The ones
who get hit also cry out sometimes, there's nothing one can do
about it. Apart from that it would have given her the creeps, a pile
of shit could have called stop! like the blast from a horn, because
trippers like to crouch under such bushes, if they want to save the
money for the restaurant but nevertheless want to relieve themselves and not their purses. No. I think it must have been further
over there, it gets flatter too, there's a little clearing surrounded by
green bushes, oh, look, the buds, so delicate, so green already!
The country policeman illuminates the way ahead, but he still
doesn't see anything which might count at some point. Here and
there a sweet wrapper flashes up in the beam of the searchlight as
if it wanted to mock the searcher, it still bears the warm trace of
hands, this cough drop cellophane. It won't decay for centuries
and will still be able to delight our grandchildren with its sparkle,
this ancient number from yesteryear, if they happened to come
here at night with their torches, discharged from the thousand
suns, brighter than any disco.

Kurt Janisch, don't let yourself be interrupted, keep on looking. He searches, all the more avidly the more hopeless it appears,
as if he now had to save his own thoughts at least, which threaten
to escape him. No, we don't think, we'd rather dig with our bare
hands in the frozen dirt of the winter which has hardly passed.
Quite pointlessly Kurt Janisch tears at the low branches, shakes

them like fists, how can something be lying there or even fall down? Do handkerchiefs grow on trees here? This man likes to surround himself with trees, in order to enjoy the feeling of plenty, even when one owns nothing. He is always, in the first instance, after houses, and what has he got so far? Well, now I have to mock: Nature, nothing but nature, whose body he now kicks, with his heavy climbing shoes, the tree trunks, in an ever more furious fit of rage. He races around in the wood like a wild animal, throws himself against the fir trees with a crash, though he doesn't get far, the branch work is terribly dense, impenetrable, he scrapes around in the half-frozen mud, which, thawing in the body heat, protrudes from his fingernails, because they can't hold any more. Now he hits out with his fists as well, again and again, blood is running down his wrists. He resounds like a note, running after its own echo, because it hasn't heard it and is entitled to it in the mountains, two copies attached!, into the forest by the river, again and again, it looks as if he wanted to passionately embrace the trees, the country policeman, yet, like many people, the trees confuse hate with love and cuddle up to him, the bad man, clasp him, who is plucking out all their little twigs and kicks their trunks for no reason at all, which after all are only lightly clothed in bark and lichens. They are not dressed sturdily enough. Now he is even scraping away the earth at the roots, our Kurt Janisch. Anyone who sees it will think it odd, perhaps there are even traces of blood, then the country policeman would really have achieved the opposite of what he wanted. This forest promises him only anni-hilation, and it promises that he, Kurt Janisch, will afterwards be cleanly cleared away. It's not like drowning, no, all the many ani-mals come who also want to eat, and they eat simply everything, but go into the water, no they wouldn't do that. It works the other way round as well: Do you see this trout? The rear end of a mouse is hanging out of its open jaws. How did that happen? How on earth? I don't know how the jaws are supposed to close again. At any rate I'm not going to pull the mouse out. There, everywhere, is a great shepherd, who has left his sheep in the lurch, but he didn't let them go into the water. He is there for them, even if not always, and he stands by the ring, until finally an abandoned lower jaw, you must be joking!, grins at him out of the undergrowth, the upper part plus teeth has long ago been dragged away by other animals, hey, you, I've bitten the dust, my dentist wouldn't have liked that at all. He's even forbidden me to do it. Must have been a deer, if you like a deer above all else then please look the other way now, because this is exactly what it could have been, no, it wasn't, no matter, it threw away its body long ago, perhaps because you didn't love it as much as you thought. So, this flame would have gone out now, the teeth are gone too, the hooves have galloped off. Today another animal was luckier than this one. So it goes. One always wins, the others only lose. The flame of life, before it is blown out by a mouth puckered for a kiss, which was always easily able to deceive one, is indeed a very sensitive little flame, there's not much gas left, it's all used up, and consumption has already been paid for and debited from our account. What's puffing there as if of stronger, higher flames? A scornful night sky, which according to the position of the moon tells us the time and that Our Time in Pictures Part Three will soon begin in this little box here, and then a completely new age will dawn, and if we finally want to see this new age, then we must make our way to a more inviting location with more fashionable furnishings.

And there we have it already, THE LOCATION, LOCA-TION, a pretty kitchen-living room, quite deliberately fitted out in a rustic look and nevertheless sighing with dissatisfaction, since it would rather collect itself into a nice crowd of kitchens by Dan or someone, preferably one for each family member, they wanted to form a kitchen circle, each one in his very own house, for the time being we only have one and a half housing units, because the son's house still belongs to someone. Into this kitchen enter, in their own character, without feeling ashamed, sure of their adventurousness, the TV guests of VERA, the hostess from the beyond, who collects the waste water of human beings and, giving a blessing, sprinkles it on the heads of millions, solemn water, which we crowd around, only in order to see: Others are even more desperate than we are. How fantastic is that, overjoyed I write a whole novel, if necessary. This one. They are not ravaged by hate, the family people in this kitchen, they are delighted with their new property. Patrick, the child, will get a whole room just for his video games. The son's wife will get the whole cellar as wash and ironing room. The country policeman's wife will perhaps get a conservatory, in order to sit quite alone with the television and find out if she wants to be a millionaire or to receive from the television a country barn dance, which will spur her on, quite alone, to laugh heartily, until she herself is locked up in it again. The country policeman's son will get a whole floor to himself, in order - the hobby of every other young man - to assemble electronic circuits, which will seem completely beside the point to everyone else, because they already exist. There he can also pursue his second hobby, playing a home organ. But because this hobby is always running too far ahead of him, he's going to give it up again soon. The country policeman himself will simply get everything he wants and will feel unusually burdened by all his property. A sleepwalker, a chiselled body of stone (with a way of speaking for women), who has to bear a whole house, and yet one alone will never be enough for him, although he would not be able to bear any more. We see: dark heads bent over a building plan, which they have boldly removed from a drawer and even more boldly will alter with their own felt-tips; in this bath they will soon splash, and in this extension with a bay window they will make quite personal gestures to one another, which, another personal present, nothing from a shop!, will be received as slaps in the face. We see eyes, which do not turn away from straight and dotted lines, but complete them or make completely different subdivisions, just as they please, according to their own yardstick. My soul tells me that these people are not for a moment thinking of themselves, but only of their descendants, who, in the shape of Patrick, the country policeman's grandson, loaf around in front of the television, let the fate of strangers bounce impudently off them and instead absorb a whole pound of biscuits, but only those that they know from the adverts, which are explicitly and exclusively directed at our young people. The country policeman now turns up at home again, as if by magic, he's wet, rumpled and dirty, but he never has to give explanations anyway. Showers and changes his clothes, while in between what happened with the stag falls from his lips like dried clay. That doesn't particularly upset anyone here, at most, that the stag survived, that's very rare. Fancy that. The things life is capable of! Until now we've only credited death with surmounting such difficulties. Life ultimately does rise above everything, if one has been able to obtain it in the hospital, but the things a skilful mason, a joiner, a carpenter are capable of, if one lets them, that is more than thinking, it is the activity of the industrious and hard-working, of which I have often spoken here, but it has paid off every time. Apart from that, others have done it even more often, haven't they? It's difficult to talk about ordinary things. About the lamplight, which blows away the darkness, the TV, which shoos away melancholy, the conversations at the family dinner table, which snarling chase away the intellect, the clothes, which hide the ill-shaped bodies of people or sometimes also such a compact, home-carved work of art as Kurt Janisch, whom one could exhibit just like that in the museum of local art and culture, if only he were a little more homely, or finally about a building plan, which subsequently discards its own house, I could talk about it endlessly, oh how beautiful it all is, because one can always work hard at oneself and at others. And how happy I am nevertheless to be allowed to say all that here. Thank you so much for everything.

7.

Please permit me to say the following once again, because it is important to me and because I can't now find the passage where I said it once before: If your vegetables are enriched by high dosages of nitrates, then you must on no account eat them! It's a sign that thanks to excessive use of fertilisers the ecological balance of the water has become upset, and with it of course your vegetables. It is therefore excessive and damage to health may result (if this has not already occurred), if the very good water, that we have, is polluted. What we douse our food in, we should even keep particularly pure, so that it does not dose us. Natural bodies of water: superabundant plant growth. Yuck. How this body of water must feel, I'd rather not try to imagine. The water wants to be as hard-working and decent as the people who drink it, but the people don't help it, they don't give it a hand. Animals would be paralysed with shock, if they could read that. They have to drink water, too, after all. Aquatic plants would die off, excuse me, I can explain that: Instead of ceasing to absorb oxygen, like those of us who have died, they now really start, just as the rest of Austria, full of love and greed, receives the tourists, our dear guests, who visit us, unless the government doesn't suit them. It doesn't suit me either. So I'm a stranger here myself. As already mentioned, excessive use of poison causes the whole orchestra of nature to strike up all at once, and even Bruckner wouldn't have wanted that. There is too much too much too much of everything. We have enough too. More than enough. We've had enough. If you are contemplating wallowing in excess: You're better off taking the whipped cream and leaving the oxygen! Besides my little bit of water here, in this machine, is also overloaded with poison. Instead of answering genteelly, when I'm asked, I tip my whole life, which is itself long dead, into this dead water zone, but deader than dead, that can't be. It would be a good thing if for once it a decent flow got going into this zone, if the water at last got a decent employment policy, so that its trophic level finally improves. Otherwise we always only remain what we were - trophies of history, displayed as a warning to other countries. And what we grabbed we couldn't take with us, or could we? No, we're not going to give this Klimt painting back now. We must have got something out of it, for making all that effort, until almost no one escaped with their lives. How we would rather have more turbulent times again, how we would like to profit from the movement of the river, until the last particle of water in us, our upright little Austrian homebody souls, is carried along (that's how coarsely our bodies of water are spoken about, I swear it), in addition to the main movement (acquisition of property), by the dear little secondary movements, the belief in God, the heavenly Father, whom we have soft-soaped for so long for our own entertainment, until He finally gave us back to ourselves, newly redecorated, as good as new, no, better!, and we had nothing more urgent to do than hand ourselves over to a new leader, voluntarily, as if we were one and a half years old, at the outside, and couldn't understand what he's saying to us. As if nothing had ever happened. There are some who still can't get enough, we've already described them and now only have to clear away our own refuse. It resembles the leguminous plants, tenacious, yielding, slimy, but in this water, in the lake, it can't be done away with, at least not for a while. This refuse consists of owner-occupied houses, of which one always provides security for the other, until the banks, exhausted, raise a small white flag and decline. The banks are asexual, that is, they do not allow themselves to be mollified either by men or by women. They are not oriented towards propagation and regeneration, like the plants of the earth, they are programmed for concentration, so, now they've caught someone again, who thought up some dirty trick with the interest redemption, he won't get far with that. If he were richer, they wouldn't have got him. They even caught the fraudulent chicken farmer and his brother, but not his powerful backers. The Freedom Party Building Society has been wound up, a pity really. They're also feeling the country policeman's collar, but he always removes his jacket very quickly, and the banks can once again take a walk. Yes, that's completely true, he is a person, a truth, a work, a property, yet in reality nothing belongs to him. Gather round me, if you want to hear once again, how many people this country has killed, no doubt you're asking yourselves why then I'm always only talking about the one person. He's not that important, after all. No, you're not asking yourselves that, and I can understand that. No one asks me about anything whatsoever. I have already described what you will find in this standing water, which has urgent need of a second leg to stand on, but now it's finally going to be found, the relic, the victim, that's quite different from just talking about it. On the other hand one imagines it to be worse than it is, finding a corpse; and I have hesitated so long to describe it, until I almost didn't feel like it, here, on the low shore of my resolves. Please throw the first stone now, but in such a way that it can hop around on the surface of the water a couple of times, as happy as a new federal chancellor.

The spoilsport, Gabi's corpse, who was searched for as a living person and so could of course never be found, not even with all the photos on the masts, almost the whole way up to the Semmering Pass, pops up now as a dead woman, although the dead are of course inactive and don't respond to anything any more. In the deep water of our mountain lakes there are places where one never finds them, the dead, doesn't matter, we have enough of them, I mean there are plenty of them. There in the mountain lakes, the shores drop almost vertically, these lakes can be 600 feet deep or more. There are holes in the lakes. They have the power to make people disappear without trace for ever, at the Last Judgement there will then be great astonishment, when the prettily packaged women all bob up from the bottom, in order to avenge themselves for their discontent in the water's cold hell. How great will be their disappointment, when others, the hosts of angels in their fast four wheel drives, which have been acquired for them, so that they can get everywhere on that day, when the trumpets shall sound without pause, will first of all want to take revenge on them. Because, going by the book, the misdeeds of the living are not erased by the death of others. But the business with Gabi affects me so badly nevertheless, I really don't know what to say now, but simply can't let it out like cigarette smoke, quickly, as if in passing; description is difficult of course, if one has never seen a real dead person. A film is only a weak substitute, a little bench in Shudderwood Station. So horror turns up today, weighs me down unusually heavily, and yet I can't look away, although actually I wanted to read the newspaper. Two men who, after a big meal at the inn, wanted to stretch their legs a bit (they will soon have to be unhappy that on this occasion they couldn't stretch their legs under the table), their wives have remained sitting and gossip away, this time without making use of the corrosive rage at their families, which so often overcomes e.g. me, now walk down to the lake, on a cold, soon to be green path, which is already depressed at the thought of all the police boots which will shortly be tramping around on it. So. I now read, because I'm used to reading, from the two men's faces, what they're thinking when, close to the shore, they discover, re-emerging as unexpectedly as it disappeared, first of all just bobbing up and down, a man-sized roll of green shiny tarpaulin, such as is used, fairly pointlessly, because it's never quite waterproof (I can tell you a thing or two about that, since I had to bail out water from my balcony three times) as covering on building sites. The tarpaulin is tied up with wire. What's that? It is at any rate first of all curious. Because something is as big as a human being doesn't mean that it has to be one. But anyone seeing this roll imagines this plastic cover has been made the size it is so that exactly one human being or four square yards of soil or a five foot three inch tree trunk fit underneath, the one has no protection any more, the other would have been very much in need of more protection, the tree trunk has no more wishes except for the nice damp earth, which it will never see and feel again. The circle of readers stands up to get a better view, the tarpaulin hides something, which for days seemed to have been swallowed by the earth, but the earth was unjustly accused. The water had the human roll the whole time and was playing yoyo with it, but the string was a wire tightly wound, and so the water was soon fed up with the game. It didn't work, there's nothing one can do with this packet and, whatever is inside it, we can't unpack it. We just have to pick up our textbook again, which tells us what killed us, who are all of us waters, in such a way that we consist almost only of water - nitrogen, phosphorus, potassium and organic stuff, we got a fresh load of the latter three days ago, but don't know what to do with it yet. Apart from that, like many children, we are basically glutted, for which there are good reasons. These are the words of the water to us and to the two men, who don't understand its language. But the language of this plastic roll they understand instinctively and take a step backwards and are suddenly silent. What's that. The two men have already eaten, that's a good thing, because at this moment their appetite would have disappeared, if they hadn't earlier on arrested it in good time and taken advantage of it for their own ends. The lake is not deep, nowhere, and yet no one has made the effort to coax this roll a little further out. There it is now, a possible covering for a human being, but not a good one.

At first the two men try to pull the flotsam ashore with the help of a broken-off long stick, but they can't reach far enough. It's as if the roll is not for them. The men say to themselves: Today of all days, it's not our day. Birds circle over them screeching, it's still cold. Too cold for the time of year, even here. We imagined angels differently, as we were fleetingly brushed by thoughts of reprisal and wanted to kill someone, but then refrained from doing so after all. These are black angels. Inside this plastic sheet rests a human face and a human body, that's what it looks like to me, this sheet. The men think, it can't be what it looks like. The men know that what it looks like is probably what it will be. Soon we will know exactly, says the law of reality. They squat down and strain to look under the water, which is especially dark and opaque, but the sheet encloses something they can recognise exactly, and with terrible certainty they understand whom they are dealing with, with death, this always cocked weapon, which is playfully turning in a circle, staring first at one, then the other, a nervous finger pointing at their cold bodies, whose turn is it today. I would like to be the first to know: Perhaps already the two men on the way home? They really shouldn't have drunk that third glass, this walk was supposed to serve, not least, as a sobering up. Well, that's exactly what it's doing. And as if with one blow of a hammer drill four eyes drill into the sight of the water-foam roll. It's a simple package, yet what will it not set in motion! In future 82 detectives of the regional force, of which 20 will be assigned solely to this one case.

Cell phone on, call out, horrors already prepared, packed, frozen and discovered by two persons. Please come immediately, we see what's been hidden and would so like to know what's inside. Their wives are always merely covered up by quilts and these always reveal what's familiar, which grows more rancid with every day and which, furthermore, in order to get some pleasure out of it has to be flattered for hours. The things one has in mind, one never ever gets. It would be a good thing to remove this covering, that would bring us considerably closer to our bobbing, restless goal. We hear a frightful voice speaking, accompanied by a blue light and, as if that were not enough, a siren. We hear how the voice is trying to tell us something: You're dealing with death here, be quiet, perhaps it's still there and is going to fetch you. Oh, how exciting. Well, it won't be as bad as all that, says another voice from an extra-small telephone, which can be snapped open, so that it looks bigger, and which may well appear more eerie than this manifestation under water, which is observed by birds not by fish, because there are no fish in this special element I'm thinking of. The Country Police force is at liberty to come, in fact, they must, and they do. Mr Kurt Janisch is not on duty today, the man has the luck of the devil. Otherwise he would have had to take acting lessons in good time, and that too he has been able to save himself, in addition to his many other savings, which unfortunately are always gone when he needs them. He has only negative savings, that is, debts. More than hairs on his head. He wishes someone would take them off him. But instead houses are supposed to come and stay. Fortunately these are ponderous, stationary fellows, they are supposed to pour in some time nevertheless, to serve as security for further houses. So something comes of nothing, no, a something comes of a nothing. But nothing, nothing at all comes of it. Not yet, but our prospects are good. Two men rise to their feet on the shore of the lake, who have done their duty as citizens, and no doubt they will sooner or later stand up impatiently to the authorities, that is their human duty, that's why everyone does it. They only agree with the authorities, the people, when someone, who doesn't belong to us, is to be carefully deported. So now the authorities come jolting and bumping down what is no more than a track and will detain these men unnecessarily for hours. This track is the only one on which the Country Police can get here, if they don't want to go on foot, which would break a few points from their uniform epaulettes, which they will certainly still need on our eastern borders and that with Slovenia, quite close to here, in order to establish their authority. These officers after all have to patrol 90 miles of border in Styria in super uniforms, with parkas and peaked caps. The whole Spielfeld district is already quaking at their steps. The training in the annexe of the Bad Radkersburg Police School lasted six months, that must have paid off at some point, because then they can protect the riches of the natives really very effectively and accompany the latter, once they have enjoyed it all in peace and quiet, with a raised signal disc into the Kingdom of God (which belongs to them alone in any case), so that no one can put a spoke in their wheel. So. Here it is, exactly, in the water. Take a look. Do you see it? What is it. We'll need the boat. After some back and forth and pushing and now heave and crossing the dead water zone, in which simply nothing stirs, the load is dragged by boat into the microscopically small harbour and pulled out. Divers aren't needed. At the top there's hair, that's already the first thing we see. But now we already know everything and lose our self-control. Jesus, hair, must be real! One of the men throws up on God and his friend and the feet of the policemen, who manage to jump back in time, but are already talking into their radios and have to listen to the din and crackle that breaks out of them like game out of the undergrowth. Soon the place will simply be swarming with men in uniform (and later also with the high-ranking civilians). A bit of smooth forehead under the saturated hair can also be seen, which didn't go under the plastic sheet, or not enough of an effort was made to tuck it in. Here someone perhaps wanted too much to own a human being and instead took this human being away from themselves, if you follow me. Perhaps this human being was simply thrown away, because someone had no more use for her any more. Once again: The killer did not take the human being away from himself (that would not have bothered the killer, he evidently had no more use for his prey) but the victim from themselves. This person would miss themselves, if they were still conscious. No idea why. The eyes literally get stuck into the roll, but cannot take it over all on their own. Impossible. We can't grasp it. The birds are disappointed, the lake, however, is relieved, its rid of the responsibility, and it doesn't, on top of everything else, have to absorb even more fertilisers. Photographers, the search for clues, indescribable excitement in a short time overfertilises the village as well and sweeps it along, heavy with all the stored up shit, which one will get to hear there, as in a spring avalanche, which in a swelling torrent, out of which poke our sins like trees and lumps of concrete, surges down the pedestrianised former high street. People who a moment ago were crouching out of sight, so that no one would see them answering the call of nature, now resolve never to do such a thing again. Someone can be lurking behind every bush, and in conclusion one ends up in the lake. Someone who has wrapped someone up and thrown them in will then also mendaciously maintain not to have known someone beforehand at all. We don't need that. To be denied in death like Jesus by his disciples, let yourself be killed, then you'll get the surprise of your life, what people will broadcast about you. But the people here are rather taciturn. You don't get anything out of them so easily. After the first photos the roll is opened and a body and a face of great charm are unpacked. Body and face still bear their delicate peaceful beauty, the face of the young woman looks as if she's sleeping, but in truth everything about her has long been divested of life. Someone has stirred up life against her, and so it went off in a huff. Not with her any more! The black ankle boots aren't there, but there is the denim jacket with the long shawl collar, which we'd already missed, but not the handbag (where is it? It's never found!). The policemen see immediately who it is, they've had the young missing person on their computer screens and now they see her in natura, in this nature which takes offence at them. Let them sleep, the dead, there are too many for one to know something even of even one strand of their hair.

In future more than 2,000 people will be questioned in relation to the case, but what can one learn from people? They lie as soon as they open their mouths. It's always the same, it's what they've read and what they've seen on television, and they confuse that with what has happened to them and what really should have been in the newspaper, because it would have been much more interesting. Really it should only have been a matter of time, until the murderer would have been caught. It must have been a stranger. But there are hardly any strangers here and only a few tourists, and they are immediately conspicuous, because of their racy-sporty or rural-hunting costume, in which they dream of higher strata, to which they do not belong, and to whom the hunting grounds belong, no, they have no grounds here. In winter the frost's tender, sensitive hands chase away the strangers, in summer the rain, which mows down everything, even the bare earth. And anyone who's still left is driven off by us in person. Perhaps this girl, Gabi, wanted to see the whole wide world, but had not suspected that this small one would already be a size too big for her. Eyes bore into eyes and discuss and ask something. Names are mentioned, people are summoned for questioning. The Country Police are only doing their duty, the officers say again and again, when they once again stop in front of the hillock of a human being, who acts the boss in front of them, mole hill as Matterhorn; not much will come of all that. Each tells his own truths, one more, the other less, the truths are, once one has got to know them, so hard to express, because they are probably not true at all. People are called, and they rush over in a state of agitation. Then they are sent away again. They all knew our Gabi, her mother and her boyfriend knew her particularly well, and they are questioned particularly well. They say, no one knew our Gabi as well as we did: There certainly wasn't another man. The two of them are sitting in the kitchen-living room again. They can no longer kiss the rim of the half-full cup of cocoa, which Gabi left standing, the last time she was seen. She made it that evening, before she left. She didn't finish it. The cup was rinsed. Where did she go after that? She shouldn't have gone out again, we definitely told her: stay at home or take your boyfriend with you. One or the other. The boyfriend didn't even know that she wanted to go out again, as he claims, although it's not much of a claim. She would never do anything without me, says the boyfriend. Funny. The boyfriend is at first naturally the main suspect, he doesn't, however, give the impression of having done it. He is altogether quite quiet. He was also quiet at school, except when he was required to say something. He did not have any greater difficulty than usual in expressing himself in the spoken exercise, which he delivered in the first lesson. There would have had to be something in the way he looked or in his voice. Nothing. He would automatically have had to make himself small in the face of something big like death, turn pale, stutter, something, sweat or stammer, if you like. His face seemed familiar to everyone, just as always. But who knows who he is, no, not the friend, who among us knows who he is. We, that is, everyone except me, knows how to make pheasant wrapped in bacon, but we don't know who we are. So, I am one of the few who really doesn't want to know. It's one reason why we always need variety, well, I don't need it. Perhaps we can find ourselves somewhere else? But to do that we always have to travel somewhere else. We also always knew everything about Gabi, apart from one essential detail, thinks the head of the regional CID even into his sleep, that is, even into his temporary death. It's the only way he can put himself in the position of the victim, by plunging into sleep and the next day hoping to have found a clue in his brain which he has not yet followed up. Again nothing. He's close, he knows that, but still: nothing. I'm sorry. I would tell you, if I could. But I can't penetrate this dimension. A carton full of little wrapped sugar cubes from various cafés in places in the neighbourhood, collected for the fun of it, which was no doubt as small as these sugar cubes, these keepsakes, which themselves don't keep their shape, but are happy if they don't have to dissolve and can first get to know two or three people to whom they are served, assuming their first owners have not damaged the wrapping with the signs of the zodiac too badly. But Gabi was always in these establishments alone, or with her boyfriend. There was never another man with her. At least no one whom we observed or whom we can remember. Her boyfriend claims she had recently perhaps been a little less passionate in love-making than usual, he says it shamefacedly. That points to something, but perhaps only that she had been a little lethargic or there was a lot to do at work. She wrote a letter, to a girlfriend: Mother and boyfriend hem me in, don't give me room to breathe, check up on me, pester me to do things, no idea what, it seems to be enough for them that I'm there, but I know, I'm their mistress, I know so, precisely because they pester me. Computers order these names, figures and dates, which in turn are shown to other men and machines. Many others note number plates and ask about the owners, who try not to look the fool. Too bad. One cannot know everything about a person, and one can know absolutely nothing about everyone, what does that mean. Even for someone smart it's hard to express, I already said so, and I'm not smart; I'll just have to take even better care to look smart, in order to understand life, although I already spend a fortune, otherwise in future I won't be admitted to life at all, and will have to let everyone else go in front of me. Would anyway be a bit late for life now, wouldn't it? If only I had learned something! When the mother wakes up, it hits her that her daughter is dead and she, the mother, can immediately go to her boyfriend in Germany, in Bavaria, but on first thoughts it's no fun at all, on second thoughts the fun will return. Yes, the two of them will return, perhaps after a really pleasant holiday together, Mr Fun and Mrs Joy of Living. The mother would in any case have moved away soon, why shouldn't parents be birds of passage for once? They want to move on sometimes, too. The mother has her own boyfriend and has put down a deposit on a house for Gabi, that should be enough, the couple, that was definitely the plan, would certainly have kept an eye on Gabi, lovingly hugged her, and Gabi would always have found ways and means of being horrid to them and to demand careful handling in return. Other people are also likewise burdened, no wonder that one would rather have their apartments instead of them; a wonder that most of them are still in one piece, given how often fate has struck them and wrested their few weak and delicate weapons from their hands, before they could even read the instructions. So. Many are in hospital. Mr Westenthaler has smashed his kneecap for the umpteenth time, always the same one. All the rest are dead now, I decide, and so I save myself a lot of work, and they've already been cleared away by the good housewife's hand of death. So I no longer have to describe them. Thank you very much. The rest still lie under their burdens and wait for someone to put them back on their feet again and deliver them to someone who will perhaps be pleased about it. There isn't anyone like that, who sticks with one like the oak with the mistletoe. One cannot neglect oneself nevertheless, otherwise not even in the misty future will this long-desired partner turn up, who talks to one in a nice and friendly fashion. One must then on no account neglect him and not oneself either. When can one take a rest? It would be better if people had been on their feet long before that, then they would have had time to find someone better than the one they have. Only he who knows longing. Who knows what they suffer, the people? Oh, the one who knows and loves us is far away. In the water. Hardly is someone gone than one longs for him. Or not, who knows. No injuries of any kind could be identified on the girl's body, no visible ones at least. Someone got too close to her, but, to the forensic doctor's surprise, he by no means acted in a brutal way. What's even more surprising: in all probability no sign of sexual intercourse before death, not even traces of a violent attempt to penetrate her or ejaculate in or anywhere on her. The water obliterated these traces. Why did someone pull Gabi's trousers down to her knees and her pullover and shirt over her breasts? And yes, the open bra as well. Why these diligent pieces of work, which perhaps had nothing to do with diligence, but with necessity? And afterwards it wasn't necessary to pull up the woman's clothes again properly, why indeed, only the doctor is going to see her now, someone like that. It wouldn't have cost anything, to make her look decent again and lay her out, the dead woman we see here. Two movements, one above, one below, but there are some who no longer have them at their command, ever since women can dress and undress by themselves. Did the taut weapons of a man take aim at this body, which came as suppliant or even as someone indifferent, which said no, and when I say no, does that mean no? You know, one can even lose self-control with suppliants in the face of their humility, which nevertheless demands everything, even as they throw themselves away, perhaps in order to create space for a whole lot more. Was it really necessary to pull down and push up her things so unkindly? And then this gentle, yet absolutely certain death, each one of its holds grips tightly - death, this free climber. He must be skilful, the fellow, sometimes he has to leave the scene of his activities very quickly afterwards. The young woman has not simply been choked or throttled, with the pressure and strength of firmly grasping hands, for several minutes, but gently through slight pressure of an open hand or a forearm on the throat, right on the nerve conductor centre, which has its home there; dingalingaling sound the nerve ends with their integrated wiring, and then they're quiet and don't make a sound. No messages for you. Not on the display either. Time and date. In the year 2000 it will perhaps, at least for a while, be difficult to find the people whom death has marked with its expiry date. The computer will perhaps fail, felled, outwitted by time itself. And in 2001 it might get even worse, let's wait and see. Perhaps even death itself won't be working properly, because it will have been programmed with the wrong data. The young woman lying here with sodden head, armpit and pubic hair (so wet, it's as if nothing had ever grown there) lacks all marks of struggle and strangulation, which are virtually always found in such cases. Only a slight bruise on the right side of the head suggests that the head (in a car against the door cross-bar?) was struck hard and that then the dazed, but not unconscious woman was gently suffocated in this curious and unusual way. It can even have happened unintentionally, can't it? No, not that. An accident of love, which wanted something else than it could achieve? At any rate the girl didn't drown. The characteristic drowned lung, the over-inflation of the lung, the indistinctly defined, reddish to blue-violet discolorations on her body (Paltauf blotches) caused by haemorrhaging, are completely missing. No froth formation either? No, don't see any. The froth would arise during drowning through an intensive mingling of the fluid swallowed with chyme, gastric mucus and air. But did not arise here. Nothing to be seen. Any other questions? Make sure she's well preserved, but later I won't be able to answer them either.

Back to the country policeman Kurt Janisch: In the course of these days, as if there were a negative agreement in this respect, no more money is lent to him. Yet the sum of compliments, which women bestow on him, whom he stops, pulls over to the roadside, and leaves standing again, in ever more rapid succession (he hardly takes the time any more to find out what significance each acquaintanceship could have for him, stares at driving licences, at gold necklaces, fur collars, rings, watches, which grow towards him like tough, self-confident creepers, which know that not even the machete of someone running amok could destroy them. He hears excuses, which are delivered in a never-changing singsong, but he doesn't listen to these half-truths and excuses, he at last knows his own off by heart and doesn't need those of strangers, he prefers to note where the supposedly, presumably lowered eyes of the women are wandering, from the country policeman's penetratingly blue iris straight down to his fly, direct connection, these greedy, grasping eyes of women, and yet why are they so carelessly screened, with nothing but a protective coating of mascara, which probably only lends these glances weight and is intended to store them in a little fairy-tale forest, which one immediately wants to enter. But there one will probably have to pay admission, instead of taking something away and carrying it home, so we'd better just leave it), these extensive acquaintanceships add up, they mount like the snow up in the Alpine sphere, just as cold and just as pointless. Well, some get pleasure out of plunging in and down, strapped to my undercarriage, downwards, ever downwards, that already makes up half the profit. The country policeman, however, would need the whole profit for himself alone. For the athletes it has to be downhill. Or uphill, depending on the sport. But we can also certainly go up in the ski lift or the chair lift. Conversations develop, the women like the look of the country policeman, but they seem instinctively to scent his increasing desperation, at the moment that's too much for them for a nice date, you know, it's a bit too complicated just now, I've lived my life, it wasn't easy, and if I try again, then it shouldn't be such a strain this time. I have my job. And from time to time I just want to lie quietly in front of the TV and cry and laugh, one's never lonely with the TV anyway. That these women are supposed to invest something in this man is something they evidently suspect, previously they only rarely suspected it, and they recoil, these women of the country road, some humbly, some good-naturedly, few boldly. Yet they are supposed to risk their whole fortune to save the country policeman. It's not a good start, because it doesn't start at all. I'm telling you for the umpteenth time, this man is a sombre figure, his uniform has already signalled that to me before a couple of times. Is he trying to get off with me, the women ask themselves, at whom he shoots his bright blue glances with the catapult of his strong, thick blond hair and eyelashes, glances which are supposed to be self-explanatory, but which can only write out fines, glances after which, with gestures which by now already begin irresolutely, he hooks into the warm flesh of breasts, to pull the blouse away a little and look into the cleavage, inside the cuddly soft sleeveless woollen pullover. How much wood does this one have outside her hut and how much gravel on her drive? Where is the old certainty of appraisal gone? The country policeman never used to be wrong before. Mr Janisch, do you receive me, over and out? Everything has to go ever faster now, one thing virtually follows on the heels of the other, yet at the same time one must not forget the hottest iron in the fire, this one particular lady, not just for special moments, but at all events, that might turn up, and to whom it would be best he came as supplicant, she would like that, it would signal to her that he has been reduced in price and that she can at last afford him. It often happens to those with ambitions. They often appear so small to us in comparison to their desires and goals, which they spread out before us, dressed up as important concerns, so that we pay them due attention. And so we, too, slowly take less and less interest in them, these concerns of strangers. The woman, who loves, knows and herself performs music, on a leash, always close beside him, the country policeman would like that, he wouldn't have to bother about her any more, and if the music wants to sniff a little longer at one corner or another (isn't this sonata movement a little faster, and this finale a little slower, so that each note can be heard separately?), she's immediately roughly pulled back by the collar. I can't really grasp it yet, but this woman has perhaps, now of all times, at the wrong moment, discovered something like her dignity, that's what she calls it at least, and this discovery makes her so happy, like everything that's new. It won't last long. Sit! Basket! Music will do that for her, and wherever one tells it to, as long as it's the right person saying it; and it's always well behaved and comes straight back, when the CD player is set at start again, it only comes to her, the music to the woman, who alone understands music and it's all she understands. So why shouldn't the country policeman keep coming back? Why should he not start to worry, when this time she doesn't open the door to him, who so often only wants to put her down? Unlike him, music only wants itself, and so we can imagine it was written for each of us alone, only we can understand it properly. It makes no difference to music, it's easily satisfied, and it likewise wants to be repeated exactly the same each time in our concert halls, so that it always sounds as on the CD, which we have at home, although many people swear, each time it's quite different from the time before. So that really everyone, even someone without ears at all, remembers it and, so as to be able to remember it even better, buys the corresponding CDs, as model for reality. An eternal cycle, in great as in little things. The country policeman doesn't want to come to himself any more, he'd rather stay away, and one can say: He doesn't know himself, otherwise he would still want to get to know himself. There's a new young colleague, but he really wants to get to know him better, recently, as if by accident, he blew lightly on the back of his neck, he was close to laying his cheek for a moment on the soft spot above the collarbone, but he didn't dare. He then merely gave the young colleague a jab in the ribs and conducted a mock fight with him, with fists, and laughed, after that for half a day he didn't need to let his head droop. It should really be enough for the country policeman, that he has a little house, a family, a grandson and that the cars whizz past him and he has the power to stop them at any moment, with nothing but a small movement. But he absolutely must have another house as well and another and another, why, he can't live in them all at the same time, this house-moving maniac. To tear the see-through plastic wrapping from women he doesn't know, before too much has been seen of them, to scatter the contents around, and all that work just to move into the packaging, which is still full of the crumbs of another's life. He wants to get hold of the property of women, this man, at which he possesses great skill, which now, however, increasingly seems to be leaving him. Men don't give up what they've got. But recently the women, as already said, seem to suspect something, not what this man intends, they would never guess that; but whatever it is, inconsistent as this sex is according to legend, they for their part no longer want anything at all from the country policeman. They don't know that they don't want anything from him, so that they don't have to give him anything for it. Love's mercy, this whore, which just takes anyone, but wants to give as little as possible for it, turns up, hardly has the church been unlocked, what, no customer here yet, to whom she could be of service? God should rather have been hung up by the feet, not only to accelerate his death, but also to still humankind's longing for love more quickly, in the nuclear age, since although war is in principle a thing of the past, everything can still at any time be smashed to pieces. When people see something as horrible as someone crucified upside down, they will realise how good things are for them and have no demands at all any more, is what I think. They've evidently already got used to the one dying upright, loyally obedient to his father, the credulous of this church, who have always got unsecured credits and are only waiting to be able to jump in themselves as apocalyptic bill credit sharks and drive the whole world, which never gave them a present of anything, to bankruptcy. Whole poultry empires sank into the dust or into the dead leaves of the embezzler hedges of the Freedom Party's economics spokesman, Rosenstingl, and even our Lord had to bite the dust, without finding a single grain, just like the poultry that nobody wanted, it's a very human religion, Christianity, isn't it? He died for absolutely nothing, nothing at all, God. It's got a lot to do with us, this religion, don't you think? Little bells ring, and women look at one very strangely, when the priest is attractive, yes, even the most good humoured. Everything's going down the drain, anyway. Eye for an eye. People have already got used to every imaginable horror. Love is the only thing they want to experience again and again and then once again after that, this time, however, exclusively with the right partner. They want the beloved to look cheerful, otherwise it's no fun for them.

But today this country policeman does not look at all cheerful to me. No one will one day have him as a husband, because he's already married and asks his wife almost every third day how she is. Then he's away again, from place to place, where he stops cars, as if he could stop himself. To see in love of all things the fulfilment of his financial longings, in a caring hand, which hands him stocks and shares, anonymous saving bank books and golden watches, in a soft body, which offers him its fantastic, firm, magnificent covering, provided with a super veneer, so that he, the country policeman, at last has security, what do you say to that? You are bored by such tenderness? What can I say to that?

No further lights went out, Gabi's will be the only one, I hope, though one can never know what will occur to the unappreciated mixed-up minds of the desperate. Other women have disappeared here, at greater intervals, no, I'm not saying anything more about that now. Growling, the tyres get stuck into the ground, don't want to let go, then hurry on nevertheless, where to, fortunately it's still the winter tyres on this cold track, on which they rush away, in two deep well-worn icy ruts. The air rises up against the vehicles, which are driving along poorly cleared detours, which force them to go up into the mountains, by way of the forest tracks, where snow is still lying, on hidden routes, which outsiders don't know. It plays happily with them, the oncoming air with the few cars, caresses their shiny, coloured bodies, one of them belongs to the country policeman, his face is quite expressionless, what does it matter, no one sees it. A woman is supposed (he called earlier) to be stretching out expectantly towards him in her house, and she is supposed to snuff it, but not too soon. That would perhaps be the best long-term solution, for the house as for the woman. But not too soon. He just came off duty, now we're driving straight to her. Can it be that she didn't open up yesterday, although she was definitely at home? No. That's impossible. That she was eating thoughtfully at home, piling salami and ham on bread to the accompaniment of her favourite music, by candlelight, which is romantic, but only à deux, since it's a pleasure to make a fuss. Except every flame is a potential fire hazard, let's be honest, and should be avoided, if Christmas is over and a person hasn't disposed of his Christmas tree in time. The country policeman will at all events try, after some walking up and down and scouting around, to get into this house, which today he wants to conquer in a surprise attack. It's all taking too long for him. His fingers are itching, to angrily beat the woman, if she doesn't want to give up her house voluntarily, he clenches his fist

on the driving wheel, just not to feel once again the steely firm-
ness of her nipples scratching around between his fingers, are
such tiny taps, which have remained shut to every child for life,
only later to fall into the hands of a freebooter for free, I too now
almost feel their contentless pointed stoniness between my fingers,
I have properly sealed and hung these two old sacks, these skin-
coloured airbags with the milky-blue veins, the producers made
quite an effort there on their silken assembly line, which - there's
not much to be done about that now - forthwith and to the end
will no longer contain anything that could even remotely serve
anyone as nourishment. They are to serve purely for pleasure, the
two of them, but please not for the pleasure of the country policeman again, who's not interested, and it's not a pleasure either, he
doesn't care if they make more agreeable acquaintanceships, how
nice for them. But the house for him! I wish I could say the same
about myself. They would jump into the country policeman's
hands with joy at any time, the two dumplings, because he at
least, one among millions of the like-minded, who from time to
time get instructions to confess something which they haven't
done, so that they can remain silent about what they have done,
he at least knows exactly how to turn a woman's switch, between
thumb and index finger, look, it's quite easy to be a creator, when
the corresponding creature is already present, but doesn't know it
yet. The desert lives, and in order to live, it must already have
contained all this energy, this momentum. No? This desert wants
to be decently serviced, if you please, that's the least that can be
expected, otherwise perhaps it will wait in vain. You won't believe
it, but to make it bloom requires only a little skill and the affection of a talented handyman, who knows the way things are and
will perhaps be moved once again, just once more, pleaseplease,
through kissing and pleading, at last to step a little closer, even if
he's already standing on one's toes with all his weight. We would-
n't even have noticed that. Please, gentlemen, come and pinch my
nipples, pinch them really firmly! And we'll manage to go a little
further down as well, my dear fingers, that little race track, not

worth mentioning, down to the fleece, this matted material at the end of the stomach, made of organic fibres, which would melt in the heat, if anyone could ever warm to them. Well, we won't set the whole house alight, to get a woman on heat and to guide the turbulent flow movements of a cock into her, until everything goes down the river bank and disappears in the water. The house is supposed to remain standing. Then we won't need much more to be happy.

What do you want? The woman appears in the door, as if surrounded by a whole troop of guards. Why. This security will, as always, disappear completely in about ten seconds. She'll be trembling then and not know why. That's a start. The man pushes past her, as if he were avoiding a vehicle in the snow, he doesn't brush against her, will have to bump her later on, because it's expected of him that he'll be rough. And he couldn't act any differently anyway. He hates her. He could keep still, yet the coarseness would break out without him doing anything about it and crash through the thin fence in front of the feeding enclosure, while the more docile hinds are still politely showing their admission tickets, after forming an orderly queue. Have you already heard about Gabi. This is her bag. She forgot it here, you remember, the day before yesterday. Did she. Give it to me, I'll hand it over to my colleagues dealing with the case. I don't know where Gabi could have gone afterwards. Do you know? She must have been somewhere. Why haven't you moved out yet. Be quiet. I'm talking now. I told you, the next time you should already be undressed, when I come, why don't you do what I say. On the contrary, you did what I said. Give me a kissy pleaseplease. I always want to be among the first, right there at the front. Perhaps that's my mistake. If my father were still alive, then my life would have been completely different. In my father I would have had someone, whose got a similar character to mine, who understands me and protects me. He was killed in the war. I miss someone whom I never knew, more than someone whom I know

now. Most of all I miss someone who doesn't exist at all. Not yet. But one mustn't give up hope. Says the woman, whose home is warm, cosy and clean. No one is listening to her. The country policeman tugs absent-mindedly and clumsily at her top, which she has lifted up especially for him, she thinks there's something there just for him, that he will absolutely want to study. But he doesn't read, not in her eyes, not on her body, because he knows this book, every book, by heart beforehand. He gulps down the woman, at the kitchen table, where everything is prepared. She quickly has to put the plates on the sideboard again, as she hears the material of her skirt tear, she clears everything away, though there's no charm in the arrangement, she can't bother with that now, when it comes to the last little bowls with olives, miniature corn cobs, more olives and pickled pumpkin chunks, she can no longer see where she's putting them and hears the clattering of china, but it's only the good-humoured collision of two ships, meeting at night on a sideboard instead of at sea, not the grinding squealing of things shattering. Hopefully, that will not all come flying down now and make a terrible mess, she's still thinking, as he's already shoving up her dress, pulling her panties past her knees and turning her round, all as usual, so that this time, too, he doesn't have to look at this charmless face, which would like to ask him something and doesn't dare, well, and now he presses the upper part of her body, her chest, which he has briefly and hurriedly kneaded, after he had first lifted the whoppers out of the bra and, squeezed together like two pancakes, because he's loaded the whole of the woman's weight onto them and basically squashed them flat, giving them a form, which was not originally intended, throws her down on the unfloured table top, and her head as well, gripped by the neck, like a whip, the hair gripped by another hand, giving additional assistance, down, down with you, you tramp, down, while she's still quickly trying to explain the Nice Weekend Programme that she's prepared for him, together with the starting times, feverishly, as if what counted was to plan the whole weekend in five minutes and immediately put it behind one as well and if possible also quickly attach the instructions for the video recorder. So. She'll be quiet in a minute, the woman, and her hair falls over her, beside her on the table top, where to begin with she still tried to support herself with her hands, in order to take a little of the weight of her body off the hard table, to relieve the pressure. She can do that, if she likes, she won't keep it up for long, she has to bear his weight behind her as well, so, and now spread the legs and relax the inner muscles, otherwise you'll get a whack on the arse. I see she still finds this task difficult, and in such an uncomfortable position as well. Yet she planned everything carefully, even if quite differently. A leading role was to be played by a mountain hotel on the Semmering Pass. But God thinks and the director does what he wants. Rejected. Too expensive. Lend me the money. I can't leave. What could I say to my wife. Are you going to open up now, I don't have to get in there, you're the one who always wants it, what are you waiting for, I don't need you. Financially speaking I'm facing ruin anyway. A pile of ruins. And what are you going to do about it. The woman feels him breathing heavily on her neck and biting into the two tendons that attach her head to her body. Please. Please don't. Ow. Good, if one's honest. But one should at least know beforehand what one wants. You want it or don't you? Yes but. But why do I always have to suffer like this? Why is my hair so tousled, right after going to the hairdresser? Why is my new skirt torn? Why does the country policeman not feel sorry for the woman? Why does she love and sacrifice herself and not entertain any suspicion? Why is this woman so weak and often has very bad moments when she is alone? Why did he promise her a weekend on the Semmering, if he in any case never wanted to go there? Why did she not know that he wouldn't want to go there? Why does her fear not subside? Why don't we often go abroad, where we, too, could feel like new? Perhaps because we like each other enough, to just stay here? Why do we love and sacrifice ourselves? Why don't we change our approach, even if we have to admit to ourselves that we are deceived and exploited? Why does this man always stick his cock, after he has wiped it with a piece of absorbent paper (take a look at the screen, yes, that's the paper I mean, the one with the particularly absorbent honeycombs, your ears are nothing compared to it, and your mind ditto, one can even pour water onto it and put a pound of vegetables on it) from a kitchen roll, in so quickly again? Why does he always pat her head briefly like that, as if he would really like to hand out a couple of good slaps instead, that can drive one crazy? When will she come down to earth? After the journey back, which isn't necessary, because the woman is already at home? Why doesn't she have a photo of him? Why has he never given her a present, not even flowers or a piece of cake from the café? Why does she always have to wipe herself, without him helping her? Where have the paper handkerchiefs got to again? There's only this kitchen roll, and its little dress is absorbent, that's true, but a bit stiff. And this careless pincer-pinching of the left nipple between the fingernails, did he absolutely have to do that, too? The pain is terrible, I've never felt anything like it, it'll turn red and swell up, and the next time he does it again, in the same place, hello. Yes, pinching and no kissing was definitely part of it. It simply occurred to the man, specialist and pleasure-seeker in one, and he immediately did it, it's not work for him, merely something to do. It occurred to him and he immediately carried it out. We can understand that, it was perhaps the final playful surprise, which an artist bestowed on his completed work, before yet again no one will buy it from him. When will the difficult everyday life of the woman continue? Tomorrow? The day after tomorrow? Next week? The music still radiates in its case, but cannot penetrate the darkness. In a moment it will once again be allowed to pour out its treasures before these two people, who have not found their way to one another. It can hardly wait to break out behind the cordon of the CD player and be allowed to flood this home, desired like hardly another, like an angry torrent of people, protesting against the government and prevented only by a couple of wire fences from sweeping away everything that is not in keeping with their will. Nazis out. The country policeman's cock has slipped in and out again, this loose bird, which knows its way around its little house, which is just as big as it is itself, but no bigger, a wonder, however, that it can move around in it at all. It doesn't only want to eat, at least it sometimes leaves something behind, its little doing, its dropping, that's the way they are, the birds. Basically they are no different from us. They can control themselves just as little, and yet our gaze rests on them with pleasure, as they hop to their nesting places and away again. They leave their shit behind, but they themselves never stay. And: No, they don't treat anyone. They're treated, the dickey-birds, fetch their grains, sunflower seeds, nuts, cereals. The feed is there, so the birds are there, too. If there were no grains for them, they just wouldn't come. Nature has absolutely no mercy on us, not even in little things. Nothing comes from nothing. And if there were no grounds for existence, we wouldn't exist either. We do possess the honest aim of slipping through fate's fingers, but this country policeman is someone who gets a grip on things, on the neck, on the hair, on the arse, he doesn't leave off and he doesn't leave any bit of us out. Nor does he leave any of this cut meat, which he gulps down standing, straight from the sideboard, where the plates have been shoved under and on top of one another like icebergs. It surely doesn't matter where the plates are standing. Wherever they are, there I'll come and eat. Would be a waste otherwise. No problem. What's the problem about that. Only God, shocked at everything that He's forced to see, has determined at which bird table He expects himself to be distributed, in wafer form, as food. We're not allowed to take Him home and perhaps even stick Him in the oven to heat Him up. Yesterday a lawyer drew up an agreement. Please take a seat, sit down and don't listen to me any longer. Just do it. I'll be brief. But not just yet. Please wait.

8.

Life can't be buckled on and off like a pair of skis, on which one glides through nature, through this fantastic, sometimes however snow-covered wealth of amino acids and vitamins, which cannot be won by adventure alone. One has to take the amino acids and vitamins as an extra, unlike the plants, which are able to produce these materials themselves. They take the elements which they need, and which have to be available in a form they can use, and off we go. Fresh soil contains all that in sufficient quantities, leached-out soils don't contain it, they are exhausted, because for too many years the same thing was always expected of them, they would urgently need variety. Aha. This soil is now acidic. That's not so good. The acid content must be reduced, absolutely, yet the way it's done is usually wrong. People bend over their soil, which is always too little for them, always too small, yet they've usually erred on the side of generosity already and expected too much of it, above all when the soil is in the water. Every day one gets dirty and cleans oneself, it never goes very deep. The people now gather in the village and talk about a young dead woman. The ceaseless circles in the water which spread out from her seem to have no cause, at least the cause is not known. The young dead woman has already become quite indistinct. The more she's talked about, the more sensation-seeking and meaty the talk, the more she seems to disappear from the little interests in life among which she existed when she was alive. This Snow White lay for a couple of days in the dark, cold water, a long, long time, no, only a relatively short time, and has not decomposed. The corpse remained fresh in the water, but as a corpse nevertheless. No prince could awake her, and if he were to take the girl to his chamber, she would rot, smell, become worm-eaten, post-mortem lividities, greenish discoloration of the abdominal wall would follow. Rigidity for a while, so that one could stand Gabi upright. Blooming churchyard roses on the cheeks, no, not them, because there were no wearisome and impractical death throes. The jeans limp as leaves in their water bag, in the green plastic sack. This Snow White died gently from the throttling of the glomus caroticum, an itself agreeable ganglion. The vagus, the tenth cranial nerve, is immediately paralysed, and one dies a reflex death on the spot. So no further attempts to kill this girl were necessary. No poisoned comb, no poisoned apple, until no more breath came from the child's mouth. No shock, except to us, when the girl falls to the ground and the slice of apple flies from her mouth in a high arc. There was no object which led to death, it was the arms of a hunter of men, and no forceful blow on the back at the right moment could return life to this body. First there was a small, then a more violent disturbance, a mouth which seemed made to kiss, yet we see no poison component, which could have made the girl very ill, we see only that no more breath descends this living human shaft, down this breathing pit. The breath has gone, the death roses are resplendent or not, it all depends. But unfortunately the investigators will only know and interrogate the official boyfriend, who weeks later will carry the coffin with five school friends and not stumble, so that no piece of apple may jump in a high arc from a mouth and bring the girlfriend to life again. At the moment he is still stunned, the boyfriend, but it could be an act, let's keep on asking him questions, we don't have anyone else at the moment, let's ask this good-looking, ambitious lad, who's not a prince, but has something to offer nevertheless, in which as a precaution he had installed Gabi like a chip, which will hopefully work. Let's ask him, why he could cope with the spoken exercise in the first period so dispassionately and calmly. Only now does the boyfriend notice: This component, Gabi, has unfortunately broken down and with it the whole apparatus. When one notices something, it's always already too late. Nothing works any more. Those whose lives are up to the minute know all about these electronic devices, but if even a tiny thing goes wrong, they have to fiddle around for a very long time, and they then become really uneasy and quickly substitute a couple of other parts in the device as if it were a hen, hoping the device won't notice, and really take offence. Just a moment! Good. Life can go on. Everything is working again, if I may say so. Let us make another attempt and equate Gabi with Snow White, let the waters race upwards, against their intentions, let us hurl them upwards, so that they are new and pure again, exactly, for once in a lifetime back to purity, out of all the lavatory bowls and wash basins and bath tubs: up, up and away to heaven, so that they can fall to earth again. If one then takes the new module, the one which at present prevents her from functioning, the poisoned piece of apple, out of the girl again, will it function again, the child? No, still not, perhaps one would have to fit a completely new part into the one who does not resemble a dead girl, only a sleeping girl, it would have to be fitted in, so that this positive impression is maintained, only better, more perfectly, most perfectly of all, if life returned. Please, sit down! What's still missing? The calm of harmony between Gabi and her boyfriend, which has been irrevocably shattered. Now and beyond that she walks at best invisibly beside the young man, which at least has the advantage that she can go away unnoticed, when he happens to be washing his car again. Whose duty is it to stay? No one can be forced to do so. Some went away involuntarily, our dear dead, most of them, they didn't want to either, but had to. They certainly wanted to know what it's like on the other side, but they didn't really want to experience it themselves, at most through the media, that would have been more comfortable than having to go there oneself to the dark, the other side, sister of sleep, in which every animal can carry on the infinity, no the finiteness of its existence. But every human being can't do it, he has to stop and retire from the game. No matter what he last did, death is inside him as a sickness, and each sickness immediately reminds him that unfortunately he has to die, but hasn't got to the end yet. Do you really believe that we emerge from death as spirit, if in life we haven't already got to know the spirit? Where should it come from, so suddenly, above all, when death, like that of Gabi, came quite unexpectedly? Above this stretch of water, in the lake in which the dead girl lay for a couple of days, nicely wrapped, as if the water was instead supposed to be kept from her, took up her residence, before being conveyed back to the shore by the attractive force of several country policemen and their paddles, there hovers no ghost, no, not that, but I don't see a spirit either, no matter how hard I try. A man of God could not be fetched any more either. After that only hikers walked round the lake path, three men in knee breeches, climbing boots and anoraks, but they didn't see anything. They probably didn't look into the water, but into the finders and viewfinders of their binoculars and cameras, but they didn't find anything. It doesn't matter that there was no spirit there, since if man had spirit, he would be God and would be immortal, which has meanwhile got a little boring even for God. There would have had to be a meaning in Gabi's life, in which she would have been able to follow and observe the process of her own life. She would have had to have the feeling: all in one, not one for two, no, one just for one alone, because that's often how women think, I believe, when they wish for wedding presents or at least a firm warm body there, where it absolutely doesn't belong, and also where, if it does end up there, it usually doesn't want to stay; this body is different, and it wants to make other, better sexual contacts, as does that one there. He won't find it difficult, he's been alone for a long time. The country policeman. He quite likes the woman and the one over there as well, but the inclination on her side is much greater. Please be my wife, who still wants to hear that nowadays. Well, she wants to hear it and agree immediately. But I don't want to grant her that experience now. A middle class life together in comfortable circumstances, of a kind she once left, after all, because life as an artist appeared so very tempting to her, but then wasn't. It is not foreseen by me that people abandon themselves to one another, it is foreseen by someone else, however, that in death they give themselves back to their species, from which they have only borrowed themselves for a short time. As so often, it's precisely when one is finally supposed to give oneself back that one can't find oneself, one has already had to pay a fine for being overdue, without having even begun to get to know oneself in the book of life. One may not like oneself, but one is very far from wanting to give oneself up because of it; and everything appears dreary and empty to people, a watery, an ice desert, a motorway, on which a ghost driver is getting ready to transform the isolation, the little people existence of the living, of this mother with the infant in the baby seat, of this driver of a delivery van full of ladies' clothing, but without a lady companion (ow! not again!), of this student, who has just picked up his clean washing from home, into something merely alive and immediately after that something dead. These people, these damaged, but then ultimately still unexpectedly dead people, because I think no one foresees their last moment, at least they're no longer around for it, they'll still manage it, to go back in time, before their birth. Some of them no doubt don't know for quite a while that they are dead, and their colleagues, who meet them, probably don't know it yet either, they're not usually in any newspaper, where one could look up their dear names, and even on the screen only their crushed, sometimes burnt-out wreck is shown, as if that had been the most important thing about them. Do you believe you thereby help nature to be become aware of itself as its own spirit? If you don't even show the spirit on TV, so that everyone can buy one or one like it? How should we reach it, if this wet snow avalanche was not announced in advance by the weather man? And God, too, you only show made of gold, silver or marble, yet he worked so hard and took on so much, precisely to leave matter, the material, behind him and to be able at last to return to himself again, in spiritual form, as spirit, who's in good shape (at any rate he's got no competition in human beings, against whom he could measure himself, he made them, after all!), in order to fly around everywhere, into people, out of people again, just as he pleased. So please, in or out, as far as I'm concerned: I'm not an airport, I'm not even a taxi rank. One step further, no not as far as that either, don't you see, that's where the precipice down to the Höllental begins, the hunting rights have been leased by an industrialist from Germany, who has retired from business and who now only wishes to devote himself to his living young wife and his dead animals of every age. The ground belongs to the Federal Forests (actually: the Habsburg Family Fund, but you can forget it, unless Zvonomir Habsburg, no sooner than he can speak three words, demands it back from you in person, then Flobert pistol in hand you will step outside your little house, which you had to save so hard for, and blow him away, the splendid pretender to the throne, yet a trace of his breath will then be able to blow you away, and the cameras will want to be there, too, but arrive too late, yes, that is ALL, that we'll never get: consideration), the shoes in which you're standing you bought at Dusika Sport, you could have got them cheaper at Shopping City Süd, the car drivers belong to the country policeman, who gets money for them as well, and so in this way you'll manage to get nature to kill itself and even to regard that as its only goal. It will cast off its covering of visibility and sensuality, push through like the last caterpillar through the last cocoon or whoever does it, until the construction of the butterfly has been completed. The imago then appears in a glow, beating its wings, the full-blown image of the finished creature, over the lake, but for the young dead woman it's no incentive, she cannot of her own accord slip out of her pupa, the plastic sheet and float around. She will be floating matter in the water, if she's not found in time, which has hereby occurred. That is how I decided it. In death this young girl cast off her pupa wrapping, but unlike the Son of Man she did not become God, a pity really. Her death should be seen in a rather more negative light, let's see if the negative has a point, too, yes, I see it, it could be the peak of what a human being can reach as nature, and that is the peak of an iceberg. From this frozen mountain peak he can see God much better, because he will have come considerably closer to Him. Believing that won't make you happy either. Her nature, the nature of the young dead woman, will burn itself up, as if it were a ship, she will go out of herself, behind herself, floating if necessary and reappear as spirit, young, pretty, smart, hard working. And here we have it, the finished young moth, pretty as a picture, nice to see you!, we usually only get oldies here, you dear newborn spirit, whose shoes and handbag are missing, choose something in the wardrobe department, we have millions of ownerless bags and shoes in stock, which we have taken away from people. At first I thought, Gabi still has her shoes, but they're gone too, sorry, my mistake. Who knew that shoe soles bear clues, which can be traced right back to the murderer? I should have known. Someone else knew. Who pulled off her shoes, and where are they now? I would incidentally urgently advise you not to take this step into the unknown, which Gabi had to take, oh no, too late, now you know it already, the unknown, are lying amidst fallen rocks down below and can try out everything on yourself. But all in the proper order. You must on no account become spirit first and then die, otherwise people will see you as you transform yourself and then wander around endlessly and without floodlights, illuminated only by the little red lamp in front of the tabernacle, which God moved out of long ago because he found a bigger apartment, flutter over the snow-covered slopes, which won't make you any better or more beautiful either, in the night, when one can't see very clearly anyway, but of course one does see the dead. They have a bright radiance about them, though not a happy one. The dead. Actors and audience in one. They so rarely become spirits, because, as already mentioned, they nowhere find spirit, which they could slip into like ichneumon wasps. Then they would eat up the spirit, in order to survive. Death could certainly apologise to us, if it comes too soon, one doesn't do that, the housewife is still busy putting on make-up, doing her hair and stirring the mayonnaise, nothing will come of it, I can see that at a glance. I've already said it several times, I think: Only with death and the Olympic Games is taking part all that is required, but I'll now add that, thanks to the admission ticket to our own death (for which we queued a long time at the abortionist's, who in the end sent us away again, because we were already too far advanced and unfortunately had to be born), we have also become part of the self-realisation of God, yes, that's his hobby and his job and once again of course it's entirely at our expense. Even God cannot be expected to pay the prices at the Manhattan Fitness Club. Presumably you, who are individually so dependent on others that you have to read books, to have at least a clue about the spirit, are anyway no more than fertiliser for the salvation process, which consists in having to dissolve oneself, take one's leave, as you please, done already, how can one so completely distort the necessity of dying? It is my only very personal consolation, please forgive me. This young, dead woman, I have to laugh at her stupidity, to entrust herself to a beast of prey, to put a little hand on its fly, why would an animal, which nearly always goes about unclothed, ever have needed something like that, its heart hardly beats any faster, when it brings down its quarry, and when the animal has to work, it can't pee at the same time, that's taken care of, I think, by the north adrenalin or the south adrenalin, which it then produces. The animal. It would carry out these actions again at any time, to get something moving, says the animal. Someone who works for a Moslem charity organisation or the like and also earns money through it is also living dangerously, says another animal, a Fuchs - fox - from Gralla, after his own hands exploded and he went the way of all flesh, following his hands, which pointed the way. The application of force is always unpredictable. That's the way it is. How fortunate, that the fox spoke to us a little beforehand, about his very own truth, which strangely enough doesn't appear more peculiar to me than this whole country, in which I find myself at present. It's better if the country is concerned with itself for a bit, in order not to alarm others.

So now the doctor cuts this young dead woman open from top to bottom, the skull is sawn open, there's no cause for hope anyway, and a silver friendship ring is pulled from her hand, which once felt something, to be given back to her family. Death. It draws its terrors, I think, solely from its linking of individuality and no longer being. If we were all equal, we would be indifferent to death, because we could only die as species and not tell one another about it. Just look, how this spirit for example, it's a very new one, a group of people thought it up, when they realised that they would never be more like God than in this film about pilots, in which they were able to achieve power over themselves and the likes of us by a kind of surprise attack. For once at least! You can see for yourself, how the little bit of spirit, which was produced, will try in vain in further episodes every evening before the news to reach us, in order to outdo the news in advance in horrors, and so today, too, it rehearses it again from the TV set, because without rehearsal it can't do it: inflating itself. The spirit is unceasing rehearsal (one can tell its knowledge of the futility of its attempts from looking at it, I believe), desperate efforts, without success. If you don't understand it immediately, you can also read it up on Austrian Broadcasting's Teletext service; the spirit is very concerned to make it exciting for us, so that we at last take note, of whatever. Announced e.g. today: Train crash in Norway, so you shouldn't travel to Norway. Have you understood that at least? But it's no use, because tomorrow there's something quite different again, even more horrifying, but somewhere else. The TV is the immortal spirit's favourite place to stay, perhaps even the place where it originated, because it doesn't seem to want to leave. No wonder, it's nice and warm, it's almost as if it were still inside the head. But perhaps television is also the only place where, against its better judgement, the spirit can still hope that we pay attention to it. And so it makes its compulsory contribution to the process of growth and decay, we watch the Universe programme and see that the beautiful butterfly has already emerged and has inflicted a terrible fate on a cabbage leaf, and so we give it a good hiding. We would have managed that even without the television. But the spirit doesn't know that. Now it's offended! Yet I like it so much. You can also get by without it, but I don't say so. Basically everything can happen by itself. Once the spirit was the whole world, today it is e.g. a family soap, which scorches its feet, if it doesn't immediately keep on running, to the next episode, always ahead of the adverts, chased by them as by a bad-tempered lioness. Always keep moving, until we are allowed to see the Lord God, who will possibly provide a poorer picture, less clear (even though the set isn't broken!) than in the nice nature film before. Apart from that God's only on once a week, on Sunday evening before the prime-time film. And if He appears earlier, we switch Him off. And if He nevertheless drops by unexpectedly, He some-times comes disguised as a bishop, so that we can get used to the sight of Him, and that in the shape of Mr Horst 'Derrick' Tappert, who has begun a completely new career, because this time he, too, would like to show a bit of spirit, at least more than before. It seems to be infectious. He would almost have died, this washout, he comes to us for bit of starch. Here I have to agree with Hegel's critics, all the pain, all the suffering, all the hardship, all the everything, all the death in itself, none of it will result in even one innocent dumb sheep less writhing on the slaughtering block of history. God created, and then He didn't waste another thought on what He had done, I'd risk laying a bet on that. I've gone on often enough about it, now that's that, once and for all, I have to accept it, and that is fortunately also the absolute end, and I don't ever want to write something down again. Now, poor child of this world that I am, I would at last like to meet the world spirit in person, so that it sends me a completely new bright idea, how I could shape my talent for invention - which I once, during carnival, in front of lay people, disguised as spirit, because for sure no one would have suspected that I was underneath - even more purposefully and ambitiously, above all in terms of content, that's my weak point, here I state a doctrine, which goes: I don't believe that myself! Or better, I avoid the spirit as I have done so far and instead show myself, quite stunned by my significance, personally, just as I am. I am I. We are we. I signify nothing, but I have a certain significance, as you see yourself. Perhaps I am even more important than you! Until now at least I've got quite far like that, and I don't have a car. If I don't believe it, why should you believe that one can get anywhere, without ever putting anything in the tank? Your travel group met half an hour ago on platform four, but now this train, too, has left. So if contrary to expectations the world spirit does come after all, because I haven't come to it, I shall do everything to send it, which kept me waiting so long, back to where it came from, with a single haughty glance. Now I don't want it any more. Off you go. To church. Because that's a place I never go to. So I shan't meet it and so will no longer have to relinquish my own thoughts. Bravo? Did I hear rightly? Bravo? So now I don't need the spirit at all any more. I am acquitted, goodbye Rome, away, away to the Maldives, into the sun! To live at last, as a whole party with very many suntanned people in it shows us every day. I can't dive, don't swim very well. In addition I haven't maintained my species. I didn't, however, receive any child allowance for it, like the mother of Gabi, our young Snow White, whose awakening from a medical point of view is here formulated in an imprecise and scientifically somewhat shaky way, perhaps because she didn't wake up any more at all. No dwarves, who cut a stay in pieces, so that the girl first breathes, then comes alive again. We have no mention, no indications of renewed activity of the heart in the wake-up phase, nor is there any breathing as further sign of a resuscitation process. Where is the corresponding opening of the eyes? Who hears the famous exclamation, with which the seemingly dead like Liz Taylor, she, too, a sister of death, return to life: I was only sleeping? Where are the journalists, now that I want to awaken? No, our smaller, younger sister of death is not sleeping in her black wet coffin, in her green knacker's sheet. She really is dead. Absolutely. The absolute pure and simple. Eternal as the spirit, to whom unfortunately, although I have so little ability to believe in it, I've taken a fancy, as to malt cough sweets, only: What did it do to me? She has, admittedly, been on TV, several times now, but she can nevertheless no longer reach us, this young dead woman. In each one of us we all die, dies our quite unkind kind, but not mine, I did not found any nor carry any on. That others have decently done so is no comfort to them, when the scythe hisses round their ears. But usually we're not sitting comfortably anyway, why should we be just at the moment of our death, then we've got other things to do: weeping, breathing, praying, paying attention to heart activity, checking the funeral parlour, hoping for a resurrection scene and knowing that it won't happen this time either, taking leave, fighting against it, refusing to stand for interruptions, screaming and scratching the bed, water or snow blanket AND: at every, really every opportunity propping oneself up with a new significance, which is not due to one and will soon be replaced by a coffin lining, which is supposed to absorb bad smells and stinking fluids. One had no significance and does not have one now either, with the exception of one's nearest and dearest, to whom one meant something, who are also, however, pleased, that we're gone at last and that they'll have no more trouble with us and we couldn't take our money with us and have left it behind.

It's all been said, perhaps someone said too much and is now holding his hand to his mouth in dismay, but God's always in His Son's way, who's simply younger and better-looking, he's gathered a group of disciples around him, whom he's keen on, and God is already regretting having taken him back and taken him in. He Himself became younger as a result, at least He looks like it, but it's also more of an effort keeping up with the young people until one's 47. Jesus wants to do sports, Jesus wants to make work for himself and catch souls, Jesus is constantly dragging in errors and cobbling together eternal truths out of them, always the DIY freak, well, he's not very skilful, the way he does it. And at the moment the Country Police are going tirelessly from house to house and conducting interviews, they've got to do that themselves, no one will do it for them. Narrative debris rains down on them, sometimes followed by stubborn, persistent silence, just like the rockfalls at the moody Neuberg Rock, from which they sometimes come thundering down for days on end and then for days there's nothing, and decorate car roofs with dents, but there the Lord God has much nicer decorations, big halos, which He could break off, if He intervenes too vigorously in our life. He doesn't do it anyway. Here is the office of the company for which Gabi worked, and He's already hanging here too, the man on the cross, in the boss's office, not in the sand, but hanging in the corner. A plain, modern cross, bought in a craft shop, and the prominent victim is so full of pride at his stiff price that he's almost bursting out of the screws with which he is fastened to his instrument, which is, I believe, by now more immortal than the sportsman on it, we could just drop him; yes, you are seeing properly: beneath it a candle and a heart-shaped vase, with a bunch of dried flowers sticking in it, that's how the personal secretary likes it, who distinguishes herself from all the other women in the company and likes to emphasise this distinction in her appearance, she has e.g. cemented her hair with hair lacquer. And then there's yet another figure who is distinguished from the secretary by not appearing at all any more: a young dead woman. The company is in a state of agitation because of it. If the young commercial apprentice is already dead, why poke around in her life and leave behind prints, which could then be mixed up with those of the murderer? It really was only a vague hint by a girlfriend. We're going to follow it up now, we followed up quite different ones, which led us nowhere, and we've often had our heads in our hands, always one bit of head in two hands or a bucket of sand, which extinguishes everything it gets hold of. Can't you remember anything concrete, anything? Any detail, no matter how small, could be important, please try to remember. One colleague remembers that Gabi was the only person in the company who, because she was still attending technical school, got her travel by rail and bus reimbursed. The officers are instantly electrified: do you still have these tickets? Of course we still have them. Take a look: Neatly stuck to A-4 pages are all the tickets. Gabriele Fluch collected fifteen schillings for every ticket. One takes what one can get, and then runs and sees how far one can go with it. Not far enough. The officers take the sheets away and decode the number codes stamped when the tickets were cancelled. Result: More than half the tickets were bought at quite different stops, often even going in the opposite direction beyond Mürzsteg and Frein. Now we've got another clue and immediately attach a belt, so that we don't lose it again and can hold on to it; given how our own ships of life sometimes pitch and roll, we can do with it. It turns out there are several colleagues who regularly gave the girl their used tickets. They say they didn't give it a second thought and never asked any questions. Only one female colleague, with whom Gabi often ate her sandwich at break-time and afterwards emptied her yoghurt tub, throws a little find at the officers' feet, which she'd been chewing on for quite a while, so that there's not much left of it: She has someone who gives her a lift, she said that to me once, Gabi, but I shouldn't tell anyone. And another colleague remembers once having met Gabi at work, before the Mariazell bus had even arrived. (Is later confirmed by several employees.) Now the narrative water begins to flow, even among Gabi's colleagues; almost all manifestations of water appear pretty to me, above all the high-proof ones, ice is also nice to look at, perhaps to eat or for ice-skating as well, but not for walking on. And I don't really like steam, then I'd rather go on stumbling through the narrative debris, there I know where I am and what I'm doing, it slips away under my feet more often than I would like, but it's not as perfidious as steam, which obscures things, and ice, which comes up at me from below and unexpectedly smacks me in the face. Why is this road suddenly folded up, it's not a spare bed? An employee states that he saw Gabi one afternoon in the post office in Mürzzuschlag, where she was posting company mail. She left the building before him. He himself drove straight home. On his way he passed Gabi's parents' house and saw her already crossing the road; it was long before the bus was due. The girl must therefore have been brought home by car, but by which one? At the time Gabi was not yet a spirit being, they're up to every trick, and so couldn't overtake herself, since she was not yet in eternity and still knew where front and back, past and future were, even though she would no longer experience her future in person. What does an outsider know. The only concrete lead from the neighbourhood so far also relates to this car: A neighbour diagonally opposite confirms that once in the morning he saw Gabi come out of her house and without hesitation and hanging around get into a car parked around the corner. This neighbour, a retired woodcutter and still active poacher, like most of the men here, states the girl had certainly given the impression that she had been expecting the car at just this spot. So she got in without hesitating or even talking to or conferring with the driver. When that was, what kind of car and who was sitting in it, the neighbour knows none of that. Most of the other neighbours say nothing. It's always the same. The country police officers, among them Mr Janisch, whom everybody here knows, a good-looking man (strange, how often this attribute is applied to him. As if one had a blood purity medal to award, but knew he didn't need to accept it; because once he at last has an opportunity to do so, he will only accept cash or good old real estate, which always comes more than one at a time, because one piece of real estate alone would not be a match for Mr Janisch; and he will take every opportunity to press up against younger colleagues, to pass his hands over their hips and to let them properly feel his little fellow, from behind, as if they didn't have any eyes there. None of them dares say anything!), knock at the door, talk to the people on their list and hear not a word more nor less, which would be less than zero. The people listen to the questions, but mostly they don't react at all, as Kurt Janisch and his colleagues soon readily have to agree. Their statement sheets are as empty as the Gobi desert, and their content tells us less than that of a prayer book, because we don't believe the people, as God doesn't believe us either. The doors are silently closed behind the officers, and Kurt Janisch and his colleague go away from the houses again and their buttoned-up inhabitants. It is a world of silent witnesses, none of whom have seen, how regularly for more than a year a girl didn't get onto the bus only a hundred yards away, but into a strange car, which really no one recognised. A pity. We all have cars ourselves, except me, and so cannot call each and every one that doesn't belong to us by its first name. Other girls often kept a place for her in the bus, but they never saw either who gave Gabi a lift, when she wasn't with them. Nor did they talk about it. And her mother and her boyfriend: heard nothing and saw nothing, for over a year. That's odd, isn't it? This one cup of cocoa, half drunk, which was all that was left from the party, luckily it exists, so that the forensic doctor is able to state, with considerable certainty, that Gabi was probably already dead one hour after leaving the house, at the very latest one and a half hours.

Since no person can cope with his life, he should really wish to get to the end of it. But no, this uncertainty of existence is supposed to go on endlessly, and precisely in the shape of the person as whom one lived. Death only breaks off what in any case was never going to finish. The great unknown, the murderer, the phantom, who tore and caroted Gabi, where the arteries divide at the neck, why search for him who put an end to a certain young woman? She must have been at a certain place at a certain time, unfortunately we only know her final address, the lake, the water, the watery dump, yet her whole life passed at a certain time and in a certain, rather small place. Her death doesn't mean that now she is everywhere and nowhere, there and gone, but her death has put an end to her having lived at a certain time in this village in the Alpine foothills. Strange how much people like to think of death as an entrance to eternity. I prefer to stick with the corpse, that's something that's there, for a while, the finality is superfluous, when one knows: It is the case that this body decomposes, till it, too, has liquefied and at some point disappeared, washed away, dissolved. I stick with this body, not in the posture of a mourner, as dogs do it, but more out of interest. No matter how insignificant this dead girl may have been, something of her is there nevertheless, which we can hold on to, she is such and such, and she is simultaneously not at all. Matter tied up in a plastic sheet, from which hair is floating at the top and socks are sticking out at the bottom. The shoes are gone. I cannot say anything about this bound spirit, nothing good, nothing bad. I can't see it, after all. I assume it is finally freed from its finiteness, but I fear it has not become infinite as a result. A puzzle, that the Country Police neither want to nor can solve. They want to find the murderer and what inspired him to snuff out the spark of another soul and perhaps other souls besides, because: Where are all the women who have disappeared? In retrospect on their photos they have such an odd expression on their face, we'll make a photocopy right away, so that we'll know, if we see one: That's one of the missing. For the times of the lifts Gabi got this much is known: There was no time for love. From the well-substantiated departure and arrival times of the very punctual girl it emerges that at these times the two never had more than twenty minutes free time together at most. Probably the time gained on the short stretch was just about ten minutes. What can you do in ten minutes? Briefly place the weight of your own body on another one, in order to keep the latter quiet as if with a dummy, to pacify it at least for a little while, until it cries out again? Take in one's mouth a very precious body part, which doesn't belong to one, anxious, but curious every time as to the taste (not everything comes in bags, otherwise it could easily be taken with one on every errand, but one could leave it standing somewhere), and whether something comes out and if so, what does it smell like? Lodge in Gabi's cunt as in a kind of institute, from which one is released having given an undertaking and with at first dark, later pale spots on one's trousers, but only so as to be able to return at any time? Simply a man, who wants to talk to a girl about something? I don't believe that. Gabi never went out without her mother, her boyfriend, her girlfriends, says her mother, says her boyfriend, say the girlfriends. They also say that in newspaper interviews, right after Gabi's disappearance. If that's true - then why did the girl make such a secret of these lifts she got? Presumably because the man had something to lose, perhaps because he was a close neighbour of Gabi and didn't want to be recognised, although or because everyone would have known him anyway. They just didn't know that it was him. It was no stranger. One can have a scrap with father and mother, a stranger dumps one like a piece of scrap, somewhere, such people have no environmental consciousness. Someone familiar won't manage that, because he knew the girl's purpose in life and never wanted to meet her again! Just don't turn into a purpose in life! He preferred to clear the girl out of the way for his own safety, the murderer, rather that than become his all and all, which yields nothing. So, now we'd rather put the body into this long-prepared green plastic refuse bag, which comes from a building site, because building sites are my whole life, to say nothing of the houses in the making, that's something one can hold on to, yes, the bones, the hair, the finger and toenails can stay too, but not as long as a house that was well built in a good mood. For all eternity, where the believer will be able to meet all these houses, or they meet him, boom!, a negation of the negation, because the perpetrator isn't building a house and probably won't get one as a present any more. The concepts of finiteness fall out of my hand like the builder's hammer at five o'clock in the afternoon. Finally I don't know what to say any more. I just say, there must still be this one minute left: Nothing is left. Death is natural, yet this was no natural death. Do you think Gabi wanted to own somebody who already belonged to somebody else? I don't believe that. I'm not a believer, that's why I always cut myself so badly when I come up against the limits of my existence. Then I believe that things go on, I so much want to follow the believers, to where they're going. But it's not possible, and at the borders you can't go any further either. As if I were a foreigner, from outside the wonderful Schengen states. Is there someone there. No, no one's there, because everyone wants to amuse themselves and hence at present and for all time to come are not and will not be at home. One can only amuse oneself outside, our European house is almost always too small for that, and now it's also too small for Austria, the model child, which never did anything and never will do anything. But neither do we want to allow others, since we are no longer welcome anywhere, to be at home with us, the inhabitants of Austria (then we would have to evacuate our common house! Anyone could come!). Anyone else there, who in return would perhaps like to see me happy? He wouldn't have to watch, because he wouldn't be at home when I came? Who, if I cried, would hear me? No one? Perhaps because no one has noticed me yet? And the perpetrator of this murder evidently didn't want to be noticed either, which doesn't surprise me. If he carried away any wounds of his existence, then they can't be seen at any rate. Otherwise we would immediately have him by the collar, as he runs bleeding through the estate, while something bigger looms up over his figure, the Beast, panting, which has lost its parking space and will never stop in its search for a new one. And if it has found one, then it would already always be too small, it would have to be a whole house at least. If a human being has to die of himself, why should he not be capable of creating a simple house with his own hands and the partly foreign capital of the building society? But its launches put out to sea, laden with interest, compound interest and gallons of our blood and our tears, and one never gets the interest, because so far the agreement always had to be renegotiated prematurely each time. With a pension fund that wouldn't have been so easy to manage, they are a work of the Devil. So it's easier to die than to get hold of a house. In death one still hangs around for a bit, with building work the ground gives way beneath one's feet, because it's already been secured with another plot, which was already heavily burdened or was insufficient in some other way. Mr Schneider, the real estate shark, he always bid against himself, so that the prices of his real estate to the banks should go sky high. Who says real estate is fixed property! Against that a dead woman, every dead woman: She only moves when she's thrown into the water, and then she moves gently, very slowly, to the rhythm of the waves, the water moves her, of their own accord the dead don't move, this dead woman doesn't move. The water carries her around, gives her a shove when she weeps, so that she's quiet again. The water is sweet. I wish I would dare to enter it more often and risk entrusting myself to it. And all the purification plants, I wouldn't even see them. Do they want to clean the water? Then no living things could exist in it any more! I don't want to permit them, these purification plants! Yet without them, things somehow wouldn't work either, we would have bits of shit floating beside us, and we would soon have water where now there's still land, one would have been exchanged for the other, trash and smut for clarity and truth. No, we're not going to do it like that, give oligotrophic and mesotrophic waters in return for eutrophic ones. No, we're not doing that. We're holding on to one lot, and the others can go somewhere else, so that we can send our dirt there and can feel good again here. We don't need anyone else, the water and I. Do we? Perhaps I, too, will be discovered one day, if someone dares to penetrate me. Who knows.

9.

Let us treat small figures as something big. We become uneasy, because we ourselves could be among them, without having grown big. Likewise. To have remained forever small, despite everything: the judgement. Whatever we produce, it finds no takers, no one takes it. No buyer. We protest many things, we didn't mean it like that, but the EU tugs at us with its maternal hands, we can't even blow our noses any more, without being sternly watched by it. What have we got up to this time? A tasty dessert pancake. Mr Fuchs with his arm stumps which went down a bomb wouldn't have managed that, he's not allowed to belong to us, although all his work was on our behalf. Now he's hanged himself on a hook in the wall. He peeled off the cable covering of his electric razor with his teeth, unpicked all the plastic with calm patience. At the end death was thirsting day and night for the sight of him. His chin he had described as Germanic, the nose does not express anything, Germans of the North, of the East, non-Germans and the remaining Slavs have one exactly the same. The battle is already over. Mr Fuchs from Gralla says he doesn't need weeping and wailing, nothing comes of it. The battle is already over, he certainly thinks that he fought and risked a great deal. That too is over. The tourist trade is over a bit too now, because we're being boycotted in Europe. But that something, too, will pass, Europe will get used to us, it will also get used to people wandering around hanging their heads, because they don't have a job. If you please, we'll give them one. Without money no customer, to whom we could get back to.

Let's drive to the capital, the woman says to herself early in the morning. Before, as every day, the feeling of anxiety comes, we'll get into the car. Life owes it to her to drive, she's sat long enough and looked at it. Now everything should move a little faster, even if not as fast as at the Villach carnival, where everything races fast-forward past us, so that it doesn't occur to us to want to grasp anything. Here's the grey ribbon of the motorway already, which looks quite like the lake, which on some winter days also looks like a concrete surface. Hello. The car gets the ribbon under its tyres and resolutely measures it out, perhaps at the end it will give a little encore, the way in an old-fashioned haberdasher's the sales assistant adds a little extra, but not on the speed. It's never quiet, because here, too, the woman has immediately inserted a cassette and is listening to a piano concerto. Although I don't know her character, and so could not describe it, I think, in some photos, but not on others, it's as if she's waiting for something, but it's probably because one's not supposed to move for a photograph, yet at the same time at least look animated. Yet not every quiet person is waiting for something. Some wait at last to be allowed to move into themselves. They have made provision for that. Before one places the furniture inside oneself, the joys and longings, one should at least hoover up everything that could remind one of earlier days. Best to give everything a new coat of paint. If that's not possible, one keeps on painting the outside.

I don't know why the woman, who has now already reached the suburbs of the capital, absolutely wants to drive to where she used to live, a spread-out suburban development on the western edge of the city. There no limit has ever been set to the human imagination, that's nice, but what arose is not so nice. Alpine high pressure systems-built villas with ready-made and clamped-on all-round balconies, laden with truckloads of begonias and geraniums, with which the house glows red, please hurl down a bolt of lightning, God, a more powerful charge, so that something more beautiful in us can dream of not having been here at all! Please, this impression in me must be erased immediately. Other houses again are a copy of big city houses, only much smaller. I plead in friendly fashion for the expression of this early Roman front garden, fountains, concrete bracing, rose hedge stress relief to be taken from me again, before it falls out of my eyes and onto my feet. On my feet it won't get far, this ecstatic expression. This is a nice little house, too, they've added extra storeys of between 70 and 150 square yards per storey and they could have gone on over ten storeys, the dear owners. It is surely satisfactory to unsatisfactory to be able to make a skyscraper out of an Alpine hut, at least it would satisfy me, I wouldn't have to look for any second person, because my house would then really be enough for me. The woman always drives off with her car. Already in Spital on the Semmering she's longing for her partner, whom she would likewise, in order for once to enjoy life to the full before it's too late, want to expand into a house, in which she can live, cook, eat, sleep and afterwards escape scot-free. She suspects, however, that he would prefer to own one storey of her house rather than her as a whole. He wants to have everything for himself. Even if he got her for free, he would still only be interested in the bonus, the house, so as to be put in it. This is a marriage that will not take place. The woman will have to admit it to herself, I won't leave her in peace until she does. She comes up to me here, sees my social circle, stops short, because only one person is important to her, then she turns round and disappears again into the morning twilight, a pity, because I almost had her in my hands! I had almost caught hold of her, I already felt her fingertips. I hurry after her, surprised that the woman has escaped me, putting my

hand to my mouth, as often, when I laugh in my sort of institution, where I live. No, it's not an institution, because apart from
me there's no one here apart from the Catholic Charitable organisation, which says: here I am and wants money from me and has
sent a Giro transfer form. The woman and I, are we one? We are
not yet at one, as to whether we have the same plan, but it would-
n't surprise me. So. First we follow the arrow for Centre, but then
take the turn-off for the Wiental. There, too, a river rushes, but
can only bite its immediate surroundings, and even then only at
flood, three times a year, at the most. Otherwise one hardly sees
it. Is it necessary, then, that the river, too, is as nice as the woman?
The river could easily be more cruel as far as I'm concerned, just
a moment, here's someone who would like to talk to me, he'll
soon be past. I duck down behind the driving wheel, perhaps he
won't recognise me. He walks on. I go on. The water will eat us
all up and swallow us yet. Like these two men, two of many, who
have disappeared and never surfaced again, in the water, this
gate, through which some stride, the others, however, through
another, where to? Imagine a Sunday evening, a collapsible
canoe, which, full of water, is lying in a bed of reeds, a last resting place, so to speak, half sunk in the flesh of the water, at its
widest the construction measures thirty-three inches. Two pad-
dlers set out in it and have disappeared, two young men, which is
something we would like to be, but not these ones, you're about
to find out why. They set out on a winter's day, a cold wind was
blowing, the water was ice cold, perhaps there would soon be ice,
unbelievably still. Do you see the many children's hands, holding
up their rubber ducks, or the arms that go with them, and they
stick out of their water wings like corks stuck in by their parents,
do you hear the squealing, the splashing, the laughter, do you see
the sand pits? Or do you see, for example, the female figure skater,
who in a fast spin cuts a hole in the ice, in which she herself will
be the cork? That would mean that it wasn't summer, as it isn't
now either. So we take everything back again, it's only words on
paper. Now it's gone, I don't even need to understand it. Before

my anxiety returns, which is dear to me, but basically always keeps me away from water. Let's just stay, nothing is going to happen to us, with the two men in their collapsible boat in the water. There's a fire burning somewhere, there's a tent somewhere, I'm also at home somewhere, where I can turn up the heating, but not here. Something is being heated up on a primus stove, human hands curve over the flames, a pot reveals something, then it's on to the next stage of a journey, during which the signs of life become increasingly rare, disappear, also the most curious habits people can adopt, e.g. washing their hands before eating. A couple of pebbles scraped together, branches oddly crossed on top of one another, two bottle shards, a plastic bag half-filled with wind, I don't need to explain it, because it will soon disappear into finality, and with that it will be superfluous. No effort any more. I, too, have a long journey behind me. A ship of life floats by, a boat that glides, threatened by ice and the depths, I hope it will come back. Markings on a hydrographic chart, which tries to convince us that water is solid, blue in colour, and one could lodge in it as in a room and appear where and whenever one wants. Oh, if one could be part of a couple, it doesn't matter with whom, perhaps like these two young men, who have disappeared, thinks the woman while driving. The two packed up their collapsible boat like a seabag and travelled by train, until they reached the water. Then onto the water with their awkward baggage. The trail, which places no value on itself, disappears, a trail for which only packing and sending itself forth are the most important thing, no matter where to, just away! That's then supposed to be the end of any cosy pillow business, and here it is already idly circling, the boat, drifting along, later, much later, within a radius of fifty yards, paddles, rucksacks, a tent, cooking utensils, food, an ID card and a cheque card of one of the missing can be located, nothing more. You, water, what have you been up to again? Why are there such gaping holes at the bow and on both sides of the boat? As if someone or something had cleanly slit open the bow, as if with a razor blade. We're not the Titanic, and if we were, then we could earn a lot of money with having disappeared. Yet ice can form on shallow waters, more quickly than where it's deep. Did it form? When a stretch of water freezes over so quickly, then the layer of ice is very thin, like a film, and so sharp that one can cut one's hand on it, that's even happened to me with paper, in pleasant, comfortable warmth. I really didn't need anything more than paper to do it. If such a collapsible boat collides with such a layer of ice, then things happen relatively fast. The water comes in, and the people have to get out. The boat is full. Let's take a look at the weather: in the morning not much cloud, intermittent sunshine. Until the early afternoon persistent early mist and low stratus cloud. After it disperses the daytime temperature rises to about 6 degrees plus. At night the temperature may fall below freezing in places. Then it's a question of either 300 yards forward or 300 yards back, because even fit sportsmen don't last long in ice-cold water, only a few minutes. After that they, too, are gone, the minutes and the people. They're still gone today, with their families I think of them now, please do so, too, wherever you are. If you have never thought of anyone, then it's good practice for the beginner. The beginner doesn't have to think of millions, he only has to think of two young men. Think of the dead immediately, e.g. of the drowned, of whom two here can no longer speak for the others and who don't allow themselves to speak either. The mobile phone is switched off. If you look down into the water, the shadows there, they're not people, they're tree trunks, which sank, there, yes, look, that is only a sunken, rusted boat, and that there, on the right, those are just boulders. Whether the dead ever emerge again, that would indeed interest me. They can do so from the past, no question. But can they do it from the water? Gabi certainly can, no problem. Take her case, pack up her worries or let someone else pack them, have worries or give someone else worries, take a deep breath, get wrapped up in a green tarpaulin, but a human being is no aeroplane, the air doesn't bear and keep him, a human being is not a boat, this water doesn't bear him, a human being is a piece of meat, himself made almost entirely of water and air, if he can get hold of them. Some do not come back at all from the dead, it simply can't be predicted. Current, depth of water and temperature, all play an important part, which unfortunately was not often granted people in their own lives, I almost believe that for some their burial is the best thing they'll ever experience. The colder the water, the slower the process of decomposition and hence of the gas formation, which usually forces the dead up to the surface, where they can happily have their say, if they meet someone. Why then does the latter run away? There was so much to tell him. Don't be afraid of death! There are so many already dead, you'll manage it too. Everyone has managed it so far, even a complete idiot like you, like me, can do it if he has to. Make sure that your body is stored, but not too long! You were already unreasonable beforehand, but now there's an extra difficulty, about which you won't be able to say a single word. If the water is cold, the body does not decompose, instead an adipose formation takes place, in which the soft parts, where fat had developed, are turned completely to wax, that is, what had grown is now firm and remains almost unchanged in appearance, imagine that. Later there follows a kind of chalk stage, which, however, I am unable to describe, because I have not yet penetrated so deeply into nothingness and can also only grasp what exists, if I can see it or can put myself in a state of a caring relationship to it. I can't. But I could also turn to a pathology textbook for help, only: It wouldn't help me. This drowned angler drifted under the surface of the water for four months, and he is still as good as new. This girl in the lake with her dead dear soft lips - I urge this delicate area, this beautiful milieu of a lake, to at last hold its mouth, it has already spoken far too often here, but it wouldn't have been necessary, the lake doesn't say a word anyway, unlike me, but earlier it did let something slip, as I see - though it was only in the ice-cold water for a couple of days, but even if she had stayed in the water longer, her body would probably have been almost preserved, although this water is permanently at the tipping point, hop into purity, skip into greater gassiness, eutrophicity, where there are rather too many living things than too few, how often am I still going to say it, well, no doubt you'll reproach me with having done so far too often already: fertiliser, fertiliser, fertiliser!, but no animals, no, one can't see any of the creatures in here with an unarmed eye. It tipped this girl out in time, the water. Silent forest, why is no boat found in you? But there it is, exactly! Someone used this boat on the night of the murder. Rings of ice can form around the reed blades, but not now. Next year again. Goodbye. There are some who would like to stand close beside one another and are not allowed to. Admittedly, as already said, I don't know the character of this woman who's driving here, but from her photo I don't have any negative impressions. It's OK. She continues driving. The car, like every means of locomotion, wants to be active instead of inactive (there's something out of place there, but not my glance, I hope), so now we're already down in the Wiental, which is too jammed to allow one to do more than crawl along. The morning rush hour has started. More stop than start. This woman set out from her house, believe it or not, at five am. In the Federal States of Styria and Lower Austria she avoided the early rush hour, but in Vienna she was hit by the whammy of Hadikgasse. Going out of town is still relatively OK, going into town, just take a look towards Schönbrunn Palace, where the giant tourist buses, instead of decently waiting at the edge of the city, are scuffling for bathtub-sized parking places, which, since they are so small, can't be found with the naked eye at all. So we'll leave them to our Vienna tourists, for as long as they're coming at all, and drive on ourselves, we know our way around. Vienna is different, it has a cherry with a heart-shaped pip as its symbol, what is the silly Big Apple against that. Or we can just let the people get out in the second lane and drown out the cries of the disabled and/or enraged by revving our engine, which we can comfortably allow to run up against these and other fates, a moment's patience, please, we're about to drive on anyway, in half an hour or so, and if you hold us up, it'll only take longer. Then we'll drive to the car park amidst the greenery, in order to poison trees, shrubs, grasses and bushes there where they have grown and not where there aren't any. The chestnuts in the Wiental were the first thing to die under a layer of lead and the greedy teeth of the sapper moth, more are to follow. The dead trees will certainly not come after us, to take revenge. Living things are replaced by imposing dead ones or also modest ones, but nevertheless dead ones, that is a principle of this city, which has entered into a rather lasting marriage with death and for more than fifty years has wanted to get a divorce, but it never has the documents ready, and when it thinks it finally does have them all and can, for one last time, which will last a very long time, have an energetic and cheerful last fuck, then new clues emerge, that at one time this city lived almost entirely on stolen money and may only die when it has paid back its debts, which can sometimes assume the size of congealed pictures, all these stolen items of value, meanwhile turned sour as milk, curdled in time, because their owners went missing, instead of them. How can one not turn sour. There stands a minor official and says: Come back next week, then we'll have got the latest painting unveilings in and we'll see what was underneath, perhaps yours, who knows. A smart-looking woman like you, dear Vienna, will be able to wait a bit longer for the new marriage, you'll surely manage to get a bridegroom next year as well, and if we have to personally break off every bit of ornament beforehand. You'll say yes again this time, too, for whatever reason, we're certain of that. No, we can never be completely certain, otherwise later on they'll say things we said, which in this form we never said in the first place, and if we did, then we didn't mean any harm. Even the opera ball doesn't mean any harm. You see! Do you see how, in its curiosity for the new, the present caught up in itself stands there in ecstatic unity with the future and opens the doors, as the Greeks would have said? The greed for the new, yesyes, it is true, let's be honest, that curiosity is not really directed at something in the future as a possibility, but in its greed curiosity craves the possible as something already real. Or something like that. Take a look. There's a man, he sees houses not as a possibility for living in, but, although they don't even belong to him and perhaps never will, as something that already belongs to him, and that because it MUST belong to him. So now the doors are open and you're taken aback, because someone has climbed on top of you, who absolutely wanted to get in, faster than you. And then we send you on a peace-keeping mission on another continent, let you spin for hours with the white washing, thoroughly plough you up a couple of times and look: You will still look exactly as you do now! And this house will also stand there just as solidly and be unable to take advantage of any possibility for relaxation. And no, there's no chance that you'll ever change. You'll have all the more need of the Persil voucher, so that you can still be washed whiter than white tomorrow as well and emerge unscathed from the soap-sud-spitting death mill, in which you swung together and were hung together, quite unjustly. There'll be a total write-off, if you don't watch out, but there's no total guilt, because of course this deer or this pushchair on the pavement or this two-headed creature on this building distracted you from the car that was driving too slowly, a small car, almost breaking down under the weight of the luggage on the roof rack, yes, that one, in front of you, just a moment, but unfortunately the wrong one.

The woman is now moving forward more quickly, she knows the exit, not many people do, to the right off Hadikgasse, follow the Meinl Blackamoor sign, the supermarket that goes along with it is at the back of the brand new apartment block, which the woman hasn't seen before. She still knew the old block, built for employees of the Austrian Fed. Railways, this street is called Käthe Dorsch Gasse, exactly. If she doesn't take the turning in time, then she can drive all the way to Lower Austria on the motorway and drive back from the Maschik side, as people say here, that is, from a long way out of town, by way of the villages before and around Vienna, via Hadersdorf, Mauerbach,

Unterpurkersdorf and Oberpurkersdorf (do you know it? A man wants to buy a railway ticket to Peking. He goes to the ticket office window in Purkersdorf and asks for a single to Peking. The man behind the window says, You're having me on, the best I can do is sell you a ticket to the Polish border, after that you have to see yourself how you go on, with the Trans-Siberian, the Trans-Mongolian or by dog sledge, I don't care. To cut a long story short, the rail customer gets to Peking, enjoys himself like the half-wit he is, because he's got as far as Peking, but then he wants to come back. He goes to the ticket office at the main railway station in Peking and asks for: A single to Purkersdorf, please. Asks the man behind the window: Ober or Unterpurkersdorf? Boomboom. What? What did you say? Please yourself.). Here's Hüttelsdorf Station and we cross out the complicated street plans leading past it and make our own, which will likewise turn against us sooner or later. Then follow Linzer Strasse away from the city for a bit, up a steep road, on which the residents politely get down on their knees and beg in vain for the 30 limit to be adhered to, here our children play in front of their own houses and our pensioners go out of their flats and into them again, and others also cross the road, who don't want to die yet either, and don't have any eyes in their head, but the road belongs to them, they know that at least; it doesn't matter, all the people here, as far as the eye can see, belong to us, that is, to themselves, decent, eager to get on and hard working as they are, as a reward for which they are allowed to live here, in the healthy western suburb, and naturally we don't want them to be encroached on or even harmed by outsiders. Who abides by that. No one. We are all precious, and when we possess something and lose it, we have to replace it. Time is passing now, too, yet again, well what do you know, we nearly didn't recognise it this time either. The way it's looking today. We must go to the hairdresser right away and get a manicure, so that we're perceived as well-groomed women, untouched by time. Yes, we have to subject ourselves to this torture, otherwise there'll soon be too much earth under our fingernails bitten down to the quick, from working in the garden. There's nothing illegal about the black under our nails, we got the dirt under our nails from gardening, and we're going to go on with it now, this healthy activity, before we ourselves end up under the earth. Before that we should still be looked at nicely a couple of times, and be acknowledged as women. Today once again we clearly rise above the men. Do you see us? Today it can be taken for granted that we have a profession and are independent. The amount that I've written about that, and it was all completely unnecessary.

Well I never, it's you. The woman has stopped the car on a very steep narrow road, where she once lived. Here, this little house, inherited from her parents, in order to keep it, now keeps others better than she could have done. A roofer's van is parked outside, evidently the roof is to be renovated at last. The woman sold the house two years earlier to settle in the country, an old dream, which is now over. The seduction of dreams lasts for years, the seduction of people happens more quickly. Now, while I wasn't watching, the woman has been recognised by a former neighbour, who's taking her dog for a walk. The dog is brand new and bored. Have you dropped by for a visit? I haven't seen you for at least a year. You're looking well. Oh, thank you. But this short dialogue, almost all of which I have left out, ensures that the woman doesn't dare to stop and look at her former house for a little longer. Nice people bought it from her, look, they've got children, who are intended to grow up in the healthier air of the suburb, which supposedly comes straight from Schneeberg Mountain, but has for some time been living in sin with the Flötzersteig refuse incinerator (the partner is usually the last to know!), and in their own house. Look, there's a tricycle in the front garden, mummy didn't insist on the child bringing it into the house, although the garden gate is less that three feet high and anyone could climb over. Nice, harmless people, have they ever suffered because of something? Nearby four frog sculptures and two crow sculptures, in amusing poses, they're talking to each other, just look how nice they've made their stay here, because they don't need to go anywhere. The house disappears beside the woman, who reluctantly, she would rather be alone now, allows herself to be pulled along by the neighbour on the short lead of a rather one-sided conversation. No surprises emerge from this mouth still familiar from earlier days. It is as if time, which before could still walk, has now stood still and only the people had gone on, well, perhaps they've gone further than was good for them. The people haven't noticed that time has stood still, they were so deep in conversation like these two women. Who hears a weak cry, which has no need to emphasise itself, and so remains almost inaudible? No one. The women walk on, the dog is supposed to be taken up to the camping meadow of the Municipality of Vienna and run, play or scrap a little with colleagues. It is to enjoy itself in the good air like a song suddenly loudly sung across the meadow. Without any echo. The dog is allowed to repeat the exercise every day. The lucky thing. The trails disappear before they were drawn, people come closer to themselves, because no one else does it, no, they run after each other and never catch anyone. No, that's wrong, too, they would gladly come closer to one another, but it's usually not wanted. Everyone wants to look for something of their own, a house of their own, a child of their own, a partner of their own, entirely for themselves alone. No one is satisfied with a room of their own any more. Everyone would even prefer to have their own TV channel, because they never like what's on offer. The dead are particularly inconsiderate, because they evade us and the media, which report on dead things (or have you ever seen a more live person than the folk song sprayer Karl Moik, the last thing you saw, before you fainted? Well, and even he's dead, as soon as he ended up on the TV screen, although his face is still thrashing around, as if he had to escape a shark), so have you ever seen anything alive outside of the nature programmes, which had to be specially dedicated to life, otherwise we wouldn't know that this landscape lies here and nevertheless lives? We wouldn't have seen it, unless, thanks to the considerable magnification which the camera granted them, ants, beetles and larvae would fill the screen, blown up to giant size.

Please lend your ear and meanwhile watch, as the woman now ascends the meadow, which tops off the hill, no, it doesn't go any higher, it only goes downhill again on two thousand more pages, which, however, I shall spare you. So, now we're there. The grass is meagre, but already really green, greener than in green Styria, the spring is definitely further advanced, and now it is already somewhere else altogether. Summer will soon be here, but I shall likewise be somewhere else altogether, I hope I shall meet it there, too, the summer. The dog is let off the lead and toddles off, on the way he has already raised his leg several times at the side of the road, now that the whole hill, the whole meadow are available to him, he'll proceed more selectively with his urine. He looks for a lady to whom he could be married for two minutes, that's silly, none there. The dog finds a like-minded companion, sniffs around his genitals and then right away they hurry off together. The woman's former neighbour has long ago joined a club, which consists of dog owners. These are people who prefer dogs to other people. They get on, also invite each other round in turn. The woman takes her leave, relieved that the neighbour has found her doggy conversation group and has blended into this nice little circle, with many good wishes, visit us more often, don't you want to come for a coffee afterwards, no thank you, I just wanted to drop by the old place, before you've all completely forgotten me, haha. A human formation strides through the play area of their animals, who mostly in playful fashion pounce on one another and form interesting alliances, just look at those two attacking a third, why on earth, no, they won't do anything, they won't do anything! Don't worry. They never bite, and if they bite today, then tomorrow they'll again never have done it, be like new or almost like new, because the vet will meanwhile have stapled two clips in their pleura. The group moves off, the people put their heads together and chat, the animals don't put themselves together, because now is not the right time for that. Some are weighed down by their corpulence, they are not at all weighed down by problems, they are very spoiled and well fed and altogether: happy, although one cannot talk to them in their native tongue. The woman, who is barked at once or twice, because the animals have never seen her on their patch and are confused by the unfamiliar figure, who has not got a four-legged friend on a lead and isn't carrying a lead in her hand either, by which one could recognise a like-minded person, this person, who has perhaps never understood how to attach someone or something to herself, animals sense that, their hearts become completely indifferent and they take their leave without any visible sign, they simply take off, the figure stops now and looks down at the city, whose southern segment, which lies before her now with the perfect clarity which sometimes follows the sunrise, which has released these pictures, which now break out impatiently from behind the cordon, and far beyond, as far as the irregular silhouette of the high rises at Alt Erlaa, the underground goes all the way out there now, which on the other side goes as far as Ottakring, a real triumph for the inhabitants, because it's just the place they always wanted to get to. Now at last they can. Here the corpse-like finger of the lighting tower of Engineer Gerhard Hanappi Stadium, the scanty car parks in front of it are completely out of sight. To the right the West Motorway, one can see a bit of it, before it disappears between the hills of the Vienna Woods, over there is the Auhof, look, they've built a Cinecenter there, the red neon sign can be easily made out, even in the daytime, because it's never turned off, and the lime green neon lights of the last petrol station before the motorway can be admired in all the magnificence and citrus freshness which a company has provided them with.

The horizon gently rocks the eyeballs of the woman, who has stopped to look across the city, which once, in part, at least, was hers, to sleep. Yet she convulsively opens her eyes wide, she wants to see everything, everything. And her gaze should also be garnished with church spires, domes, roofs, gasometers, Second World War tower bunkers. The dear places of culture, to which the woman once strode as to work in the fields, are not to be seen. Wrong part of town. The head hair of the city flows somewhere else, one would have to follow the Wiental further, but the Wiental doesn't follow one either. On the left there, the Steinhof, with the lunatic asylum and the famous, unfortunately dilapidated church built by Otto Wagner, which every child knows, and not many children will still get to know (apart from those who in the Nazi period were injected to death, after starvation, cold, sick (no, they weren't sick, but they were given drugs which made them vomit unceasingly, unstoppably) and beating cures, which no one had to invent, because they already existed, a relatively large number of these children are still represented by their brains in jars), because it will soon collapse, the church, one would have to go over that way, in order to see St Stephan's Cathedral, but there the view is vigorously limited and checked by a small hill together with an old quarry, by a hill which presses forward, perhaps because it thinks that people could not bear so much beauty. And then we have to call emergency again. The mixed canine/human group has meanwhile disappeared around the bend, it'll be about ten minutes before it re-emerges, although individual animal heralds, who have run ahead, again and again impatiently appear on the horizon with little sticks and the doggy rearguard, which has remained behind, is bending over something that it wants to eat, but will not agree with it. The woman is completely alone. She is not in Paris or London, she's in Vienna. She would have quite liked to travel to Paris and London again. Well, it probably won't happen now. In the country there's always something good and useful to do, is what she thought, until someone else took it from her, who is extremely interested in everything she has. Where it was necessary he took it in hand, also her, that is what one does in the country. To take something in hand and carry out tasks which are so complicated that the woman never saw through them and from now on doesn't want to see through them. She often cried out, when he, with his wealth of movements, climbed over her and, not to be softened by anything, tossed her little burden around, depending on which side he wanted to penetrate her, while she pleaded for him to give her love, but nothing comes of nothing. Through him she found her soul, she tells herself. It's no use, she doesn't know what to do with her soul. In her he found a building, which he could slip into. So one dwells in the other, in order to live at last. Only there are some who need more for that than others, who only need a partner in order to be filled with light and the capacity for love. Like this empty vessel, which she is without him, the woman, this dull cup, which is filled with nothing but itself and cannot even see to the bottom, why she does something like that. She doesn't see to the bottom of things any more. She has poured herself out, but no one wiped her up. Perhaps it's all a form of madness, well, at best a little form, into which children press their sand in order to push it into their neighbour's eye. Town and country, what more did I want to say, that has nothing to do with psychological self-analysis, which I have hereby brilliantly mastered? The land is its activities, because it has to be constantly created, wrested from the soil, also from the animals. The city is: the activities of others. It is already there. Even if there's always new building going on, the city is what was always already there. Reflecting things flash in the sunlight, panes of glass, roof ridges, tin roofs, cars. Another reflects on houses, let him have them. He's no mere employee, that he would have to earn them. He's a civil servant. He has called something forth and thrown away the bones, no need to bone up himself, up to every trick, imposing no moderation on himself. A shared happiness will not be created, savings will not be put down anywhere. That's too bad, the bank can't always be giving, it has to take as well, of course always more than it gives, otherwise it wouldn't be a bank, but a Church charity organisation, but not it either: We've got administration costs to bear and the rest is borne by others. Where do you expect it to come from? The city is more and more coming to life, the clock is moving forward, laughter, cries, the calls of the dog army are approaching again. Has she really been standing here for ten minutes already, the woman? It's not enough, it's never enough, but at least she will have gone for a short walk here. Crows rise comfortably and expertly through the air. They settle on one of the trees and talk to one another, by copying us and breathing in a bit of air at the same time and, how amusing, eating a shrivelled apple, which they've found somewhere. If the bird on the top of the magnificent blue spruce (a sly cultivated species from some country or other, which didn't want to have it there and so expelled it, a plant, which could surely suddenly begin to speak and go away, so that I don't have to see it any more, but I'll have to go sooner than it will!, it has got a permanent foothold here, the stinging, disgusting thing) now opens its beak in order to caw, the apple will fall to the ground. The woman laughs involuntarily, when this is exactly what happens. A black dog hurries up, the crow unfortunately has to shout at it and so loses its precious piece of fruit. That's how fast it happens sometimes, although we don't advocate that animals should be dispossessed. And yet most of them even have to give up their lives, for one reason or another. As we do, only more humbly and painfully, we owe them a debt of gratitude, that they sacrifice themselves for us. And even if they do it involuntarily, it's still nice of them, isn't it? Whom are we supposed to eat? We can't even take what we sit on or what we've set our heart on with us, but some don't know that and measure people by their possessions. And then they prefer to take the possessions and just leave the people. So now a person stands there, looks stupid and out across a central European city, calmly examines it and doesn't believe that her eyes are really right in what they see. It doesn't matter. It doesn't mean anything, if in a city one looks at the other inhabitants. It doesn't mean anything, if in the country one looks at the other inhabitants, it only counts more, because there are fewer people. That's why the woman moved away back then. In order, perhaps, to be more important somewhere else, where there's less competition than here. That's OK. It worked, she can still play the piano as well, which is rarer in the country than a shot fired from a rifle. Desires were told her, and that she would be important for their fulfilment, but not essential. Now we'll make another impression and go to the hairdresser we always used to go to. It's likewise in this suburb, only on the other side, a small new building with shops on the ground floor. We're now proceeding there, please follow us at last. The dogs are coming, we're going now. We're going to look nice. We'll have our hair and our eyelashes and our nails done, and then we'll go away again, to serve them up in peace and quiet, somewhere else, to someone else. After the full treatment this hair will have become so healthy and strong that one could hang oneself with it. For one bird just one hair would be enough for this purpose.

We're coming slowly, we're coming alone, we'd rather come as a twosome, which has the small advantage, four eyes see better than two. What happens, if one doesn't want to see anything at all? I wish you all something big and important, but very few of you will get it. At her old hairdresser the woman can be fitted in between two customers who aren't in a hurry. The salon has just opened, in order to lend youthful elasticity to locks, which it has to create in the first place. Wash, cut and set. You're really due another perm, no, it won't come out yet. Instead we'll give it a nice reddish tint. If you think about your property, it'll certainly be a plus, everything would be a plus. The one whom you would do it for didn't notice it in the holy disorder in which he lives, and of which he is not a part. But we rub the dye on our head nevertheless, it's no big deal. It can't do any harm, but it won't do any good either. The water pours maternally out from the hand shower (as cool as possible, please, it's better for the hair!) and takes the backward-leaning head in its arms with gentle murmuring, envelops it, gently strokes it. For the moment it can't concern itself with the expression on the face, the water, it has the task of rinsing out the surplus dye and leaving some of it over, a remnant, which is, however, the essential part of this procedure. The concerned express themselves in newspaper columns, but not for this woman, who would at last like to express herself through her body, but remains an onlooker, who at the sight of Claudia Schiffer turns pale to the roots of her hair. It's not easy to read while one's hair is being washed, nor when it's being cut either, but then under the drier, we can look through a couple of magazines, so that we know what we'll have missed, when we no longer need the new spring wardrobe. Aah, nice and warm, the towel, that's always a good moment, the drying, and the cutting is quite interesting, too. Now the nails at last get their due. Still biting your nails? You're quite a big girl now, madam! Not every heart is heartfelt, but this one suspects that it won't have much more time to be friendly to the right person. Out of her imprisonment in herself, into which unfortunately she let another, the wrong one, at the wrong time, the woman forces a few nice words out of herself, as if she were a person like every other. The words hop out of her mouth into inhospitable reality, it sounds as if someone had let them depart without eagerness, without anger. No, it sounds more as if an insect were dropping its shell, but the creature is too small for that to cause even the softest scratching on the ground. So. Finished. Please take a look at the back as well, all right? The hairdresser holds up the round mirror behind the woman's head, the apprentice brushes over the pullover because of the tip, everything takes its course, but which one, where does it end. Time will tell, no, it doesn't tell anything. Very smart, thank you. Out of good manners a good tip is distributed. The woman feels as if someone with a sharp knife had scraped the last meat from her bones, and now the last bone is to be boiled down as well. Well, there are enough round here who are hard boiled, in fact, they're the majority. Let's give the dog the bone. Perhaps it at least will enjoy eating us. We just end up in the soup. There's something comical about wishing for something. One won't know yet that one's probably not going to get it. Over long distances, across which the wind whistles and the wild beasts hunt, this human being here is called a nice, polite woman. Once she allowed the country policeman to take a nude photo of her, in which drawer will that be found? At any rate, right at the bottom. No fear, it's been thrown away long ago. It was snapped for a special reason, but for which? Perhaps the man took it, to spur himself on again and again, to be able to look at her, when he is weary of the sight of her. He surely won't have taken it, if he didn't have to? Or to laugh at her with others, at the inn, in the station, while changing beside the lockers? In the shower?? That would be nice!

On a romantic tour or a dream holiday one can get to know one's dream partner, but what to do if one already knows him? Then one simply never makes the trip again to all the romantic places. Perhaps this man feels a need to forget being alone, perhaps it's no effort for him to go to bed with her, perhaps he would have quite liked her, if he had got to know her. No, the future tells me: well, not that! Don't worry so much about it, worry about something else, you must have your own souvenirs, and take good care of your savings bank books. The woman has for a long time behaved with excessive reserve, and now the opposite is the case, she can't stop herself busily and tirelessly looking for the man everywhere. But probably the interest on her side will be much greater, yes, that's the way it is. She will fall passionately in love with him, she will become a climbing plant, will smother with kisses, until the man will have to fear for his limbs, and that's exactly how it turned out. But no, the man is afraid of nothing. He drives for miles around, in order to be afraid, but is never afraid. She would go on for years, lying in wait for him everywhere, offering him her chambers, in which he will never want to live, unless they had previously been abandoned by her, the woman, for his sake. She knows that very well. She wouldn't be able to stop herself. She would always be shooting out of a place of ambush like an adder and shoving her tongue in his ear, because he'd liked that a single time, but not a second time, at least not from her, but perhaps he secretly wants it after all, who knows. She knows that he doesn't want it. No, he's quick and rather bright, and he would already know now, if he ever wanted it again. He knows what he wants, and what he doesn't. She would, if possible, press herself so firmly against him, till he would feel the hard walls of the house right through her. Brick, concrete, plaster. He would like that better. The woman could furthermore make it very clear that she is ready to repeat something like that at any time. Yet she is herself a repeat of this wonderful model in this photograph, only she looks quite different. Where on earth is the architect's plan of the house, yesterday it was still in the drawer. The man makes the communication and signs it with his dear name, which is not yet worth anything, but will soon be worth something when he has her house and her off his back: I would like, of course, I would certainly like to marry you. Believe me, if it was up to me, immediately. If I only could, not now, but perhaps somewhat later it'll perhaps work out, that we become a couple. But I would rather be one with you, how shall I put it? Couple is too little, we have to fuse with one another and become entirely one. What, that's impossible? It is possible. In this house it can be realised. This house is clean, spacious and comfortable, why should I, of all people, not want to live here. I have calculated that's the fastest way of coming by a house, which then later my grandson, Patrick, is to get, then everybody in the family has one, because the old dear will soon take her d.t.'s away with her to hospital and then out to the cemetery. Her house, however, she will have to leave here with Ernst, who has been waiting a long time for it. Nobody digs a grave so huge that a house will fit in, for that we would need a company of the Yugoslav Federal Army, they're used to that. Best of all I would like to enter the house and then sew it up behind me, like a living body from the upper middle class, such a treasure, whoever could raise it, would have hit the jackpot, even if under very special conditions. Am I still talking about the house or about a human body now? My mummy always mixed it up, too, and peed everywhere, in every corner, that's why I don't know so much about it. I only know one thing: bricks last better and longer than flesh, high-grade steel lasts even longer, so why stick with people, even if they are good for us and good to us? Even this paint on the kitchen cabinet will last longer than I will. A fir grows green, who knows where, in the wood. A rose bush in which garden? They are chosen, sure, remember, oh soul, to grow and blossom by your grave or something like it, I am not so choice that I know it all by heart.

I bring everything together once again but, as usual, can't hold it and let it drop at the last moment, boing: The woman wants to feel sheltered and yet at the same time nevertheless feel free. She wants to feel a great deal else besides, I'm sorry, it's not possible. She's the type who wants to be led, as her dear parents led her, I'm sorry, it's not possible. So now the situation is as follows: In return for his friendliness the man demands her property, which is her house. The woman would in future never be able to forget the exceptional harmony of this relationship, so it's better that there's no future any more, for the woman knows: I could never forget it, this great happiness. The woman is not deceived by her feelings but certainly by the matter itself. Should one bleed to death like a beast freshly slaughtered, while the sun plays around the still untouched real estate? Should one wither like a plaster cast, while the real concerns that one has all go under, one after the other? It's much too cold for that. Should one sit down at all in a car, when it hardly feels the small burden that one represents? Should one wave to someone from the window, who doesn't even look, because the eyes of the house are shut and don't sense that the heavens lie heavy upon them, do you see the little clouds there on the window pane? There are none. These are streaks, which the cleaning material has left behind, although in front of millions of witnesses it promised never to do such a thing. It is not heaven which appears on this glass, one must be fair, no one promised it to us either. If someone lies once, he's not believed a second time, even when he's telling the truth, I say to this slimming drink, which, yes, that one, too!, didn't keep its word to me and my girlfriend, and now it's my turn to get a word in, I hold it fast like a dear close family member, which I don't have. So it's my turn to speak, but I didn't notice in time and now I'm talking nonsense. I beg your pardon. But for you too there is bound to be a programme, on which you can present your concerns. If companies and politicians lie in public, then you don't have to stick to the truth in this talk show either. What? You have your own truth? But you are certainly not the only one, that is also something you'll come to understand in the course of this programme, which we can now finally dispatch. You should take that in. We shall also need a new dress and so we'll buy it at Fürnkranz on Kärntnerstrasse, that's a very exclusive shop. The woman wouldn't normally shop here any more, it's not worth it for the country. The dress is of brightly coloured, flowered silk and rather expensive, but it was worth it to me. It is the crowning, but not of Jacob's Monarch coffee, it is the crowning of a woman, who for once in her life would like to be queen or at least a Snow White, who doesn't care whether she sleeps or wakes, because Snow White wouldn't know which was which. So sleep my child, but first we have to drive back home, where the bed is, the mid-day traffic isn't so bad, and once we're on the motorway, then we'll get ahead somehow, the crash barriers will tell us how.

No one cares for the woman, so she must somehow care for herself, she must take something, with plenty of alcohol, a wonderful red wine, vino classico something, that's healthy. Even a glass a day increases life expectancy. But no, that would really not have been necessary! First the woman dresses nicely and does her hair once more in the proper sequence, so, now lipstick, eye shadow, mascara. Go to the toilet, only then the silk panties, matching the chemise, which we're already wearing and which we bought at the same time. Before we admit defeat, we spend a lot of money on pretty underwear. Even women who resemble a sheer rock face, because one can't land on them, are turned soft as laundry in the hands of the mighty fabric softener which pours a small capful into the final wash (the only one to be really gentle to us!). If we cap it all and put on this little hat, then we really do look silly, then the stuff runs down over our ears. Aha: Now for once you look at yourself with your empty eyes, and you don't like what you see? Why don't you like it? Well I think, I think the decision of this woman, who is merely groping for life, yes, this woman here, she's just got her fingers burnt again!, the decision was the right one. Where is the note, on which we wrote down everything ourselves, where is the little tube, which we stole from our best friend, who had an epileptic dog, which is dead now too, from the cabinet in the bathroom? We don't need to ask, because we've already known it all the time. The drug is phenobarbitone and in pure form, whereby the veterinary drug supplier, R. & Co. in V., smoothly circumvents the law on addictive substances, quite legally incidentally, well, not quite, in the hands of an experienced vet this drug can blossom and do an animal good, in our hands it can only turn to ashes, which isn't hard, every cigarette can do the same; the theft was not legal, no, it was permissible theft for immediate consumption, we're not going to make ourselves punishable after death, since it will have become completely unnecessary! A little tube of tablets is raised to the mouth and the contents are swallowed one after the other, the alcohol runs cheerfully and comfortingly, nono, it doesn't hurt, no need to worry, alongside and snaps at the funny round things, sliding down the throat there, hurrah. Why is life suddenly so cheerful? We always have to stop when it's nicest, says a child, who appears in the doorway and goes to the piano, also feeling her way, but she will surely hit the right keys, otherwise there'll be trouble. Otherwise there'll be trouble. Yes, indeed, you heard: Trouble! Unsatisfactory. Favourite music is heard. If one really wants to go, one can make everything nice and comfortable for oneself, can't one? The shoes should fit, because it's a long way. Such a bonne vivante, we wouldn't have thought it of her, suddenly she's like a rubber stamp, which would like to press itself down somewhere, we've chosen this point in time, of all times, when we can't stand up any more, in order to look at our own impressions from a distance. So something is left of us after all, how nice. Well, then we'll just have to make an impression here, where we're lying down, it doesn't matter: That was not only THE man, that is THE man, he will be the man for the rest of my life, the only man I really love, I would always be comparing all other men to him. He shall also get the whole of my earthly possessions, in particular this house and everything in it, no, not me, he can have me accompanied out first, the funeral is already paid for, the grave is ready. He gets what remains, at least I have got this beautiful new silk dress, this shining red tint in my hair and in this glass, both of which cost me a bit, perhaps he will resent these expenses, everything already belongs to him; my best black pumps, although I have already worn them a couple of times, and which are perhaps familiar to the audience at concerts or the opera, to one or two among you, ladies and gentlemen, if you, like me, who is quickly embarrassed by something, have looked disconcertedly at the floor, because the horn-player has fluffed his entrance. That's how I would like to fall to the floor, like a wrongly played note, but I'm already lying in bed and cannot get up. I won't get out of it again. I have locked up my telephone, who knows what I would have got up to otherwise. I would perhaps, with a foolish smile and apologetic words, have called emergency, but the emergency will soon be over anyway. I would injure myself, if I lost the beat and went my own way, in order, just look at me, here I am, shall I swallow a switched-on light bulb, so that you see me at last? Then I would rather swallow this all-purpose adhesive, which would still be detected in my bone marrow in thirty years' time, if someone went to the bother of taking a closer look there, of all places. But no one ever wanted to get to the bottom of me anyway, which, besides, is no deeper than a footbath. No one there, who would open my mouth and remove the poisonous little pieces, an unusual procedure, but one sometimes used for resuscitation. The woman. She doesn't look like a corpse, only like someone sleeping, I would say, if something like that existed, like a sleeping corpse, rather attractive in fact after death, which smooths the features, only a holy bleeding to death would get as many points. But then one would have a blue pallor or something. Soon there won't be another wake-up phase, since there will be no more waking up. So, now this is it. The eyes cannot be opened any more, so that someone who is not particularly interested can try to read something in them. Now you know why, in the world of fairy tales and legends, the long-time sleep of characters so often turns out to be a tricky, secretive kind of staying alive, it's down to appearance. We have the choice: fall down dead, fall down in a faint or pretend to be dead or be dead. No need to worry, she's only sleeping, the old maid, without a kiss of assent, but with the attested assent in the envelope on the pillow beside her. She proudly pinned her hopes on her property, the mother's child, and she was right, the property may leave now. No one will be waiting at the door, watch in hand, for it to come home. It can also, as far as I'm concerned, come into other hands, because even property sometimes needs a bit of variety. A shudder passes through the woman, I call her by her name one last time, oh, it's slipped my mind, perhaps I never knew it, it's not written down here, is it?, I was merely notified by her, to write this down. Careful, sleep will come now, be quiet, I'm still speaking, sleep is knocking at this door, immediately goes purposefully up to the brain stem, scrambles further, in order first of all to create favourable physiological conditions for itself. Come sweet sleep, walk on in. When all is silent and only one speaks, it's called a teaching period, any volunteers? No one? Well, then chemistry will speak in my place, I don't mind, and it says breathing flat to arrested, circulation weak to collapsed (temperature below normal and deterioration of kidney activity to the point of anuria, hence the name Barbara anuria). Let's leave it at that. Where she's lying we no longer have to concern ourselves with the Holzer blisters, an all too late and somewhat unsuccessful wedding dress, also the signs of the 'dying heart' will have been superseded in the ECG by the dead heart. There was no dependency on the drug, would also be very unusual today, these drugs have gone right out of fashion. There can be no reason whatsoever which would be compelling enough to prescribe such drugs to pregnant women, please don't do it, if you are a doctor. Whose compelling whom. One can't even compel someone to wear a skirt instead of trousers. A woman sinks to her own feet, but is prevented from doing so by her bed, the dress too is not permitted to fall in a forward way. This person will be forwarded, the address is already written out, one can still put one's finger on the best of her, it is brick, is glass, concrete, steel and plaster. No more than that. Ridiculous, that the birds should chirp or that one person should lead another to his mouth and then the latter still doesn't find the entrance.

It was an accident.